P9-BZG-699
York

York

"My study," he commanded. "Now!"

Tory bit her lip, lifted her skirts and hurried down the hall in front of him. Cord followed her into the study and slammed the door.

"Sit down."

She dropped into the nearest chair as if her legs had been severed at the knee and forced herself to look up at him. He seemed even taller than he usually did, his eyes fierce and dark.

"I think it's time we talked about the necklace. The one you and your sister stole from Baron Harwood."

Her head swam and her palms went damp. She smoothed them over her crisp black taffeta skirt. "I don't know what you're talking about."

"Don't you? I think you know exactly what I'm talking about. I'm speaking of the very valuable necklace that was stolen from Harwood Hall." His jaw hardened. "And there is also the not insignificant crime of the attempted murder of the baron."

Tory swallowed, tried to look calm even when her insides were quaking. "I don't know a Baron Harwood," she lied.

He didn't believe her. She could see it in his face. Dear God, she wanted to tell him the truth more than anything in the world. But if she did, if she told him she and Claire were Harwood's stepdaughters, he would be honor bound to send them back. She couldn't let that happen. She and Claire would have to run again, leave London and find someplace new to hide.

Watch for the next book in this dramatic new trilogy by KAT MARTIN

THE DEVIL'S NECKLACE

Coming August 2005 from MIRA Books

Kat Martin

The Bride's Necklace

MIRA®

ISBN 0-7783-2125-8

THE BRIDE'S NECKLACE

www.MIRABooks.com

Printed in U.S.A.

To my great friends Meryl Sawyer, Ciji Ware
and Gloria Dale Skinner for their help
on this trilogy. Love you guys!

Prologue

England, 1804

A soft creak in the hallway awakened her. Victoria Temple Whiting sat upright in bed, straining toward the sound. The faint noise came again, footsteps passing her bedchamber, continuing down the hall, pausing in front of the door to her sister's room.

Tory swung her legs to the side of the bed, her heart racing now, pounding in her ears. There was no lock on Claire's door. Their stepfather, the baron, wouldn't allow it. Tory heard the click of the silver knob turning, then the soft glide of shoes on carpet as someone walked into the room.

She knew who it was. She had known this day would come, known the baron would finally act on the lust he felt for Claire. Desperate to protect her sister, Tory rose quickly, grabbed her blue quilted wrapper off the foot of the bed and raced out into the hall. Claire's room was two doors down. She made her way there as quietly as possible, legs trembling, her palms so slick she could barely turn the doorknob.

She wiped her hands on her wrapper and tried again, successful this time, opening the door and stepping silently into the darkness of the room. Her stepfather stood next to the bed, a long, shadowy figure in the dim light coming in through the mullioned window. Tory stiffened at his low-murmured words, the fear she heard in Claire's voice.

"Stay away from me," Claire pleaded.

"I won't hurt you. Just lie still and let me do what I want."

"No. I w-want you to get out of my room."

"Be quiet," the baron said more sharply. "Unless you want your sister to awaken. I think you can guess what will happen to her if she comes in here."

Claire whimpered. "Please don't hurt Tory." But both of them knew he would. Her back still carried the marks of an earlier caning, the punishment her stepfather, Miles Whiting, Baron Harwood, had delivered for some minor infraction she could now scarcely recall.

"Do as I say then and just lie still."

Claire made a sound in her throat and Tory fought down a wave of fury. Slipping around behind the baron, her nails digging into the palms of her hands, she inched closer. She knew what her stepfather meant to do, knew that if she tried to stop him, she would suffer another beating and sooner or later he would still hurt Claire.

Tory bit her lip, forcing down her anger, trying to think what she should do. She had to stop him. No matter what happened, she couldn't let him touch her sister.

Then her gaze lit on the brass bed warmer next to the hearth. The coals inside had long grown cold, but the bowl was heavy with the ashes left inside. She reached down and gripped the wooden handle, silently lifting the instrument up off the hearth.

Claire made another whimpering sound. Tory took two steps closer to where the baron leaned over Claire and swung the heavy brass bed warmer. Harwood made a sort of grunting noise and toppled over onto the floor.

Her hands shook. The bed warmer hit the floor with a soft clunk, spilling spent coals and black ash all over the Aubusson carpet. Claire leaped up from the bed and started running toward her, threw herself into Tory's arms.

"He was…he kept touching me." She made a funny little choking noise and held on tighter. "Oh, Tory, you came just in time."

"It's all right, darling. You're safe now. I won't let him hurt you again."

Trembling all over, Claire turned toward the man lying on the rug, a dark streak of blood running from the gash at his temple. "Did you…did you kill him?"

Tory gazed at the baron's still form and swayed a little on her feet. She took a breath to steady herself. It was dark in the room, but a sliver of moonlight slanted in through the mullioned window. She could see the scarlet stain spreading beneath Harwood's head. His chest didn't seem to be moving, but she couldn't tell for sure.

"We have to get out of here," she said, fighting an urge to run. "Put on your wrapper and get your satchel out from under the bed. I'll go get mine and meet you at the bottom of the servants' stairs."

"I—I need to change out of my bedclothes."

"There isn't time. We'll change somewhere along the road."

The journey wasn't unexpected. They had each packed a satchel three days ago, the night of Claire's seventeenth birthday. Since that night, the lust in the baron's dark eyes had grown every time he looked at her. They had begun making plans that very evening. They would leave Harwood Hall at the first opportunity.

But tonight fate had taken a hand. They couldn't wait a moment longer.

"What about the necklace?" Claire asked.

Stealing the baron's most prized possession had always been part of their plan. They needed money to get to London. The beautiful diamond-and-pearl necklace was worth a small fortune and was the only thing of value they could easily carry with them.

"I'll get it. Try to be quiet. I'll join you as quickly as I can."

Claire rushed out the door and headed down the hall. Tory cast a last glance at her stepfather and raced out behind her. *Sweet God, don't let him be dead,* she thought, sickened to think she might actually have killed him.

Tory shuddered as she hurried away.

One

London
Two months later

Perhaps it was the necklace. Tory had never believed in the curse, but everyone for miles around the tiny village of Harwood knew the legend of the beautiful diamond-and-pearl necklace. People whispered about it, feared it, coveted and revered the magnificent piece of jewelry crafted in the thirteenth century for the bride of Lord Fallon. It was said the necklace—The Bride's Necklace—could bring its owner untold happiness, or unbearable tragedy.

That hadn't kept Tory from stealing it. Or selling it to a moneylender in Dartfield for enough coin that she and Claire could finally escape.

But that had been nearly two months ago, before the two of them had reached London and the ridiculously small amount of money Tory had been forced to accept for the very valuable necklace had nearly run out.

In the beginning, she had been certain she could find a job as a governess for some nice, respectable family, but so far she had failed. The few clothes she and Claire had been able to take along the night they had fled were fashionable, but Tory's cuffs had begun to fray, and faint stains appeared on the hem of Claire's apricot muslin gown. Though their education and speech were that of the upper classes, Tory didn't have a single solitary reference, and without one, she had been turned away again and again.

She was becoming nearly as desperate as she had been before she left Harwood Hall.

"What are we going to do, Tory?" Her sister's voice cut through the self-pity rising like a dark tide inside her. "Mr. Jennings says if we can't pay our rent by the end of the week, he is going to throw us out."

Tory shuddered at the thought. She had seen things in London she wished she could forget, homeless children picking food scraps out of the gutter, women selling their frail bodies for coin enough to last another bitter day. The thought of being tossed out of their last place of refuge, a small garret above a hatmaker's shop, into the company of the riffraff and blacklegs in the street was more than she could bear.

"It's all right, dearest, you mustn't worry," she said, putting on a brave face once more. "Everything has a way of working out." Though Tory was truly beginning to doubt it.

Claire managed a trembly smile. "I know you'll think of something. You always do." At just-turned-seventeen, Claire Whiting was two years younger but several inches taller than Tory, whose build was more petite.

Both girls were slender, but it was Claire who had inherited their mother's stunning good looks.

She had wavy silver-blond hair that reached nearly to her waist and skin as smooth and pale as an alabaster Venus. Her eyes were so blue they put a clear, Kentish sky to shame. If an angel dressed up in apricot muslin and donned a warm pelisse, she would look like Claire Whiting.

Tory thought of herself as a more durable sort, with heavy chestnut-brown hair that often curled when she least desired it, clear green eyes and a smattering of freckles. But it wasn't just their looks that set them apart.

Claire was simply different. She always had been. She inhabited a world mere mortals could not see. Tory always regarded her sister as ethereal, the kind of girl who played with fairies and talked to gnomes.

Not that she really did those things. It just seemed as if she could.

What Claire *couldn't* seem to do was take care of herself in any responsible fashion, so Tory did it for her.

Which was why they had fled their stepfather, made their way to London and now faced the threat of being cast out into the street.

To say nothing of being wanted for the theft of the valuable necklace—and perhaps even murder.

A soft August breeze blew in off the Thames, cooling the heat rising up from the cobbled streets. Comfortable in a big four-poster bed, Cordell Easton, fifth earl of Brant, lounged back against the carved wooden headboard. Across from him, Olivia Landers, Viscountess Westland, sat naked on a stool in front of her mirror, slowly pulling a silver-backed hairbrush through her long, straight raven-black hair.

"Why don't you put down that brush and come back to bed?" Cord drawled. "Once I get through with you, you'll only have to comb it again."

She turned on the stool and a seductive smile curved her ruby lips. "I thought perhaps you wouldn't be interested again quite so soon." Her eyes ran over his body, sweeping the muscles across his chest, following the thin line of dark hair arrowing down his stomach, coming to rest on his sex. Her eyes widened as she realized he was fully aroused. "Amazing how wrong a woman can be."

Leaving the stool, she walked toward him, long black hair swinging forward, the only thing hiding her very seductive body, making him harder than he was already.

Olivia was a widow—a very young and tasty widow whom Cord had been seeing for the past several months—but she was spoiled and selfish and she was fast becoming more trouble than she was worth. Cord had begun to think of ending the affair.

Not today, however.

Today he had stolen a couple of hours away from the stack of papers he had been poring over, badly in need of a diversion. Livy was good for that if nothing more.

She tossed her black hair over her shoulder as she climbed up onto the deep feather mattress. "I want to be on top," she purred. "I want to make you squirm."

What she wanted was the same thing she always demanded, rough, hard-pounding sex, and he was just in the mood to give it to her. The problem was, once they were finished, he had begun to feel oddly dissatisfied.

He told himself he should cast about for some new female companionship. That always raised his spirits—among other parts of his body. But lately, he simply couldn't get into the thrill of the hunt.

"Cord, you aren't listening." She tugged on a tuft of curly brown chest hair.

"Sorry, sweeting." But he wasn't really contrite, since he was certain nothing she had to say would interest him in the least. "I was distracted by your very lovely breasts." To which he directed his full attention, taking one of them into his mouth as he lifted her astride him and slid her luscious body the length of his powerful erection.

Olivia moaned and began to move and Cord lost himself in the sweet charms of her body. Livy peaked and Cord followed, then the pleasure began to fade, disappearing as if it had never existed.

As Livy climbed from the bed, the thought he'd been having of late began to creep in. *Surely there is more than just this.*

Cord shoved the thought beneath the dozens of other problems he had been facing since his father had died and he had inherited the Brant title and fortune. Following Olivia out of bed, he began to pull on his clothes. There were a thousand things he needed to do—investments he needed to consider, accounts he needed to review, tenant complaints and shipping invoices.

And there was his ongoing worry about his cousin. Ethan Sharpe had been missing for nearly a year and Cord was determined to find him.

Still, no matter how busy he was, he always found time for his single great vice—women.

Convinced a new mistress was the answer to his recent bout of gloom, Cord vowed to begin his search.

"What if it's the curse?" Claire looked at Tory with big blue worried eyes. "You know what people say—Mama told us a dozen times. She said the necklace could bring very bad fortune to the person who owned it."

"You're being ridiculous, Claire. There is no such thing as a curse. Besides, we don't own it. We just borrowed it for a while."

But it had certainly brought misfortune to her stepfather. Tory gnawed her bottom lip as she remembered the baron lying on the floor next to the bureau in Claire's bedchamber, a trickle of blood running from the gash in the side of his head. Dear God, she had prayed every night since it happened that she had not killed him.

Not that he didn't deserve to die for what he had tried to do.

"Besides, if you remember the story correctly," Tory added, "it can also bring the owner good fortune."

"If the person's heart is pure," Claire put in.

"That's right."

"We stole it, Tory. That's a sin. Now look what is happening to us. Our money's almost gone. They're going to throw us out of our room. Pretty soon we won't have even enough to buy something to eat."

"We're just having a little bad luck, is all. It has nothing to do with the curse. And we're bound to find employment very soon."

Claire looked at her with worried eyes. "Are you sure?"

"It might not be the sort of work we had hoped for, but yes, I am extremely sure." She wasn't, of course, but she didn't want Claire's hopes to plummet any lower than they were already. Besides, she *would* find work. No matter what she had to do.

But three more days passed and still nothing turned up. Tory had blisters on her feet and there was a rip in the hem of her high-waisted dove-gray gown.

Today is the day, she told herself, summoning a renewed determination as they headed once more for the area she believed most likely to provide employment. For more than a week, they had knocked on doors in London's fashionable West End, certain some wealthy family would be in need of a governess. But so far, nothing had turned up.

Climbing what must have been the hundredth set of porch stairs, Tory lifted the heavy brass knocker, gave it several firm raps, then listened as the sound echoed into the house. A few minutes later, a skinny, black-haired butler with a thin mustache opened the heavy front door.

"I should like to speak to the mistress of the house, if you please."

"In what regard, madam, may I ask?"

"I am seeking employment as a governess. One of the kitchen maids down the block said that Lady Pithering has three children and may be in need of one."

The butler's gaze took in the frayed cuffs and the rip in her hem and lifted his nose into the air. He opened his mouth to send her away when his gaze lit on Claire. She was smiling in that sweet way of hers, looking for all the world like an angel fallen to earth.

"We both love children," Claire said, still smiling. "And Tory is ever so smart. She would make the very best of governesses. I am also looking for work. We were hoping you might be able to help us."

The butler just kept staring at Claire and Claire kept on smiling.

Tory cleared her throat and the skinny man dragged his gaze away from Claire back to Tory. "Go round to the back door and I shall let you speak to the housekeeper. That is the best I can do."

Tory nodded, grateful to have gotten even that far, but a few minutes later, when they returned to the front of the house, she was filled with an even deeper despair.

"The butler was ever so nice," Claire said. "I thought for certain this time—"

"You heard what the housekeeper said. Lady Pithering is looking for someone older." And there never seemed to be a job for a servant as lovely as Claire.

Claire gnawed her bottom lip. "I'm hungry, Tory. I know you said we have to wait till supper, but my stomach is making all sorts of unladylike noises. Can't we have a little something now?"

Tory closed her eyes, trying to resurrect some of her earlier courage. She couldn't stand the look in her sister's eyes, the worry mingled with fear. She simply could not tell her they had spent their very last farthing, that until they found work of some kind they couldn't buy so much as a dry crust of bread.

"Just a bit longer, darling. Let's try the place the housekeeper mentioned down the block."

"But she said Lord Brant doesn't have any children."

"It doesn't matter. We'll take whatever jobs we can find." She forced herself to smile. "I'm sure it won't be for long."

Claire nodded bravely and Tory wanted to cry. She had hoped to take care of her younger sister. While Tory had often worked long hours at the day-to-day task of running Harwood Hall, Claire wasn't used to the hard work done by a servant. Tory had hoped to spare her sister, but fate had led them to this dismal place in their lives and it looked as if they would have to do whatever it took to survive.

"Which one is it?" Claire asked.

"The big brick house just over there. Do you see those two stone lions on the porch? That is the residence of the earl of Brant."

Claire studied the elegant town house, larger than any other on the block, and a hopeful smile blossomed on her face.

"Perhaps Lord Brant will be handsome and kind as well as rich," she said dreamily. "And you shall marry him and both of us will be saved."

Tory flashed her an indulgent smile. "For now, let us simply hope the man is in need of a servant or two and willing to take us in."

But again they were turned away, this time by a short, bald-headed butler with thick shoulders and beady little eyes.

Claire was crying by the time they reached the bottom of the stairs, which was a rare thing, indeed, and enough to make Tory want to cry along with her. Funny thing was, if Tory cried, her nose got all red and her lips wobbled. But with Claire, it just made her eyes look bigger and bluer and her cheeks bloomed with roses.

Tory grabbed her reticule and began trying to dig out a handkerchief for Claire when one magically appeared in front of her face. Her sister accepted it gratefully. Dabbing it against her eyes, she turned her sweet, angelic smile upon the man who had provided it.

"Thank you ever so much."

The man returned the smile as Tory could have guessed he would. "Cordell Easton, earl of Brant, at your service, dear lady. And you would be...?"

He was looking at Claire the way men had since she was twelve years old. Tory didn't think he realized there was anyone else there but Claire.

"I am Miss Claire Temple and this is my sister, Victoria." Tory silently thanked God that Claire had remembered to use their mother's maiden name, and ignored her sister's disregard of the proper rules of introduction. The man was, after all, the earl, and they were desperately in need of his employment.

Brant smiled at Claire but had to force himself to look in Tory's direction. "Good afternoon, ladies."

"Lord Brant," Tory said, hoping her stomach wouldn't choose that particular moment to growl. Just as Claire had imagined, he was tall and exceedingly handsome, though his hair was dark brown and not blond, and his features were harder than one of Claire's imaginary princes would have been.

His shoulders were exceptionally wide, with no padding that she could discern, while his build was solid and athletic. All in all, he was a very impressive man, and the way he was looking at Claire made a knot of worry ball in the pit of Tory's stomach.

Lord Brant continued to gaze at Claire as if Tory had disappeared. "I saw you leaving my door," he said. "I hope you weren't crying over something my butler might have said. Timmons can be a bit of a muttonhead at times."

Tory answered while Claire continued to smile. "Your butler informed us there were no positions available. That is the reason we are here. We are in search of work, my lord."

For a moment, he actually looked at Tory, his gaze running over her slim figure and upswept brown hair, sizing her up in a way that sent spots of color into her cheeks.

"What sort of work are you talking about?"

There was something in his eyes…something she couldn't quite read. "Any sort of position you might need to have filled. Chambermaid, kitchen maid, anything that pays a respectable wage for a respectable day's work."

"My sister wishes to become a governess," Claire said brightly, "but you don't have any children."

His gaze returned to Claire. "No, I'm afraid I don't."

"Anything would do," Tory said, trying to keep the desperation out of her voice. "Recently, we have come upon rather unfortunate circumstances."

"I'm sorry to hear that. You have no family, no one who might be of assistance?"

"I'm afraid not. That is the reason we're looking for work. We were hoping that perhaps you might have something available."

For the first time, the earl seemed to understand exactly what they were about. He gazed at Claire and his mouth curved up. Tory thought that perhaps that smile did to women what Claire's smile did to men.

Only Claire's was completely guileless, while the earl of Brant's definitely held a calculating twist.

"As a matter of fact, we *are* in need of help. Timmons just hasn't yet been informed. Why don't you both come with me?" He was offering Claire his arm, which didn't bode well as far as Tory was concerned.

She knew the effect her sister had on men—not that Claire was even remotely aware of it. It was the reason they found themselves in such dire straights in the first place.

God's breath—the girl was an angel. Cord had never seen skin so fair or eyes so blue. She was slender, yet he could see the swell of her breasts, outlined beneath her slightly frayed apricot gown, and they looked utterly delectable. He had been searching for a new bit of muslin. He hadn't expected a divine creature like this to appear at his front door.

Cord paused inside the entry, the sisters gazing up at him from where they stood beneath the crystal chandelier. A few feet away, Timmons cast him a look of disbelief. Cord turned to Claire, but she had wandered over to a vase filled with roses and appeared to be enthralled with a single pink bud.

The other sister, he saw, was eyeing him with what could only be called suspicion. He gave her a friendly, innocent smile, all the while calculating how long it would take him to lure the blond beauty into his bed.

"So, my lord, you were telling me about the position you have available."

He focused his attention on the dark-haired sister…what was her name? Velma or Valerie or…? Victoria—yes, that was it.

"As I was saying, we are definitely in need of help." He looked her over. She was shorter than Claire, but not too short, and not nearly so…fragile. That was the word for Claire. This one, Victoria, looked *capable,* at least in his estimation, and she was obviously protective of her sister.

"My housekeeper, Mrs. Mills, gave notice nearly two weeks ago. She'll be leaving in a few more days and I have yet to find a suitable replacement." Victoria Temple was far too young for the position and undoubtedly she knew it. But he didn't give a damn and he didn't think she would, either. "Perhaps you would be interested in the job."

He didn't miss the staggering relief that washed over her face. It gave him an odd sort of pang.

"Yes, my lord, I would most assuredly be interested. I've done similar work before. I believe I could handle the job very well."

She was attractive, he saw as he hadn't before. Not the raving beauty her sister was, but her features were refined, her dark eyebrows winged over a pair of lively green eyes, her nose straight and her chin firm. A stubborn little chin, he thought with a hint of amusement.

"What about my sister? I'm afraid I can't accept the position unless there is a place here for Claire as well."

He heard the tension that crept into her voice. She needed this job—very badly. But she wouldn't stay without her sister. Apparently, she hadn't realized yet that Claire was the reason that she had been employed.

"As housekeeper, you will be able to hire as you wish. Another chambermaid would probably be useful. I'll summon Mrs. Mills. She can show you around and discuss the duties you will need to perform. As this is a bachelor household, I imagine it would be better if I introduced you as *Mrs.* Temple."

Her lips slightly pursed as she recognized the necessity of the lie, which obviously didn't sit well with her.

"Yes, I suppose it would. As that will pose a problem for Claire, you may refer to my sister as Miss Marion. That is her middle name."

He motioned toward Timmons, who left to collect Mrs. Mills. The broad-hipped housekeeper arrived a few minutes later, a speculative look on her face.

"Mrs. Mills, this is Mrs. Temple," Cord said. "Beginning on Monday, she will be taking your place."

The housekeeper's speckled gray eyebrows drew together. "But I assumed Mrs. Rathbone—"

"As I said, Mrs. Temple will be your replacement. And this is her sister, Miss Marion. She's being employed as a housemaid."

Mrs. Mills didn't look all that happy, but she nodded her acceptance, then motioned for the women to follow her and started climbing the stairs.

"We'll get your sister settled in first," the housekeeper said. "Then I'll show you to your room. It's downstairs next to the kitchen."

"Come, Claire." The dark-haired sister's command drew the blonde's attention from the flower-filled urn. "Mrs. Mills is going to show us our rooms." Though the words were directed at Claire, her eyes were fixed on Cord and he thought that they held a trace of warning.

The notion somehow amused him. A servant with that kind of pluck. For the first time in weeks, Cord found himself thinking of something other than the business of being an earl and his worry about Ethan.

He cast a last glance at Claire, who climbed the stairs

with her elegant head bent forward as she studied the patterns in the carpet. Cord watched the way a silver-blond strand of hair teased her cheek and felt a familiar male stirring. Thinking of the intriguing possibilities the future suddenly held for him, he smiled.

Then he thought of the stacks of paperwork waiting on his desk and the smile slid away. With a sigh, Cord headed for his study.

Two

It was early the following morning that Mrs. Mills began her instruction and Tory learned the scope of her duties. Fortunately, she had managed a fairly large household at Harwood Hall, though the penny-pinching baron kept the staff to a minimum, resulting in long, exhausting days for all of them.

Though Claire had never worked at Harwood, she accepted her duties without the least complaint, collecting peas and beans from the kitchen garden, haring off to the marketplace for a pot of butter Cook needed for the evening meal, enjoying the camaraderie of working with the other servants.

Since their mother, Charlotte Temple Whiting, Lady Harwood, had died three years ago, they'd had very little social life. Tory had been away at Mrs. Thornhill's Private Academy when her mother had fallen ill. After her mother's death, her stepfather had insisted that Tory forgo the balance of her term at school to stay home and manage the household in her mother's stead.

Claire, he said, could receive private instruction. Where the girls were concerned, the baron was miserly in the extreme, but Tory now knew he also hoped to find his way into her sister's bed.

A shiver ran down her spine. *Claire is safe now,* she told herself. But in truth, the theft of the necklace and the possible death of the baron hung over them like a shroud that darkened each of their days. Surely, if the man had died, she would have read about it in the papers—or been apprehended for the deed by now.

Then again, perhaps the baron had recovered and simply said nothing of the crime, hoping to avoid a scandal. He was obsessed with the title he had gained on the death of her father. He was Baron Harwood now. He would not wish to sully the name.

Her mind strayed to the necklace. From the moment Miles Whiting had first seen it, he had been fascinated with the beautiful string of pearls interspersed with glittering diamonds. Tory thought that perhaps he had purchased it for his mistress then couldn't bear to part with it. Whatever the truth, the necklace always seemed to have an odd sort of hold over him.

Surely the whispered tales of violence and passion, vast fortunes gained and lost that revolved around the necklace were nothing more than fantasy.

Then again… Tory glanced around, thinking of her present situation, her face damp from the coal fires burning beneath the pots boiling on the stove, her hair springing out of its coil and sticking to the back of her neck. She thought of Claire and worried at the earl's intentions—and wondered, just for an instant, if perhaps the curse was real.

* * *

Tory worked with Mrs. Mills, going over each of the tasks she would be responsible for as housekeeper. Keeping the accounts, preparing menus and receiving deliveries, inventorying the larder, looking after the linens and placing orders for household supplies were among an endless list.

It wasn't until several hours later, as she headed upstairs to begin an inventory of the west-wing linen closet, that she encountered the earl, lounging in the doorway of one of the bedchambers. Her sister was changing the linens inside the room, she realized, and her whole body stiffened.

"Is there something you need, my lord?" Tory asked, certain she knew what he was about.

"What? Oh, no, nothing, thank you. I was just..." He flicked a glance at Claire, who was staring out the window holding an armload of dirty sheets. "What is your sister doing?"

Tory followed his gaze, saw Claire standing there with a mesmerized look on her face. Reaching out, she caught a moth on the tip of her finger. She didn't move an inch as she watched the tiny wings float up and down.

Worry tightened Tory's chest. They needed this job. They were out of money, out of options. They simply had nowhere else to go.

"You needn't fear, my lord. Claire is a very hard worker. She'll see her tasks completed. It might take her a little longer than someone else, but she's very conscientious. And she'll do a very good job."

The earl looked down at Tory. His eyes were a sort of golden brown, a bit unusual and somehow disturbing.

"I'm sure she will." His gaze flicked back to Claire, who still stood mesmerized by the slow, graceful movement of the tiny moth.

Tory started forward, walking purposely into the room. "Claire, darling. Why don't you take those sheets down to Mrs. Wiggs? She could probably use some help with the laundry."

Claire's face softened into a beatific smile. "All right." Strolling out of the room, she breezed right past the earl, whose gaze followed her feminine movements down the hall.

"As I said, you don't have to worry about Claire."

His attention returned to Tory and a corner of his mouth edged up. "No, I have a feeling you do enough worrying about her all by yourself."

Tory made no reply, just continued past him into the hall. Her heart was racing, her stomach oddly trembling. Fear of losing their desperately needed employment, she told herself. But as her gaze slid one last time toward the tall, dark-haired earl, she worried that it might be something else.

The ormolu clock on the mantel struck midnight. Seated behind the desk in his study, Cord barely heard it. Instead, he stared into the circle of light from the silver whale-oil lamp illuminating the ledger he had been poring over since just after supper. Wearily, he rubbed his eyes and leaned back in his chair, thinking how far into the red his family fortune had sunk before he had taken over the job of rebuilding.

Until the day his father died, he'd had no idea the problems the old man had been facing. Cord had been too busy carousing with his friends, drinking and debauching, gaming, skirt-chasing and generally doing whatever pleased him at the moment. He'd had no time for family responsibilities, duties that should have been his as the eldest son.

Then his father had suffered an apoplexy, leaving him unable to speak and his left side paralyzed, distorting his once-handsome face. Two months later, the earl of Brant was dead and the crushing weight of his financially failing earldom settled heavily on his son's more-than-adequate shoulders.

In the two years since, Cord still wondered if the earl might not be alive today if his son had been there to help ease his burden. Perhaps together they could have solved at least a portion of the estate's financial problems. Perhaps if the strain hadn't been so great...

Ah, but it was too late for that now and so the guilt remained, driving Cord to do what he felt he should have done in the first place.

He sighed into the silence of the room, hearing the clock tick now, watching his shadow move against the wall as he leaned over his desk. At least there was some satisfaction in the accomplishments he had made. Several wise investments over the past two years had returned the Brant coffers to a satisfactory level. He had earned enough to pay for all the needed repairs on the three estates that belonged to the earldom and make several new investments that looked very promising indeed.

Still, it wasn't enough. He owed his father for failing him in his time of need. Cord meant to repay him not by simply rebuilding the Brant family fortune but taking it to greater heights than it had ever been before.

Not only had he discovered he was remarkably good at making money, he had formulated a financial plan, one that included marriage to an heiress, a lady of quality who could contribute to the family wealth.

He didn't imagine that goal would be particularly difficult to accomplish. Cord knew women. He felt comfortable with them, liked them—young or old, fat or thin, rich or poor. And they liked him. He already had his eye on a couple of potential mates. When the time came, it wouldn't be hard to decide which attractive, wealthy young woman he should marry.

Thinking of women, an image of the lovely little blonde asleep upstairs rose into his head. He had never seduced one of the servants before, or for that matter, such an obvious innocent, but remembering the beautiful Claire, he was willing to make an exception. And he would take very good care of her. He would see she had a comfortable town house and be generous enough in his allowance that she could take care of her older sister.

The arrangement would benefit all of them.

It was Monday, Tory's first official day as the earl of Brant's housekeeper. It was just past noon and so far things hadn't gone well. Even though the earl had introduced her to the staff as *Mrs.* Temple, Tory had known it would be difficult for a young woman her age to gain their loyalty and respect.

Hiring a woman of her mere nineteen years just simply was not done. The servants were resentful of taking orders from someone they saw as completely inexperienced, and though that was scarcely the case, beyond proving herself as time went on, there was nothing she could do to change their opinion.

To make matters worse, the servants all expected the job would be given to Mrs. Rathbone, a senior member of the below-stairs serving staff. And Mrs. Rathbone was obviously furious to have been overlooked.

"Tory?" Claire came rushing down the sweeping spiral staircase. Even the mobcap she wore over her silver-blond curls, the crisp black taffeta skirt and plain white blouse, couldn't dim the glow of her beautiful face. "I finished sweeping the guest rooms in the east wing. What shall I do next?"

Tory gazed round the lavishly furnished mansion, noting the freshly cut flowers on the table in the entry, the gleam of the inlaid parquet floors. At first glance, the interior of the house looked clean, the Hepplewhite tables glistening, the hearths cleaned of coal dust, but on closer inspection, she had discovered a number of things amiss.

The silver badly needed polishing, none of the guest rooms had been freshened in weeks, and the chimneys needed sweeping. The rugs were due for a very thorough beating and the draperies desperately needed to be aired.

She would see it done, she told herself. Somehow she would win the servants' cooperation.

"I haven't done the rooms in the west wing," Claire said from her place on the stairs. "Shall I go up and sweep in there?"

Tory didn't really want her to. Lord Brant's room was in that part of the house and she had vowed to keep her sister as far away from the earl as she possibly could.

"Why don't you go down to the butler's pantry and

help Miss Honeycutt finish polishing that lovely Sheffield silver?"

"All right, but—"

"My room could certainly use a bit of sweeping," the earl drawled from where he stood on the staircase just above Claire, his unusual golden eyes running over her sister's suddenly flushed features.

Claire dropped into a curtsey, momentarily lost her balance and almost tumbled down the stairs. Fortunately, the earl reached out and caught her arm, helping her regain her footing.

"Take it easy, love. You needn't kill yourself trying to get there."

More color stained Claire's already rosy cheeks. "Forgive me, my lord. Sometimes I—I'm a little clumsy. I shall see to it right away." Claire raced back up the stairs, passing the earl, causing him to turn and watch her climb upward. His lion's gaze followed her until she disappeared, then he turned and fixed his attention on Tory.

"I trust you're settling into your new position."

"Yes, my lord. Everything is going along quite well." That was a lie, of course. The servants barely acknowledged her existence and she wasn't sure how much work she could actually get them to do.

"Good. Let me know if there is anything you need." He turned and started climbing upward, heightening Tory's worry about his intentions toward Claire.

"My lord?"

He paused near the top of the landing. "Yes?"

"There are...I have a couple of items I should like to discuss."

"Perhaps a little later." He took the last several steps, started striding toward his room.

"They are rather important," Tory called after him, beginning to follow him up. "Perhaps you might break away for just a few moments."

Brant stopped and turned. He studied her for several long moments and something told her he knew exactly what she was about.

A faint smile curved his lips. "That important, are they? I'll be down in fifteen minutes."

Cord shook his head, his amused smile still in place as he reached the doorway of his suite. She was quite remarkable, this new housekeeper of his. Cheeky little thing and far too perceptive for his liking. The door stood open. His gaze slid across the room to the ethereal creature in the mobcap pushing the broom with light, rapid strokes, piling up the tiny bit of dust that was all she could find on the carefully polished oak floor.

She was lovely in the extreme. And unlike her slightly impertinent sister, completely in awe and even a little afraid of him. He wondered what he could do to put her at ease.

He started into the room, then stopped as he realized she hadn't noticed his presence, which allowed him the pleasure of watching her. The broom continued its movements, then stilled as Claire stopped to study the little silver music box on his writing desk in the corner. Lifting the lid, she stood transfixed as the notes of a Beethoven lullaby spilled out.

She began to sway, the broom moving side to side as if it were her dancing partner, her lilting voice softly humming along with the tune in the box. Cord watched her lithe, graceful movements, but instead of being captivated as he had been that first day, he found himself frowning.

As lovely as she was, watching her was like peering into a fairy's private kingdom, like watching a child at play. Cord didn't like the notion.

She saw him just then, jumped and slammed the lid closed on the box. "I—I'm sorry, my lord. It—it was just so lovely. I opened it and the music poured out and, well…I—I hope you aren't angry."

"No," he said with a faint shake of his head, "I'm not angry."

"My lord?" At the sharp tone of Victoria Temple's voice, his eyebrows went up and he swung his attention in her direction. He found himself inwardly smiling at the fierce look on her face.

"What is it now, Mrs. Temple? I thought I told you I'd be down in fifteen minutes."

She smoothed her features into a bland expression. "Quite so, my lord, but I was bringing up this load of freshly washed laundry and I thought I would save you the trouble of walking all the way back downstairs."

She held up the laundry as proof of why she had come and he caught a whiff of starch and soap and a hint of something feminine. "Yes, well, that was extremely thoughtful of you."

And fairly creative. She was a protective little thing, and no doubt. But then he had known that from the start.

With a last glance at Claire, whose face, even drained of color, still held an ethereal beauty unlike anything he'd ever seen, Cord closed the door, leaving the girl to her work. He followed Victoria Temple down the hall, then paused beneath a gilt sconce on the wall.

"All right, Mrs. Temple, these very important questions you have…what are they?" He imagined she'd had time to think of something in the moments she had feared for her sister's safety. He found himself intrigued to discover what she might have come up with.

"To begin, there is the issue of the silver. I assume you wish to keep it polished at all times."

He nodded very seriously. "By all means. What would happen if a guest arrived and the tea service were not up to snuff?"

"Exactly, my lord." She glanced over his shoulder toward the room in which her sister still worked, Claire's humming faintly audible through the door. "And there are the guest rooms to consider."

"The guest rooms?"

"They are desperately in need of airing…if that meets with your approval, of course."

He bit back an urge to laugh and instead kept the serious expression on his face. "Airing… Of course. I should have thought of that myself."

"Then I have your permission?"

"Absolutely." As if Victoria Temple needed his permission for anything she might wish to do. "Why, should a guest catch the scent of less-than-clean air in any of the bedchambers, the humiliation would be unbearable."

"And the chimneys. It's important that—"

"Do with the chimneys whatever you wish, Mrs. Temple. Keeping the house clean is extremely important. That is the reason I hired someone as obviously capable as you. Now, if you will excuse me…"

She opened her mouth, probably thinking he meant to return to where Claire continued to work, then snapped it closed when she saw he was heading, instead, downstairs. Chuckling to himself, he made his way toward his study. Behind him he could hear her sigh of relief.

Cord just smiled. He wasn't sure what to make of either of the two young women, but one thing was certain. His life hadn't been dull since the moment they arrived.

Tory rose early the following morning. As befitted her status as housekeeper, her below-stairs room just off the middle hallway was large and surprisingly pleasant, with a well-furnished sitting room and a bed with a comfortable mattress and pillow. A porcelain basin and pitcher painted with lavender flowers sat on the bureau against the wall, and pretty white muslin curtains hung at the half windows.

Tory poured water into the basin, completed her morning ablutions, then walked over to the black skirt and white blouse that were the uniform she wore each day. She frowned as she picked up the clothes, realizing these weren't the ones she had hung beside the door last night.

Instead, these were freshly laundered, smelling strongly of starch and soap. They crackled as she took them off the hook, so stiff they looked as if they were fashioned of pieces of wood instead of the soft cotton fabric they had been sewn from.

Sweet Mother Mary! Of all the childish... Tory cut herself off, ending her silent tirade before it had actually begun. She didn't know which of the staff had done this, though Mrs. Rathbone, the most senior of the staff, seemed the most likely. Her dislike of Tory was a clear case of jealousy, but it didn't really matter. All of them resented her. They probably spent half the morning devising ways to make her quit. They didn't know how badly she needed this job, how desperate she and Claire were for money.

They didn't understand it was possible they might even be fugitives from the law.

At least they seemed to have accepted Claire. But then, Claire was so sweet and generous nearly everyone did. It was Tory they considered the problem, the one they needed to get rid of. Still, no matter what the others believed, no matter what they did to her, she wasn't going to quit.

Gritting her teeth, Tory pulled the blouse on over her shift and shoved her arms into the sleeves, stepped into the skirt and fastened the tabs, the garments crackling with every move. The blouse scratched under her arms and the collar chafed the back of her neck.

She knew how she sounded, snapping and popping with every step. As she passed a gilded mirror in the hallway, she discovered how awful she looked. The sleeves of the blouse stuck out like wings and the skirt poked out front and back like a stiff black sail.

"What in God's name…?"

Tory froze at the sound of the earl's deep voice, turned to see him striding toward her, dark eyebrows raised in disbelief. *Dear sweet God—of all the rotten luck!* Didn't the man have anything better to do than lurk around the hallways?

Cord stopped in front of her, leaned back and crossed his arms over the very impressive width of his chest.

"Perhaps, Mrs. Temple, when you were asking me all those housekeeping questions the other day, you should have asked my advice on how to manage the laundry. I might have suggested you consider using a bit less starch."

Tory felt the color rushing into her cheeks. She looked like a complete fool in the ridiculous garb, which was perhaps the reason the earl looked even more handsome that he had the day before.

"I am not in charge of the laundry, my lord. However, I assure you that in future, I shall see that more care is taken in the training of your staff in that regard."

A corner of his mouth curved up. "I would think that a very wise course."

He made no move to leave, just stood there grinning, so she simply stared back at him and lifted her chin. "If you will excuse me, my lord."

"Of course. I imagine you have airing and polishing to do—and laundry instruction of course."

Her face colored again. Turning, she left him, trying to ignore his soft chuckling laughter and the crackle and popping of her skirts.

Still smiling, thinking again of Victoria Temple in her god-awful, overstarched clothes, Cord continued down the hall to his study. He had a meeting this morning with Colonel Howard Pendleton of the British War Office. The colonel had been a good friend of his father's. He had also worked closely with Cord's cousin, Ethan.

Aside from the hours spent rebuilding his family fortune, the balance of Cord's time was spent trying to locate his cousin and best friend, Ethan Sharpe. Ethan was the second son of Malcolm Sharpe, marquess of Belford, his mother being Cord's aunt. When Priscilla and Malcolm Sharpe were killed in a carriage accident on their way in from the country, Lord and Lady Brant had taken in the marquess's children, Charles, Ethan and Sarah, to raise as their own.

Since Cord had no siblings, he and the children had become extremely close. There had been the occasional bloody nose, and once Cord had accidentally broken Ethan's arm in a wrestling match that ended up with the two of them landing in the creek. Cord would have suffered a well-deserved birching had Ethan not sworn he had fallen in accidentally and that Cord had been trying to save him from drowning.

The incident had cemented Cord and Ethan's friendship, though Ethan was two years younger. Perhaps it was partly to prove himself that he had joined the navy as soon as he graduated Oxford. That had been nine years ago. Since then, he had left the navy but not His Majesty's Service. Ethan Sharpe captained the schooner *Sea Witch*, serving Britain now as a privateer.

Or at least he had been until he and his ship disappeared.

A soft knock sounded on the study door. His short, stout butler, Timmons, stuck his head through the opening. "Colonel Pendleton is here, my lord."

"Show him in."

A few moments later a silver-haired man in the scarlet tunic of a military officer walked into the study, gold buttons glittering on the front of his coat. Cord rounded his desk and walked over to greet him.

"It's good to see you, Colonel."

"You as well, my lord."

"Would you care for some refreshment? A glass of brandy or a cup of tea?"

"No, thank you. I'm afraid I haven't much time."

Cord passed as well, his mind on Ethan, his worry building each day. For nearly a year, he had been searching, refusing to consider the possibility that the missing ship and its crew might simply have perished in a storm. Ethan was too good a captain, Cord believed. Something else had to have happened.

Both men seated themselves in comfortable leather chairs in front of the hearth and Cord got directly to the business at hand.

"What news, Howard?"

The colonel actually smiled. "A bit of good news, my lord. Three days ago, one of our warships, the *Victor,* arrived in Portsmouth. She was carrying a civilian passenger named Edward Legg. Legg claims to be a member of Captain Sharpe's crew."

Cord's chest tightened. He leaned forward in his chair. "What did he say about Ethan and his ship?"

"That is the good news. Mr. Legg claims that on their last mission, two French warships were lying in wait off the Le Havre coast. Someone had informed them as to Captain Sharpe's arrival—or at least that is what Legg believes. A battle ensued and the *Sea Witch* was damaged beyond repair, but most of the crew was captured, not killed, including Captain Sharpe."

"How did Legg wind up on the *Victor?*"

"Apparently, once they reached the mainland, Legg and another sailor managed to escape. The other man died of injuries he received during the fighting, but Legg made it to Spain, where he came upon the *Victor*, returning to England."

"Did he say where Ethan was taken?"

"I'm afraid he didn't know."

"Was Ethan injured in the fighting?"

"Legg said the captain suffered a saber wound and other miscellaneous injuries in the battle, but he didn't believe they were serious enough to kill a man like Captain Sharpe."

Cord prayed Legg was right. "I'll need to speak to him. The sooner, the better."

"I'll make the necessary arrangements."

They talked a few moments more, then Cord rose from his chair, ending the conversation.

"Thank you, Colonel."

"I'll be in touch," Pendleton said, moving toward the door.

Cord just nodded. Ethan was alive; he was sure of it. The boy who had never shed a tear during the setting of his broken arm had grown into an even tougher man.

And wherever he was, Cord meant to find him.

Three

Tory's laundry problem was resolved. Mrs. Wiggs, the laundress, professed her innocence, hands shaking as she reached out to examine Tory's overstarched apparel.

That night the woman worked late to wash and re-press the clothes and by morning managed to come up with a second skirt and blouse for Tory's limited wardrobe, the black skirt shortened to precisely the correct length.

Today, the household, along with a small fleet of young male sweeps that Tory had employed, was immersed in the task of cleaning the chimneys. The warm days had allowed the bricks to cool so the only danger the boys faced came from falling down the three-story shaft.

There was little chance of that, Tory discovered. Like monkeys, they climbed the rough bricks, making their job look easy, which, of course, it wasn't. Several of the servants assisted them, Mrs. Rathbone among them. Tory checked each fireplace as the sweeps and servants worked.

Satisfied with the progress being made in the Blue Salon, she made her way into Lord Brant's study, where earlier he had been working. She had noticed the long hours he spent there, poring over stacks of paperwork and reviewing the sums in the heavy ledgers sitting on the corner of his desk. In a way it surprised her.

None of the wealthy elite who visited Harwood Hall did the slightest bit of work. They felt it was beneath their dignity, and instead were content to deplete whatever sums they had managed to inherit—her stepfather among them.

The thought sent a familiar jolt of anger shooting through her. Not only had Miles Whiting, her father's cousin and the man next in line for the title, managed to gain the Harwood lands and fortune, he had also wormed his way into her grieving mother's affections, convinced her to marry him, and thereby stolen Windmere, her mother's ancestral home.

Miles Whiting—if she hadn't managed to kill him—was the lowest form of humanity as far as Tory was concerned. He was a thief, a scoundrel, a molester of innocent young women. Beyond that, for the past several years she had begun to suspect he might even be responsible for the death of her father. For all that he had done, Tory had vowed a thousand times that someday Miles Whiting would pay.

Or perhaps he already had.

Resolved not to think of the baron and what might or might not have happened to him, Tory walked over to the fireplace in the corner of the study.

"How is the work progressing, Mrs. Rathbone?"

"There seems ta be a bit of a problem with this one. Perhaps you'll be wantin' ta take a look."

Tory stepped closer. Bending down, she stuck her head into the opening and peered up the chimney—just as one of the sweeps knocked down a load of soot. Black dust flew into her eyes and mouth. Coughing, she inhaled a breath and sucked a snootful up her nose. Gagging and wheezing, she backed away from the chimney and turned a furious stare on Mrs. Rathbone.

"I guess they musta fixed the problem," the older woman said. She was scarecrow-thin, with a sharp nose and wispy black hair shoved up beneath her mobcap. Though no smile appeared on her lips, there was an unmistakable gleam of triumph in her eyes.

"Yes..." Tory agreed through clenched teeth. "I guess they must have." Turning, she started out of the room, her hands and face covered with soot. The way her luck had been going, she wasn't at all surprised to see the earl of Brant lounging in the doorway, his broad shoulders shaking with mirth.

Tory cast him a glance that would have sliced a lesser man off at the knees. "I realize you are lord here, but in this I would advise you not to utter a single word."

Tory walked past him, forcing him to step out of her way to avoid getting soot on his perfectly fitted, nut-brown coat. The earl kept smiling, but made no comment, wise enough, it seemed, to heed her words.

Upstairs in her room, cursing her stepfather and the circumstances that had brought her this low, Tory changed into the second set of garments Mrs. Wiggs had very opportunely provided. She took a moment to compose herself, then returned to her work downstairs.

It occurred to her that in the entire Brant household, her only ally was the butler, Mr. Timmons. But he was a meek, rather mildly mannered man and he mostly kept to himself.

It didn't matter, Tory told herself as she had before. Nothing they could do was going to make her leave.

Cord reclaimed his study within the quarter hour, the chimney sweeps gone off to some other part of the house, Mrs. Rathbone wisely going with them. He wasn't certain if the older woman were responsible for what had happened to his housekeeper, but he had a strong suspicion she was.

He didn't like the idea of the Temple girl having problems, but he couldn't help grinning as he remembered her black face and hands, the white circles of her eyes staring up at him in fury.

She wasn't having an easy time of it. Still, Victoria Temple seemed capable of handling the job he had given her and he didn't think she would appreciate his interference. She was an independent little baggage. He rather admired that about her. He found himself wondering where she had come from and why it was that she and her sister both possessed the manners and speech usually reserved for the upper classes. Perhaps in time, the information would surface.

Meanwhile, Cord had more important things to do than worry about his servants, no matter how intriguing they might be. This afternoon, he planned to interview the sailor, Edward Legg, in regard to the whereabouts of his cousin. Concern for Ethan loomed at the front of his mind and he meant to explore every avenue that might lead to his return.

Cord glanced toward the chessboard in the corner, a

game in progress still laid out on the board and only half finished, the intricately carved pieces resting in the exact location they had been for nearly a year. The long-distance game had become a tradition between the two men, played whenever Ethan went to sea. In his letters to Cord, Ethan made known his moves, and in Cord's reply, he countered. Their skill was fairly well matched, though at present, Cord was ahead two of the last three games.

In the current match, Cord had moved his queen and posted the information in a letter, which had been delivered to Ethan via military courier. But he had never received a reply. The chessboard sat in the corner, a silent reminder of his cousin's disappearance. Cord had left instructions that the pieces not be touched until Captain Sharpe's return. He sighed to think when that might be.

Seating himself behind the desk, he turned his thoughts away from Ethan to the stack of paperwork he needed to do, investments to be considered, accounting to be reviewed, but it wasn't long before his mind began to wander, returning once more to the scene earlier in his study.

A faint smile tugged at his lips as it occurred to him that his housekeeper had had the audacity to issue him a command—and that he'd had the good sense to obey it.

At least the house was beginning to look better, the downstairs floors so shiny Tory could see her face, the household silver once more sparkling. Getting the servants to complete their assignments was like pulling the teeth of a chicken, or however the saying went. Still, little by little, the work was beginning to get done.

And Claire seemed happy in her new home. So far, Tory's worries about the earl had not surfaced. Perhaps he was simply too busy to pay attention to a serving girl, no matter how beautiful she was. Still, she didn't trust him. The earl was an unmarried man and exceedingly virile. There was every chance he was simply another lecher with designs on Claire.

The evening meal was over. Along with most of the servants, Claire had retired upstairs for the night, but Tory still wandered the shadowy halls. She wasn't the least bit sleepy, or perhaps it was her stepfather that stirred her restless thoughts, worry that she had accidentally killed him—though at the time, there hadn't been much of a choice.

Surely if he were dead, the authorities would have been searching for his murderer or might even have found her by now. She hadn't seen anything in the newspapers, but she had only read them sporadically since her arrival in London. Mostly, she had simply been trying to survive.

Deciding that perhaps a book might help her fall asleep and hoping the earl wouldn't mind if she borrowed one, Tory held the oil lamp out in front of her and climbed the short flight of stairs up from the basement. As she passed the earl's study on the way to the library, she realized a lamp had been left burning on his desk. She was making her way in to snuff it out when she noticed the chessboard in the corner.

She had seen it before, had admired the exquisite inlaid board and its ebony and ivory pieces, and wondered which of the earl's acquaintances might be his opponent. But days had passed and the pieces had not been moved.

Tory wandered toward it. She was very good at chess, had been taught by her father and played often with him before he had been killed. Looking down at the board, she couldn't resist seating herself in one of the ornate high-backed chairs to study the moves the earl and his silent opponent had made.

On closer inspection, she saw that although the pieces had been dusted, small circles at the base of those remaining on the board gave evidence the game had been interrupted some while back.

Tory studied the board. Assigning the ebony pieces to the earl, which somehow seemed fitting, and prompted by a sense of competition that was simply part of her nature, she reached over and moved one of the ivory horses. Up two and over one, fitting the beautifully carved knight into a spot that jeopardized the opposing black bishop.

She ought to move the piece back. The earl would undoubtedly be angry if he discovered it was she who had made the move, but some mischievous part of her simply would not let her. He could always put it back, she thought. If he made a fuss, she could simply say it got shifted in the dusting. Whatever he might think, Tory didn't return the knight to its former position.

Instead, sleepy at last, she snuffed the lamp on his desk, picked up her own and headed back down to her room.

The gold crest on the door gleamed beneath the lamp on the side of the Brant carriage as it rolled up in front of Cord's town house. It was well after midnight. After his unproductive interview earlier that afternoon with Edward Legg, who'd had little more to add to his tale besides how gallant and courageous Captain Sharpe had been during the ship's ill-fated battle and how much Legg admired him, Cord's mood had plunged straight downhill.

With his pursuit of Claire Temple somehow stalled and not wishing to put himself back in the clutches of his former mistress, he had decided to pay a badly needed visit to Madame Fontaneau's very exclusive house of pleasure.

Cord wasn't sure what had changed his mind, why he found himself detouring, instructing his driver to take him to White's, his gentlemen's club, instead. But there he had sat some hours later in a deep leather chair, sipping a glass of brandy, immersed in a game of whist, brooding and losing his money.

His good friend, Rafael Saunders, duke of Sheffield, had been there, as well, doing his best to cheer him out of his dismal mood, but his friend had miserably failed.

Instead, Cord had finished his drink, ordered his carriage brought round and returned to his town house. Now, as the coach rolled to a stop in front of the three-story brick building and the footman opened the door, Cord descended the iron stairs and made his way inside the house.

He tossed his kidskin gloves into the crown of his beaver hat and left them on the table beside the door. He glanced up the staircase, knowing he should try to get some sleep. He had important papers to review at his solicitor's first thing in the morning and he hadn't been sleeping very well.

But instead of going upstairs, he headed down the hall to his study. Earlier, for whatever reason, his mind had veered away from his need for a woman to the work he needed to do, to Ethan and, amazingly, to his two latest employees.

The latter in itself amazed him. Had it simply been lust for Claire, he might have understood, but the lovely, ethereal girl appealed to him less and less while the older, slightly impertinent sister intrigued him more and more.

It was ridiculous. And yet as he watched Claire Temple glide through her work like a princess in a fairy tale, the thought continued to nag him that seducing the lovely Claire would be completely unfair. Where women were concerned, Cord was a man of vast experience, while Claire...well, he wasn't certain the girl completely understood the differences between male and female.

In truth, seducing her would be like pulling the wings off a beautiful butterfly.

Out of sorts with women in general and cursing himself for not partaking of some badly needed sexual relief before returning home, Cord eyed the stack of papers still sitting on his desk. He removed his coat and tossed it over a chair, loosened and pulled off his cravat, rolled up his shirtsleeves and prepared to settle in for a couple of hours of work.

As he crossed the study, his gaze slid over to the chessboard in the corner. He continued a few more paces before he found himself frowning, turning back to where the inlaid board sat between two ornately carved high-backed chairs.

Cord studied the pieces on the board. He knew exactly where each one rested, had stared at them so many times he could close his eyes and see them in his sleep.

Tonight something was different, slightly out of place. Cord stiffened in anger as he realized one of the pieces had been moved.

He told himself he must be wrong, but seeing the knight that now threatened his bishop, he remembered the game he and Ethan had started, the game they might never finish, and a muscle ticked in his cheek. Certain one of the servants had moved the piece, he stormed out of the study, his temper in high dudgeon, strode down the hall and started toward the stairs leading down to the basement.

Thoughts of Ethan kept him going, past the below-stairs' first and second hallways, past the kitchen. Anger still pumped through him as Cord reached the end of the corridor and hammered on Victoria Temple's door. He didn't wait for her to answer, just lifted the latch, strode through her small sitting area and on in to her bedchamber.

The pounding must have awakened her. As the bedroom door slammed back against the wall, he saw her jerk upright in her narrow bed, trying to blink herself awake.

"Good evening, Mrs. Temple. There is a matter of some importance I wish to discuss."

She blinked several more times. "N-now?" She was dressed in a thin white cotton night rail, her usually clear green eyes heavy-lidded with fatigue, her mouth rosy from slumber. A single thick braid of chestnut hair hung over one shoulder while stray wisps curled around her cheeks.

He had thought her merely attractive. Now he saw she was far more than that. With her finely carved features, full lips and straight, patrician nose, Victoria Temple was a very lovely young woman. If she hadn't been so overshadowed by the otherworldly beauty of her sister, he would have noticed long ago.

She shifted on the bed and his blood began to thicken. In the moonlight streaming in through the bedchamber window, he could see the outline of her breasts, the dark shadows of her nipples, the pale arch of her throat beneath the small pink bow on the front of her gown. Desire sank into his loins, pulled low in his belly.

"My lord?"

He dragged his gaze back to her face, saw that she was staring up at him as if he had lost his mind, and a fresh bout of anger rippled through him.

"Yes, Mrs. Temple, we need to discuss this now—this very instant."

She seemed to finally awaken. Glancing down, for the first time she realized the state of her undress and that a man stood next to her bed. With a small squeak, she jerked the covers up over her very lovely breasts.

"Lord Brant—for heaven's sake! It is the middle of the night. Need I remind you it is highly improper for you to be standing in my bedchamber?"

Highly improper and extremely arousing. "I am here for a reason, Mrs. Temple. As I said, there is something of importance I wish to discuss."

"And that would be…?"

"Surely Mrs. Mills instructed you in the matter of my chessboard."

She paused in the act of scooting backward, taking the covers with her, then continued until her shoulders came to rest against the headboard. "What…what about it?"

"Mrs. Mills and the rest of the servants received strict

instruction that those pieces were not to be moved under any circumstance."

"Are you...saying someone did?"

"Exactly, Mrs. Temple, and I expect you to ferret out the culprit and see that he doesn't do it again."

"You are here...in my room at—" she broke off, glanced at the small clock on the bureau "—half past three in the morning, because someone moved a chess piece? I don't see how that could possibly be of such importance that you would come barging into my bedchamber in the middle of the night."

"What you do or do not see is none of your concern. I don't want those pieces moved—not until my cousin is returned."

"Your cousin?"

"That is correct. Captain Ethan Sharpe of the *Sea Witch.* He and his crew are missing."

She said nothing for several long moments. "I'm sorry." He wasn't sure what she saw in his face but her features softened. "You must be very worried about him."

There was something in the way she said it. Or perhaps it was the way she looked at him when she did. Whatever it was, his anger seeped away as if a hole had been pricked in his skin.

"Yes, well, I am, and I appreciate your concern. At any rate, if you discover the man who moved the piece, please inform him not to do so again."

She eyed him in the moonlight, took in his weary expression. "Perhaps it would be good to finish the game, my lord. Sometimes memories do more harm than good. You can always begin anew once Captain Sharpe is returned."

He'd had the same thought himself. The chessboard was a grim reminder, a haunting note that never let him forget Ethan was missing, perhaps even dead. "Just do as I say, Mrs. Temple."

Cord took a last long look at the woman propped up in bed and thought how incredibly desirable she looked. In the moonlight, her eyes were luminous green pools, her lips a little pouty. He wanted to pull back the sheet and lift her night rail, to feast his eyes on the delectable body outlined by the thin cotton garment. He wanted to remove the ribbon at the end of her braid and run his fingers through the heavy dark strands of her hair.

His body tightened with arousal and Cord turned away. As he left the room, he shook his head, wondering what the devil was happening to him lately. He had never been the sort to have designs on his serving women, but lately, two of them had caught his fancy.

He amended that. One had appealed to his appreciation of beauty, like a finely crafted vase or an exquisite painting. The other intrigued him with her saucy tongue and overly protective nature. Now that he had seen her in her bedclothes, his prurient interests had also been aroused.

He should have gone to Madame Fontaneau's, he told himself as he climbed the stairs. Then again, he far preferred a relationship of sorts with the women he took to his bed. As he headed upstairs, he thought again of Victoria Temple.

With Olivia Landers gone from his life, he remained in need of a mistress. Now that his misplaced desire for Claire had vanished, he began to think that perhaps he had merely fixed his interest on the wrong woman.

Where Claire was shy and fearful, Victoria was bold and not the least afraid of him. Beneath her prim facade, he sensed a passionate nature he would very much like to explore.

And of course, he would take care of her, set her up in grand style and see that she wanted for nothing. She could take care of Claire, as she wanted so badly to do. He would be doing them all a favor.

Yes, Victoria would be a far greater challenge than her sweetly innocent sister. In fact, judging from the fiery look in her eyes when he had burst into her room, she might very well run him a merry chase. Still, Cord loved nothing better than a challenge, and in the end, he would have her. Victoria Temple might as well resign herself to her fate.

Tory immersed herself in her work the following day, making an inventory of the wine cellar, receiving deliveries from the butcher and the milkman, trying to keep her mind off the earl and his appearance in her room last night.

Just thinking about it made her pulse race. Sweet God, the man had been beyond angry. Surely moving a single chess piece hadn't set off such a reaction?

Tory thought perhaps it was more a response to his worry for his cousin than the fact that the piece had been moved. It was obvious the men were close friends. She knew what it was like to lose a loved one. She had lost her father and not long after, her mother. She knew how badly it hurt.

And yet she wasn't sorry that she had moved the piece. Perhaps in a way, the outburst had been good for him, a means of helping him vent his frustration. She could still recall the way he had looked—a virtual fire-breathing dragon with the light of battle glowing in his golden eyes.

His coat had been missing, his shirtsleeves rolled up over nicely corded forearms. Snug black breeches hugged a narrow waist and the long, solid muscles in his thighs. He had been breathing hard, expanding the width of an already powerful chest.

As furious as he was, for the first time since they had met, he had looked at her. Really looked at her. And the heat in his tawny eyes had made her feel as if her bones were slowly melting. She had felt as if her heart might pound its way out of her chest, as if her entire body might go up in smoke. Then, to her utter mortification, her nipples had peaked beneath her night rail.

Secretly, she had worried about the strange pull she felt whenever she encountered the earl. Now, sweet Lord, her worst fears were confirmed. She was attracted to the earl of Brant!

It was ridiculous. Completely absurd. She wasn't even sure she liked him. She certainly didn't trust him, and aside from that, the man was an earl while she was merely a servant. Even as the daughter of a baron, after hearing the gossip about him, Lord Brant was the last man who should interest her.

Was it only earlier that morning Miss Honeycutt had stood just inside the butler's pantry giggling at the tale she had heard from Alice Payne, lady's maid to the Viscountess Westland?

"Alice says 'e's quite the stallion, is the earl. Says 'e can tup all night and still be rarin' for more in the mornin'. Says her ladyship were sore for a week the last time 'e come to call."

Like every other young woman, one day Tory hoped to marry. Someone kind and considerate, a gentle sort of man, she had always imagined, a man much like her father, who never spoke a harsh word to either his daughters or his wife.

Certainly not a man like Brant with his fiery temper and equally fiery passions.

Fortunately, aside from the hot looks he had cast her way last night—due, she was certain, to the natural instincts of a male in the proximity of a young woman in a state of semi-undress—Lord Brant had eyes only for Claire. In that regard, Tory vowed to remain vigilant. If Brant were half the rake he seemed, Claire yet remained in danger.

Tory strengthened her resolve to do whatever it took to protect her sister from the earl.

Four

"Tory?" Claire flew toward her up the stairs. Three days had passed since the earl had barged into her room and things seemed to have returned to normal. "Thank goodness I found you!"

"What is it, darling?"

"It's Mrs. Green and her daughter, Hermione. They had to leave for the day. Mrs. Green says she is coming down with an ague and she thinks Hermione has contracted it, as well."

"An ague? They both looked perfectly healthy this morning." Then Tory remembered that she had assigned the women the job of preparing two of the upstairs guest rooms for the arrival of Lady Aimes, one of the earl's cousins, and her little boy, Teddy. It was simply another attempt to make Tory leave, but there was nothing she could do about it now.

She looked down the stairs to the grandfather clock in the entry. The day was rapidly slipping away. The rest of the staff was busy, grudgingly doing the work she had assigned them. Any attempt to rearrange their schedule would simply cause more trouble than it was worth.

"I'll take care of it, Claire. You go ahead and finish helping Mrs. Wadding. She is outside beating carpets."

Claire hurried off to her tasks and Tory made her way downstairs to collect a broom, mop and pail.

All the rooms in the house were lovely, and the two she had chosen for Lord Brant's guests overlooked the garden, one of them done in peach and cream, the other in shades of robin's-egg blue.

Deciding the little boy should have the blue, she began her work in there, opening the windows to let in the summer breeze, fluffing the feather pillows, dusting the landscape paintings on the wall and the marble mantel over the hearth. She did the same to the second room, grateful that at least the linens had already been changed, then began the job of mopping the inlaid parquet floors.

She was down on her hands and knees scrubbing a particularly stubborn stain when a pair of shiny men's shoes appeared in her line of vision. Her gaze traveled up a set of very long, very masculine legs, over a broad chest and extremely sizable shoulders.

Tory sank back on her heels as she looked up at the earl. "My lord?"

"What the devil are you doing?"

She glanced down, saw that her skirt was wet, her white blouse damp and clinging to her breasts, so translucent she could see the shadow of her nipples.

Brant must have noticed. His gaze fixed there and some of the heat she had seen before reappeared in his eyes. Tory's face heated up as he continued to stare at the damp fabric plastered over her bosom.

Tory swallowed, tried to pretend nothing was wrong. "Two of the chambermaids took ill," she explained. "In their stead, I am completing the work necessary for the arrival of your guests."

"Is that so?" The earl's jaw hardened, and instead of answering, she found herself wanting to back away. A little squeak escaped as Brant caught her arm and hauled her to her feet.

"Dammit, I didn't hire you to scrub my floors. I hired you to run my house. As I see it, there is a very large difference."

"But—"

"There is a virtual bevy of servants in this house. Find one to take care of the guest rooms." He frowned at the look of horror that appeared on her face. "Never mind. I'll send someone up myself."

To her utter amazement, the earl strode out of the bedchamber and down the stairs. She could hear him bellowing for Timmons and a few minutes later, Miss Honeycutt and Mrs. Wadding both came bolting into the room.

Determined to act with at least some portion of her authority as housekeeper, Tory instructed the women to finish mopping the floors in both bedchambers, then sprinkle a few drops of lavender scent on the embroidered linen pillowcases.

With menus to plan for the week and shopping lists to compile, she left them to their work and returned downstairs. She was on her way to change into a dry blouse when she passed the open door to the earl's study. Her steps seemed to slow all by themselves and she found herself wandering inside, over to the chessboard in the corner.

She was surprised to discover the white knight hadn't been returned to its former position but remained exactly where she had placed it. Even more amazing, the earl had countered the move.

Not that he knew it was she who had made it. Clearly, he believed one of the male servants had made the play, having made the reference to a man several times in his tirade that night—which irritated her more than he knew. Perhaps he thought it was Timmons who challenged him or one of the two new footmen who had recently been hired.

Whatever the case, in moving his bishop in response, her challenge had clearly been accepted. Either that, or a trap was being laid to discover if the culprit had the nerve to gainsay his orders again.

Tory pondered the latter, worried she might lose her position. Surely the man wouldn't fire her over a simple chess game. Convinced she could talk her way out of trouble if she had to and never one to back down from a challenge, she seated herself in front of the board and contemplated how to counter the earl's countermove.

It was late in the afternoon the following day, the June days lengthening and growing warmer. With so many projects in the works, Cord rarely had time for visitors. His cousin Sarah was the exception.

Seated on a pale blue brocade sofa in the Blue Salon, Sarah Sharpe Randall, Viscountess Aimes, was the sister Cord never had. Blond and fair, Sarah was tall for a woman yet slim and fine-boned. As children growing up, he had always been protective of her, the only girl among three rowdy boys, but in truth, Sarah was entirely capable of taking care of herself.

Cord crossed the high-ceilinged room beneath a crystal chandelier, stopping in front of an ornately carved sideboard to refill his glass of brandy.

"How is Jonathan?" he asked, speaking of her husband. "Well, I trust."

Lifting a delicate, gold-rimmed porcelain teacup, Sarah took a sip of her chamomile tea. "Aside from grousing over the fact he had prior commitments and couldn't come with us, he is fine. He sends you his regards."

Cord took a drink of brandy. "Teddy has certainly grown since last I saw him. I hardly recognized the boy."

Sarah smiled with pleasure. Her husband and son were the most important people in her life. "Teddy looks more like his father every day."

"You have a fine family, Sarah."

"Yes, I am fortunate in that. Perhaps it is time you began to think of having a family of your own, Cord."

Carrying his glass, he walked over to the sofa. "Actually, I've been thinking quite a lot about it. I'm trying to work up the courage to enter the marriage mart. So far I haven't quite found the nerve."

"At least you're considering the notion. That is more than you have ever done before."

"More than considering. I've decided to wed. It's merely a matter of choosing the right woman."

"Have you anyone particular in mind?"

He thought of Mary Ann Winston and Constance Fairchild, the two young women currently at the top of his list, but he was far from ready to mention any names. "Not yet."

"Tell me you've given up that silly notion of marrying an heiress. I can tell you from experience, loving someone is far more important."

"Perhaps to you." He sipped his drink. "I'm afraid I wouldn't recognize the emotion, though I can tell you're happy with Jonathan. It shows in your face."

"I'm very happy, Cord. Except for missing Ethan."

It was the reason for Sarah's visit. She had come to discover news of her brother, which they had briefly discussed over breakfast earlier that morning. Cord set his brandy glass down on a piecrust table.

"I wish I had more to report. At least we know that the *Sea Witch* didn't go down in a storm. According to Edward Legg, Ethan was alive when he was taken off the ship."

"Yes, and I suppose in a way that is very good news. My brother is a strong man and we both know how determined he can be. We must believe he is still alive. Which means, all we have to do is discover where he might have been taken."

Cord only wished it were that easy. He took a courage-building breath, preparing to explain the difficulties they would be facing in their renewed effort to locate her brother, when a soft knock sounded at the door.

"That will be Pendleton," Cord said, grateful for the interruption. "I received a message from him this morning. Perhaps he has received more information."

Cord opened the door, allowing the silver-haired colonel to enter. Pendleton made a polite bow to Sarah, his glance taking in her upswept golden blond hair, fine features and the feminine fit of her pale green silk gown.

He spoke for a moment to Cord, then addressed himself to Sarah. "I presume, Lady Aimes, that Lord Brant has informed you of the latest word on Captain Sharpe."

"Yes, he has. We were both in hopes you might be bringing news of his whereabouts."

"Unfortunately, not quite yet. We have, however, as of this morning, been able to place an informant on the shores of France with the specific duty of locating the prison where Captain Sharpe may have been taken."

Sarah's features seemed to draw in. "*Prison.* I suppose I have denied the thought far too long. I cannot bear to think of my brother suffering in such a place."

"Dear lady, you mustn't despair. Once we are certain of the captain's whereabouts, we shall find a way to rescue him."

Sarah nodded, managed a wobbly smile. "Yes, I'm certain you will."

Cord spoke up just then. "In the meantime, Colonel Pendleton has promised to keep us informed of whatever news he receives and I shall do the same."

The meeting lasted a few minutes more, then Pendleton left the study. Needing to check on Teddy, Sarah followed him out, leaving Cord alone.

The news of Ethan again had been good. For the first time in nearly a year, he felt they were finally making progress.

As he thought of Ethan, his gaze strayed toward the chessboard. Something looked different. He found himself walking in that direction, stopping next to the board. Then he saw that a piece had been moved yet again and a fresh shot of anger poured through him.

He'd been certain the Temple girl would relay his middle-of-the-night demands to the servants. Just to be sure, he had baited a trap for the culprit, daring him to disobey his rules again. The ivory knight remained as it was, but in response to his countermove, the ivory queen had been advanced three spaces.

Cord found himself studying the board. It was an intriguing move. His bishop remained in danger, and if he weren't careful, his castle just might fall. He told himself to move the pieces back to their original position. Ethan was the man he should be playing. But he couldn't quite convince himself. Perhaps with this latest news of his cousin, it was a good sign the game had begun again.

He wondered if Timmons had taken it upon himself to challenge him in an effort to renew his spirits where Ethan was concerned, or if, as he had believed that night, one of the new footmen simply could not resist.

A niggling thought surfaced. Claire Temple wouldn't have the slightest notion how to play a sophisticated game like chess, but her sister… Surely, Victoria Temple wasn't masterminding the game.

Few women played, even fewer did so with any amount of skill, yet the latest moves said this player knew what he—or she—was about. That his opponent might be Victoria Temple was, though somewhat farfetched, decidedly intriguing.

Cord sat down in one of the ornate chairs and began to assess the board. The clock ticked and time slipped past. Lifting his black knight, Cord countered his opponent's latest move.

Tory stretched and arched her back, trying to work out the kinks in her neck and shoulders. Today had been even more difficult than the day before, the atmosphere below stairs openly hostile, Mrs. Rathbone's silent anger grating on everyone's nerves.

As housekeeper, Tory could fire the serving woman and hire a replacement, but somehow that didn't seem fair. What she needed to do was win the woman's loyalty—but she had no idea how to go about it.

Badly in need of fresh air, she walked over to the French doors leading into the garden, then found herself shoving them open and walking out beneath the warm summer sun. White clouds floated by overhead, one shaped like a dragon, the other a damsel in distress. Not liking the image, she wandered through the garden, which was lush and green with colorful crocuses blooming along the gravel paths and bright purple pansies yawning at her feet.

She shouldn't be out there. She was a servant, not a guest. Still, it had been so long since she had enjoyed the splash of water in a fountain, smelled the scent of lavender in the air. Pausing next to the round, tiered fountain, she closed her eyes and inhaled a deep breath of air.

"Are you Mrs. Temple?"

Tory's eyes shot open. She looked down to see a small, dark-haired boy standing beside her. "Why, yes, I am." She smiled. "And you must be Master Teddy Randall."

He grinned and she saw that two of his front teeth were missing. He was perhaps five or six, with great blue eyes and a smile that lit up his face.

"How did you know my name?" he asked.

"I overheard your mother and Lord Brant talking about you at breakfast," she said.

"I heard people talking about you, too." He looked up into her face. "Why doesn't anyone like you?"

Tory's smile slid away. "The earl was talking about me?"

He shook his head. "A lady named Mrs. Rathbone and the cook. They said you were Lord Brant's doxy. That's why he hired you. What's a doxy? I thought it was some kind of dog."

Her face must have been seven shades of scarlet. How dare they say such a thing! Thoughts of firing the woman resurfaced, but Tory tamped them down.

"Well…a doxy is…is someone who does things she shouldn't. But that is not at all the truth. And it is the very reason you must never listen to gossip." She reached down and took hold of his hand. "You mentioned dogs," she said, desperate for a change of subject. "Do you like puppies?"

He vigorously nodded.

"Well, then, you are in luck. There is a new litter just birthed out in the mews."

Teddy grinned and a dimple appeared in his cheek. "I love puppies. 'Specially little black fuzzy ones."

Tory smiled. "Come on, then." Still holding on to his hand, she started leading him through the garden. "Why don't we have a look?"

They were just walking into the shadowy interior of the carriage house, Teddy clinging to her hand, when she spotted Lord Brant on his way out.

He paused just in front of them. "Well, I see you two have become acquainted."

Mrs. Rathbone's words came rushing back, sending hot color into her cheeks. She wanted to shout at him, tell him the gossip was entirely his fault, but in truth it was her fault as much as his, since she never should have accepted the housekeeping job in the first place.

She kept her features bland. "Yes, we met out in the garden." The words came out a bit sharply. She wished she had the nerve to quit. She couldn't possibly do that. She had to think of Claire and what would happen to them if she did. "Teddy and I have come to look at the puppies. If you will excuse us, my lord."

But he made no effort to move, just stood exactly where he was, tall and broad-shouldered enough to easily block their way.

"I heard the coachman's mongrel had a litter. If you don't mind the company, I would enjoy seeing them myself."

Oh, she minded. She minded a very great deal. The servants were already gossiping about them. Seeing them together would only fuel the wagging tongues.

Still, she could scarcely order him out of his own carriage house. She and Teddy started forward and the earl fell in beside her. She stiffened at the feel of his warm hand settling at her waist, guiding her through the shadowy interior, past a shiny black carriage parked at the far end of the building.

She could hear the faint rustle of her skirt against his leg and her heart kicked up. When his arm lightly brushed her breast as he helped her through the doorway into another, smaller room filled with harnesses and hay, a rush of heat slid into her stomach.

They reached the enclosure where the puppies lay sleeping next to their mother, a thin, black-and-white-spotted hound, but the earl didn't move away. She tried to widen the distance between them, but there simply wasn't room.

"They're only a few days old," he said softly, his warm breath fanning her cheek. Embarrassingly, she trembled.

"Could I hold one?" Teddy asked, staring down at the mongrel pups as if they were purebred.

"They're too little yet," Brant said, reaching down to affectionately ruffle the little boy's dark hair. "Perhaps the next time you visit."

"Do you think I could have one?"

The earl chuckled softly, and Tory felt an odd lift in her stomach. "If your mother says it's all right. Why don't you go in and ask her?"

Teddy grinned up at him, turned and tore out of the carriage house, running pell-mell back inside and leaving her alone in the shadows with the earl.

"I—it is time I went back in. I have a great deal of work yet to do."

"You're looking a little flushed," he said, his golden eyes fixed on her face. "Are you feeling all right, Mrs. Temple?"

He was standing so near she could measure the beats of his heart, study the sensual curve of his bottom lip, see the way his mouth faintly lifted in one corner.

"It's…it's a bit close in here. I believe I could use a breath of air."

His lips curved even more. "Of course." He stepped away from her so quickly she nearly lost her balance. The earl's hand shot out to steady her. "You seem a little faint. Here, let me help you."

"No! I mean…I'm fine. Really I am."

"At least let me help you outside."

Sweet Lord, Brant's help was the last thing she needed. Mostly, she just wanted to get as far away from him as she possibly could. Why did that seem such a difficult task?

She tried to ignore his nearness, the strength of the hand at her waist, guiding her out of the mews, into the sunlight behind the fountain in the garden, but she couldn't dismiss the flush in her cheeks or the soft heat in her stomach.

She felt a little better outside, a little more in control. The earl very politely stepped away.

"Feeling better?"

"Yes, much, thank you."

"Then I shall leave you to your work. Good afternoon, Mrs. Temple."

Tory watched him walk away, her heart still pounding, her knees weak beneath her skirt. The man had played the perfect gentleman and yet she could barely catch her breath. Dear God, if he did, indeed, have intentions toward Claire—

Tory walked back to the house, more worried about her sister than she had ever been before.

A summer storm rolled over the city, thick black clouds blocking the thin slice of moon. Thunder rumbled outside the mullioned windows as Tory made her way through the shadowy darkness to the earl's study. The grandfather clock in the entry began the twelve chimes of midnight.

It was the Season in London. Lady Aimes was attending a house party with friends and, as was his custom, the earl had gone out for the evening.

Earlier, most of the servants had retired to their rooms, Tory among them. As she had lain in bed, she told herself to stay exactly where she was, to ignore the earl's latest chess move. But the challenge was simply too great.

As soon as the house fell silent, she pulled her quilted wrapper over her night rail, picked up the whale-oil lamp in her sitting room and headed for the stairs.

Now as she entered the study, she could see the chessboard, the glow of her lamp casting the tall ebony and ivory pieces into shadow. She ignored the cold wooden floor beneath her bare feet, quietly made her way to the board and seated herself in one of the high-backed chairs.

Setting the lamp down on the table, Tory studied the board, barely aware of the rustle of branches against the brick walls outside, the glimpse of moonlight between passing clouds. Gazing at the pieces, she knew a moment of satisfaction. The earl had taken the bait. The trap she had laid had won her his castle.

She picked up a pawn to capture the piece, then realized that in doing so she was leaving an opening that could net him her queen. Tory grinned. The man was no fool. She would have to be more careful. She was deep in thought, planning the strategy that would win her the game, when a husky voice rumbled into her awareness.

"Perhaps you should take the castle after all. There is always the chance your opponent will fail to see the danger in which you've left your queen."

Tory's hand froze above the chessboard. Turning very slowly in her seat, she looked up into the face of the earl. "I don't...I don't think that he will. I think that he—you—are a very good player."

"Do you? Then that is the reason you ignored my wishes and continued to play after I specifically told you not to?"

Tory eased up out of her chair, hoping to feel less at a disadvantage. She realized her mistake the instant she was on her feet, for only a few inches separated her from the earl. He didn't back away, just kept her pinned there between the chair and the solid wall of his chest.

"Well, Mrs. Temple? Is that the reason you disobeyed my orders? Because I am such a very good player?"

She swallowed. He was a tall, well-built man and she knew firsthand how very volatile his temper. She had learned from her stepfather the consequences of angering such a man. Still, for some strange reason, she wasn't afraid.

"I—I can't exactly say why I did it. Chess is a game I enjoy. I was challenged in a way. Then you came to my room that night and I…I thought that playing again might be good for you."

Some of the tension seeped from his shoulders. "Perhaps it has been. Why don't you sit down, Mrs. Temple? You are prepared, are you not, to make your next move?"

Her own tension eased, replaced by a different sort of nervousness. Unconsciously, she moistened her lips, running the tip of her tongue into the corner of her mouth. In the lamplight, the gold of his eyes seemed to darken. He watched her with such sensual awareness that a little frisson of heat sparked in her belly.

"Yes, my lord. I'm ready." It was insane. She was barefoot and dressed in her nightclothes. It would be no small scandal if someone chanced upon them.

Unable to stop herself, knowing the risk she was taking, she sank back down in her chair, hoping her hand didn't tremble as she reached out and picked up her bishop. She angled it along an open row of beautiful inlaid squares, and captured one of his knights.

The earl chuckled as he seated himself on the opposite side of the chessboard. "You're certain taking the castle wouldn't have been the smarter move?"

Her confidence returned. "Quite certain, my lord."

The earl studied the chessboard, then moved his queen, neatly capturing one of her pawns.

The play went on. The wind howled and wrenched the leaves from the branches of the trees, but in the small circle of light in the earl of Brant's study, Tory felt oddly protected.

She moved her castle. "I'm afraid that is check, my lord."

Brant scowled. "Yes, so it is."

The play continued, pawns and pieces falling as if in a savage battle. It was well past two when the final move was made.

"Checkmate, my lord."

Instead of being angry, as she somewhat feared he might be, the earl merely laughed. He shook his head as he looked over to where she sat on the opposite side of the board.

"You continue to surprise me, Mrs. Temple."

"I hope that means I also continue to retain my position as your housekeeper."

One of his dark brown eyebrows went up. "Perhaps you should lose to me once in a while, simply to ensure you keep your position."

She smiled. "I don't think you would like that in the least."

The earl smiled, too. "No, not in the least. I shall expect a rematch, Mrs. Temple, in the very near future."

"I would be delighted, my lord."

The earl rose and helped Tory to her feet. She found herself in exactly the position that she had been in before, so close she could see the deep gold of his eyes. They seemed to hold her where she stood, to fix her feet to the carpet beneath the table. She felt his hand on her cheek, tilting her face up, then his mouth settled gently over hers.

Tory's eyes slid closed as soft heat enveloped her. He didn't reach for her, just continued to kiss her, his lips moving slowly over hers. He sampled and tasted, coaxed her to open for him, then slid his tongue inside. She started to tremble. Unconsciously, she reached her hand out and clutched the front of his evening coat. He made a deep sound in his throat and his arm came around her, pressing her more fully against him.

It was in that moment, as she felt the hard length of his arousal, that Tory's senses returned, slamming into her with the force of the wind outside the window.

Breaking away, she stumbled backward, desperate to be free of him, to regain her self-control. "My lord! I—I know what you must be thinking, but you are…you are sorely mistaken if you believe that…that I… If you think for an instant that I would…would…"

"It was only a kiss, Mrs. Temple."

Only a kiss? It felt as if her world had just turned upside down. "A kiss that shouldn't have happened. An indiscretion that will not…not occur again."

"I'm sorry you didn't enjoy it. I assure you I did."

Heat rushed into her cheeks. She had enjoyed it—far

too much. "It isn't proper. You are my employer and I am your housekeeper."

"That is true. Perhaps there is something we could do to remedy that."

What on earth was he saying? The word *doxy* popped into her head. "You aren't…you aren't suggesting…? You can't possibly mean that I should…?"

Knees wobbling, she squared her shoulders and picked up the lamp. "I'm afraid I must bid you good-night, my lord." Turning away, she marched past him. As she crossed the study, she could feel his eyes on her, burning like fire into her nightclothes.

"Good night, Mrs. Temple," he said as she walked out of the room.

Five

Standing in the darkness of his study, Cord struck flint to tender, lighting another lamp now that Victoria had carried hers away. He smiled to think how the evening had progressed. Having returned early to the house on purpose, he had been hoping to catch out his chessboard culprit. Secretly hoping it might be Victoria Temple.

She had surprised him with her skill. And pleased him. He liked intelligent women. His cousin Sarah was bright and interesting. As had been his mother, dead now seventeen years. He could imagine passing enjoyable hours with Victoria at the chessboard—after he had spent even more enjoyable hours in the lovely lady's bed.

Getting there, however, might not be as easy as he had imagined.

Cord walked over to the carved wooden sideboard against the wall and poured himself a brandy. He had hinted at the notion of an arrangement tonight. Surely the girl was not so naive she didn't understand that as his mistress her situation would be immensely improved for both her and her sister.

Next time he would explain the advantages in practical, no-nonsense terms, but he had a niggling suspicion it wouldn't do any good. Victoria Temple had principles. She was an unmarried woman, regardless of the *Mrs.* he had placed in front of her name. Sleeping with a man not her husband wasn't something she intended to do.

Oh, she was attracted to him. He knew women well enough to know when a woman returned his interest—which he most definitely had. His *interest* yet remained hard and throbbing inside his breeches, reminding him of the soft warmth of her lips, the way they had perfectly melded with his, the way they had trembled.

His arousal strengthened, making him harder still. He wanted Victoria Temple. He couldn't remember a time when a woman had appealed to him quite so much.

Unless, of course, it was all merely an act.

Cord liked women, but he also knew how devious some women could be. No matter her upper-class manners and speech, he had found Victoria on the street. Was she playing a game, or was she truly the innocent she seemed?

For now, he would trust his instincts in that regard, follow the plan that would solve both of their problems, and begin a subtle campaign of seduction. It was, after all, in Victoria's best interest. She had obviously been gently reared, no matter her current unfortunate circumstances. She belonged in stylish gowns, riding in a smart black carriage. And with the money he gave her, she could also provide those things for Claire.

The thought gave him pause. Just exactly who were

Claire and Victoria Temple? Cord made it a policy to know the strengths and foibles of the people around him. Perhaps he should hire a runner, see what he might find out. He would give the matter some thought.

He glanced down at the chessboard. Seduction was not so different from a game of chess, he thought, the man making a move, the woman responding, the play going back and forth until one of them was victorious. He saw himself clearly in that role, but it wouldn't be easy. If he wanted to win the prize, he would have to plan carefully.

Cord smiled. *To the victor go the spoils.*

Tory rose early the following morning, yawning behind her hand, her eyes puffy from the little sleep she had managed to get last night. Mostly, she had tossed and turned, torn between embarrassment and thinking what a fool she had made of herself in Lord Brant's study.

Dear God, what must he think of her, allowing him such liberties? She certainly hadn't been raised to behave that way. Her mother and father, as well as the years she had spent at Mrs. Thornhill's Private Academy, had taught her to behave like a lady. Whatever weakness had come over her, Tory vowed it would not happen again.

With that resolve, she made her way up the servants' stairs to the main floor of the house. She must check on the housemaids, see that the wardrobes were dusted and freshly lined with paper. She needed to see to the candle supply and be certain there was a sufficient amount of writing paper and ink.

She was passing through the entry when Timmons

rushed up with the morning paper tucked beneath a short, stout arm.

"Ah, Mrs. Temple. Would you mind terribly? I've a quick errand to run and I'm a bit pressed for time." He handed her a copy of the *London Chronicle.* "His lordship likes to read the paper while he takes his morning sustenance," he said as he dashed to the door, leaving behind the paper, and Tory with the job of seeing that his lordship got it.

And here I was hoping I would never have to face him again. Tory sighed. Hardly realistic if she wished to retain her position. At least after last night, he knew she had no interest in becoming anything other than his housekeeper.

Timmons's bald head flashed in the sunlight as the door closed behind him, and Tory headed for the breakfast room, a cheery salon done in shades of yellow and blue overlooking the garden. Perhaps the earl wouldn't yet be there. If she hurried, she could leave the paper beside his plate and not have to see him.

She walked toward the door, opening the paper as she went, making a quick perusal of the headlines. Tory froze two paces outside the door.

Baron Harwood Arrives in London, Tells Strange Tale of Robbery and Attempted Murder.

Her heart jolted to a screeching halt, as did her feet, then started beating in a heavy, sluggish rhythm. According the *Chronicle,* the baron had received near-fatal head injuries during the course of a robbery at Harwood Hall, his country estate in Kent. His attacker had inflicted a great deal of pain and rendered him temporarily incapable of memory. He had only just recovered enough to proceed to London in search of the villain responsible for the deed.

There was mention of the valuable pearl necklace that had been stolen but no accusations against his stepdaughters. It appeared the baron valued his reputation far too much to stir up that sort of scandal. Instead there was simply a description of the two young women he believed responsible for the crime. Unfortunately, the descriptions fit her and Claire to a T.

At least I didn't kill him, Tory thought with relief, then wondered with a trace of guilt if perhaps it would have been better if she had.

Just then the door to the breakfast room swung open and the earl strode out. Tory jumped, jammed the newspaper behind her back and forced herself to look up at him.

"Good morning, my lord."

"Good morning, Mrs. Temple." He looked down at the table. "Have you seen my morning paper? Timmons usually leaves it on the breakfast table."

The paper seemed to burn her fingers. "No, my lord. Perhaps it is in your study. Shall I go and see?"

"I'll go." The minute he turned and started walking, she hurried away, hiding the newspaper in her skirts, hating to deceive him yet grateful the exchange between them had been so matter-of-fact.

At least part of her was grateful. The other part resented the fact he could look at her as if he had never pressed her up against his tall, hard-muscled body, never kissed her lips, never slid his tongue inside her—

Tory broke off, aghast at the train of her thoughts. She was a lady, no matter her current position—not one of the earl's scarlet women. And thinking about last night was the last thing she wanted to do. Determined to put the incident behind her, she headed upstairs to find Claire, to warn her sister of the article in the paper.

Leaving London would undoubtedly be the safest course. But they had yet to receive their next pay and what they had earned so far would barely get them out of the city.

In the end, she decided the best plan was to remain where they were, hiding virtually in plain sight, hoping no more articles would appear in the paper or that if they did, no one would equate the baron's odd tale to their appearance in Lord Brant's household.

Tory shuddered, praying no one would. Not only would she find herself tossed into prison, but the baron would, at last, have complete and utter control of Claire.

Three days passed. No mention was made of the article in the paper, but Tory's worry remained. Still, she had a job to do and she had to see it done.

Now that Lady Aimes's brief visit was over, she ordered the linens changed in the upstairs guest rooms, set herself to the task of completing an inventory of the kitchen larder, then went in search of Claire.

"Excuse me, Miss Honeycutt, have you seen my sister? I thought she was working in the Blue Room."

"She was, Mrs. Temple. She was polishing the furniture when 'is lordship happened past. She was staring out the window. You know how she loves to look out into the garden?"

"Yes?"

"Well, 'is lordship asked if she would care to take a

stroll. Said something about showing her the robin's nest he had found."

Tory's worry shot up, along with her temper. Why, the womanizing rogue! Only days ago he had been kissing her and now he was out in the garden trying to seduce poor Claire!

Hurrying in that direction, Tory made her way directly to the French doors, pushed them open and stepped out onto the red-brick terrace. The scent of lavender struck her, mingled with that of freshly turned earth, but she saw no sign of Claire.

Her worry heightened. If Brant had touched her sister...harmed her in any way...

Taking the gravel path, she hurried toward the fountain, knowing the garden lanes came together there like the spokes of a wheel, hoping she might be able to tell which direction they had gone. To her surprise, they were standing in plain sight, just a few feet off the path, Claire gazing up at the cluster of leaves and twigs that formed a shallow bird's nest.

Claire was standing a goodly distance from the earl, staring up into the branches of a white-barked birch. At the sound of Tory's leather-soled shoes crunching on the gravel, the earl looked away from Claire and fixed his gaze on her.

"Ah, Mrs. Temple. I wondered when you would arrive."

She tried to smile, but it felt as if her face would crack. "I came in search of Claire. There is work yet to do and I am in need of her assistance."

"Are you? I invited your sister to join me. I thought she might enjoy seeing the robin's nest the gardener discovered."

Claire finally looked in their direction, her eyes big and blue and filled with awe. "Come and see, Tory. Three tiny blue-speckled robin's eggs. Oh, they're marvelous."

Ignoring the earl, who, instead of being annoyed at having been caught out, wore a faintly satisfied expression, Tory exchanged places with her sister, stepped up on the footstool the gardener had placed at the base of the tree, and peered into the nest.

"They're wonderful, Claire." She stepped down, eager to be away from the earl, feeling an unfamiliar twinge of jealousy. As lovely as Claire was, Tory had never been jealous of her sister. In truth, she wasn't now. Lord Brant might have fixed his interest on Claire, but her sister had no such interest in him.

"The earl's a nice-enough man, I suppose," Claire had once said, "but he makes me nervous. He seems so…so…"

"Yes, well the earl can be a bit intimidating at times."

"Yes, and he's so…so…"

"Lord Brant is…well, he is definitely a masculine sort of man."

Claire nodded. "I never know what to say or what I should do."

The earl's deep voice banished the memory. "Come, Miss Marion. As your sister appears to have need of you, I'm afraid our pleasant interlude is over."

He was looking at Claire and smiling, but there was none of the heat Tory had seen in his eyes when he had looked at her. Taking Claire's hand, he helped her down from where she once more stood atop the stool, peering into the bird's nest.

He made them a last polite bow, as if they were guests instead of servants. "Have a pleasant afternoon, ladies."

As soon as they were out of earshot, Tory turned to Claire. "Are you all right?"

Claire just looked at her. "It was nice of him to show me the nest."

"Yes…yes, it was." Tory wanted to say more, to warn her sister in some way. Claire had already had one bad experience, though fortunately nothing too damaging had occurred.

It was hard to believe Lord Brant was anything like her stepfather, and yet—why else had he been out there with Claire?

Darkness thickened outside the window. A soft fog crept through the streets, blanketing the houses and ships. After supper, Tory had retired downstairs to her room to continue reading the Mrs. Radcliffe novel she had borrowed from the library. At a little past eleven she fell asleep on the sofa in her sitting room.

She stirred as a soft rap at her door began to filter into her senses, then awoke with a start, thinking it might be Lord Brant, realizing by the timid knock it could not be. Quickly pulling on her wrapper, she hurried to the door. She didn't expect to find her sister outside in the hallway.

"Claire! What on earth…?" She pulled her sister into the room and closed the door, alarmed by the stark look on her face. Tory hurried over to the oil lamp burning low on the bureau and turned up the wick, throwing soft yellow light into the sitting room.

"What is it, Claire? What's wrong?"

Claire swallowed, her eyes huge and frightened. "It's…it's his lordship."

Tory's stomach tightened. "Brant?" In the lamplight, she could see the pale hue of her sister's cheeks. "What about the earl?"

"Lord Brant sent me a message. I—I found it under my door." With trembling fingers, Claire held up the folded sheet of paper and Tory pulled it from her hand.

Claire,
I should like a private word with you. Come to my bedchamber at midnight.

It was signed simply, "Brant."

"I don't want to go, Tory. I'm frightened. What if he…what if he touches me the way the baron did?"

Tory reread the paper and her temper went scalding hot. God save them, she had been right about the earl all along!

"It's all right, darling. You don't have to go. I shall go in your stead."

"B-but aren't you afraid? What if he beats you?"

Tory shook her head. "The earl may be wicked, but I don't believe he is the sort to hit a woman."

Though why she believed that she had no notion. So far she had misjudged the man completely. She had come to believe he was different from other men, more open-minded, a bit less condescending. It bothered her more than it should have to discover that he was also completely lacking in scruples.

Whatever sort of man he might be, tonight she intended to teach him a lesson in the consequences of trying to seduce an innocent young girl.

* * *

Cord flicked another glance at the clock on the mantel, as he had done at least twenty times. It was two minutes after midnight. Wearing only his shirt and breeches, he reclined on the bed, hoping his plan would work, that his latest strategy would win him the game.

That sacrificing a pawn would net him the queen.

It was a dangerous move and he knew it. Still, Victoria Temple was a difficult opponent and he had been forced to come up with a different approach than he had intended.

Cord grinned at the sound of four sharp raps at his door. Not the soft, tentative knock Claire would have used, but the firm, furious tapping that could only belong to her sister.

"Come in," he drawled, then waited as the door swung open and Victoria marched in. She stood in the shadows so he couldn't see her face, but he recognized her shorter stature and the belligerence in her stance.

"You're late," he said with a nonchalant glance at the clock. "I specifically instructed you to be here at midnight. It is now three minutes past."

"Late?" she repeated, the fury in her voice unmistakable. "Three minutes or three hours, the fact is Claire is not going to come."

Victoria stepped toward him, out of the shadows and into a shaft of moonlight streaming in through the window. He saw that her hair was unbound, curling softly around her shoulders and glinting with burnished highlights. He itched to run his fingers through it, to know the silky texture. Beneath her wrapper, her breasts rapidly rose and fell with her breath, and he wanted to cup them, to bend his head and take the fullness into his mouth.

"I am sorry to disappoint you, my lord, but your plan for seduction has failed. Claire remains safely upstairs in her room."

Cord came up off the bed and paced toward her, a lion with his prey in sight. "As well she should be."

"What are you talking about? You sent Claire a note. You told her to come. You planned to seduce her. You—"

"You're wrong, lovely Victoria. I told her to come because I knew you would not let her—that you would come in her stead." He reached her then, settled his hands on her shoulders, felt the tension thrumming through her. Very slowly, he drew her toward him. "It's you I want, Victoria. It has been almost from the start."

And then he kissed her.

Tory gasped as his mouth settled softly over hers. For several moments, she simply stood there, letting the heat flood through her, absorbing the taste of him, only dimly aware of the hard male body pressing into hers. Then she remembered why she was there, that it was Claire the earl truly wanted. Tory pressed her hands against his chest, turned her head, and shoved hard enough to get free.

"You're lying!" She was breathing fast. She told herself it was anger. "You're just saying that because I am here and not Claire." She took several steps backward. "You...you would take whatever woman happened to appear in your bedchamber."

The earl shook his head, stalking her, matching her step for step until her shoulders came up against the wall and she couldn't retreat any farther.

"You don't really believe that? We were playing a game, you and I. You were the prize I wanted, not Claire."

"That can't be the truth. Men always want Claire."

"Claire is a child, no matter her years. You're a woman, Victoria." He pinned her with his lion's gaze, caught her chin, held her so she couldn't glance away. "Deep down, you know it's you I want and not Claire."

She swallowed, stared into those hot golden-brown eyes and fought not to tremble. She remembered that same look the night he had come to her room, remembered the way he had kissed her in his study. She remembered the vague hints that he wanted her as his mistress, and God in heaven, she believed he was telling the truth.

The earl tilted her chin up, bent his head and captured her lips. It was a gentle, persuasive kiss, softly taking, convincing her with every touch, every taste. He kissed the corners of her mouth, pressed his lips against the side of her neck.

"If you're telling the truth," she whispered, "why didn't…why didn't you send the note to me?"

She felt the faint pull of his smile. "Would you have come?"

She wouldn't have, of course. "No."

"I didn't think so." And then he kissed her again.

Tory's hands came up to his chest, fluttered, flattened against the front of his full-sleeved shirt. Sweet Lord, it was heaven, the softest, hottest kisses, his lips hard-soft, perfectly fitted to hers, coaxing and demanding, giving and taking all at once.

"Open for me," he whispered, his tongue sliding over her lips, sending warm shivers across her skin. He deepened the kiss and pleasure made her legs go weak. Her arms slid up around his neck and he pulled her more snugly against him, tasted her more completely, let her taste him.

Tory trembled.

She knew she should stop him. He was the earl of Brant, a rake and a rogue, a man who would ruin her if she let him. He cared nothing about her. He only wanted to satisfy his lust. And yet she sensed a need in him, had since that night he had barged into her room.

Her own need surfaced, pulsed to life with every stroke of his tongue, deepened with the feel of his hands on her breasts, smoothing over them, molding them through her robe, sending little curls of heat sliding into her stomach. Her legs were trembling. He kissed the side of her neck as he parted the blue quilted wrapper and slid his hand inside, over her thin cotton night rail to cup her breast, his thumb stroking over her nipple.

"God, I want you," he said, pulling the little blue bow at her throat, reaching in to caress the fullness of her breasts. Her mouth went dry. She couldn't swallow. Her nipples swelled, pressed into his palm. "Give yourself to me," he said softly. "I know you want to."

God's breath, it was the truth. She had never wanted anything so badly. She wanted to see where all this heat would lead, wanted him to touch her, kiss her all over. He was every wicked dream she'd ever had, every wanton fantasy. She had known that about herself, that she wasn't like Claire, that she had desires and wants, and she wanted the earl of Brant.

Tory shook her head, tried to step away. The earl held her firmly in place.

"Don't say no. Let me take care of you. You'll have a better life. And you can take care of Claire. Neither of you will want for anything."

He was saying it straight out. He wanted her to become his mistress. He didn't want Claire, he wanted her, Victoria, the sturdy sister, not the beautiful one. The notion left her feeling light-headed. Considering the life she faced and the desire she felt for him, it wasn't a bad proposition.

Tory simply could not do it.

She was surprised to feel the hot sting of tears. Shaking her head, she eased a little away, forced herself to look up, into that sinfully handsome face.

"I can't. In a way, as wicked as it might be, I wish I could, but..." Another shake of her head. "It just isn't something I can do."

He ran a finger gently down her cheek. "Are you certain? It isn't so wicked between people who share similar needs, and you've Claire to think of. It would ensure both of your futures."

Claire. She felt guilty. She should do it for Claire.

But perhaps that was just an excuse.

Either way, she simply could not compromise her principles in that manner. And, of course there was the not-so-small matter of the robbery and attempted murder of her stepfather. She stifled a sudden urge to blurt out the tale, to throw herself into his arms and beg him to help her.

She couldn't take the risk. "I am quite sure, my lord."

Very gently, he bent his head and kissed the tears on her cheeks. "Perhaps in time you will change your mind."

Tory stepped away from him and drew in a shaky, courage-building breath, though in that moment she wanted nothing so much as to let him kiss her again, let him make love to her.

"I won't change my mind. Say you will not ask me again. Say it, or I shall have to leave."

There was something in his expression, a turmoil she could not read. Several long moments passed, then he sighed.

"If that is truly your wish, I won't ask you again."

"I want your word as a gentleman."

The edge of his mouth barely curved. "After tonight, you still believe I am one?"

She managed a tremulous smile. "For reasons I am at a loss to explain, I do."

He turned, moved even farther away. "All right, I give you my word. You are safe from me, Mrs. Temple, though I am certain to rue this day for as long as you are employed in my household."

"Thank you, my lord." She turned to leave, telling herself she had done the right thing, feeling more wretched than she had since the day she had received word that her mother had died.

The echo of the softly closing door slid through him like the edge of a blade. His body still pulsed with desire, ached with unspent need. He had wanted her so badly, more even than he had guessed. And yet the feeling that washed through him now could only be described as relief.

There was no denying that over the years he had become somewhat jaded, somewhat insensitive where women were concerned. But he had never stooped so low as to attempting the seduction he had planned tonight.

He could have justified the results. As his mistress, Victoria, along with her sister, would have been well taken care of. He would have seen to their financial security, even after his liaison with Victoria was over.

And yet, in some perverse way, he was relieved that she had not agreed. In the weeks she had been in his employ, he had come to respect, even admire her. She did her job—no matter the little cooperation she received from the rest of the servants. She was intelligent and clever, spirited, and loyal to those she loved. And she had a strong set of morals—she had proved that tonight.

She deserved far better than the brief sexual liaison she would have had with him.

Still, he wanted her. Even as he stripped off his shirt and breeches and prepared himself for bed, his body throbbed with desire for her. He remembered her innocently passionate kisses and groaned with the ache the memory stirred.

But Victoria Temple was safe from him now. Cord had given his word and he would not break it. She would remain his housekeeper, nothing more.

Six

In some ways, at least, fate seemed to be on Tory's side. As the days continued, nothing more surfaced about the theft of the necklace or the attack on Baron Harwood. Undoubtedly there would be gossip among the *ton*, but Lord Brant was far too busy to pay attention to rumors and scandal.

Brant. Tory did her best not to think of him. She didn't want to see him, didn't want to look into those tawny eyes and remember his scorching kisses, the way her body had melted into his the moment he had touched her. She didn't want to feel the awful, wicked temptation that she had felt that night.

Or battle her desire to be with him that way again.

Fortunately, she had succeeded in hiding her turbulent thoughts from Claire. Her sister had been waiting when Tory returned downstairs. She had told Claire the note had simply been a misunderstanding, that the earl had written *midnight* but meant *midday* and that he had merely been interested in discovering whether she and Tory were happy in their jobs.

It was an utterly ridiculous story, one that only someone as completely naive as Claire would believe. Tory felt guilty for the lie, but thanked the Lord that her sister had accepted it and put the matter to rest.

Since that night, she saw the earl only when they chanced to pass in a hallway. Each time he was exceedingly polite and reserved. Maddeningly so, Tory secretly thought.

In his study, the chessboard sat forlornly in the corner, and whenever Tory saw it, she battled the urge to move one of the pieces, to challenge him again. She didn't, of course. She knew where that would lead and the road was one that could only end in disaster.

Then this morning, at the bottom of today's *London Chronicle,* a reference was made to the search still being conducted for crimes against Baron Harwood. Fortunately, Tory made this morning's newspaper, like the last, mysteriously disappear.

Still, she wondered how much longer she and Claire could continue hiding in Lord Brant's household. They were madly saving every farthing should the need arise for a hasty escape, but the longer they were gainfully employed, the more money they would have and the better their chances of getting safely away.

And there was always the slim hope the baron might tire of his search and simply return to Harwood Hall, or that he might believe they were hiding somewhere in the country. Tory prayed each night that happenstance would occur.

In the meantime, the earl had left word that he would

be having a small dinner party that evening. The guest list included his cousin Sarah and her husband, Lord Aimes; Colonel Pendleton of the British War Office; and Lord Percival Chezwick. The Duke of Sheffield was also invited, along with Dr. and Mrs. Geoffrey Chastain and their eldest daughter, Grace.

The last name on the list gave Tory's heart a jolt. She knew Gracie Chastain. They had attended finishing school together. At Thornhill's, Gracie had been her dearest friend.

That seemed eons ago. Another time, another life. After the baron had forbidden her return to school, Tory had heard little of Grace beyond an occasional letter. With the troubles facing her at home, Tory's replies had been sluggish at best and the friends had drifted apart.

Still, Grace would know her immediately, even in her dreary housekeeper's uniform. Tory would have to make a point of staying well away from the dining room.

"Ah, there you are, Mrs. Temple."

Tory stiffened at the sound of the familiar deep voice coming up behind her. Taking a steadying breath, she turned to face the earl.

"Good afternoon, my lord."

"I just wanted to check, make certain you have everything in order for tonight."

"Yes, my lord. I was just making out the place cards."

"You understand how the guests should be seated?" He seemed so aloof, so distant, as if he had never had the slightest interest in her at all. She wished her interest in him would fade as quickly.

"The guests should be seated by rank, my lord."

He nodded. "Then I shall leave the matter in your hands." Turning, he walked away. Tory watched him disappear down the hall, trying not to notice the width of his shoulders, the long legs and graceful way he moved. She tried to ignore those strong hands and the memory of them caressing her breasts, stroking over her nipples. She tried not to think of the overwhelming pleasure he had made her feel.

"Tory!" Claire flew toward her down the hall. Her sister had been working below stairs, where Tory had asked her to help with preparations for the dinner party. Which really meant she was to make certain the serving women got the necessary work done.

"What is it, darling?"

"Mrs. Reynolds just quit. She was angry that you wanted her to add more spices to the partridge stuffing—the thyme and rosemary? Then she refused to add more rum to the fruit-soaked cakes. When she found out you wanted her to put lemon juice in the sauce for the asparagus, she took off her apron, threw it on the table and slammed out the back door. Mrs. Whitehead, her helper, went with her."

"They left? Both of them?"

"They said they wouldn't be back till…till hell freezes over, and then only if you were no longer in his lordship's employ."

"Oh, good Lord." Tory raced for the stairs leading down to the kitchen. "I can't believe it. I may not be a cook but I know what tastes good. The food Mrs. Reynolds prepared was edible, but it was basic and entirely too bland. I thought…I've been reading this wonderful French recipe book I found in the library. I thought by adding a few more spices, a bit more pungent flavors, everything would taste far better."

"I guess Mrs. Reynolds didn't agree."

"I guess not."

The kitchen was in chaos when Tory arrived, pots boiling, steam rising, flames leaping up beneath the skillets on the stove. Miss Honeycutt's eyes looked liked saucers and Mrs. Conklin's thin hands were shaking.

"Gor, Mrs. Temple," the older woman said. Broad-hipped with kinky blond hair and a faint cockney accent, she had been one of the few serving women who had ever been polite. "What in the world will we do?"

Tory glanced round the kitchen, saw the bowls of raw oysters still waiting to be made into soup, the asparagus not yet trimmed, the joint of beef roasting over the spit jacks in the wall, sending black smoke up the chimney.

She straightened her shoulders, tried to sound calm and confident, which she wasn't in the least. "Does any-one else on the staff know anything at all about cook-ing? Mrs. Rathbone, perhaps?"

"No, missus. None of us but Mrs. Reynolds and Mrs. Whitehead and both of them are gone."

She released a steadying breath. "Well, then, first we shall remove those skillets from the fire so the sausages don't continue to burn, then we shall finish the dinner ourselves."

"But, missus...we don't—Miss Honeycutt and me—we don't usually work in the kitchen. We don't 'ave the least idea what to do."

Tory grabbed a towel, folded it and used it to grab the handle of the heavy iron skillet and set it off the flames.

"Well, it can't be that hard, can it? Not when most of the food is at least half prepared."

Mrs. Conklin warily eyed the stove. "I dunno, missus...."

Tory lifted her skirts, walked purposefully across the kitchen, picked up Mrs. Reynolds's apron and tied it round her waist.

"We'll simply have to do the best we can. Between the four of us, we'll figure things out as we go along." She forced herself to smile. "I have every confidence this dinner will be one his lordship's favorites."

But several hours later, as she wiped grease off her hands and brushed flour off her apron, she knew that would have been far too easy.

Instead, she filled a silver terrine with too-salty oyster soup, loaded a silver tray with slices of overcooked beef and another with roast partridge still pink in the joints. As she scooped scorched sausage stuffing into silver bowls, Tory ordered the footmen to keep the wineglasses filled to the brim and prayed the guests would be so inebriated by the time the food actually reached their fancy gold-rimmed plates they wouldn't notice.

At least working in the hot, steamy kitchen all day, she and Claire, Miss Honeycutt, Mrs. Conklin, and the newly hired footmen, Mr. Peabody and Mr. Kidd, whose services she had enlisted, had developed a certain camaraderie. And during that time, she had gleaned all manner of gossip.

There were few secrets in a household the size of the earl's. Chiefly notable was Lord Brant's ongoing search for his cousin, Captain Sharpe. Even more intriguing, Miss Honeycutt, through bits and pieces of conversation picked up between the earl and his cousin, Lady Aimes, informed her that Lord Brant intended to wed an heiress.

"His father, the late earl," Mrs. Conklin put in, "left his son in a bit of a pickle—God rest the poor man's soul. Lost most of 'is money, ye see. But the son—he's a smart one. He fixed things back the way they was before."

Still, his goal, it seemed, wasn't simply to replace the losses but to make the Brant fortune increase.

It was information she almost wished she hadn't learned.

"Here come the footmen." Miss Honeycutt's voice drew her thoughts back to the chaos in the kitchen. "'Tis time to serve dessert."

They began to scurry around, helping Mr. Peabody fill the dessert trays while Mr. Kidd hefted one of them up on his shoulder. All four of the women grinned as a silver dome was placed over the rum-soaked fruit cakes—very rum-soaked—and carried in to the guests.

"Those ought ta finish 'em off," Mrs. Conklin said. "By the time they get through eatin' those and drink a bit more wine, they won't notice the molded heart looks more like the face of a pig."

Claire cast Tory a glance, clamped a hand over her mouth, but couldn't stifle a giggle. As hard as she tried not to, Tory started laughing, too.

It was true. The molded heart looked exactly like a pig. Miss Honeycutt and Mrs. Conklin joined in, filling the room with gales of mirth.

The laughing came to a very sudden halt when the kitchen door slammed open and the earl walked in. He took one look at the stacks of dirty pots and pans, the food strewn all over the counter and the flour on the floor, and his eyebrows climbed toward his forehead.

"All right—exactly what the devil is going on?"

Claire's whole face turned pink. Mrs. Conklin and Miss Honeycutt began to tremble in terror. All Tory could think was how her hair was sticking out in ugly little curls beneath the mobcap she had retrieved during the afternoon's debacle and that her skirt and blouse were spotted with grease.

"Well, Mrs. Temple?"

"I—I'm sorry, your lordship. I realize the meal didn't turn out quite as well as we planned, but—"

"Quite as well as you planned!" he roared. "My guests are reeling drunk, and the meal—if you could actually call it that—tasted like something you dug out of a slop bucket."

"Well...I suppose some of it was pretty awful, but—"

"But?"

"At the very last moment, the cook quit and so did her helper, and the rest of us...well, we tried to do the best we could." She flicked a glance at the other three women. "To tell you the truth, with a little more practice, I think in a pinch we could rub on very well."

A flush rose under the bones in the earl's handsome face and a muscle tightened in his cheek. When he spoke, his voice was deceptively calm.

"I'd like a word with you, Mrs. Temple—in private, if you please."

Oh, dear, he was angrier than she thought. Tory braced herself and tried not to let her nervousness show. Walking ahead of him, she shoved through the kitchen door and preceded him down the hall, far enough away that they wouldn't be overheard.

She squared her shoulders and turned to face him. "As I said, I'm sorry about the dinner. I had hoped it would turn out better."

"Did you, indeed?" Hard, golden-brown eyes bored into her. "I gather you are having more trouble managing your duties than I imagined."

Something in the way he was looking at her…as if she might as well have been Mrs. Rathbone or one of the footmen. As if he had never made advances, as if he had never kissed her, never caressed her breasts. Something in the blandness of his expression made all common sense rush out of her head.

"Actually, I am not having the least amount of trouble. Some of your staff, however, are having trouble accepting me as their superior—and the fault is entirely your own!"

His eyes widened. "Mine!"

"It wasn't fair of you to hire me in Mrs. Rathbone's stead and the rest of the servants know it."

One dark eyebrow arched in disbelief. "You're not suggesting I dismiss you?"

"No! I mean…no, I need this job. And I believe I am better suited to the position than Mrs. Rathbone ever will be. In time, I intend to prove it. Once I do, the problem will be solved."

Lord Brant frowned. He studied her face for several long moments. Then he turned and started walking. "You needn't trouble yourself further, Mrs. Temple," he said over his shoulder. "Tomorrow I shall solve the problem for you."

"What!" Tory raced after him. Grabbing his coat sleeve, she forced him to turn around. "You can't possibly interfere! You'll only make things worse!"

"I guess we'll just have to wait and see."

"Wh-what are you planning to do?"

"Ten o'clock tomorrow morning," he said, ignoring her question. "Make sure the entire staff is present. In the meantime, I would appreciate it if you began your search for another cook."

Tory watched his tall figure disappear back up the stairs, returning to the dining room. Dear God, why had she said those things? She wouldn't be able to sleep a wink until she found out what the earl planned to do.

The dinner was a disaster, and yet as he sat in the dining room, enjoying brandy and cigars with the men, Cord couldn't help a flicker of amusement. Seeing Victoria so utterly disheveled and completely undone, with flour on her nose and her hair a riot of curls, was almost worth the awful food.

That even under such circumstances she'd had the courage to speak her mind simply amazed him. She was, he realized, quite an amazing woman.

The dinner was an utter failure but the company was pleasant. Though his good friend Sheffield was laughing a little more loudly than he usually did and young Percy Chezwick was flat-out in his cups, it was obvious his guests were enjoying themselves.

Pendleton was a gentleman as always. "I'm expecting a courier in the next few days," he said as the men finished their brandy and prepared to rejoin the ladies in the drawing room. "I'm hoping for word of your cousin."

Cord felt a rush of excitement. "You think your man may have found out which prison he's being held in?"

"Max Bradley is extremely capable at this sort of thing. If anyone can discover where Captain Sharpe is, Bradley is the man."

"Then I look forward to hearing from you, Colonel."

Pendleton nodded and wandered away, leaving Cord with more hope than he'd had in as long as he could remember. He was returning to his guests when Percival Chezwick, a friend of Sarah's husband Jonathan, walked toward him a bit unsteadily.

"I must tell you, my lord, I have fallen completely in love." Percy rolled his eyes. "Merciful heaven, never before in my life have I seen such a face. Like an angel, she was. When she smiled, I swear my heart very nearly stopped beating. And she is here, right under your very roof. You must tell me her name."

Claire. It had to be. From the moonstruck look on young Percy's face, there could be no other conclusion.

"The lady's name is Claire, but she isn't for you, I'm afraid. You probably didn't notice, but the girl is a member of my housekeeping staff. She's an innocent, Chez, not the sort for a tumble or two, and I'm afraid your father would scarcely approve a match between you and a serving maid."

Percy's gaze strayed toward the hall, but Claire was nowhere to be seen. It was completely out of character for the young man to mention a woman at all. Cord imagined the wine he had drunk had given him a shot of courage.

In a way it was a shame the pair's status was so far apart. Percival Chezwick was a dreamer like Claire, a naive young man with his head in the clouds who wrote poetry but was too shy to read it. He was blond, blue-eyed and attractive to the opposite sex, if a bit thin and pale.

He was also the youngest son of the marquess of Kersey and a match between him and a chambermaid would hardly be the thing.

And oddly enough, Cord had come to feel protective of Claire. He wouldn't stand by and let one of his friends take advantage of her. In fact, it would please him to see the girl well settled. Perhaps in time, he would help her make some sort of match. His thoughts strayed to Victoria. He could find her a husband, as well. Somehow the notion didn't please him nearly so much.

Cord followed Colonel Pendleton and Lord Percy into the drawing room. Sarah and Jonathan were there, both blond and fair, a golden couple still enamored of each other even after eight years of marriage. They were talking to Dr. and Mrs. Chastain, while Grace, it seemed, had slipped off to the ladies' retiring room.

Cord sighed. His cousin was matchmaking for him again. Sarah didn't seem to understand the daughter of a physician held not the least appeal for him, no matter how attractive she was. He was going to marry an heiress. Lately he had been thinking more and more of Constance Fairchild or Mary Ann Winston. They were both blond and attractive and each possessed of a considerable fortune.

An earl was no small prize in the marriage mart. Either girl would likely accept his suit, and his wealth would expand considerably the moment the ceremony was performed.

He owed his father. He intended to repay him in the only way he knew how.

Walking over to the sideboard, he poured himself a brandy, his mind slipping away from the past to the disastrous supper he had hosted tonight. He thought of the excessively rum-soaked cakes and grinned as he made his way toward his guests.

Grace Chastain crossed the entry toward the sweeping spiral staircase on her way to the ladies' retiring room. The evening was becoming interminable. Not only was the food beyond god-awful, she'd been seated next to Colonel Pendleton, who was a passable conversationalist but wanted mostly to discuss the war, which Grace did her best to forget.

Now that supper was over, Sarah would begin her matchmaking—the reason she and her parents had been invited in the first place. Her mother had been ecstatic, of course, pressing her every minute to talk more to the earl. It wouldn't have mattered if she had. Everyone in London knew the earl would settle for no less than marriage to an heiress.

Grace just wished the evening would end.

Straightening the bodice of her high-waisted plum silk gown, she lifted the pearl-trimmed skirt and started up the stairs just as a movement in the hall caught her eye. Turning, she spotted a familiar slender figure and sucked in a breath.

"Tory! Victoria Whiting, is that really you?" Racing back down the stairs, she ran after the woman hurrying along the hall in the opposite direction. Grace caught her arm and spun her around in the middle of the corridor.

"Tory! It's me—Gracie. Don't you recognize me?" As she enveloped her friend in a hug, several seconds passed before she realized the warmth wasn't being returned.

Grace let go and took a step backward. "What's the matter? Aren't you glad to see me?" It was then that she noticed Tory's clothing, the crisp black taffeta skirt and white cotton blouse. "All right—what's going on? Why are you dressed like a servant?"

Tory sighed and her shoulders sagged. "Oh, Gracie—I was hoping you wouldn't see me."

"What are you doing here? Surely you aren't really working as a member of his lordship's staff?"

"There's so much to explain. So much has happened since I left the academy." She glanced toward the drawing room. "There isn't time tonight. Just promise me you won't tell anyone I am here."

"If you're in some kind of trouble—"

"Please, Grace. If you're still my friend, promise me you won't say a word."

"All right, I won't say a word—on one condition. Tomorrow you meet me and explain what's going on."

Tory shook her head. "It would be better for both of us if you just pretended you never saw me."

"Tomorrow, Tory. The King's Inn is just round the corner. It's quiet and out of the way. No one will see us. I'll meet you in the dining room at one o'clock tomorrow afternoon."

Tory made a resigned nod of her head. "All right. Tomorrow. King's Inn. One in the afternoon."

Grace watched her friend walk away, her mind spinning with a dozen different thoughts, each of them laced with worry. It had been years since she had seen Victoria Whiting. She wondered what could have happened to Tory in that time, wondered if her best friend's life had become as complicated as her own.

Seven

The following morning Cord sat at the desk in his study, reviewing the estate ledgers for Willow Park, his country estate in Sussex. He had already found one not-so-small discrepancy between the amount of hay being ordered for the sheep on the property and the number sold at market. For the past several years, he had been growing less trustful of his estate manager, Richard Reed. Cord made a mental note to make a trip to Sussex to check out the matter for himself.

He glanced at the clock on the mantel, then rose briskly to his feet. Ten o'clock. Time to solve Victoria's problems with his staff once and for all. Striding down the hall to the entry, he found the servants lined up to greet him, their faces filled with worry at what he planned to do.

Good. They ought to be worried.

He flicked a glance at Victoria, who looked more resigned than fearful. He forced himself to remember the promise he had made her, and tried not to recall the feel of those soft pink lips or the silkiness of her hair as he'd fisted it in his hand.

"Good morning."

"Good morning, my lord," they replied in unison.

"Let me begin by saying I am extremely disappointed in the lot of you. In the weeks Mrs. Temple has been running my household, instead of trying to help her, you have done everything in your power to make her job more difficult."

A murmur went through the crowd and dark looks flashed Victoria's way. He saw her square her shoulders.

"Still, the work got done and for the most part very well, I might say. I told her she could fire any or all of you, should that be her wish, but she refused. Instead, she suggested your grievance might have some merit."

A dozen pairs of eyes fastened on his face. "Although Mrs. Temple has obviously had a good deal of experience, she is younger than most of the women employed in so important a position and hiring her might have seemed somewhat unfair. She suggested that in order to correct the situation, I should consider giving all of you a raise."

An audible murmur went through the group. Heads swiveled. Faces gazed at Victoria as if she were someone they had never seen before, and inwardly he smiled.

"Your raises take effect immediately. In return, I expect you to give Mrs. Temple your full cooperation. That is all."

He cast a last glance at Victoria, saw the relief and maybe a hint of admiration in her eyes. As he walked back to his study to face the mountain of paperwork on his desk, for the first time in weeks, his footsteps seemed a little lighter.

He had almost made it to the study door when Timmons approached from behind him.

"Begging your pardon, my lord. A messenger has arrived with a note from Colonel Pendleton. I assumed you would wish to see it right away." He handed over the wax-sealed missive. "Shall I tell the messenger to await your reply?"

Cord cracked the seal and quickly scanned the note, which said that Pendleton had just received news of Ethan and requested a time that would be convenient for him to call.

"I won't be making a reply. At least not in writing. Have my phaeton brought round front. I'll see to the matter in person."

It was only a few minutes later that Cord climbed up on his high-seat phaeton and picked up the reins of the glossy black gelding harnessed in front. He wove the reins between the fingers of his gloves, then slapped the leather strips against the horse's rump, setting the conveyance into motion.

The trip to Whitehall took longer than it should have, the streets being clogged with heavy drays and hackney carriages, freight wagons and traveling coaches. Once he reached his destination, he tossed a coin to a linkboy and instructed him to watch his rig, then walked to the far end of the building and climbed the stairs to Pendleton's office.

The colonel didn't keep him waiting. Gold epaulettes gleamed on his scarlet tunic as he invited Cord to take a seat in front of his desk. "I wondered if you could stand the wait."

"Not a chance. What news, Colonel?"

"As I had hoped, the courier arrived this morning. Ethan is being held in the prison at Calais."

His heart leaped. "Is Bradley certain?"

"As certain as he can be. He hasn't seen the captain himself, but word is, he is there."

"How soon will he be ready to go in after him?"

"As soon as he receives instruction from us where the pickup is to be made. In the meantime, he'll make the necessary arrangements."

"You mean he'll bribe the guards to turn their heads so Ethan can escape."

"Exactly so. He'll want a moonless night. Safer all round. That should be coming up soon."

"I've a schooner standing by with a capable captain and crew. Tell Bradley we'll be ready whenever he gives the word."

"I'll see that he gets the message. I'll let you know as soon as I receive a reply." The rescue mission was unofficial, since Ethan was no longer officially a British officer. They had the colonel's help, but he could only go so far.

Cord stood up, his pulse humming with excitement. Ethan was alive. Soon he would be home. Unfortunately, he would have to wait to tell Sarah as she and Jonathan, who were visiting for several days, had taken little Teddy to Merlin's Mechanical Exhibit for the day.

Cord left the office and headed for his town house, his body still pulsing with nervous energy. If Victoria had agreed to his proposal, he would exhaust himself making passionate love to her for the rest of the afternoon. He remembered the feel of her breast in his hand, the softness of her lips, and went hard inside his breeches.

Cord cursed and forced the memory away. Perhaps tonight he would visit Madame Fontaneau's, as he should have done long before this. The women there were beautiful and talented and he could have his pick.

It was amazing how little the notion appealed to him.

It was early afternoon, a warm June day with a breeze blowing in off the Thames. Returned from her brief half-hour outing to the King's Inn, all the time she dared take meeting Grace—Tory untied the strings of her drab gray bonnet and tossed the hat on the table in her sitting room. As much as she had hoped to avoid her friend the night before, she couldn't deny it was good to see her. And their friendship seemed as solid as ever, even after three long years.

In the end, she had told Gracie the truth and sworn her to secrecy.

"I can't believe all that has happened," Tory had said.

"You only did what you had to in order to protect yourself."

"I know, but that won't keep either of us out of prison."

"We'll think of something," Grace promised. "In the meantime, I'll try to find out what the baron's been up to. If you have to leave the city, you know where to find me. Just send word and I'll do what I can to help."

Grace hadn't changed. Once she had been a loyal and trustworthy friend. Apparently, she still was.

She looked about the same, a bit taller than Tory, her hair a rich auburn touched with hints of gold. She had always been pretty. Now, at nineteen, her gawky girlhood was gone, replaced by an attractive maturity. Tory thought that the only trouble Grace would have finding a husband was finding a man she wanted.

The week stretched toward an end. Seeing Grace had kept her spirits buoyed these past few days, but counting, mending and marking the linen, then sorting through the bins and drawers in the dry stores in the heat of the afternoon had worn her out.

At least the servants had been treating her more fairly, thanks to Lord Brant and the fact the staff was beginning to realize she wasn't carrying on an affair with the earl—somewhat to her disappointment.

She was heading below stairs to make a final check on dinner preparations when the front door slammed open and the earl strode in. She squeaked as she realized he was bearing down on her—as mad as she had ever seen him.

"My study," he commanded. "Now!"

Tory bit her lip. Lifting her skirt she hurried down the hall in front of him. Brant followed her into the study and slammed the door.

"Sit down."

"I—I think I'd rather stand, if you don't mind."

"I said sit!"

She dropped into the nearest chair as if her legs had been severed at the knee and forced herself to look up at him. He seemed even taller than he usually did, his eyes fierce and dark, his jaw clamped tight.

"I think it's time we talked about the necklace."

Her head swam. For an instant, she feared she would fall right out of the chair. "Wh-what necklace?"

"The one you and your sister stole from Baron Harwood."

Her palms went damp. She smoothed them over her crisp black taffeta skirt. "I—I don't know what you're talking about."

"Don't you? I think you know exactly what I'm talking about. I'm speaking of the very valuable diamond-and-pearl necklace that was stolen from Harwood Hall." His jaw hardened. "And there is also the not-insignificant crime of the attempted murder of the baron."

Tory swallowed, tried to look calm when her insides were quaking. "I don't know a Baron Harwood. I have never even heard of him."

"I don't know him, either, but that is hardly the point. The fact remains, according to information I happened to overhear at my club, information that apparently was printed in the newspaper—editions I somehow managed to miss—the crimes were committed and two young women are suspect. One is tall and blond, the other dark-haired and a few inches shorter." He stared hard into her face. "Sound like anyone you know?"

Tory forced an eyebrow up. "You think Claire and I are the women you describe? Why would you believe we had anything to do with it?"

"Because the blond is said to be extravagantly fair of face." A corner of his mouth edged up. "And the brunette is reported to be ruthless in the extreme."

Tory's spine went stiff. "You think I am ruthless?"

His lips curved into what might have passed for a smile. It wasn't a friendly smile. "Desperation drives people to do desperate things. You looked pretty desperate the day I met you on the paving stones in front of my house."

She sat up a little straighter in the deep leather chair,

keeping her eyes on his face. "If the necklace were as valuable as you say and I had, indeed, stolen it, I wouldn't have been desperate. I would have been quite well settled. That only makes sense."

Lord Brant pinned her with a glare. "Or perhaps something happened to the money you received from the sale. Perhaps it was stolen or you spent it or—"

"Or perhaps I am innocent of the crime. Perhaps I never took the necklace, never sold it, and therefore never had any money at all."

He didn't believe her, not for an instant. She could see it in his face. Her heart was hammering, her cheeks flushed. She wondered if he could tell how terrified she was.

She nervously smoothed a loose curl into the coil at her nape. "These women…they were servants in the baron's household?"

"I presume so." His voice faintly softened. "If you are in trouble, Victoria, perhaps I can help. Tell me the truth. I don't believe you are the sort who would commit these crimes without cause. Tell me what you have done and let me see what I can do to straighten things out."

She wanted to. Dear God, she wanted to tell him the truth more than anything in the world. She wanted to throw herself into his arms and beg him to save her. If she did, if she told him she and Claire were Harwood's stepdaughters, he would be honor-bound to send them back to the baron. She couldn't let that happen.

"I would tell you, my lord, if there were any truth to the tale. In fact, there is none. Claire and I are not the women in question. We are not the ones who committed the crimes."

A muscle tightened in his cheek. "Lie to me, Victoria, and I will see you punished to the very limits of the law."

The blood drained from her face. He would see them put into prison. They would languish there for years, perhaps even die there. Dear God, it took all of her courage to look into the hard lines of his face and lie to him again.

"I am telling you the truth."

The earl stared at her for several moments more, then turned and walked away. "That will be all," he said harshly, keeping his back to her. "For now."

Legs shaking, Tory rose unsteadily to her feet. As silently as possible, she made her way out the door of the study. She and Claire would have to run again, leave London, find someplace new to hide.

Tears blurred her vision as she hurried down the hall toward the stairs leading down to her room. She would have to tell Claire. She had no idea where they might go, no idea how to get there. Somehow she would have to find a way.

In the meantime, her behavior had to remain completely normal. She would do her job exactly as she usually did until the workday was over.

Tonight she would tell Claire the awful news. Then they would have to leave.

Dammit to hell! Cord slammed a hand against the walnut bookshelf in his study. He didn't know if he wanted to throttle Victoria for lying or admire the courage it had taken to stand up to him in one of his towering rages.

Few men had the nerve. Sarah was the only woman

who had ever been brave enough, and only because she knew he would never hurt a woman. Victoria had feared him, as he had meant for her to do. Still, she refused to cower and instead found the strength to defy him.

He knew she was guilty. She was a very poor liar. He could see the deceit written clearly on her face. What he didn't know was why she had done it, and as he had said, he didn't believe she was the sort to commit such crimes without cause. He ought to call in the authorities, he knew, but the notion left a bad taste in his mouth. Before he decided what action he would take, he needed to ferret out the truth.

He would, he vowed, pacing over to his desk. He would hire a Bow Street runner, and he knew exactly the man. Seating himself behind the desk, he snatched the pen from its silver holder and dipped it into the inkwell, then scratched out a message for Jonas McPhee, instructing him to discover all he could about Harwood, the theft of the necklace, and the serving women who had allegedly stolen it.

He had used McPhee before and been satisfied with the results. Cord sealed the message with a drop of wax, then rang for a footman to see it delivered to Bow Street. Once the facts were known—assuming he had judged Victoria correctly—he would find a way to help her.

In the meantime, he'd have Timmons keep an eye on her, make sure she didn't try to leave while he was away.

Cord sighed, his mind returning to recent events. Yesterday, Colonel Pendleton had stopped by with the news Cord had been waiting for. The prison escape was set. The schooner, *Nightingale,* that Cord had hired for the trip would be sailing for France tonight. If all went well, Ethan would be free and aboard the ship sometime tomorrow evening.

As soon as he finished supper, Cord returned to his study. It was dark tonight, not the hint of a moon. A fog had begun to creep in, a thick cocoon hanging over the streets of the city. A hammering at the door of his study drew his gaze from the window and an instant later Rafael Saunders, duke of Sheffield, strode in, a man as tall as Cord, dark-haired and powerfully built.

"Everything's set, I gather." Rafe walked straight to the sideboard to pour himself a drink.

"Everything on this end's ready to go," Cord replied. Rafe had been determined to come along. He was a friend of both Ethan and Cord's, a capable sort of man. If anything went wrong, Cord would be damned glad to have him along.

"We're to anchor in a cove near Cap Gris-Nez, south of Calais," Cord said. "A boat will deliver Ethan to the schooner sometime after midnight. All we have to do is turn round and take him home."

Rafe swirled the brandy in his glass. "Sounds too easy."

Cord had been thinking the very same thing. "I know."

"Let's just hope we get lucky—or that Ethan does."

Cord nodded. "It's early yet. I've got a couple of things to do. The *Nightingale* is anchored on the Southwark quay near the bridge. I'll meet you there at midnight."

Rafe downed the last of his brandy and set the empty snifter back on the sideboard. "I'll see you on the ship."

Cord watched him leave, his thoughts on both his cousin and the women in his employ. Over the next few days, he hoped to see both of his problems resolved.

* * *

Tory stepped back into the shadows of the hall outside the study and watched the tall, elegantly dressed figure of the duke of Sheffield stride off, his expensive Hessian boots ringing on the black-and-white-marble floor. She shouldn't have eavesdropped, wouldn't have if her situation had not been so dire. But until she and Claire were safely away from London, she had to know what the earl was about.

To her relief, his meeting with the duke had nothing to do with them, but involved Lord Brant's ongoing plan to save his cousin.

A plan that had him sailing to France that very night.

Tory mulled over the news as she climbed the stairs to Claire's third-floor bedchamber. The workday was over. It was time they left the house, got as far from London as they possibly could. Grace would be angry that Tory had not sent word of her departure, but she refused to involve her friend unless there was no other choice.

She knocked on her sister's door. Claire pulled it open. She was already dressed in her night rail, her pale hair plaited into a single braid. Tory stepped into the room and quietly closed the door.

"What is it?" Claire said. "You don't look quite yourself."

Tory sighed. "I'm afraid I am bringing bad news."

"Bad news? What sort of…?" Her face went suddenly pale. "You don't mean they have found out who we are?"

"In a roundabout way, I'm afraid they have. Or at least the earl has become suspicious. We have to get away before he discovers the truth."

Claire's lovely blue eyes filled with tears. "Where shall we go? Oh, Tory, what shall we do? I like it here. I don't want to leave."

"I know you don't, darling, but we haven't got any other choice. We have to leave or we'll be arrested. And I think I know a place where we will be safe."

Claire sniffed. "Where?"

"France."

"France? I thought we were at war with France."

"*England* is at war with France. You and I aren't at war with anyone. And the earl is sailing there tonight." Tory explained her idea, how they would steal aboard the ship and hide in the hold, then once the ship was anchored in the cove, they could slip over the side and swim ashore.

"But I can't swim, Tory!"

"No, but I can." When she was at school, she and Grace sometimes sneaked down to the river in the afternoons. One of the village boys had taught them to swim. Claire had always wanted to learn but had never quite worked up the courage to let Tory teach her. "It won't be that far to shore and I can help you get there."

"I don't know, Tory…."

"It'll work, Claire. We both speak excellent French. No one will suspect we're English. We'll go to Paris. Perhaps I'll find that job as governess that I hoped to find before."

Claire nervously moistened her lips. "Do you really think it could work?"

"I'm sure it will. Now, you get dressed and pack your satchel, then come to my room downstairs."

As she left Claire's bedchamber, Tory thought of the

earl and wondered if he might have instructed someone to watch them while he was away. She was beginning to know how he thought. She wouldn't put it past him. Timmons would be the logical choice. She would have to make sure the butler didn't see them leave.

The wheels of the hackney carriage whirred into the tense silence around them. Finding a conveyance for hire had not been easy, but in the end, Tory had been able to flag down a hackney about four blocks from the house. According to the conversation she had overheard in Cord's study, the *Nightingale* could be found near the bridge at the Southwark docks. It was an unsavory section of town, scarcely a place for a pair of young women. They would have to be careful, go straight to the ship, and pray they could sneak aboard without being caught.

"Are we there yet, Tory?"

"Soon, darling."

"How will we get aboard?" Claire asked, speaking the question Tory had hoped to avoid.

"Don't worry, we'll figure out a way once we get there." And the fog would definitely be of help. It grew thicker as the hackney approached the dock.

"The *Nightingale* is supposed to be down by the bridge," Tory told the driver, growing more nervous by the moment. "Can you tell which one it is?" A sea of ships' masts bobbed along the quay. In the heavy fog, how on earth would they find the right one?

"Harbor master'll know where 'tis. I can stop and find out if ye like."

She felt a wave of relief. "Yes, please."

A few minutes later, they were on their way again, headed for the *Nightingale*'s berth in the spot the harbor master had indicated.

Tory thanked the driver, gave him a little extra for his trouble, and she and Claire climbed out into the misty dark night.

"I think I see it," Claire whispered.

Tory read the name on the stern. "Yes, and there are only a couple of crewmen on deck and they appear to be quite busy." Tory reached over to adjust the hood of Claire's cloak, making certain it covered her sister's bright hair, then adjusted her own. Gripping her sister's hand, they started toward the ship.

Eight

The deck of the *Nightingale* rocked pleasantly beneath Cord's feet. He had always loved the ocean—its beauty and its vastness, the salt spray in his face and the cry of the gulls overhead, though his passion couldn't compare to Ethan's, who lived and breathed the sea, had loved ships and sailing since he was a boy.

It was natural that Ethan, the marquess's second son, had joined the navy as soon as he graduated Oxford. Cord wondered how he would take the news of his older brother's death while he was in prison and that he was now the marquess of Belford, a man with an entirely different set of responsibilities. Fortunately, the family also had shipping concerns, so Ethan wouldn't feel entirely a fish out of water.

Assuming he was still alive.

Cord paced the deck, listening to the creak of the tall spruce masts, the clatter and clank of the ropes and pulleys in the rigging. The night was as black as the devil's den, the sea an endless dark phantom rolling beneath them. A sharp breeze built as they headed east. Soon the surface of the water would be frothy with whitecaps that would remain unseen in the inky blackness.

Cord inhaled the damp, salty air, listened to the sound of the waves as the ship plowed through the water, and prayed their journey would not be in vain.

Claire squeezed Tory's wrist. "Did you hear that?"

Tory shifted in the darkness in the bottom of the ship. "It's just the timbers creaking in the hull."

"I think it's rats. I hate rats, Tory."

Since the snuffling sounds probably were being made by the furry little beasts, Tory made no comment, just leaned back against the wooden planks that formed the side of the ship.

Getting aboard had been easier than she had imagined. The two sailors working on deck were busy loading supplies into the galley. A lantern had been burning on the forward mast, guiding them to the ladder leading down into the hold. Another lamp hung at the bottom of the stairs, dimly illuminating the interior. Hurriedly, they had surveyed the contents of the hold, then hidden behind a stack of heavy bags of grain.

But one of the sailors had come down and snuffed the lantern and it was pitch black in there now.

"We won't be down here long," Tory said. "As soon as the boat anchors in the cove, we can sneak up on deck and slip over the side of the boat. We'll just have to be strong until then. Think of it as an adventure."

Claire had always liked adventures—at least pretend ones.

"Yes, I suppose that's what it is. I've never been on a ship before, and once we reach France, we'll be safe."

"That's right, darling." All they had to do was elude Lord Brant and the captain and crew of the *Nightingale*; then get safely to shore, make their way across a completely unknown landscape—avoiding the dangers on the roads—and try to find a village that might provide gainful employment.

Tory sighed into the silence broken only by the whoosh of waves against the bow. What had seemed so plausible in the safety of the house now seemed a near impossibility.

At least they wouldn't have to swim. Tory had noticed a little wooden dingy tied to the stern of the ship. Once the schooner was anchored and the crew settled in, she planned to use the dinghy to get them ashore.

Then again, she had planned a lot of things in the past few months and so far very few of them had worked.

"The seas are getting rougher." Cord stood next to Rafe at the aft deck rail of the ship. Both men were dressed in snug breeches tucked into knee-high boots and full-sleeved shirts beneath woolen coats.

"We expected a bit of weather," Rafe said. "The *Nightingale*'s sound and we're more than halfway there." The wind had picked up the minute they had reached the mouth of the Thames, sending them speeding on their way.

"We'll have to anchor in the cove until tomorrow night. I hope no one spots us and wonders what the devil we're about."

"If Bradley's as good as the colonel says, he'll pick a place where the ship won't be easily seen."

Cord stared out across the water. "I suppose I'm just a little nervous. I want this to go the way we planned. I want Ethan to come home."

Rafe set his big hands on the rail and looked out over the sea. "So do I."

Cord studied his friend's strong profile, the solid jaw and straight nose outlined by the ship's lantern hanging from one of the two tall masts. "There's something else I've been wanting to talk to you about."

Rafe's blue eyes swung to his face. He must have seen something there, because a corner of his mouth curved up. "Whatever it is, I'm betting it involves a woman. Don't tell me you've finally fallen in love."

Cord smiled and shook his head. "It's nothing like that, though it does involve a woman. And I'll admit she's a fetching little baggage. The problem is she's in trouble with the law."

"You're jesting."

"I wish I were. She's wanted for robbery and attempted murder."

"Sweet Jesus, man, how the devil did you get involved with a female like that?"

"She isn't a female like that or I wouldn't be involved. Or at least I don't think she is. I need you to do me a favor."

"Name it."

"See what you can find out about Miles Whiting, Baron Harwood."

"Harwood? I'm afraid I've never met the chap, though I've heard whispers about him here and there."

"So have I. None of them good, I might add."

"As I recall, there was something written about him recently in the papers."

"That's right. Two women robbed him and one of them hit him over the head. Harwood claims he suffered a loss of memory for several months. Now he's in London, trying to catch the culprits."

Rafe cast him a long, assessing glance. "This woman…I take it she is one of the two who coshed him on the head."

"She denies it, but I'm fairly certain she is."

"And she means something to you?"

Cord said nothing for several moments. "Put that way, yes, I guess she does."

"Then I'll ask round a little, see what I can find out, but in return, I expect to meet her. Any woman who can stir your interest this much has to be someone very special."

Cord made no reply. He just hoped Timmons was doing his job and Victoria would be there when he got back.

"I don't feel so good, Tory." Claire leaned back against the timber planking and slid her hand down over her stomach. "I think I'm going to be sick."

Oh, Lord. When she planned their escape, getting seasick never occurred to her. As it was, Tory seemed to be adjusting to the roll and sway of the ship without a problem, but Claire wasn't doing so well.

"You're not going to be sick," Tory said firmly, wishing her confident tone matched her mood. "It's just so dark in here. I think that makes it worse. Close your eyes and maybe you'll feel better."

Claire closed her eyes. "Oh…" she moaned.

"Think about something else. Think about that pretty lace shawl you saw in the window of that shop on Bond Street. Think how nice it would look draped round your shoulders."

Claire moaned again and covered her mouth with her hand.

"All right, I'll see if I can find a bucket." Tory moved away from the hull on her hands and knees, dragging her skirt out of the way and trying to remember where she had seen the bucket when they had sneaked down the ladder.

She felt her way over the bags of grain and continued toward the ladder, groping along the floor, ignoring the muck and the scurry of rats she hoped Claire wouldn't hear. She said a silent *thank you* when her fingers touched the rim of the wooden bucket, which sat on the floor below the lantern.

A box holding flint and tinder sat beside it. She remembered seeing it next to the lamp. Knowing she shouldn't, Tory retrieved the box, shoved up the glass and lit the lamp. A soft yellow glow filled the hold as she replaced the glass, and immediately she felt better. If anyone came down, he would probably think the lantern was left burning by mistake.

She hurried toward Claire with the heavy wooden bucket, climbed over the sacks of grain, into the safety of their hiding place, and set the bucket on the floor right next to Claire.

"Are you all right?"

Claire nodded. "The light makes it better." She managed a wobbly smile. Then she gagged and leaned over the bucket.

* * *

It was late, only a few more hours till dawn. With all the excitement, Cord wasn't very sleepy, but tomorrow was going to be a long day and he needed to be alert. Figuring he had better get a couple of hours of rest, he unbuttoned his shirt, pulled it off, and tossed it over the back of a chair. He had started on the buttons on the front of his breeches when he heard a rap on the door.

Striding across the cabin, he opened the door to find Rafe and the first mate, Whip Jenkins, standing in the passage.

"What is it?"

Rafe started grinning. "One of the crew found a couple of stowaways. After our earlier conversation, I have a hunch you might want to talk to them." He stepped back, turned and urged a slender woman forward.

"What the devil…?" He knew that face. "Bloody hell, Victoria!" Looking over her shoulder, he caught a glimpse of Claire and saw that she was trembling, and paler than he'd ever seen her.

"She's seasick," Victoria explained. "She needs to lie down."

Fury made it hard for him to speak. Cord flicked a glance at Rafe, who nodded.

"I'll take care of her," Sheffield said, turning toward the first mate. "The blonde can use my cabin. I'll bunk in with you until we get this worked out."

Jenkins nodded and Rafe started leading Claire away. She twisted to look back at them. "Tory?"

"It's all right, dearest. No one's going to hurt you."

"Sheffield's cabin is right next door. She'll be fine." His look turned hard. "It's you who had better be worried."

He stepped back from the door, and Victoria lifted her head and regally walked past him into the cabin. Cord closed the door a little harder than he meant to, barely able to contain his temper.

"Do you have any idea what you've done? This ship is on a mission—a very important mission. Do you realize the danger you have put yourselves in?" He reached for his shirt, pulled it on but didn't bother to fasten the buttons. "We're too far at sea to turn round and take you back. There is simply too much at stake."

Victoria shifted under his intense regard, but she didn't speak.

"God's teeth, I've seen some cork-brained schemes, but this one tops the list. The London docks are swarming with pickpockets and blacklegs. It is hardly a safe place for two unescorted young women—nor is a ship full of randy sailors."

He moved closer, till he stood right in front of her. Gripping her chin, he forced her to look up at him. "Give me one good reason why I shouldn't throttle you within an inch of your life."

Victoria swallowed. "We had to get away. This seemed like a good idea at the time."

"A good idea? This seemed like a good idea?" He made a sudden movement and she flinched.

"Dammit, I'm not going to hit you—though taking you over my knee is a monumental temptation."

Victoria said nothing. He saw how frightened she was, saw that her hands were trembling, and some of his anger faded.

"Sit down before you fall down." He urged her into

a straight-backed wooden chair and she sank down gratefully.

"Thank you."

"All right. Now you can tell me why you and your sister felt it was necessary to run away from my house, sneak aboard this ship and set sail for France. And I don't want any more fabrications. I want the truth, Victoria, and I want it now."

He could see her mind spinning, groping for some sort of plausible explanation. But she was exhausted, worried and fearful, and much of her usual pluck was gone.

"The truth, Victoria. Nothing else will do."

Her eyes slid closed. A resigned sigh whispered past her lips. "I'm the one who stole the necklace. I'm the one who hit the baron over the head. I used a bed warmer. A big heavy brass one."

"A bed warmer."

She nodded. "I had to stop him. It was the only thing I could think of to do."

He refused to feel a flicker of sympathy. "Why?"

"Why?"

"Why did you hit Lord Harwood over the head with a bed warmer?"

"Oh. Because he was…he was…he would have hurt Claire."

Cord took a breath, fighting for control. "All right. Start at the beginning and don't leave anything out. Tell me exactly what happened."

Tory clasped her hands in her lap, trying to keep them from shaking, trying to decide how much to say. Her glance strayed round the cabin, though there was no way she could possibly escape. The room was small but comfortable, with a wide berth and a built-in teakwood dresser. Curtains hung over the porthole and a basin and pitcher sat on the dresser.

"I'm waiting, Victoria."

She took a deep breath and silently prayed he would help her, as he had once offered to do. There was really no other choice but to tell him the truth. Well, most of it, at any rate.

"We were working at Harwood Hall." She glanced up at him from beneath her lashes. It looked as though he had yet to discover she was the baron's stepdaughter and she didn't intend to tell him—at least not yet. The law gave the baron complete control of his stepdaughters. Lord Brant might feel it his duty to return them.

"In the beginning, Lord Harwood was kind to us. Then he started looking at Claire."

"Most men look at Claire. She's difficult not to notice."

"The way Harwood looked at her made your skin crawl. Those cold black eyes, that tight little puckery mouth. Claire grew more and more afraid of him. I knew it was only a matter of time before he forced himself on her. We were planning to leave as soon as we could, but..."

"But?"

"But we needed more money. We figured if we could make it a couple more weeks, we'd have enough to get by. But two days later I heard him sneaking into Claire's bedchamber and I...I went into the room to stop him."

"And hit him over the head with the bed warmer."

She swallowed, her nerves inching up again. "It was the only weapon I could find at the time. I was afraid I had killed him."

"What about the necklace?"

She looked down at her hands, saw them gripped tightly in her lap. "I'd seen it once when I…when I cleaned the master's suite. We were desperate—just as you said. I took the necklace and sold it to a moneylender in Dartfield."

She explained how she had been forced to settle for a ridiculous sum, then spent the money during the weeks she had tried to find work. She looked up at him, trying to be brave, fighting not to cry.

"None of this is Claire's fault. She doesn't deserve to go to prison." Tears welled and spilled onto her cheeks and the earl's broad shoulders subtly straightened.

"No one is going to prison."

She started crying then, she couldn't help it. Not a soft little feminine cry like Claire would have done, but big, heaving sobs that shook her whole body. She didn't protest when the earl lifted her into his arms, sat down in the chair and settled her on his lap.

"It's all right," he said, cradling her head against his shoulder. "We'll figure this out. No one is going to prison."

Tory sagged against him, slid her arms around his neck and just kept crying. She had carried the burden so long. It felt so good to tell someone, to think that the earl might actually help her. She pressed her face into his neck, inhaled the scent of salt spray and cologne.

His shirt hung open. His chest was mostly bare and corded with layers of muscle. His breath felt warm as he whispered soothing words, and she wanted nothing so much as to turn her head and press her lips against his smooth, taut skin.

She wanted to kiss him, wanted to feel his mouth moving over hers as he had done that night. She wanted him to touch her, to caress her breasts until her nipples turned hard and swelled into his palm. She wanted him to do the things he had only hinted at that night.

"It's all right, love. Everything is going to be all right."

She nodded but the tears kept seeping from beneath her closed eyes.

She felt his hand on her cheek. He caught her chin, tipped her face up. "It's going to be all right," he gently repeated. His eyes held hers, gold into green, and she thought in that moment that he wanted to kiss her as badly as she wanted to kiss him.

He didn't.

And yet he wanted her. She moved a little and brushed against his heavy arousal. The earl lifted her up as he rose from the chair and set her on her feet, and still he made no move to touch her.

He had given his word. Apparently, he didn't intend to break it.

Not unless she wanted him to.

Oh, dear God, she wanted that so much. Tory closed her eyes and leaned toward him, just as a soft knock sounded at the door. She jumped and guiltily turned away, embarrassed at what she had almost done. The earl crossed the room to see who was there. The door opened and the duke of Sheffield stood in the passage.

"The girl...Claire. She's getting sicker." Sheffield turned his gaze to where Tory stood across the room, a handsome man with a strong jaw, a cleft in his chin and amazing blue eyes. "She's asking for her sister."

She returned her attention to the earl. "I need to go to her…if that is all right with you."

He nodded. She wished she knew what he was thinking.

"The first mate is bringing some crackers and tea," the duke said. "Perhaps that will help."

"Yes, perhaps it will." She looked over at the earl but his expression remained inscrutable.

"We'll talk again on the morrow," he said.

Tory just nodded. She didn't want to leave. She wanted so stay with the earl. Which meant she had better run as fast as her feet would carry her in exactly the opposite direction.

By the time the ship was anchored in the cove later that day, the seas had calmed, but the sky remained overcast and a stiff breeze whipped across the deck. After his conversation with Victoria late last night, Cord had tried to get some sleep, but his thoughts were too jumbled.

Worry for Ethan mixed with worry for Victoria and Claire.

He had believed Victoria's story. They were well enough acquainted that he knew what lengths she would go to in order to protect her sister. Hitting a man over the head with a bed warmer—bloody hell! Harwood was lucky she hadn't shot him.

Cord chuckled at the thought, then sobered. Even if the story were true, it was the word of two housemaids against that of a nobleman. The girls were in serious trouble.

Still, Cord believed if he greased enough palms, promised enough favors, hc could see the matter settled.

He turned at the sound of footfalls and watched Victoria approach. She was dressed in the clothes she had been wearing in his cabin, the clothes she had been dressed in the first time he had seen her, a high-waisted dove-gray gown, simply cut and slightly frayed but of obvious quality.

She looked pretty and innocent and he thought of all she had suffered these past few months. He recalled how good she had felt nestled against him last night, and how much he still wanted her, and his groin tightened. He couldn't remember wanting a woman so badly and yet he knew it wouldn't be fair. Victoria deserved far more than he could offer.

At least he could offer his help.

She stopped beside him and smiled. "Good morning, my lord." Her hair was no longer braided, but pulled back and clipped on each side, leaving soft dark curls to fall loose around her shoulders.

"How is your sister?" He had sent Whip Jenkins to check on the women this morning and word had come back that Claire was feeling much better.

"She is much improved. It is calmer here in the cove. Or perhaps she is beginning to get her sea legs."

"Let us hope so. There is still the return trip home."

Victoria glanced away. "Yes…I suppose there is that." Her gaze returned to his face. "I've been thinking, my lord…perhaps it would be better all round if Claire and I simply stayed in France."

"What are you talking about?"

"You wouldn't have to involve yourself in our problems. One of the crew could row us ashore and we could make our way inland, the way we had planned. I could find a job—"

"As a governess, I suppose. I believe that is what you had in mind before."

A hint of color rose in her cheeks. "I could find some sort of employment."

"No."

"You don't believe what I told you?"

"I believe what you have said."

"Then why won't you let us stay here?"

He didn't know why he was getting angry, he just knew that he was. He reached out and caught her shoulders, hauled her a little closer.

"Because you would be putting yourself in the gravest sort of danger. Two women, unescorted. No idea where you are going, how to get there, or who might help you. I simply won't have it. You are going back to London and I am going to help you straighten this out."

She swallowed. "What if…what if you can't?"

His hold on her gentled. "Then I will personally see you reach France or somewhere else where you will be safe. Trust me, Victoria. I'm an earl and a man of some means. If I explain matters to the authorities, they will listen."

She bit her lip. She looked as if there was something else she wanted to tell him, but in the end she kept silent.

"I can help you, Victoria. As long as you've told me the truth."

"I've told you exactly what happened."

He ran his thumb along her jaw. Her skin felt smooth as silk, soft as down. With the wind in her hair and her lips moist with spray, God, she was pretty. He wondered how he ever could have thought her merely attractive.

And he wanted her so badly he ached.

"If that is the case, then you have nothing to worry about."

Victoria turned to look out at the sea, her gaze sliding off toward the coastline. The shore along this section of land rose out of the water in jagged, flat-topped cliffs, though several steep trails led down to the beach where a boat rested on the sand, waiting to be used tonight. Gulls swept over the crags and ravines, their shrill cries reaching all the way out to the ship bobbing quietly at anchor.

"There is something else you need to tell me."

Victoria turned and her clear green eyes searched his. "What is that, my lord?"

"Who you really are."

Some of the color faded from her cheeks. "I don't know what you mean."

"It's obvious you and Claire have been gently reared. What happened to your parents? Why were the two of you left alone?"

She moistened her lips and the heaviness returned to his groin. "My father was a landowner in Kent. He died five years past. One night in late May, footpads set upon him on his way home from the fields and he was…he was killed."

She kept her eyes fixed on the shore. "My mother was devastated. All of us were. Two years later, my mother died. We had no relatives, no one to care for us. We did the best we could on our own."

He didn't mean to touch her. He simply could not resist. "I'm sorry," he said, drawing her against him.

She turned into his arms. "Someday I hope to see the men punished who were responsible for my father's death."

He couldn't blame her. He would feel exactly the same if someone he loved were murdered, though he imagined it would not happen. Not after so many years.

"I lost my father two years ago," he said. "I didn't realize how much he meant to me until he was gone. Toward the end, he got into a good deal of financial trouble. He never mentioned it and I was too wrapped up in myself to ask. He suffered an apoplexy. I think the strain was simply too much for him. If I had been there to help, perhaps it wouldn't have happened. I don't know. I don't suppose I ever will."

Victoria looked up at him. "You faced a number of problems when you inherited the title, but you overcame them. You rebuilt the fortune your father lost."

"How did you…?"

"There are very few secrets, my lord, in a household the size of yours."

His mouth edged up. "I suppose that's so."

"Why is it you've never married? I've seen you with Teddy. It's obvious you like children. And there is the matter of an heir." Twin spots of color rose in her cheeks. "I suppose it is none of my business."

"Actually, I have a number of obligations. Providing an heir is only one of them. But I would like to have a family someday. All I have to do is find a wife with the necessary requirements."

"You're searching for an heiress. I heard that as well. Someone who can add to your holdings."

"I owe a debt to my father. I mean to see it paid. Marrying well is important in accomplishing that end."

"I see."

He wondered if she really did. If she could imagine

how it felt to know you had failed the person who meant the most to you in the world.

No matter what happened, he would not fail again.

"You're cold," he said, noticing the gooseflesh on her arms. "Why don't you go inside?"

She nodded. "I believe I will."

Cord watched the feminine sway of her hips and wished she had agreed to become his mistress. Perhaps if Victoria were waiting for him at night, he could fulfill his obligations—and marry himself a wealthy wife.

Nine

Supper was over. Tory walked her sister back to the cabin they would share for the balance of the journey. Once the ship left the cove, Claire had begun to feel queasy again and Mr. Jenkins had given her a dose of laudanum. As soon as she put on her night rail, she curled up in her bunk and fell almost instantly asleep.

Tory wasn't the least bit sleepy. Earlier, she and Claire had dined at the captain's table with Brant and his friend, the duke. Afterward, the earl had asked if she would like to join him on deck.

All evening he had been solicitous in a way she hadn't expected. He felt sorry for her, she imagined, though the last thing she wanted was his pity. It was his help she needed and he had already agreed to that.

If she could trust him to keep his word.

Tory believed that he would. There was something about Cord Easton, something that spoke of honor and duty, something that urged her to put her faith in him. It was there in his eyes whenever he looked at her, along with something more, a need, an impossible longing that pierced straight into her heart. He desired her in a way no other man ever had.

And she desired him.

She knew it was wrong. She had been raised to save herself for the man she married. But even if the earl knew she was the daughter of a baron, even if he somehow managed to clear her name, he had made it plain the sort of woman he meant to wed. And an heiress was something Tory would never be.

Brant wasn't for her, she knew, and yet even as she said the words, she found herself reaching for her cloak, whirling it round her shoulders, pulling open the cabin door.

She would be strong, she told herself, ignore the longing she read in his eyes. And the sharp ache of yearning in her heart.

It was well past midnight and still no sign of the boat bringing Ethan. Claire was asleep in the cabin the two sisters shared, but Victoria still stood next to the earl on deck. Having overheard his conversation with Rafe in the study last night, she knew he had come to help his cousin escape from prison. Oddly, he was glad she knew. Having someone there who understood somehow made the waiting easier.

His gaze went to where she stood next to the rail. The night breeze sifted through her hair, and burnished highlights gleamed in the light of the lantern hanging from the mast.

"Are you certain you don't want to go in? It's getting late and it's damp out here."

She pulled her woolen cloak a little tighter around her. "It isn't really all that cold and the sea is calm. I would rather stay up here."

He thought that she was staying because of him, helping him pass the endless time until the boat arrived. He had never had a woman friend before. If it weren't for the constant lust he felt for her, he would think of Victoria that way.

"Look!" She pointed toward the water. "Someone is rowing out from shore!"

He turned toward the rail just as Sheffield walked up, tall black boots thumping on the holystoned deck. "It looks like they're coming," Rafe said, echoing Victoria's words.

Cord peered into the darkness. "I can't tell if Ethan is in the boat."

"Two men are coming. That's all I can see."

Cord's pulse quickened as he watched the man at the oars row the wooden dinghy closer to the schooner. As soon as the smaller boat pulled alongside, he tossed the heavy rope ladder over the rail and prayed he would see Ethan's face looking up at him.

Disappointment shot through him as the sailor who had manned the oars remained aboard and the other man, a stranger, climbed the rope ladder to the deck.

"Max Bradley," he said. A gaunt man, his face was hard and weathered, his fingers long and scarred. Thick black hair grew over the collar of his dark blue woolen coat. "I'm afraid I've brought bad news."

Cord's insides tightened. "Is he…is he dead?"

"I don't think so. It looks as if they've moved him somewhere else."

"When?"

"Less than two days past."

He felt as if a lead weight was pressing on his chest. They had lost their chance. Ethan yet remained in prison. He swallowed, tried not to succumb to a feeling of overwhelming despair.

"We knew it was too easy," Rafe said. "Now we'll have to make a second trip."

A second trip. Cord's head came up, Sheffield's words stirring a flicker of hope back to life. It burned brighter by the moment. "Yes…that's right. We'll just have to come back again. Where did they take him?"

"I'm not sure," Bradley said, "but I'll find out. This isn't over, my lord. Captain Sharpe is one of the best men we have. We want him home and safe almost as badly as you do."

Not nearly so much, Cord thought, feeling the tension of the past few days seep out of him, leaving him mired in fatigue.

Bradley glanced toward the open sea behind them. "I'd suggest you make way while it's still dark. Once I've located Captain Sharpe, I'll send word to Pendleton, as I did before."

"We'll be ready," Cord said. "Good luck."

"Thanks." Bradley slipped back over the side, descended the rope ladder with a skill that said he was no stranger to a ship, and settled himself in the dinghy.

Cord watched the boat disappear in the direction of the cove, the darkness closing around them once more. Around him, sailors raced into the rigging and started unfurling the sails. The anchor chain creaked as it turned round the capstan, hoisting the anchor, and a few minutes later, the ship began to move, heading into the open sea. Cord turned and started walking toward his cabin.

"My lord?"

Victoria's voice floated toward him. He had forgotten she was still there. "I'm sorry. I don't know what I was thinking."

"You were thinking of your cousin," she said softly.

Cord's gaze slipped back toward the shore, but if the dinghy had landed, he couldn't see it. "If only we had been a few days sooner."

"You'll get him next time."

He nodded. "Next time...yes. I wonder where he is tonight."

"Wherever it is, I pray he is safe."

Cord took a breath, silently echoing that same prayer. "Come. I'll walk you back to your cabin." Though he didn't really want her to go, he settled a hand at her waist. Victoria made no move to leave, just stood there looking up at him. Her eyes searched his face and he wondered if she could read the weariness there, the terrible disappointment.

"I was wondering if...I thought that perhaps I would join you in your cabin instead."

A long moment passed. At least a dozen heartbeats. Cord stared down at her, unable to believe he had heard her correctly. "Do you know what you're saying...what would happen if you came to my room?"

"I know what I'm saying." She reached up and cupped his cheek. "I am asking you to make love to me."

His feet seemed frozen to the deck. He felt like a callow schoolboy on his first assignation. "Victoria...are you certain? Are you sure this is what you want?"

"I've tried to convince myself it isn't, but it is not the truth. I want you to make love to me. I am very certain, my lord."

He moved then, close enough to touch her, cradle her face between his palms. "I'll take care of you. Both of you. I promise you won't regret—"

She silenced him with a finger against his lips. "Don't say more. Please. We don't know what lies ahead, what troubles we may face on the morrow. Tonight is all we have, but it is ours. If that is what you want."

God's blood, he had never wanted anything so badly. Cord reached for her, drew her against him, captured her lips in a desperately passionate kiss. She tasted like honey and roses, and his body throbbed with desire for her.

Wordlessly, he swept her into his arms and strode across the deck to the ladder leading down to his cabin.

By the time the earl carried Tory along the passage, opened the door and set her on her feet, she was trembling. Some wild insanity had pushed her to this moment, but she was here now and there was no turning back. She had sensed his desperate need tonight and she had responded. And she had told him the truth. She wanted the earl to make love to her. Wanted it more than anything she could remember

In the darkness inside his cabin, he closed the door, slid off her cloak and his coat, then crossed to the bureau and lit the small brass ship's lamp perched on the top.

The light cast a glow on his face, outlining the masculine hollows and valleys. He looked so strong, so unbearably handsome, but when he came to her, uncertainty flickered in the depths of his golden eyes.

"You aren't doing this simply to ensure my help once we return to London? You don't feel this is some sort of payment?"

Anger warred with hurt. He thought she would sell her body in order to save herself and Claire. She wanted to turn and walk out of the cabin, would have if it weren't for the awful need she read in his face.

"You will help me or you will not. One has nothing to do with the other."

His relief was so obvious it eased the pain. It seemed impossible, but perhaps she wasn't the only one afraid of being hurt.

"My name is Cord. Say it."

A slight flush rose in her cheeks. She had called him that in her dreams. "It's a very fine name... Cord...."

He bent his head and brushed her mouth with a feather-soft kiss. "What about your sister? She'll miss you if you stay."

"Once the ship reached the open sea, Claire felt queasy again. Mr. Jenkins gave her a dose of laudanum. He says she will sleep all the way back to London."

The earl ran a finger along her cheek. "Then tonight you are mine."

Tory closed her eyes as he drew her into his arms and kissed her. Not a soft, gentle, seductive kiss, but a hot, deep, taking kiss, a plundering, ravishing kiss that filled her with heat and need. Her knees went weak and she slid her arms around his neck to keep from melting into a puddle at his feet.

"Say my name."

"Cord..."

A deeper kiss followed, wet, fierce, abandoned. She was trembling, her head spinning.

"I know I should go more slowly," he said. "I'm having the damnedest time."

She smiled then, went up on her tiptoes to kiss him. Got a ravaging kiss in return. He pressed his lips against the place beneath her ear, kissed the side of her neck, captured her lips again. He worked the buttons on the front of her gown and the fabric parted, exposing the soft swells underneath.

Tory moaned as he cupped a breast, molded and caressed it, stroked his thumb across her nipple. The tip peaked and distended, began a faint throbbing that made her want to press herself against him.

Almost magically, the gown fell open and he slid it off her shoulders, eased it down over her hips to pool in a heap at her feet. Her chemise went next, leaving her in only her garters and stockings. Tory fought an urge to cover herself from his hot lion's gaze.

"I dreamt of this," he said, reaching out to cup a breast, caressing it gently, making her nipple throb with pleasure. She was breathing fast, faintly dizzy, unsure exactly what to do. She swayed toward him as he bent his head and took the fullness of her breast into his mouth.

"Oh, my..." Tory laced her fingers in his hair, unsure whether to push him away or pull him closer. His tongue circled her nipple as he suckled and tasted, drew on the peak, and sensation shot through her, amazing bursts of heat that slid into her stomach and floated out through her limbs.

His hand slipped over her belly, through the tight dark curls at the juncture of her legs, and he cupped her there. He suckled her breast as his fingers parted her, slid gently inside, and a little mewling sound rose in her throat.

Tory clung to his shoulders, trembling so badly he swept her up in his arms.

"Don't be frightened. The last thing I want is to hurt you."

"I'm not...not afraid." Mostly she was on fire. She wanted more of his passionate kisses and bold, intimate caresses. She wanted him to touch her—and she wanted to touch him. She wanted to taste him, know the texture of his skin. She wanted to breathe in his scent.

As he set her on her feet beside the bed, she leaned toward him, reached for his shirt and began to tug it free of his breeches. Cord helped her pull the fabric loose and dragged the shirt off over his head. He reached down and pulled off his boots, began to work the buttons at the front of his breeches.

He paused and looked up to see her staring at the width of his chest. She reached toward him and he caught her hand, turned it over and kissed the palm, then flattened it over his heart. She could feel the fierce beating, so alive, so vital, so like the man himself.

Tentatively, she learned the texture of his chest hair, the smoothness of his skin, the indentation of muscle over each of his ribs, the flatness of his stomach. He made no move to stop her and yet she could feel the tension in his body, the cords and sinews beneath her hand vibrating with need and the powerful urge to take her.

"I want you," he said softly.

She reached for the last of his buttons, brushing the

thick ridge straining upward beneath the front of his breeches, and heard his swift intake of breath.

"My fearless little Victoria." He seemed pleased even as she stepped away from him, allowing him to remove the balance of his clothes. He shed his breeches and she admired the leanness of his body, the strong, powerful torso and long, tapered legs.

When her eyes came to rest on the heavy shaft jutting from between his thighs, curiosity mingled with a tremor of uncertainty.

"It's all right. We don't have to rush. We'll take this slow and easy." He kissed her then, a soft, drugging, coaxing kiss that convinced her to trust him.

Desire returned, began to swirl through her, slip like mist over her skin. He eased her down on the berth and followed her down, bracing his weight on his elbows, kissing her all the while. His hands were everywhere, smoothing over her skin, stroking her breasts, moving lower, parting her softness and slipping inside her, sending waves of pleasure crashing through her.

She barely noticed when he settled himself between her legs. She felt his powerful erection, but instead of being afraid, wild anticipation filled her. She wanted this, wanted him. What happened later did not matter.

Her passage was hot and slick, throbbing in a way she had never experienced. Cord eased his hardness a little inside her, preparing her to accept him. He kissed her long and thoroughly, caressed and teased until she was writhing beneath him, whispering his name, trying to press herself more fully against him. Then he drove himself deeply inside.

For an instant, pain stabbed through her. He had

breached her maidenhead. From this day forward, she would be forever changed. But the thought quickly faded, and with it, the pain. She was filled with him, linked in a way she couldn't have imagined.

"I'm sorry," he said, holding himself rigidly above her. "I tried not to hurt you." But there was triumph in his eyes and a look of fierce possession. In truth, he had claimed her. She couldn't let him know how thorough a job he had done.

"The pain is fading." And the pleasure yet remained, the sweet ache returning, the throbbing need just out of reach. Tentatively lifting her hips, she allowed him to penetrate more deeply and heard him groan. Then he was moving, slowly at first, easing the way, stirring the passion to life and making her tremble.

Tory picked up the rhythm, began to move with him as he drove himself on, moving faster, surging deeper, taking her harder. Something was building inside her, something hot and wild.

It tore through her so keenly she cried out his name. Arching upward, her fingers digging into his shoulders, she felt as if the world had suddenly shattered into pieces.

Cord's muscles tensed a few seconds later. He groaned as he followed her to release.

The ship's clock chimed. Still linked together, they began to spiral down, the soft throbbing pleasure slowly fading. For several seconds longer, Tory lay still, sorting through the emotions she was feeling.

"That was quite something," she said, and heard the rumble of laughter in his chest.

"Quite something, indeed."

She turned to look at him, saw the lazy satisfaction in his eyes. "I had no idea…"

"And for that I am eternally grateful."

She wasn't sure what he meant, but before she could ask, he was kissing her again. The heat returned and he slid into her again, more easily this time. She couldn't have guessed how wonderful making love with him would be.

And whatever happened on the morrow, she knew she would never regret it.

Ten

Cord had to be objective. He had to be certain Victoria had told him the complete and utter truth. Not that he didn't trust her. Well, mostly he did.

Thinking of her, now that they were returned to the house, reminded him of the hours they had spent together onboard the ship and he felt the pull of a smile. She was as passionate as he had imagined, more so, perhaps. He had hated to awaken her as the *Nightingale* neared port, but he didn't want her sister to find her gone and discover where she had spent the night.

Claire would learn the facts of life soon enough, once Tory was installed as his mistress, a situation that couldn't occur until both women had been cleared of the charges against them. To accomplish that end, he needed to know what Jonas McPhee might have found out about Harwood and his two wayward employees.

Of course it had only been a few days since McPhee had received Cord's message, two days since his return from France. The investigator had been given only a brief time to work. Still, the runner might have turned up something. Once Cord was armed with the facts, he planned to go directly to the baron.

According to Sheffield, Harwood was as tight as the hide on a drum. Money to replace the necklace—along with the threat of scandal—ought to be enough to convince him to drop the charges.

Which would return Victoria to his bed.

As he walked out the front door, he smiled to think of her working in his house, pretending nothing had changed between them, unable to hide a blush whenever she found him looking in her direction.

Though that had rarely happened in the past few days.

Victoria was avoiding him, he knew, uncertain exactly how to proceed. He had promised her he would find a way to straighten out her problems, but that only seemed to make her more nervous. He thought that there was more to her story, something else she wanted to confide in him, but so far she hadn't come forth.

Perhaps McPhee could fill in the gaps.

Cord hoped so. He thought of Victoria and felt the hot pull of desire as he shoved open the front door of the runner's office on Bow Street—and was greeted by a very serious Jonas McPhee.

"You have to tell him the rest of it, Tory."

Tory had told her sister that she had been forced to confess most of the story the night they had stowed away in the hold. "I know."

"The earl said he was going to help us, didn't he?" They were working in one of the bedchambers upstairs,

Tory oiling the rosewood furniture while Claire swept the floor.

"He said he would help and I am fairly certain he'll do what he can, but…"

"But you have left out one of the most important parts. You haven't told him Lord Harwood is our stepfather—our true and legal guardian."

"That's because I don't know what will happen when he finds out." Whatever it was, Cord certainly wouldn't be pleased. Not when he realized she was Victoria Temple Whiting, daughter of the late Baron Harwood, a member of the aristocracy.

Miles Whiting, the man next in line for the title, had arrived at Harwood Hall just weeks after her father's murder. He had generously allowed them to remain in the house, then spent the next twelve months wooing her distraught mother into believing he was her savior and finally convincing her to marry him. A n'er-do-well who had lived by his mother's largess, he had wound up with the Harwood title, estate and modest fortune, along with Lady Harwood's inheritance and fabulous ancestral home, Windmere.

Whiting had got exactly what he wanted. Tory believed he would have gone to any lengths to get it.

Including murder.

"The earl could speak to the baron," Claire suggested, "convince him we will find a way to pay back the cost of the necklace."

"Harwood wants more than money. He wants you, Claire." Just as Lord Brant wanted Tory. And the earl would be furious when his plan to make her his mistress vanished like smoke—once it was known she was the daughter of a peer.

"Whatever happens, you still have to tell him. It's only fair."

Tory stopped rubbing the spot she was polishing on the Sheraton table and turned to look at Claire. "All right. I'll tell him tonight, as soon as supper is over."

She cringed to think of it. For the past two days, she had avoided him as much as possible, which he seemed to know and somehow find amusing. On the rare occasion she ran into him, it was clear what he was thinking. She could see the heat in his eyes, the sensual curve of his lips. She remembered the exact feel of them moving over her skin, and an answering warmth stirred in the pit of her stomach.

Claire turned to the door. "What was that?"

"What was what?" Tory's gaze followed Claire's.

"It sounds like someone is calling you." Claire looked over at Tory, her eyes growing big and round. "I think it's the earl."

Tory heard it, too. She recognized the outraged bellow and a chill swept through her.

"He really sounds angry. You don't think—"

"That's exactly what I think. You had better stay up here." Wishing her heart would stop that ridiculous clatter, Tory lifted her crisp black skirt up out of the way and walked out the door, heading for the stairs leading down to the entry.

Lord Brant stood at the bottom of the staircase, his jaw clenched, a slight flush rising beneath the bones in his cheeks.

"My study," he said as she reached the last stair. "Now!"

Her pulse picked up even more. He was beyond furious, she could see. Sweet God, she should have told him the whole of it before it was too late! Lifting her chin, she preceded him down the hall and into his study. The earl followed her in and slammed the door.

"You lied to me." His voice was tight, his anger barely contained.

She forced herself to meet his furious gaze. "Only by omission. The rest of what I told you is true."

"Why? Why didn't you just tell me who you were?"

"Because you are an earl and Harwood is a baron. Because there are rules among members of the aristocracy and I wasn't certain you would be willing to break them."

One of his hands fisted. "So you believed I would turn you over to Harwood."

"I thought it was possible, yes."

His jaw went even harder. "I can tell you one thing I likely wouldn't have done. I wouldn't have spent the night making love to you!"

She winced. Perhaps it was true. Perhaps he would have refused the comfort of her body. She wondered if that were part of the reason she hadn't told him who she was.

"I don't regret what happened between us. Do you?"

"For God's sake, of course I regret it! You are the daughter of a baron! Do you realize the consequences of what you have done?"

She opened her mouth to answer, to assure him that she would never mention what had transpired between them, but a sharp rap cut off her words. Cord frowned at the interruption, turned and strode to the door. The instant he opened it, two uniformed watchmen swept in, followed by a tall, lean, black-haired man Tory had hoped never to see again.

Her stomach knotted. Cord must have sent for him. Dear God, she should have known better than to trust the earl. Why hadn't she listened to the warnings in her head? Why hadn't she taken Claire and fled the moment the ship arrived back in London?

Tears burned her eyes but Tory blinked them away. She refused to show weakness in front of her stepfather. She stiffened her spine as the watchmen approached, but before they could reach her, the earl stepped in front of them.

"You can stop right there," he said, freezing them in place. He turned a hard gaze on the baron. "I presume you are Harwood."

He managed a small, haughty smile. "At your service, my lord." He was tall and whipcord thin, his face carved in hard, unforgiving angles. He was selfish and ruthless, and yet for the year he had been wooing her mother, he had seemed kind, almost gentle. He was the sort of man who would do whatever it took to get what he wanted and she hated him for it.

"Before this progresses any further," the earl said, "I want you to know Miss Whiting and her sister are under my protection."

"Is that so?"

"I only just discovered their connection to you this morning. I planned to send word, try to work all of this out."

The smile, such as it was, remained in place. "There is nothing to work out. My wayward daughters will be returned home, where they will make restitution for the necklace they stole, and all of this will be over. I apologize, Lord Brant, for the trouble they have caused. If there is anything I can do to—"

"You can leave them in my care until this matter is resolved. My cousin and her husband, Lord and Lady Aimes, will stand as chaperones. Victoria and Claire can stay with them at Forest Glen, their Buckinghamshire estate."

Tory's heart beat with a faint ray of hope. Cord hadn't betrayed them. He was trying to help them, just as he had promised.

"You don't seem to understand," the baron pressed. "There is nothing to resolve. The girls are going home with me, their legal guardian."

Frustration crept into the earl's features, and something that looked like desperation. He wasn't going to be able to help them, just as she had feared. Her face felt bloodless and her knees began to tremble beneath her taffeta skirt. Sweet God, she could only imagine the punishment the baron would mete out for what she had done.

It would be less than nothing compared to what he intended for Claire.

She heard her sister then, coming down the hall, crying as one of the watchmen led her into the study. She looked at the earl, crestfallen with disappointment, certain that he was responsible.

"I thank you for seeing to their care," Harwood was saying. "Since the scandal of residing in a bachelor household all of these weeks would be ruinous to my daughters' reputations, I trust you will keep the matter private."

"No word will come from me."

Harwood focused his attention on Claire. "Come, my pet. It is time we went home."

Cord pinned him with a look of warning. "As I said, these women are under my protection. Should they be mistreated in any way, you will personally answer to me."

The baron made no reply, but his lips thinned as he fought to control his temper. "And should I discover they were harmed in any way during their tenure here, you, sir, will answer to me!"

As if he cared, Tory thought. But perhaps he was concerned that the earl had stolen Claire's virginity, as he himself had planned to do. That would surely upset him. He would, no doubt, be amazed to discover it was his elder stepdaughter who had fallen prey to the earl.

Harwood urged Claire out the door and Tory started after them, but the earl caught her arm.

"I won't leave you there. I'll come for you. I'll find a way to help Claire."

He would try, perhaps. He would do his best to aid them. But the courts were strict in matters of family and there wasn't the least chance he would succeed.

"I'll be all right. It's Claire who needs you."

"I'll come," the earl said even more fiercely, his eyes dark and hard. Worry tightened his jaw as he reached out and touched her cheek.

Tory looked at him one last time, memorizing the handsome lines of his face, thinking of the night they had shared, admitting to herself for the first time how much he had come to mean to her. In truth, she realized, she was in love with him.

And if Harwood had his way, she would never see him again.

Eleven

"Then it's true." Cord paced the Oriental carpet in the China Room of the duke of Sheffield's town house, a palatial residence in Hanover Square that dominated most of the block. The China Room was equally grand, with ceilings of black and gold, deep sofas in brocaded Oriental silk, black lacquer furniture and carved cinnabar vases.

Rafe shrugged his shoulders, moving the fabric of his dark blue tailcoat. "We can't know for sure, but Madame Fontaneau is a very reliable source for this kind of information."

"And she says when it comes to matters of the flesh," Cord added, "Harwood's appetites include everything from very young women to boys and anything in between. On top of that, he is known to be somewhat sadistic. This is the man who has control of Victoria and Claire."

Rafe took a sip of his brandy. "What will you do?"

Cord raked a hand through his hair, dislodging several dark strands. "What I was honor-bound to do from the moment I carried her into my cabin aboard the ship. I took her innocence. Victoria is the daughter of a peer. I'll have to marry her."

Rafe eyed him above the rim of his glass. "I don't believe she expects it. I got the impression she is quite an independent young woman."

"Perhaps marriage is *exactly* what she expects. Perhaps that is the reason she encouraged my attentions. She wanted out of her stepfather's grasp. Once she is married to me, she will certainly have accomplished that end."

"What about her sister? You've told me how protective she is. Do you really think she planned to marry you and leave her younger sister in the hands of a predator like Harwood?"

He couldn't make himself believe it, not in a million years. "No. I don't think she would ever do anything that might hurt Claire." He sighed as he picked up his glass and started for the sideboard. "I could use another drink."

"I think you're definitely entitled."

Cord lifted the stopper off the crystal decanter and poured a goodly amount of brandy into his glass. "I've already been to see the magistrate. He says his hands are tied. As Harwood is legally their guardian, there is nothing I can do."

"Except offer marriage."

He took a long sip of his drink. "Exactly." He shook his head. "I hoped to expand the family holdings. Lately, I was seriously considering making an offer for Constance Fairchild."

"The Fairchild whelp is a green girl barely out of the schoolroom. She would bore you in a thrice."

"There are ways to entertain oneself beyond home and hearth." He glanced off toward the window. "I can't believe I am failing my father again. He must be turning in his grave."

Rafe just smiled. "From what I've seen, I think your father would approve your choice."

He scoffed. "Victoria will come to me penniless. She has no land, no inheritance." He laughed then, a bitter, grating sound. "God's blood, I never thought to marry my housekeeper."

Rafe chuckled softly. "Hardly that, my friend." A big hand settled on Cord's shoulder. "I think she may very well suit you. Money or not, your life will never be dull."

Cord made no comment. Victoria had lied to him, tricked him and ruined his plans for the future. He had hoped to repay the debt he owed his father. He had made a promise and now he could not keep it.

He was doomed to fail.

Again.

The door to her bedchamber creaked open. "Tory?" Dressed in her night rail and long quilted wrapper, Claire crept into her bedchamber. The lantern next to the bed cast her slender form in shadow. Worry etched lines into her forehead. "Are you all right?"

They had made the overnight journey from London and arrived at Harwood Hall late in the afternoon. After supper, the baron had summoned Tory into his study and brutally repaid her for the theft of his precious pearl necklace and all the trouble she had caused.

She winced as she sat up in bed. "I'm all right. I'll be better in the morning." But her back burned with the angry red slashes her stepfather had inflicted. The caning she had received was no more than she had expected and she had managed to suffer it without crying out.

She hadn't fought him. She had learned he enjoyed it more if she did. Neither would she let him break her.

"I brought you some salve." Claire closed the door and walked toward her. "Cook says this will help heal the marks and take away some of the pain."

Tory sat up straighter in the bed. Pulling the bow at the neck of her gown, she slid it off her shoulders, exposing the welts. A sound of sympathy whispered from Claire's throat as she sat down on the bed beside her and began to gently dab the ointment on the vicious-looking marks.

"Why does he always beat you and not me?"

Claire still didn't really understand. She didn't realize it was her perfection that drew him. He wouldn't do anything to destroy it. At least not yet.

"He didn't beat you because he knows you don't deserve it. I am the one who took the necklace. I am the one who encouraged you to run away."

"I'm frightened, Tory."

So was she, but not for herself. "Perhaps…perhaps the earl will find a way to help us." She couldn't help wishing, praying that he would. She didn't really believe it would happen.

Claire's face brightened. "Yes, I am certain he will," she said firmly, her mind sliding away as it usually did, into a place where there was light and hope and never any pain. "Lord Brant is a very resourceful man."

An image of Cord appeared, strong and impossibly handsome. Tory forced back memories of hungry kisses and heated flesh, of wild desire and drugging passion.

She pasted on a smile. "Yes, he is, and I'm sure he'll think of something."

Perhaps he would, but how much time would it take? How long would it be before Harwood went after Claire? As soon as he had finished his assault on Tory, he had left the house, called away on business for the balance of the week, she had heard him tell the butler. Once he returned… Dear God, she refused to think of it.

Claire dabbed the last of the salve on her shoulders.

"Thank you, darling. That feels much better." Pulling her night rail up where it belonged, Tory retied the bow at her neck. "Why don't you go back to your room and get some sleep? For now Lord Harwood is gone and we are safe."

Claire nodded. She had changed in the months since they had left Harwood Hall. Some of her innocence was gone, and if the baron had his way, soon all of it would be.

Tory heard the door softly close as Claire slipped quietly away. In the darkness, she lay on her side and began to count the shadows on the wall. Outside the window, the leaves on the branches of a big sycamore tree shifted against the mullioned window, making a soft scratching sound.

Tory closed her eyes, but she couldn't fall asleep.

"Excuse me, miss." The butler, a brittle little man in his seventies who feared for his job and worked for less than normal pay, hurried toward her down the hall, pausing next to the linen closet, where Tory busily took inventory. She wasn't a housekeeper any longer, but her duties had little changed.

"You've a visitor, miss. The earl of Brant is here. I've shown him into the drawing room."

Her heart pinched, began a painful throbbing. Cord was here. She hadn't completely believed he would come.

"Thank you, Paisley. The journey from London is a long one. Instruct one of the chambermaids to prepare one of the guest rooms for his use."

Removing the apron tied over her apple-green muslin gown, she headed down the hall to the drawing room. Just outside, she paused to smooth her hair, wishing it weren't pulled back in such an unflattering coil, wishing her hands would stop trembling.

The earl stood with his back to her in front of the hearth, his long legs braced a little apart. For an instant as she entered the room, she simply enjoyed the sight of him, the wide shoulders and trim waist, his neatly groomed dark brown hair.

Then he turned toward her and all the emotions she had been fighting rose up at once, threatening to overwhelm her. Her eyes burned. It took sheer force of will to keep herself from rushing into his arms.

"My lord." The words came out more softly than she expected, but her voice sounded fairly even, hiding the turmoil she felt inside.

He strode toward her, his gaze filled with worry and something more. "Are you all right?"

She swallowed. Her back still burned. She was stiff and sore from the thrashing she had received, but the baron was always careful to make sure the marks didn't show.

"I'm fine. We both are. The day after our arrival, Lord Harwood was called away."

"When will he return?" His eyes were a darker golden brown. There were secrets in them. She wondered what they were.

"He should be home today."

He nodded. "Good. In the meantime, we need to talk."

She smoothed the front of her gown, took a steadying breath. "Shall I ring for tea?"

"Perhaps I'll have something later."

Crossing the room in front of him, she indicated they should take a seat on the green velvet sofa and they sat down next to each other, a respectable distance apart.

Cord didn't bother with formalities. "First, I need to tell you that I have been to see the magistrate. Unfortunately, he says where your guardianship is concerned there is nothing he can do."

A faint sound of distress escaped and Cord captured her hand, holding it gently between both of his.

"That doesn't mean this is over. I'm working on several other options. We'll find a way to help Claire."

She tried to remain optimistic, but her chest squeezed with fear. "How?"

"I'm not yet certain. But that is not the reason I am here."

She frowned, wondering at the change in his thoughts. "Why then?"

He let go of her hand, straightened a bit on the sofa. "I came here to propose."

"Propose?" Her mind didn't seem to be working. "Surely you realize I can't become your mistress. Not now."

The edge of his mouth barely curved. "I am not offering an indecent proposal, Miss Whiting. I am making you an offer of marriage."

Tory swayed a little on the cushion, for an instant, feeling light-headed. The earl was asking her to wed. *Dear sweet God.* She hadn't known how much she wanted that to happen until that very moment.

Then it dawned on her. He had taken her innocence. She was the daughter of a baron. He had no choice but to marry her. She hoped the crushing disappointment didn't show.

"I realize you feel it is your duty…under the circumstances…to make such a proposal. I assure you, I never expected marriage when we…when I accompanied you to your cabin. We both know I am not what you want for a wife."

"What I want is no longer important. Fate has intervened and there is no other choice except for us to wed."

She shook her head. "You planned to marry an heiress. Even should the baron feel obligated to provide a dowry, it would be of meagerest proportions, certainly nothing that would strengthen your family holdings."

"Be that as it may, our course has been set. I have already obtained a special license. On the morrow, we will wed."

She couldn't believe it. Did he really believe she would simply agree, that she would marry him knowing he didn't want her? Squaring her shoulders, Tory stood up from the sofa.

"I have not agreed to marry you, my lord, and I don't intend to. My answer to your proposal is no. I don't want a man who doesn't want me."

Cord stood up right next to her. "Oh, I want you. I can assure you, sweeting, one night with you in my bed was scarcely enough." Gripping her shoulders, he drew her toward him, bent his head and very thoroughly kissed her. Tory tried to push him away, but his hold only tightened. Her back still stung, but the heat was so overwhelming she forgot about the pain. Instead, desire swept through her, weakening her resolve, coaxing her to return the kiss.

She leaned toward him, gave herself up to him, felt a stab of disappointment when Cord pulled away. When she opened her eyes, there was a hint of triumph in his expression.

"We're going to be married. You might as well get used to it."

Tory tried to find her voice, then simply shook her head. "I won't do it."

His eyes flared. "You will, dammit!" Cord caught her shoulders again. "Listen to me, Victoria. You need to get out of this house before your stepfather seriously hurts you. Aside from that—have you considered the possibility that you may be carrying my child?"

She blinked. The thought had never crossed her mind. "Surely it takes more than once."

The edge of his mouth faintly curved. "It happened more than once, if you will recall, and even if it hadn't, the possibility would remain."

She pondered that. If things were different, she would love to have Cord's child. If he loved her. If he weren't being forced into a marriage that he didn't want.

"It doesn't matter," she said. "I won't marry you. I don't believe I am with child and there are other things to consider."

"Such as?"

She flicked a glance toward the rooms upstairs. "My sister. If…if you want to marry someone, marry Claire. She is the one who needs your help."

The earl made a harsh sound in his throat. "It wasn't Claire whose innocence I took that night on the ship. It wasn't Claire whose luscious little body wept for me, trembled for me, sang for me. And it isn't Claire I intend to wed—it is you, Victoria!"

Tory swallowed but said nothing more. He wasn't going to take no for an answer. Half of her wanted to marry him so much an ache throbbed in her heart. The other half knew she had stumbled upon the answer to how she was going to save Claire.

"All right, you win," she finally agreed. "If you are certain that is your wish, then I will marry you."

An odd emotion flickered in his eyes. If she hadn't known him better, she would have sworn it was relief.

"I'll speak to Harwood as soon as he returns. Once matters between us have been settled, we can be wed."

Tory watched him leave the room. There was purpose in his strides and a confidence about him he wore like a cloak. She couldn't help thinking of the chess games they had played. In this match, she had made the first move when she had gone to his cabin. Today he had countered. It was her turn next.

There were sacrifices to be made in any game.

She only wished it didn't have to hurt so badly.

Over the last few days, Cord had kept himself busy. After his conversation with Rafe, he'd made a second fruitless trip to the magistrate's, then paid another visit to Jonas McPhee, instructing the runner to look for any information that might be useful against the baron, hoping it would provide the leverage he needed to free Claire.

He had hired the best attorney in London to look for avenues his position as her soon-to-be brother-in-law might supply. He had arranged for a special license and bought a wedding gift. A very special wedding gift.

Wedding. Cord frowned at the thought. He had wanted to marry an heiress. Instead, he was wedding a penniless young woman—his *housekeeper,* for God's sake! Part of him couldn't help feeling angry and duped. But the deed was done and there was no changing the result.

Which was why he had returned to Harwood Hall for his necessary but entirely distasteful meeting with the baron. Cord sighed as he crossed the bedchamber he had been assigned, mentally replaying the conversation they'd had that afternoon.

They had met in Harwood's study. Cord had begun by stating his interest in a match between him and Victoria, which seemed to surprise the baron.

"When you requested this meeting, I thought perhaps you meant to make an offer for Claire."

Harwood assumed every man found her as irresistible as he did. Which only proved what a fool he was.

"Your younger daughter is extremely beautiful, as you well know, but she's young and incredibly naive. It's your older daughter who has captured my interest."

Harwood lifted a small porcelain pitcher off one of the Sheraton tables and held it up to examine it. As he had been before, the baron was dressed a bit foppishly, in a blue satin tailcoat and ruffled black cravat. Whatever Cord thought of him, it was obvious he thought himself a handsome man.

"I'm not sure that is a good idea. Victoria is young and not yet completely prepared to become a wife."

Words Cord translated as, *She runs my household without payment and I enjoy having her under my control.*

"Yes, well, she is nineteen, after all, and we both know there are extenuating circumstances. A young woman who has lived unchaperoned in a bachelor household. Sooner or later rumors are bound to surface. Should the gossipmongers get wind of the story, her reputation will be ruined. Yours and mine will suffer as well. A marriage between us would head off any possible scandal."

Harwood set the pitcher back down on the table. Both men were standing. Neither wanted to be at a disadvantage.

"I shall have to give it some thought."

"You do that. While you're at it, you might also give thought to the fact that you've another daughter to consider. As an earl and Claire's brother-in-law, the younger girl's reputation will also be protected."

Harwood toyed with the cuff on his satin coat. "There is still the matter of the necklace. Victoria must remain here long enough to make reparation."

Cord had known this was coming and he was prepared. "I'll gladly pay for the necklace. As her husband, I would, of course, be responsible for her debts."

Harwood's face immediately lit with interest, as Cord had been certain it would. For the next half hour, they haggled over the value, Cord finally agreeing to the baron's ridiculous claims of the pearls' worth.

"There is no limit to the value of such an object," Harwood said. "It is irreplaceable."

Not entirely, Cord thought, since he had already managed to find and purchase the necklace himself. Victoria had mentioned the moneylender in Dartfield who had bought the pearls for a miserly sum. As there was only one such man in the village, it hadn't been difficult to track the necklace down. Paying far more than the moneylender had for the piece, he had eventually struck a deal.

As Victoria's future husband, righting the matter of the theft was the honorable thing to do, and at first Cord had meant to simply return the necklace to the baron. In the end, for reasons he couldn't quite explain, he had decided to keep it.

As he watched the gleam of greed enter Harwood's dark eyes, he was glad of his decision. The beautiful antique necklace was far too precious to belong to such a man.

"You are willing to pay me for the necklace. Are you also willing to take Victoria without a dowry?"

Cord's jaw tightened. Financially, he had done very well in the last few years. But he had vowed to increase his family's worth to an even greater extent. He hated the reminder of his failure.

"I am not asking for one."

In the end, Harwood agreed to the marriage almost gleefully. More, Cord figured, from the realization that once Victoria was gone, he would be rid of Claire's watchdog rather than any real concern for the girls' reputations.

Cord paced the bedchamber, the memory slipping away as he sipped the brandy that had been left for him on a silver tray atop the bureau. The room he'd been provided was surprisingly nice, though the dark green damask draperies were far from new and the counterpane slightly worn. Still, everything was clean and the furniture well polished. Victoria's doing, he imagined, trying not to be amused.

He drew back the counterpane, pulled back the freshly washed linens and was surprised to see a small white note, carefully folded and sealed, lying on his pillow. He picked up the message, broke the seal and skimmed the feminine, finely penned script.

As the words sank in, images of Victoria, naked and writhing beneath him, swam into his head. Desire pulsed through him. Heat pooled heavy in his groin and he went hard beneath his robe.

> Dearest Cord,
> I apologize for my reluctance this afternoon. I am in your debt for what you are doing. And there is the matter of our mutual attraction. You said you wanted me and in truth I want you, too. Come to my room tonight, two doors down on the left. I'll be waiting for you in bed.
> Yours, Victoria.

Sweet Jesus. She had only reluctantly agreed to the marriage. Knowing how stubborn she could be, he hadn't expected such a reversal, but he was glad to see that she had come to accept her situation, and thinking of the way she had returned his kiss he knew her desire for him was not feigned. She wanted him. And God knew he wanted her.

It was getting late. Cord blew out the lamp beside the bed and crossed the Aubusson carpet to the door. Barefoot and naked beneath the robe, he checked to be certain no one saw him, then stepped out into the hall. His blood was pounding, his arousal almost painful.

Cord reached Victoria's bedchamber and quietly opened the door.

Twelve

The wind blew noisily outside the brick house, but still Tory could hear his familiar footsteps striding down the hall. She pressed her ear against the door and listened to the soft closing of the door to her sister's bedchamber. Her pulse was racing, thundering in her ears. And there was a soft ache in her heart.

You have no choice, a little voice said.

Claire would be better off with the earl. With him, she would be safe. And Tory believed that Cord was a good man, the sort of man who would be kind to Claire. She thought that he would be patient with her sister, give her time to adjust to the idea of marriage. She remembered how gentle he had been the night that they had made love.

The pain expanded, seemed to fill her chest. Tory ignored it. Cord would be furious at being bested, but she didn't believe he would take it out on Claire.

And like most of the men of his class, having a wife wouldn't necessarily change his life. The earl had several estates. Perhaps he could remain in the city and leave Claire in the country. Tory could come for long visits and Claire would be happy there.

Tory told herself all those things as she stepped out into the hall. She said them again as she moved along the corridor, holding up a small brass lamp to light the way. The master's suite was just down the hall. It wouldn't take much to wake the baron.

Tory took a deep, steadying breath, opened Claire's door and started to scream.

Bloody hell! Cord jerked away from the figure asleep in the bed and whirled around. Victoria stood in the doorway dressed in her night rail, long brown hair plaited into a single thick braid. She was shouting, pointing her finger at him, bringing half the servants down the corridor at a dead run, led by no less than the baron himself.

Cord turned back toward the bed, his mind spinning, trying to grasp what was happening. A sleepy-eyed Claire jerked upright and stared at him with a completely bewildered expression.

If you want to marry someone, marry Claire. She is the one who needs you. In an instant, Cord realized what Victoria had done.

His jaw clamped, his fury so great he felt as if the top of his head might blow off. He wanted to strangle Tory. He wanted to shake her until her teeth rattled. He wanted to shout at her until his voice went hoarse.

The baron had reached the doorway. He stood there in his nightclothes, a half-dozen servants clustered behind him in the hall.

"I—I can't believe it," Tory said, a hand dramatically at her throat. "I heard a noise in Claire's room. I opened the door and…and there was the earl, leaning over Claire's bed."

She wouldn't look at him, just kept her eyes on her stepfather's mottled, angry face. "He has compromised her, my lord. Ruined her completely. Her reputation will be in tatters."

"Tory…?" Claire's voice trembled.

Victoria cast her sister a soothing glance. "It's all right, darling. Everything is going to be fine."

Cord turned his attention from Claire to Victoria and some of his temper receded. He could see the desperation in her face, her terrible fear for Claire. And there was something more, something of pain and regret, something that caused an odd pain in his chest.

She was trying to save her sister, no matter the cost to herself. What the baron would do to her if he discovered her scheme didn't bear thinking about.

Cord went over all that had happened since his arrival at the house. He had made a calculated move in forcing the marriage and Victoria had neatly countered, outmaneuvering him completely. He couldn't help a hint of admiration.

He could make this easy for her or hard. He looked from her to the baron, saw the ruthless glint in his eyes, the fury barely contained.

"Miss Whiting is entirely correct," Cord began. "Entering her sister's room happened completely by accident, I assure you. I merely forgot which bedchamber was mine. Still, the damage has been done. I shall, of course, do the honorable thing."

The baron bristled, his tall, whipcord body snapping completely erect. "I don't think that will be necessary."

"Oh, but it is. I shall simply marry Claire instead of Victoria. The result will be the same. As an earl and Victoria's brother-in-law, your older daughter's reputation will also be protected."

"I—I can't possibly allow it. Claire is too young, too naive. Besides, nothing happened—you said so yourself. Victoria arrived in time."

Cord looked over the baron's shoulder, saw the row of servants gawking in at them. His chest was exposed in the vee of his robe, his legs and feet bare. "I don't see you have any choice."

The baron's gaze followed his, and the man's face turned redder than it was already. Cord tossed Victoria such a cold smile her lips trembled.

"Arrangements will need to be made," he said. "You may leave that to me. Good night, ladies."

He brushed past the baron, tipped his head to the servants and continued back to his room. His temper rose again, climbed until he was seething, so furious it was difficult to think. Victoria had duped him, made a fool of him again.

He wouldn't stand for it. If he was trapped, then by God, so was she!

His mind whirled, spun with possible solutions. One stood out from the rest. He latched on to it with grim determination, and the edge of his mouth faintly curved. She thought she had won the game, but the match was far from over.

It might take several tricky moves, but when the play was ended, Cord intended to possess the queen.

* * *

The London weather shifted, grew damp and still, casting a thick, sooty pall over the city. There wasn't much time, Cord knew. Every minute Tory and Claire remained at Harwood Hall put them in danger. He prayed the not-so-veiled threats he had made against the baron would keep the man in line until the wedding.

Cord paced the floor of the duke of Sheffield's study, a library two-stories high with walls lined floor to ceiling with leather-bound books. Two brass-and-frosted-glass lamps hung down over a long, ornately carved wooden table lined with high-backed chairs. Sheffield's desk sat in the corner, surrounded by comfortable leather chairs.

"What time is it?" Cord looked up at the ormolu clock on the mantel.

"Ten minutes past the last time you asked. Take it easy. The boy will be here."

It seemed like hours, but soon there he was. Blond and fair, rosy cheeked and slightly nervous, a little gangly and amazingly shy. At twenty-four, Percival Chezwick hadn't completely grown into his narrow face and lanky frame. Cord thought that once he did, he would be an extremely handsome man.

The duke welcomed him in. "Good afternoon, Percy. Thank you for coming."

"Good afternoon, your grace…your lordship." In the weeks after the dinner party, Percy had dropped by Cord's town house three or four times, ostensibly to see him on one matter or another, but in truth just to catch a glimpse of Claire.

Once Cord had found them talking together, both

of them blushing and stuttering. Percy had caught Cord's hard look of warning, excused himself and left the house.

The boy appeared nervous even now, as if Cord had summoned him there just for having secret thoughts about Claire.

"Thank you for coming, Chez."

The use of the familiar nickname seemed to relax him. "It's always good to see you both."

Sheffield beckoned him farther into the room. "Actually, our invitation was for more than just a casual visit. Cord has a matter he wishes to discuss. He thought you might need a little moral support, which is why you are here instead of at his house. He believes, once you hear the tale, you might decide to help."

"Of course. Whatever I can do."

"Don't be so hasty," Cord warned. "This matter is the sort that could affect the rest of your life."

A fine blond eyebrow went up. "You have certainly managed to pique my curiosity."

"I'm glad to hear it...since it concerns a certain lady of your acquaintance. Her name is Claire. I believe you know who I mean."

The rose in his cheeks went brighter. "Your chambermaid?"

"Yes, well, as it turns out, Chez, she is not a chambermaid at all, but the daughter of a baron. That is where the trouble lies."

Worry entered the young man's features. "Has something happened? Has something happened to Claire?"

"Not yet," Cord said. "But if we don't act quickly, there is every chance that something will." He motioned toward the chairs grouped in front of the desk. "Why don't we sit down and I'll tell you all about it."

"I'll get you a drink," Sheffield offered. "I think you're going to need it."

Percy swallowed, his Adam's apple moving up and down. "Thank you. Perhaps I will."

It was nearly two hours later that Cord and Rafe were alone in the massive study again.

"Well, I guess that's settled," Rafe said.

"Looks that way."

Rafe chuckled. "The lad was positively beaming. He's obviously smitten with the girl. He couldn't seem to believe his good fortune when you suggested a match between them. I thought he was going to come out of his chair when he learned what Harwood had in mind for her."

"Chez will have to speak to his father, but with your support as well as mine, I don't think Kersey will give his son any trouble."

"What about the girl?" Rafe asked. "Will she agree?"

"She's extremely naive, but she isn't stupid. She'll understand that she has no other choice. She can't stay there in the house—not once Victoria is gone. And she seemed to like Percy."

"He won't push her."

"No." Cord had explained how innocent Claire was and Chez had agreed to give her all the time she needed, once they were married, to accept her role as his wife.

Rafe smiled. "As shy as he is, he may never get the deed accomplished."

Cord chuckled softly in agreement. They talked a bit

longer, then Sheffield and Cord both rose from their chairs.

"Well, I suppose you have any number of things yet to do," the duke said.

Cord nodded. "Sarah is taking care of the details, a small wedding at Forest Glen, just a few friends and family. You'll be there, won't you?"

"I wouldn't miss it." He grinned. "I can scarcely believe you're finally about to get leg-shackled."

Some of the satisfaction Cord had been feeling slid away. "No," he said darkly. "I can't believe it myself."

It was a dismal day. It had been a dismal week, overcast and windy, the baron bursting into flights of temper, condemning Lord Brant as a lecher, all but pulling out his already thinning black hair. At least he hadn't figured out the truth of what had happened—that it was Tory who had manipulated the night's events.

Wishing she could block the memory, she began to climb the stairs leading up to the third floor of the house. Carrying a small brass lamp, she continued up another, narrower flight that led to the attic, determined to complete the task she had set for herself.

The wedding would take place two days hence. The thought made her stomach churn. Claire had cried and begged not to marry the earl, but Tory had finally convinced her.

"Claire, darling, you must do this. It is the only way that you will be safe. I know there is little you've learned about...about what happens between a man and woman, but you remember what happened the night the baron came to your room. You know he meant to hurt you.

He's an evil man, Claire. Deep down, you know that is the reason you are afraid of him."

Her sister's lovely blue eyes filled with tears. "I hate him. I wish Mama had never married him."

"So do I, dearest, but once you're away from him, the earl will take care of you. He'll be kind to you." He would be, she told herself. Cord had a terrible temper, but Tory had never been truly afraid of him. And she didn't believe he would ever hurt Claire.

Her throat tightened. She loved him, but it was Claire he was being forced to marry.

"What about you, Tory? What will happen to you if you stay here?"

A shudder rippled through her. She had no idea what Harwood might do. The man was vicious and unpredictable. Still, she was far more able to defend herself than Claire.

"I'll be all right," she replied. "In time, I'll find a way to make a life for myself."

They had spoken only yesterday morning, yet it seemed more like weeks. She couldn't keep track of time, couldn't seem to concentrate.

Still carrying the lamp, she reached the top of the stairs and opened the door to the attic. Only a dim afternoon light shone through the narrow dormer windows. As she entered the room, the lamp cast an eerie glow on the walls, and dust motes swirled up from her feet.

She had come in search of her mother's trunks, used each year when her parents had journeyed to London. On their return, the trunks were often stuffed with gifts and toys they had purchased for their daughters.

After her mother's funeral, Tory had meant to go

through them, sort through the clothing the servants had packed away, give some of the gowns to the vicar for distribution to the poor. But the thought of sifting through her mother's possessions had simply been too painful. She had never quite worked up the courage.

Now Claire was getting married. A young woman should have something of her mother's to wear on her wedding day. Tory ignored the pain that came with the thought and continued farther into the attic.

Her mother's jewelry was stored in one of the trunks. Her stepfather had taken anything of real value, but pretty pins and brooches, things her mother had liked to wear, remained. Tory thought of the pearl-and-diamond necklace she had stolen and imagined how lovely it would have looked at Claire's throat. The necklace was gone, but hopefully she would find something else for her sister to wear.

Tory tried not to think of the man Claire would wed. She didn't want to remember how quickly Cord had accepted the situation he found himself in and acquiesced to marrying Claire. She tried to ignore a feeling of betrayal.

After all, it was her fault this was happening—she was the one responsible, not the earl.

Still, it hurt. She had thought that he cared for her at least a little.

Tory sighed into the dim light in the attic, determined not to think of Cord. Kneeling in front of the first steamer trunk, she lifted the lid and began to search through the contents, mostly dresses and gloves, an ostrich-plumed hat, a pleated satin turban, a lovely ermine muff. The gowns in the trunk were slightly dated, purchased while her father was still alive, but they were beautiful just the same.

The second trunk held an array of kidskin slippers, stockings, garters, a pretty lawn chemise with little pink bows down the front. Tory ran her fingers over the garment, thinking of her mother, feeling the sting of loneliness she hadn't allowed herself to feel in years.

Oh, Mama, I miss you.

She wished her mother were with them now, wished her father were still alive and none of this had ever happened. Tory closed the lid of the trunk, knowing it was useless to wish for something that could never be. Her mother and father were dead. There was no one to take care of them. They had to take care of themselves.

She raised the lid on the third steamer trunk, found a small, black lace fan, a tasseled velvet spencer and several colorful shawls. Carefully lifting the items out of the way, she spotted her mother's black lacquer, mother-of-pearl-inlaid jewelry box in the bottom of the trunk. She gently touched the glossy black surface, lifted out the box and set it on the floor in front of her.

Her hand trembled as she opened the lid. She remembered some of the pieces nestled on the blue velvet lining—the black jet cameo; a pretty rhinestone brooch her mother often wore on the front of her pelisse; an embroidered collar; a string of tiny pale pink gemstones with matching earbobs.

Something beneath the necklace caught her attention. Tory lifted the gemstones out of the way and picked up a satin-wrapped object that seemed to be hidden away. She unwrapped the cloth, and when she saw what lay inside, she couldn't seem to breathe.

Tory picked up the heavy garnet ring with a shaking hand, recognizing the piece at once. The ring had belonged to her father. He had been wearing it the day he had been killed. The footpads who killed him had stolen it, along with his coin purse and any other valuables he'd had with him.

The ring had belonged to his father and his father before him. It was treasured. Her mother had despaired that something so precious had been lost.

Where had she found it? Why hadn't she mentioned it to Tory? And why had she hidden it away?

Tory felt the hair rise at the back of her neck as her suspicions grew. Glancing round the attic, she began a frantic search for her mother's diary. Perhaps she would find the answers there.

But the diary was nowhere to be seen.

Tory remembered her mother writing in the journal nearly every day, but she had no idea where the diary might have wound up after Charlotte Whiting had died.

The afternoon sunlight filtering into the room grew weaker. The day was slipping away and Claire would begin to worry. Rewrapping the satin around the ring, she tucked it into the pocket of her skirt, picked up the pretty pink necklace and tiny earbobs, and closed the jewelry box. It went back in the bottom of the trunk, beneath the clothes, shawls and black lace fan. As she descended the narrow attic stairs, she reached into her pocket. Even through the satin, the ring seemed to burn her fingers.

Thirteen

The day of the wedding dawned windy and cold. Sullen gray clouds loomed over a grim, damp world, and the sun hid behind an overcast sky. On the garden terrace at Forest Glen, a flower-covered arch sat at one end, a cluster of white wicker chairs in front of it, waiting for the small number of guests who had been invited to the nuptials.

They gathered there now, the ladies in high-waisted silk gowns, the men in tailcoats, waistcoats and cravats. From the window of the upstairs guest room she had been assigned, Tory could see the people on the terrace beginning to take their seats for the event.

Dressed in a pale blue silk gown, her hair swept into soft dark curls interlaced with white rosebuds, she was ready to face the consequences of all that she had done. The happenings of the past swirled through her head, her stepfather and Claire, stealing the necklace, her desperation in London, meeting Cord. *Falling in love.*

Setting the trap that forced him to marry Claire.

She was responsible for much of what had taken place and yet she felt as if most of it was out of her control, a path fate had led her down that had left her standing here, at the window above the garden, wishing with all her heart that she were anywhere else in the world.

A light knock sounded. Lady Aimes stepped quietly into the room and closed the door. "Are you ready?"

She nodded. But she would never be ready to watch Cord marry someone else, not even Claire.

"You look beautiful," Sarah said.

Tory swallowed. "Thank you." Cord's cousin was taller even than Claire, slender, blond and lovely in a rose silk gown with tiny embroidered flowers beneath her breast and around the hem. There was a softness in her features and a serenity about her, an inner glow of happiness that Tory envied.

"I need to see my sister, make certain that she is all right."

"I'm sorry, I'm afraid Claire has already gone downstairs."

She should have left sooner, she knew, but a terrible lethargy had settled upon her and she couldn't seem to shake it.

"They're waiting. I'll walk down with you." Lady Aimes held something out to her and Tory saw it was a nosegay of beautiful white rosebuds mixed with delicate baby's breath. It was tied with blue ribbons, set upon a circle of white Belgian lace.

"Are those for Claire?"

"Claire has her own bouquet. These are for you."

She accepted the flowers, thinking how lovely they were, holding them up to inhale the subtle fragrance.

Her hand trembled as she started toward the door Lady Aimes held open for her. She tried to summon a smile but couldn't manage even a curve of her lips as she preceded the viscountess out into the hall.

Most of the guests had taken their seats on the terrace. She could hear the soft murmur of voices coming through the French doors in the drawing room. Little Teddy stood in the hallway, waiting for his mother, a miniature of his father in the same navy blue coat, white piqué waistcoat and dark gray breeches.

He looked up at her and grinned as she reached the bottom of the stairs. "You look pretty."

She finally managed a smile. "Thank you. How is your puppy?"

"His name is Rex. He's getting bigger all the time."

"Yes, I imagine he is."

Jonathan Randall came forward. "My son is right. You look lovely." To her surprise, he bent and pressed a light kiss on her cheek.

"You're very kind," Tory said.

The viscount turned a soft smile on his wife. "You both look beautiful." He rested a hand at Sarah's waist. "Come, love." He took hold of Teddy's hand. "We had all better find our seats."

Lady Aimes smiled at Tory She thought that it held a trace of sympathy. "He's a good man. Claire will be fine."

A lump rose in her throat. Tory turned to look for Claire, but instead the earl of Brant walked toward her. He looked so imposing, so unbelievably handsome. He wore a dark brown, velvet-collared tailcoat and snug beige breeches. A white cravat topped a gold-flecked waistcoat that matched the gold of his eyes. For an instant, she forgot what was about to happen and simply allowed herself to look at him.

Then one of the servants darted past, carrying a silver tray heavy with crystal goblets, and the moment disappeared. The earl stopped in front of her and Tory forced herself to look into his face.

"I'm sorry," she said. "I know that is scarcely enough, but I wish none of this had happened." Cord said nothing. "I don't suppose, at this juncture, you are interested in an apology."

"Not at the moment."

She glanced away from him, no longer able to stand the censure in his eyes. She searched the hallway, gazed back up the staircase. "Where is Claire?"

His expression shifted, changed to a look that could only be described as triumphant. "I'm afraid your sister is no longer at Forest Glen. She has left with Lord Percival Chezwick. They have eloped to Gretna Green."

Her heart seemed to freeze, to simply stop beating. She could feel the blood slowly drain from her face. "Wh-what are you talking about?"

Cord took her arm and led her into one of the drawing rooms. "I'm telling you your sister is still getting married. Only the groom has changed."

Her legs seemed to fold beneath her. Cord urged her down in the closest chair. "How? When did they leave? I—I don't understand."

"Then allow me to explain. As you correctly deduced, your sister was in need of a husband to rescue her from Harwood. I simply believed that Lord Percy was better suited to the position. Fortunately, he agreed. I'm sure the two of them are going to be very happy."

"I can't believe this." Her head was swimming.

"Yes, well, it is most definitely true, and there is one other small thing."

"What is that?"

"As I find myself short of a bride, you will be filling the position."

"What!" She came up out of the chair.

"That's right, my lovely bride-to-be. In language you might better understand, your pawn has been captured and you—my queen—will also be in danger if you think to gainsay me again."

Tory's mind spun. "You can't...can't just... What about the scandal? First you are going to marry me and then you are going to marry Claire. The guests will all have received invitations. You...you can't simply show up with a different bride."

Cord smiled wolfishly. Reaching into the pocket of his waistcoat, he drew out a gold-embossed invitation and handed it over.

Tory read the words, more incredulous by the moment. Instead of Claire's name imprinted on the card, her own name glittered in small gold letters. "But Lady Aimes sent the invitations. She...she agreed to such a plan?"

"I explained the situation and my cousin volunteered to help. She approves of the match between Lord Percy and your sister. And apparently, she also approves of you."

Tory swallowed, her thoughts in turmoil. In her days as housekeeper, she had seen Percival Chezwick several times at the earl's town house. He seemed shy and reserved, handsome in a youthful sort of way. Claire had even mentioned him once or twice. What had she said about him? Tory couldn't recall.

She remembered the viscountess's words. *He's a good man. Claire will be fine.*

She hadn't meant Cord, but Percival Chezwick. Tory prayed it would turn out to be true.

"You're looking pale. Perhaps the gift I have for you in honor of the occasion will help lift your spirits."

Reaching into the inside pocket of his tailcoat, he pulled out a blue velvet box and flipped open the lid. A strand of exquisite pearls gleamed up at her from a bed of white satin, each perfect sphere interspersed with a glittering diamond. She knew what she was seeing, the beautiful pearl-and-diamond necklace she had stolen, the necklace that had once belonged to the bride of Lord Fallon.

Tory swallowed, unable to pull her gaze from the dazzling display. The necklace seemed to hold her entranced, to mesmerize her in some way. The diamonds winked up at her like long-lost friends. Each creamy pearl seemed to beckon her to touch it.

"The Bride's Necklace," she whispered, unable to take her eyes off the brilliant strand.

"If that is what it's called, the name is fitting." Lifting the necklace out of the box, he draped it round her throat and fastened the diamond catch. The pearls felt cool against her skin, yet in her mind they burned with accusation. She had stolen the ancient jewelry. Now it encircled her throat as a reminder of all she had done.

A faint shiver ran through her. She wanted to tear the necklace away and run from the room, from the house. At the same time, nothing had felt so right as the lovely yoke Cord had placed around her neck.

"Wh-what about my stepfather? When he sees this, he will—"

"Harwood has received full compensation for his loss…though I imagine when he spots you wearing it, he may turn a few shades of green."

"It is…it is beautiful." She wondered if Cord knew the legend, if perhaps he had given her the necklace hoping it might bring retribution for the trouble she had caused.

He looked down at her and the curve of his lips held a trace of satisfaction. "The game is over, my sweet. This is check and mate. Your stepfather is waiting down the hall, so furious he can hardly find his tongue. I believe your only move is to take his arm and let him guide you down the aisle to the bishop."

Tory swallowed. Her hand trembled as she touched the pearls at her throat. They felt warmer now, oddly comforting. The game, indeed, was over, and Cord had won. She wondered what price he would extract for his victory.

His hand settled firmly at her waist. "Ready?" When she simply stood there, completely at a loss and unable to move, his deep voice softened. "You'll be safe, Victoria. And so will your sister."

Perhaps Claire would be safe. She prayed Lord Percy would be good to her. As for Tory, the earl posed an even graver threat than the baron.

The man about to become her husband wanted to marry someone else.

The wedding passed in a blur. Thank God Gracie was there. Apparently the earl had discovered their friendship—there seemed no end to his supply of information. Once Grace understood what was happening, she eagerly agreed to act as bridesmaid, and having her there gave Tory a badly needed shot of courage.

The ceremony seemed to take forever yet be over in the blink of an eye. When the bishop pronounced them man and wife Cord swept her into a hard, almost punishing kiss. Afterward, a wedding feast was served at the opposite end of the terrace. Standing beside her, the earl casually accepted congratulations while it took Tory's full concentration just to nod and smile.

"We'll be leaving soon," he said. "Riverwoods isn't that far away. They're expecting us. We'll be spending our wedding night there."

Wedding night. The words made a knot form in her stomach. Cord would expect to consummate the marriage, though in truth the deed had already been done. They were husband and wife. Cord played the part well, but beneath his surface calm, she knew he was angry that he had been obliged to marry her. "Riverwoods? That is your country estate?"

He nodded. "There is another in Sussex."

And he would have owned more lands yet if he had married an heiress, as he had planned. Tory concentrated on the plate of delicacies her husband had set on the linen-draped table in front of her. Pheasant with candied carrots, oysters in anchovy sauce, perigord pie with truffles. The smell made her stomach churn.

Grace sat to her right, next to the duke of Sheffield. They made a nice-looking couple, she thought, Sheffield tall and dark, Grace with her fiery auburn hair swept up and her cheeks blooming with roses. Her eyes were a vivid emerald green and today they sparkled with excitement.

But Grace had no interest in the duke, other than that of a friend, and he seemed to feel the same about her. Jonathan and Sarah Randall sat to Cord's left. Little Teddy had accompanied his nanny upstairs to the nursery for a nap.

Grace leaned closer. "So how does it feel to be married?"

Tory lifted an eyebrow. "I am married? Why didn't someone tell me?"

Gracie laughed. "I vow you will know it by morning. I have never seen a man look at a woman in quite the way the earl looks at you."

Tory's gaze shot to her husband's face, but he was deep in conversation with the viscount.

"He didn't want to marry me," Tory said dully. "He planned to marry an heiress."

Cord laughed at something Jonathan Randall said and Grace studied his handsome profile. "Sometimes plans change. It is obvious he has feelings for you. I imagine he will show you exactly what they are tonight when he comes to your bed."

"Gracie!" Her friend merely laughed. She had always been a bit irreverent. It was one of the things Tory liked best about her.

"Well, it's true. The earl has a wicked reputation. They say he is quite talented in the bedchamber. Whatever happens in the course of your marriage, I imagine you will learn a great deal about pleasure."

Tory's cheeks went hot. "Gracie, please…"

Grace's burnished eyebrows drew together. She

stared hard into Tory's face. "Oh, my God, how could I be so stupid! He has already made love to you!"

"Gracie! Someone will hear you!" Tory looked away, mortified that Grace had somehow guessed. "For heaven's sake, I hope it doesn't show."

"Of course not, silly. At least not to anyone but me." Grace flicked a glance at the earl, whose gaze fell on Tory. A corner of his mouth edged up and his eyes seemed to glitter with heat. For an instant, Tory couldn't breathe.

"You must be in love with him," Gracie whispered. "That is the only way you would have let him take liberties."

Her throat went tight. She lowered her head. "I don't know how it happened. I tried to stop myself. I knew I wasn't what he wanted. Nothing I did seemed to matter."

Gracie reached down and caught her hand, which was colder than her own. "You mustn't feel bad. Once he gets to know you, he is bound to fall in love with you."

But Tory wasn't convinced. The earl was a man of lusty appetites. He had wanted her as his mistress, not his wife. He was also a man of honor. He never would have made love to her if she had told him she was the daughter of a peer. Tory wondered if he would ever forgive her.

Cord drank too much. Fortunately, a coach and four waited out front to carry them to Riverwoods. Victoria sat on the seat across from him, nervously watching his every move. She looked beautiful today, so feminine and lovely, a little uncertain. Just looking at her aroused him.

During the two-hour ride to his estate, Cord considered pulling her down in the seat and taking her right there in the carriage. She was his wife. He had every right. And he was angry. He was married to the wrong woman and it was all Victoria's fault.

He thought of Constance Fairchild, the wealthy woman he had thought to wed. She was blond and pretty, young and pliable. She would have well served his purpose.

Not like the woman he had married, the woman who had tricked him, lied to him, made a fool of him—more than once!

At Riverwoods, he continued to drink but couldn't seem to get drunk. Instead he paced the drawing room, thinking of Victoria. His *wife* waited in the suite adjoining his. She belonged to him now, no matter how it had happened, and he wanted her. He damned well intended to have her.

Cord set his brandy glass down on the Hepplewhite table and headed for the stairs. He went into the room adjoining hers, stripped off his coat, waistcoat and cravat, but left on his shirt and breeches. Striding toward the door between their rooms, he jerked it open and stepped inside.

Victoria sat before the mirror in front of her dressing table in a long blue satin nightgown, a wedding gift from Sarah. In the mirror, he saw the bodice was fashioned of white Belgian lace, exposing the roundness of her breasts and the dark areolas that crowned each one. She turned to face him, slender feet peeping out from beneath the hem, and he caught a glimpse of slim pale ankles.

He was hard before he closed the door, aching with desire for her.

Victoria rose from the stool. Her hand went to her throat and he realized she was still wearing the necklace. "I...I couldn't get it unfastened."

It glittered in the light of the candles in the silver candelabra on the dresser, and an image arose of her naked, wearing nothing but the necklace. His groin tightened, began a painful throbbing.

"I know you're angry," she said. "If I could change things, I would."

"It's too late for that. Come, Victoria."

For an instant she didn't move. Then she drew in a shaky breath and started toward him. Her hair was unbound, floating around her shoulders, dark yet shimmering with burnished lights. The nightgown moved over her breasts with each of her steps, chafing gently against her nipples, and the blood roared through his veins.

She stopped in front of him, looked up into his face. Cord slid his hand into the heavy strands of her hair and pulled her head back, crushed his mouth down hard over hers.

The kiss wasn't gentle. It was a fierce, savage, plundering kiss that let her know what he was feeling. Tory stiffened but he just kept kissing her, taking what he wanted, filling his hands with her breasts. She made no move to stop him, but neither did she respond.

Cord hauled her more tightly against him and cupped her bottom, pressing her slim frame into his sex, telling her he meant to have her. He could feel her trembling, told himself this was what he wanted, that he meant to pay her back for the lies she had told and the future she had cost him.

"Remove your nightgown," he commanded. "I want to take you wearing only the necklace."

She stepped away from him, her eyes fixed on his face. There were shadows there, and they tightened something in his chest. Reaching up, she slid the straps of the nightgown off her shoulders, let it glide down over her hips to pool on the floor at her feet. She stood there gloriously naked, looking as regal as the ivory queen he had secretly called her.

"I'm sorry you had to marry me," she said. "If I had known what would happen, I wouldn't have asked you to make love to me that night on the ship."

"Why did you?"

"I'm not completely certain. Perhaps I was afraid of the future. I wanted to know what it felt like to be with a man I wanted. I wasn't sure I would ever have the chance again."

Cord worked to hold on to his anger, but some of it seeped away. "You're my wife. I'll have you any time I want."

"Yes."

The edge of his mouth faintly curved. "But it won't be the way it was before. That is what you are thinking, is it not?"

She stood there, defiant and lovely. Young and sweet and more of a woman than any he had ever known.

"It won't be the same..." she said, "...not unless you want it to be."

The words rolled through his head. What *did* he want? He wanted her as she had been that night on the ship, wanted her returning his kisses with the same wild abandon, responding eagerly each time he touched her.

He wanted her whispering his name, her body gloving him so sweetly he groaned.

Reaching out, he cupped her cheek. "I want you, Victoria. I want it to be as it was."

Tory gazed up at the man she had wed and her throat went tight. She heard Cord's words and the soft way he said them, and hope blossomed deep inside her. She remembered the way he had looked at her that night on the ship, the need she had read in his face. It was there now, reaching out to her as it had before.

Cord kissed her again, the way she had wanted him to kiss her before, with a tenderness that overrode his passion. Tory kissed him back, tentatively at first, then a fire seemed to ignite between them. Their kisses turned wild, unbridled. She slid her arms around his neck and pressed her body into his, ran her fingers over the solid muscles in his chest.

Lifting her up, he carried her over to the bed and settled her on the mattress. He kissed her as he followed her down, bracing himself on his elbows. Cord pressed his mouth against the place beneath her ear, kissed the side of her neck, trailed a hot, damp path over her shoulders.

That's when he saw them. Tory had prayed that in the darkness they would not show.

Reaching out, he hesitantly touched one of the faint marks that had almost disappeared on her back. "Harwood," he said harshly. "Harwood did this?"

"What happened is in the past. He has no power over me now."

"I'm going to kill him." Though his voice turned soft, anger darkened his features. "I'm going to call him out." He started to get up from the bed, so furious his hands were shaking.

Tory caught his arm. "No, Cord, please! The baron's an expert marksman. He practices nearly every day. He prides himself on his skill with pistol and sword."

The edge of Cord's mouth barely curved. "You don't believe I can match his skill?"

"I don't want you hurt!"

He rose from the bed, but Tory wouldn't let go of his arm. "Think of the scandal. You've got your family to consider. And mine. Whatever he did, it happened in the past. I'm your wife now. I'm safe with you. Harwood can't hurt me again."

A muscle bunched in his jaw. "No," he said in that too soft way of his. "He won't ever hurt you again."

"I'm asking you, Cord—begging you—not to go after him. Please. It can only cause more grief."

Deep down, he knew she was right. She could see the resignation settle into his face. The scandal would be brutal. He was the head of the family. There were others to consider.

"Harwood has made an enemy. I won't forget what he's done." His finger gently outlined one of the fading marks. "If these are painful, there will be other nights..."

"They are well past hurting. And this isn't just any night, it is our wedding night."

The hunger returned to his eyes, making the gold in them glitter. He kissed her deeply and Tory kissed him back. She wanted this night, wanted to feel the pleasure he had given her before. Cord cupped her breasts, bent and took the fullness into his mouth, and she gave up a soft sigh of pleasure. He laved the tip, suckled and tasted, and heat like lightning speared out through her limbs. He continued his tender assault, ministering to each breast, making her body go liquid and warm.

She had forgot how good it felt when he touched her, forgot the overpowering hunger. He trailed kisses over her belly, moved lower, parted her legs and settled his mouth on her most sensitive spot.

Tory arched up off the bed, her fingers sliding into his hair. She bit down on her lip to keep from crying out as sweet sensation enveloped her. Cord slid his hand beneath her hips, lifting her to give him better access, and little by little her resistance faded. He didn't stop until she reached release, crying out his name as she flew apart.

Cord rose above her, kissing her gently then deepening the kiss. She felt his hardness pressing against her, then sliding slowly inside.

Fanning her desire back to life, he surged deeply, and her fingers dug into the muscles across his shoulders. Pleasure tore through her, so sweet and hot she trembled. Her body tensed, tightened around him, and she lost herself in the storm of climax.

Afterward they lay entwined, one of his long legs draped over hers. His eyes were closed, dark lashes fanning his cheeks. She wanted to reach out and touch him, wondered if in time there was a chance he might come to love her as she loved him.

His eyes came open, came to rest on the necklace that still encircled her throat. Tory reached up and touched it, ran her fingers over each satiny pearl.

"It's incredibly lovely," she said.

Cord turned onto his side and propped himself up on

an elbow. "Yes…it is." But he was looking at her, not the necklace.

She smiled as he reached out to touch it, then trailed a finger down over her breast.

"Do you know the legend?" she asked.

His gaze returned to her face and one dark eyebrow went up. "There is a legend about it?"

Tory fingered the pearls, admiring the perfect weight of them, the texture. "It started nearly eight hundred years ago when the necklace was made for Lord Fallon. It was a gift for his bride, Ariana of Merrick."

"The Bride's Necklace," he said, remembering the name she had told him.

"That's right. It was said the couple was deeply in love. Lord Fallon sent the necklace to Ariana with a note professing his devotion and she was thrilled with the gift. The wedding approached, but on the way to the castle, Lord Fallon was set upon by thieves. The earl and all of his men were killed in the fighting."

Cord studied the strand of pearls. "Not good news for the bride."

"Ariana was devastated, so distraught she climbed the castle parapet and jumped to her death on the rocks below. Apparently, she was already several months gone with child. When they found her body, she was wearing the necklace. They would have buried her with it, but it was too valuable, and so it was sold."

Cord made a low sound in his throat. "I'm glad I didn't know all this before I bought the damned thing."

Tory smiled. "The necklace is believed to carry a curse. It is said that whoever shall own the necklace will be blessed with great fortune or suffer terrible tragedy—depending upon the pureness of his heart."

Cord reached out and lifted the heavy strand, watched the way the diamonds glittered in the candlelight, ran his thumb back and forth over the creamy roundness of the pearls. "I thought it the most exquisite piece of jewelry I'd ever seen."

"Are you certain you didn't buy it to punish me for the trouble I've caused?"

Cord leaned toward her, looked down into her face. "Perhaps I did…at the time. Now I just like the way it looks round your very lovely throat."

To prove it, he bent his head and kissed the side of her neck, kissed his way up to her ear, then captured her lips. He was hard, she realized as her body came to life, began to throb with the same need he was feeling. They tried to go slowly, but passion flamed to life and their control slipped away. They reached release together, then drifted off to sleep.

They made love again just before dawn. When Tory awakened, Cord was gone. As she slipped from the bed, her thoughts were troubled. What sort of marriage could she have with a man who didn't love her? What sort of future was in store for her?

And, dear God, what was happening to Claire?

Fourteen

Claire shifted on the carriage seat and slowly came awake. She straightened as she realized she was snuggled against Lord Percy's shoulder, one of his arms keeping her in place as she slept. They were on their way to Gretna Green, just over the Scottish border. Never in a thousand years would she have believed she would soon be married to a man she barely knew.

Embarrassed, she scrambled to sit up, and he hurriedly released her.

"Forgive me," he said. "I was just…I wanted you to get some sleep."

Claire looked into his pale blue eyes and read the concern there, along with the fatigue. "What about you? You've been riding as long as I have."

Percy shook his head. His hair was a darker blond than her own, the color of gold, like pirate treasure. "I am fine. I dozed a bit while you were asleep."

He had told her to call him Percy. She thought that she should, since she was going to be his wife.

Wife. A little tremor ran through her. She barely understood what that meant. As a girl, she had imagined becoming a bride one day—sometime in the far distant future. But the day had somehow arrived and she felt like a leaf in the wind, with nothing of substance to cling to.

She tried hard not to be afraid.

She wished Tory were there. Tory would explain the things a wife must do, tell her what Percival Chezwick would expect of her.

At least her sister was safe. And Claire thought that Tory really did care for the earl. Claire had seen the way her sister looked at him. There was something special in that look, something Claire had never seen in her sister's eyes before. And the earl would take care of her, keep her safe from Lord Harwood.

"Claire?"

She blinked up at the man beside her and reined in her wandering thoughts. Her future husband was certainly handsome enough, tall and spare, with gentle blue eyes, his golden hair parted neatly in the middle.

"My lord?"

"It's just Percy, remember?"

She flushed. "Oh course…Percy."

"I asked if you are hungry. We have traveled all night. There is a village just ahead. I should think you would be ready to rest and perhaps break your fast."

The color deepened in her cheeks. She fidgeted on the seat. It had been hours since their last stop. She needed badly to attend herself.

"Thank you, yes. I am quite hungry. I appreciate your thoughtfulness…Percy."

He nodded, rapped on the roof of the carriage. It was a plush conveyance, made for long journeys, pulled by four sturdy bay horses. Percy had told her his eldest brother, the earl of Louden, had lent him the rig when he had learned his youngest sibling intended to elope—with their father's blessing, of course.

"We'll have a proper wedding when we get home," Percy had promised, but Claire didn't want a big wedding. In truth, she didn't want a wedding at all. But Lord Brant had explained she must marry Lord Percy so that she and Tory would be safe from the baron, and she trusted the earl to tell her the truth.

And she liked Lord Percy, truly she did. He reminded her of the prince who had scaled the tower to save the maiden in the story her mother used to tell when she and Tory were little girls.

The carriage stopped at an inn called The Fat Ox, where Lord Percy let a room so that she might refresh herself before they went in to breakfast. He was ever solicitous of her wishes and he had a kind way about him. She often found herself smiling at something he said or when he looked at her in that soft way of his.

They resumed their journey sitting across from each other in the carriage, and though it was the proper thing to do, she missed his reassuring presence beside her.

Lord Percy shifted on the seat and she realized he was watching her. Catching her gaze, he cleared his throat and spots of color appeared in his cheeks.

"I am happy we are to wed, Claire," he said softly.

Her face felt warm. "I will try to be a good wife, Percy."

She wanted that, wanted to make her husband happy, as wives were supposed to do.

As soon as they returned, she would ask Tory to explain her wifely duties. Her sister had attended Mrs. Thornhill's Private Academy, after all. They studied such things there. Besides, by now, her sister was a wife herself.

Yes, Claire thought, Tory would know what to do.

"Do you think she's all right?" It was the third time she had asked the question. From his seat behind the desk, Cord was beginning to frown.

"Claire is fine. Lord Percy gave his word and he is a gentleman. He will not take advantage of Claire. He will not make husbandly advances until she is ready to accept them."

"But Claire isn't like me. She isn't—"

He looked up from his work and one dark eyebrow went up.

Tory flushed. "She is more reserved than I am."

Cord got up from his desk and walked toward her. "She is not the passionate creature you are, is that what you mean?" He lightly caught her shoulders. "You are an utter delight in that regard and there is scarcely a moment I don't think of hauling you off to bed. Which means, if you don't leave me to my work, I shall drag you upstairs this very moment and make you behave like the passionate little baggage you are."

Tory flushed and backed away, uncertain whether to be flattered or insulted. "Then I suppose I shall have to leave. I wouldn't want to interfere with your duties."

Cord's mouth edged up, but she could see that his mind had already returned to the stack of paperwork on his desk. With a sigh, he returned to his chair and submerged himself once more in his task.

Tory watched him for a while, but he had already forgotten she was there. Since their wedding night, Cord had spent most of his time in his study, foraging through the mountain of papers on his desk. Now that he was resigned to being married to a penniless wife instead of an heiress, he seemed determined to make up for the loss by working even harder than he had before.

Tory sighed as she left the study and made her way down the hall. Physically, they seemed well suited. One of Cord's hot looks left her breathless. One kiss and she wanted more. Her husband seemed to feel the same, making love to her several times a night.

But he never came to her room before midnight and he always left before dawn. He had duties, he explained, responsibilities he couldn't ignore.

And there was his ongoing search for his cousin.

Captain Sharpe's present location had yet to be determined. Though the captain was thought to be alive, they were unsure in which prison he was now being held.

And uncertain how long he could endure under harsh French prison conditions.

The clock was ticking, the need to find the captain resting heavily on Cord's broad shoulders. He had important things to do, and spending time with his wife, it seemed, wasn't one of them.

Her stomach churned at the thought. If she couldn't be with him, how could she make him fall in love with her? If he didn't love her, how long would it be before he tired of her and turned to another woman?

"Beg pardon, my lady."

Standing in the hall outside the study, Tory turned at the sound of the butler's voice.

"Your carriage is arrived out front, as you requested."

"Thank you, Timmons." She was on her way over to see her sister. Claire had safely returned home to London, she and her husband living in the small but elegant town house Lord Percy had provided near Portman Square. Tory knew Claire was lonely, and uncertain about her new life. In time, Tory hoped things would improve.

She followed Timmons into the entry, picked her reticule up off the side table, then waited while he held open the door. Since her return as Cord's wife, the staff had been surprisingly cordial. Once they learned she wasn't actually a servant but the daughter of a baron, they seemed to admire the fact that during her term as housekeeper she had worked just as hard as they had, even though her blood was blue.

All but Mrs. Rathbone, who remained surly and only grudgingly respectful. Still, she had been in Cord's employ for a number of years and Tory refused to dismiss her.

Her sister waited anxiously on the front porch when Tory arrived. As she departed the carriage, Claire raced along the brick walkway into her sister's arms.

"Oh, Tory, I'm so glad to see you!"

"It's only been a few days, darling."

"I know, but it seems much longer." She took hold of Tory's hand and led her into the house, which was fashionably elegant, with a marble-floored entry and a drawing room done in ivory and gold.

A tall, thin butler appeared. When Claire simply looked up at him, he smiled. "Perhaps my lady would wish some tea to share with her guest," he prompted.

"Oh, yes! Thank you, Parkhurst, that would be lovely."

"Of course, my lady." He gave her an indulgent smile, already enthralled with his new mistress.

She and Claire went into the drawing room, which was small but stylishly furnished, with a sienna marble mantel above the hearth and crystal-prismed lamps and porcelain-faced clocks sitting on Sheraton tables.

Claire smiled as they walked into the room, but the smile seemed forced.

"You look a little pale, dearest. Are you feeling all right?"

Claire glanced away. "I am fine."

Worry filtered through her. "Is everything…is everything all right between you and Lord Percy?"

"I suppose so." She sighed as she sank down on the sofa. "It's just…"

"Just what, darling? Do you not enjoy Lord Percy's company?"

She nodded, her smile a little more genuine. "Oh, yes. I like him ever so much. But—"

The tea cart rattled just then as Parkhurst shoved it through the open doorway.

"Why don't you pour for us?" Tory suggested. "Then you can tell me all about it."

Parkhurst left the tea cart and closed the drawing room doors, making them private. Tory seated herself on the sofa next to Claire, who took care to arrange the skirt of her finely cut day dress, a pale green jaconet gathered into delicate folds beneath the bosom. Tory also wore a gown of muslin, hers in a saffron hue, the square-cut bodice heavily embroidered in silk.

Claire was married to the son of a marquess; Tory was the wife of an earl. Both Cord and Percy had gone to extravagant expense to see their wives properly clothed.

Claire took a sip of her tea. "Sometimes when I am with him...I don't know...in some odd way he makes me feel nervous. He's extremely handsome, of course, and entirely a gentleman. Still, when he holds my hand, my palms become damp. He kisses me and I like it very much, but when he stops, I find myself growing agitated that he doesn't continue."

Tory bit her lip. She knew what her sister was feeling. Cord made her feel those things and a good deal more. But how did she go about explaining desire between a man and his wife?

"What you are feeling is natural, Claire. When a woman admires a man, she often feels those sorts of things. Just follow Lord Percy's lead, and in time, it will all work out." At least she hoped that it would.

"Tonight he is taking me to the opera. I have never been to an opera and I am so looking forward to it. He has planned something for every night this week. It is all very exciting."

He is courting her, Tory thought, pleased by the notion.

"Percy said to ask if you and Lord Brant might wish to join us. The marquess has a private box and Percy thinks you would both enjoy the performance."

Oh, how she would love to attend the opera! And to sit in a private box, no less. Cord would be too busy, she knew, working late, as usual, unable to break away. She tried not to let it annoy her, but lately it did.

"He will probably be working," Tory said. "But I shall certainly try to convince him."

"If the earl cannot come, perhaps you could still come with us. I should like that ever so much."

Tory would like that, too. Still, she would rather go with her husband.

She was thinking of Cord several hours later when she returned to the house and made her way straight to his study.

"I'm sorry to interrupt, my lord."

Cord leaned back in his chair and rubbed the bridge of his nose. "It's all right. I could use a moment's break. How was your sister?"

"She is adjusting. Lord Percy is treating her very well. As a matter of fact, they have extended an invitation to join them at the opera tonight. I was hoping that perhaps..."

Cord sighed tiredly. "I'm sorry, sweeting. Unfortunately, I've a meeting with Colonel Pendleton tonight. I'm sure Lord Percy wouldn't mind escorting two beautiful women instead of one."

The matter of Captain Sharpe's rescue was certainly of more import. Tory could scarcely argue with that. Still, if he would be gone for the evening, what would it matter if she went on her own? "Are you sure you wouldn't mind?"

"Go ahead," he urged. "It'll be good for you to get out of the house."

She didn't want to go without him, but staying home alone every night wasn't much fun, either.

And so it had started, innocently enough, just a reason to get out of the house while Cord was busy working. Three or four nights a week, Tory joined her sister and her husband at an endless stream of social events.

Unlike Cord, Percival Chezwick had few responsibilities. He had a sizable trust fund combined with a small inheritance from his grandfather, and he was young and full of life.

He was proud of his beautiful wife and took every possible occasion to show her off to Society.

It was the night of the earl of Marley's house party that Percy's cousin, Julian Fox, first accompanied them.

Julian was the son of a viscount, several years older than Percy, in London for the Season. He was black-haired and blue-eyed, more sophisticated than his cousin and not the least bit shy. He was handsome and utterly charming.

Tory liked him from the moment she met him and he seemed to like her. Throughout the evening, Julian was approached by women, but though he was friendly, mostly he ignored them, remaining, instead, close to Tory and the party he had come with.

The next night, they attended the theater, Shakespeare's *King Lear,* and again, Julian went with them. If he had made the slightest overture, the least improper advance, she might have been uncomfortable, but he played the perfect gentleman.

Over the next several weeks, the foursome attended the theatre, the opera and an endless stream of soirees, house parties and ridottos. Tonight they were attending a ball in honor of the mayor's birthday. Occasionally, she noticed someone looking their way, but it never crossed her mind that people might be gossiping about them.

It wasn't until later she realized she was traveling the road to perdition.

* * *

Percy stood next to his wife in the ballroom.

"Where is Tory?" Claire's gaze searched the room. "I don't see her anywhere about."

"She is probably in the gaming room with Julian. Or perhaps they are dancing."

"Your cousin and my sister have become such dear friends," Claire said. "Still, I know she would love for Lord Brant to accompany her. Perhaps you could speak to him, tell him how happy it would make her if he joined us some evening."

Percy's pulse increased as her lovely blue eyes came to rest on his face. He nodded noncommittally but made no reply. It wasn't his place to interfere between a man and his wife. Besides, he had more than enough problems with his own marriage.

Claire took his hand. "Could we dance? Please, Percy?"

"If that is your wish, sweetheart, I shall make it my command." He smiled and led her off toward the dance floor. He agreed to anything she asked, gave her anything she wanted, though she rarely asked for much. He was head over the mark for her, completely dim-witted where his wife was concerned.

Not that she was his wife in truth. The marriage had yet to be consummated, and though he thought of little else twenty-four hours a day, the time was not yet right to press his suit.

His wife knew nothing of the physical side of marriage—though if kissing were an art form, she had become a female Michelangelo. So good, in fact, that he dared not kiss her overlong for fear he might lose control and ravish her.

He forced the worrisome thought away and smiled at her. Letting her lead him onto the dance floor, he took her hand and led her into the steps of a contredanse, enjoying the sweet way she smiled back at him whenever he took her hand. Each time she touched him, his manhood stirred and his face heated up. He worried about the snug fit of his breeches and tried to think of something besides the soft swells of her breasts above the top of her mauve silk gown.

He watched her make a graceful pirouette, her gown floating softly around her calves. For an instant, her beautiful eyes locked with his and a blush rose in her cheeks. Percy forced himself to look away and prayed with every ounce of his strength he could continue to control himself where his utterly delectable wife was concerned.

The evening progressed. Tory wandered out of the card room, wondering where her sister had gone. "There you are. I've been looking all over." Julian Fox walked toward her, smiling as he captured her hand. He was as tall as Cord, with thick black hair and stunning blue eyes, and he cut a dashing figure in his perfectly tailored burgundy tailcoat and light gray breeches.

"They are starting the entertainment out in the garden," he said. "I thought you might like to see it."

"I was playing whist and not very well. I should far prefer watching the entertainment than losing all of my money."

"Dancing Cossacks from the Steppes of Russia." Julian leaned close to whisper in her ear. "Probably no more than wandering Gypsies, but who cares?" He straightened. "Come. If we hurry we can still find a seat."

Julian led her through the doors leading out to the terrace. Tory knew he felt safe with her, able to dodge the throngs of women who vied for his attention. Aside from his good looks and charm, Julian had money and social position. He would be considered a very good catch for one of the young women in the marriage mart. But Julian seemed to have little interest. Tory wondered if perhaps a woman had hurt him in the past and now he guarded his heart very carefully.

Certainly, he had no interest in *her,* which was why she also felt safe with him. They were friends, nothing more, and, in truth, she would much rather be with her husband.

And yet marriage to Cord had been far from the sort of which she had dreamed, the kind her father and mother had shared, doing things together, enjoying each other's company more than anyone else's.

She sighed as she let Julian seat her in a chair at the end of several rows. He wasn't Cord, but he was excellent company. Tory settled back to watch the show.

Cord pushed away from his desk. It was well past one and Victoria had not yet returned. These evening affairs were beginning to annoy him.

Still, wives often attended *ton* functions without their husbands, and it was through no fault of Victoria's that he hadn't the time to go about with her in Society. He should be grateful his brother-in-law had taken on the job of chaperone. Thank God the young man enjoyed that sort of thing.

As for Cord, he was busy with the purchase he was about to make on a block of real estate in Threadneedle

Street, an empty building in an area of prestigious offices. With a little renovation, the structure would be worth double his investment.

It was highly unfashionable for a member of the aristocracy to do any sort of work, but Cord had discovered he enjoyed it. To appease the *ton,* he had passed his interest in finance off as a hobby, which seemed perfectly credible to them.

Mostly, though, his mind was preparing for the upcoming attempt to free Ethan.

Two nights ago, Colonel Pendleton had received news that Ethan had been moved inland, to a prison east of Nantes. The place wasn't nearly as accessible as the prison in Calais, but the Loire River flowed past Nantes into the sea at St. Nazaire, and if freeing Ethan could be managed, the colonel believed Max Bradley could sec it done.

And, as before, Cord intended to have a ship waiting to bring Ethan home once the men reached the coast.

He pulled the gold chain from the pocket of his waistcoat, flipped open the lid of his watch and checked the time. It was half past one. He snapped the lid closed and his gaze snagged on the chessboard sitting in the corner. He hadn't played chess with Victoria since they were wed. He simply hadn't had time.

Or perhaps that was just an excuse.

Staying busy kept his mind off his wife, kept him from getting more deeply involved with her than he was already. She'd had her hooks in him from the beginning, though he didn't think she knew. The last thing he wanted was to fall more deeply into the female trap she posed.

God's breath—he didn't want to wind up like that young fool, Lord Percy.

Cord liked things exactly as they were—Victoria pleasing him in bed while their lives ran on parallel, but separate, courses.

He heard movement in the hall and rose from his chair. Victoria was home and it was about damned time. Striding down the corridor, he spotted her in the entry, a slender, feminine vision in saffron silk and cream lace.

"I expected you sooner," he said darkly as he approached. She turned at the sound of his voice and her chin went up.

"Claire and Lord Percy wished to stay a bit longer tonight. As I was their guest, I had no choice but also to remain. Perhaps if you had come with me—"

"I was busy—as you damn well know."

"Then, it would seem the problem would be yours and not mine."

His eyes narrowed. He started to say something more, but he knew in a way she was right, and besides, she looked so delectable with her cheeks flushed and her nose in the air that his body stirred and his loins filled. She gave a little squeak of surprise as he scooped her up in his arms and started climbing the stairs.

They could discuss her late hours on the morrow. Tonight he needed his wife and he meant to have her.

Her arms slipped around his neck, her soft breasts pillowed against his chest, and his body throbbed to be inside her. There were advantages to being married he hadn't thought of before. As long as he maintained a certain distance, as long as he thought with his head and not his heart, he could enjoy himself.

Cord vowed that was exactly what he would do.

Fifteen

Tory was beginning to tire of the endless social whirl. There were nights she wished she could simply stay home, but if she did, she would wind up sitting alone in the drawing room, reading a book or working on her embroidery. Cord would be squirreled away in his study and wouldn't wish to be disturbed.

Tory sighed. She might as well go out.

Crossing the room, she tugged on the bell pull, ringing for her lady's maid, Emma Conklin, to help her select a gown for the night's affair.

"Gor, milady, but this one surely is fine. 'Tis one of me personal favorites." Emma had been a serving maid when Tory worked as housekeeper. Broad-hipped, with kinky blond hair and a faint cockney accent, Emma had once revealed her dream of becoming a lady's maid, a highly unlikely circumstance, considering her background.

But Emma loved clothes and it turned out she was a very competent seamstress. When Tory became Cord's wife, she decided to give Emma the job as her maid.

"You don't think the pearl satin would be better?"

"'Tis handsome and no doubt. But the rose silk with the pale pink overskirt and those lovely little oak clusters up the front— 'tis exquisite, milady."

Tory smiled. She enjoyed Emma's company and her refreshing candor. "Then the rose silk it shall be."

Emma helped her into the dress and fastened the buttons up the back, then Tory selected the jewelry she would wear.

Digging into the jewelry box, her hand brushed the slick white satin wrapped around her father's ring. A little chill went through her as she lifted the ring out of the box and unrolled the satin.

Set in heavy gold, the bloodred garnet flashed up at her, dredging up painful memories and all her niggling suspicions. For weeks, she had forced her suspicions to the back of her mind. She'd had Claire to protect—and herself. She'd been busy trying to keep them both out of prison. Now, along with the constant worry about her marriage, the nagging questions about her father's murder had returned to plague her thoughts.

How had the ring come to be in her mother's possession?

Why had her mother never mentioned finding it?

Tory felt more and more certain the answers lay in the diary her mother had kept—if it still existed. Tory believed her mother had found the ring among her second husband's possessions. Miles Whiting must have had the ring, and if he did, he was the man responsible for her father's murder—as Tory had for years suspected.

If only she could prove it.

The diary was the key. Somehow she had to find it.

She needed to return to Harwood Hall and go back up to the attic. She wished she could speak to Cord, ask for his help, but he was always so busy and she had caused him enough trouble already.

She rewrapped the garnet ring and put it back in the box, then reached for the blue velvet case, pulled it out and opened the lid. The diamond-and-pearl necklace gleamed up at her. She found herself picking it up, draping it around her throat.

It looked perfect with the rose silk gown. The pearls felt cool and reassuring against her skin. The diamond clasp came together with a softly muted click. She remembered the night Cord had demanded she wear only the necklace to bed, then made passionate love to her. She wished he were going with her tonight.

Ignoring a feeling of hopelessness, she cast a glance at the clock. Her sister and brother-in-law would be arriving any moment, her usual escorts for the evening. Accepting the richly embroidered, white silk India shawl Emma handed her, Tory headed for the stairs.

The week dragged past. In return for their care of her, Tory gave a dinner party in her sister and brother-in-law's honor. If her husband wouldn't accompany her in Society, she decided, she would bring the party to him.

Their guests would be arriving any minute. Tory glanced down the hall to see their very efficient housekeeper, Mrs. Gray, hustling toward her, carrying a list of last minute details. Tory answered each of her questions, then made a final check of the seating in the dining room.

Cord was upstairs dressing, but he wouldn't be down

for a few more minutes. He had returned late from a meeting with Colonel Pendleton. The men were still not ready to make the attempt to free Captain Sharpe, but they were hoping for a chance very soon.

She spotted her husband coming down the stairs just as the first guests arrived, and for an instant, she simply stood there admiring him. He was so tall and broad-shouldered, his features so strong and male. He took her arm and his gaze swept over her. She caught his look of approval, along with the gleam of desire.

The latter disappeared as they walked over to greet the first arrivals, Dr. and Mrs. Chastain and their daughter. Lately, at one party or another, she and Grace had been able to spend a good deal of time together.

"Mama is determined to marry me off to some decrepit old fool with gobs of money," Grace had said. "So long as the man has a title—that is all she cares about. You should have seen her last week at Lord Dunfrey's soiree. She insisted I sit next to Viscount Tinsley at supper. The man is blind in one eye and so ancient he couldn't remember whether he was eating baked herring or roasted goose."

"I gather you are still determined to marry only for love."

Grace's chin went into the air. "If I can't have love, I refuse to marry at all."

But so far, Grace had yet to find a man who interested her.

Not even Julian Fox.

He arrived a few minutes later, in company with Claire and Percy. Though she had spoken of Julian to Cord several times, the two of them had yet to meet.

She smiled as he walked in. "Julian! I'm so glad you could come."

He made a very gallant bow over her hand. "The pleasure is mine, Victoria."

"It is well past time you met my husband." She led him to where Cord stood next to his friend, Rafael Saunders. "Cord, this is Julian Fox."

"Mr. Fox."

"Lord Brant."

"I believe you know his grace, the duke of Sheffield."

"Yes," Julian said. "We've met on several occasions."

Appropriate responses were made, but Cord seemed strangely remote. She could tell her husband was sizing Julian up as men did and wondered what he was thinking.

It didn't take long to find out. He cornered her on their way into the dining room, drawing her down the hall away from their guests.

"So…I finally get to meet your elusive Mr. Fox."

"Yes, I am happy he could come."

"You never mentioned how charming he was."

She didn't like the way he was staring at her, the way his eyes looked harder than they usually did. "I told you he was a very nice man."

"You also never said he was six feet tall, exceedingly well-built, and one of the best-looking men in London."

Her chin went up. "I didn't think the way he looked was of any importance."

"Is that so?"

"I hoped that you would like him."

"Oh, I like him just fine." Cord didn't say more, simply took her arm and wove it through his and rather firmly guided her into the dining room.

Once she was seated, she began to relax. Cord chatted amiably with their guests, and she thought that when he wished, he could be even more charming than Julian. He seemed the perfect host, relaxed and laughing, yet she felt his eyes drift toward her again and again.

Dr. Chastain told a disturbing story about a pair of Siamese twins he had delivered.

"I dare say, you should have seen them. Joined at the head. Never seen anything like it. Died before they were two weeks old. Blessing, it was, to be sure." He was about to launch into another equally unpleasant medical tale when Julian smoothly cut in.

With a glance at Tory, he smilingly relayed the story of the cossacks who had entertained at the mayor's birthday ball, a group that turned out to be Gypsies.

"They were actually quite good entertainment," he said, "even if they were utter frauds." Everyone laughed at the story and Tory flashed him a grateful smile.

Then he mentioned the opera they had attended, *Don Giovanni.* "It was by far the best production I've seen in years. Wouldn't you say so, Victoria?"

She smiled. "It was remarkable. Of course, I hadn't been to an opera since my parents brought Claire and me to London years ago. This was even more wonderful than the performance we saw back then."

"It was lovely," Claire put in. "You should have come with us, my lord," she said to Cord. "You would have enjoyed yourself."

Cord's eyes burned into Tory. "I'm certain I would have."

Dr. and Mrs. Chastain, who had also seen the production, remarked on the quality of the performance, though Grace hadn't attended with them. Grace and her father had never been close, and in the past few years, they had grown even further apart. It bothered Grace, but there seemed to be nothing she could do.

The conversation remained lively through supper. Cord nodded and smiled, but fell more and more silent. The men remained in the dining room for brandy and cigars while the women retired to the drawing room.

Once the men rejoined the ladies, the group seemed cordial enough, yet Cord remained strangely quiet, and by the time the last guest departed, his mood was completely black. He ushered Tory upstairs and followed her into her bedchamber, closing the door behind him, then lounged back against the paneled wood, his arms crossed over his chest.

"So you enjoyed the opera, did you?"

She didn't like his tone. "Yes, I enjoyed it very much. You suggested I go, as I recall. You were busy—as usual—or you could have come with me."

"There were things I needed to do. Unlike your good friend, Julian, I have a number of responsibilities."

"Julian knows how to enjoy life. There is nothing wrong with that."

He came away from the door. "I don't want you going out with him again."

"What are you talking about? I have never been out with Julian. He has been kind enough to make us a party of four instead of three, for which I am grateful."

"You heard what I said. I don't want him escorting you anywhere. If he is joining his cousin and your sister for the evening, you will stay home."

Her temper began to rise. "You are not my jailer, Cord."

"No, merely your husband…in case you have forgot."

She clamped her hands on her hips. "What is it about him you don't like?"

"I told you I like him fine. I just don't want him out with my wife."

"Why not?"

"For one thing, I'm concerned that seeing him as much as you have been will begin to rouse the gossips. I don't want my wife's name dragged through the mud."

"Julian is merely a friend. Beyond that, he has no interest in me and I have no interest in him."

"I'm damned glad to hear it."

Her eyes widened in disbelief. "Good Lord, you're not jealous, are you?"

"Hardly. As I said, I am merely concerned with protecting my wife's reputation."

But he was still angry. She realized he *was* jealous, and more than that, it thrilled her that he was. Except for his amorous attentions, Cord had mostly ignored her since the day they were wed. It wasn't the recipe for a happy marriage as far as Tory was concerned, but perhaps at last she had found a way to stir his interest.

Excitement bubbled through her. She should have thought of this before.

She started for the bell pull above the bed to ring for her maid, but Cord caught her arm. "Turn around," he said darkly. "You won't be needing your maid tonight."

She didn't argue as he turned her back to him and began to undress her with swift, sure movements that made it disturbingly clear how familiar he was with a lady's wardrobe.

Once he had undressed her to garters and stockings, he pulled the pins from her hair, slid his fingers into the heavy strands, tilted her head back and very thoroughly kissed her.

She was breathless by the time he finished, her body pulsing with heat. Lifting her into his arms, Cord carried her through the door adjoining their two suites, over to his huge four-poster bed.

They had never made love in his room before. He had always come to her bed and left before the servants arrived. Now he didn't bother to pull back the dark blue velvet counterpane, just settled her in the middle of the deep feather mattress, came down on top of her and began to plunder her mouth.

Their lovemaking was savage, Cord taking possession of her body more thoroughly than he ever had before. He'd been disturbed by Julian's presence. Perhaps she meant more to him than he realized.

If he did, there was still a ray of hope.

If only she could find a way to make him see.

"Good night, Claire."

"Good night, Percy." Claire smiled, but as soon as the door softly closed, she threw her hairbrush against it.

"My lady!" Her maid hurried forward, bent and scooped up the brush.

Claire sighed. "I am sorry, Frances, I don't know why I am angry except..."

"Except what, my lady?" Frances was ten years older than Claire, a short, dark-haired woman with pockmarks on her face from a childhood disease.

Claire turned on the stool and looked up at her. "Do

you and your husband…do the two of you sleep in the same bed?"

The maid flushed. "Aye, that we do. And pleasurable it is, I can tell ya."

"Sometimes I wish…I wish Lord Percy would stay with me. We are married. My father and mother slept in the same bed. If Percy were here, I wouldn't wake up in the middle of the night feeling so lonely."

The maid was frowning. "'Tisn't my place to ask this, my lady, but I been thinking…. I know your mother has passed on, God rest her soul, and I was wondering if…" The maid shook her head. "'Tisn't my place."

Claire caught her arm. "You were wondering what? Tell me, Frances."

"Well…I was wondering if…well, if you and his lordship have got round to making love?"

Claire shrugged, reached for her silver-backed hairbrush, pulled it through her hair. "I suppose we have. He kisses me all the time."

"Well, kissing is part of it, that's for sure, but there is a good deal more goes with it."

The brush paused midstroke as Claire whirled to face her. "There is?"

"Indeed, my lady. I'm thinking that perhaps, with your mother gone, no one has told you the way of things."

"What things are you talking about?"

Frances bit her lip. "I don't know if I should say, my lady."

"I need to know. Please tell me, Frances. I want to make my husband happy."

"Well, you're certainly right in that. Lord Percy

would be smiling once in a while if he were gettin' what other men get from their wives."

Dear Lord, had she been failing him all the while and not even known it? "Tell me, Frances, please. I really want to know."

And so two hours later an astonished Claire bid her maid good night and climbed into bed. She tried to sleep, but every time she closed her eyes, she kept remembering the outrageous things the maid had said.

As soon as the sun was high enough to mark a decent hour for calling, Claire was going to see Tory. She needed to confirm what the maid had told her—and find out if Tory had done those things with the earl.

By midafternoon Claire knew the true and astonishing facts of life.

Not only had her sister blushingly nodded at the things Frances had told her, she had loaned her a book from the earl's library, *In the Matter of Male and Female Sexuality.*

"You should have told me," Claire had said.

"I know. I'm sorry I didn't. But it isn't an easy matter to discuss, even between sisters as close as we are. I was hoping…that your husband would handle the matter."

But Percy was even shyer than Claire.

Claire sat perched on the edge of the sofa. "What is it like?"

Tory blushed. She took a deep breath and then she smiled. "Lovemaking is wonderful, Claire."

Claire left for home and spent the day in the library engrossed in the book Tory had loaned her. As evening approached, she pled a headache, remaining home instead of going out, and retired upstairs to her room. Carrying the book, she crossed her bedchamber and curled up in the window seat.

Claire cracked open the leather-bound volume to the place she had marked when she had been forced to stop reading. Time and again her face heated up at the words printed on the page, and yet she had never read anything more intriguing.

And she wasn't going to bed until she had finished the very last sentence.

It was later that same night that Tory prepared to go out for the evening. Her afternoon had been full of surprises. Though she was relieved that Claire finally understood and even seemed to look forward to the physical side of marriage, her own marriage was turning into a dismal failure.

Slipping into a high-waisted gown of gold satin trimmed with rhinestone brilliants, Tory stood stiffly as Emma did up the buttons.

She was angry. And disappointed. The duke of Tarrington was having a ball at his magnificent residence on the outskirts of the city and Cord had agreed to accompany her. She'd been excited all week, looking forward to wearing the new gown she had purchased especially for him, mostly looking forward to just being with him.

Then tonight, at the very last moment, he had told her he wouldn't be able to go.

"I know you were looking forward to tonight, but something's come up. I'm afraid I'll have to cancel."

"You aren't going?" She could hardly believe he was

crying off when he had promised to take her. "What has come up that is so important?"

"It's a business matter, nothing for you to worry about."

"A business matter," she repeated, trying to hold on to her temper. "We have been planning this evening for the past two weeks. Grace is going. My sister and Percy will be there. Surely whatever it is can wait."

"I'm sorry, but it can't. There will be other occasions. The Season isn't yet over."

Tory reined in a shot of anger. Instead of arguing, she waited till Cord left the house then sent a note to Gracie, explaining that the earl had been forced to cancel for the evening and asking if she would ask her parents if she might be included in their party.

Grace was thrilled, of course. It would be easier to escape her parents and the line of unwanted suitors they constantly pressed upon her if Tory were with her. When the Chastains' carriage rolled up in front of the town house, she was ready and waiting, her anger lowered to a simmer.

The traffic was heavy on the roadways, with freight wagons and hackney coaches, and a number of fine carriages headed to the same destination. By the time they reached Tarrington Park, the ball was already well under way; a crush of elegantly dressed men and women who filled the sumptuous residence to overflowing, spilled out onto the terrace and into the torch-lit garden.

Tory greeted familiar faces as she searched for Claire and her husband. She smiled when she saw a friend approaching along the marble-floored hall. The handsome, black-haired man caught her hands, bent and kissed her cheek.

"It's wonderful to see you, Victoria."

"You, as well, Julian."

Cord finished his meeting but had too much on his mind to simply go home.

And he was feeling guilty about disappointing his wife.

He knew how much Victoria had wanted to go to the ball. But the real estate purchase on Threadneedle Street was getting ready to close and the seller was leaving London in the morning. At the last minute, the man had demanded a meeting to clarify some of the terms, and Cord had no choice but to agree.

At least that's what he had told himself.

Instead of going home, he directed his coachman to take him to Sheffield House. But as the carriage rolled in that direction, he couldn't help wondering if tonight's important meeting hadn't simply been another excuse to avoid spending time with his wife.

Cord sighed into the carriage. Every minute he spent with her seemed to draw him deeper under her spell.

It worried him. Bloody hell, it terrified him.

He was a man who had learned to rely on himself. He didn't like involvements, especially with a woman. He didn't like becoming too attached. He remembered how he had suffered when his mother had died. He'd been a boy back then, barely able to stand the grief. Over the years, he had learned to distance himself, to keep his emotions carefully guarded. It was the only way a man could protect himself.

The carriage pulled up in front of the mansion. Lamps still burned in the rooms downstairs, which meant Rafe was likely at home. Cord climbed down from the coach and made his way along the brick walkway to the wide front porch. Two sharp raps and the butler pulled open the door. Cord was surprised to see his best friend standing in the entry.

"I know it's getting late," Cord said. "I saw the lamps still lit." Cord eyed the evening clothes his friend was wearing. "I take it, you're on your way out."

"As a matter of fact, I am. I'm off to Tarrington's ball. I thought you were attending, as well."

Cord ignored a thread of guilt. "I planned to go. Something came up."

Rafe smiled. "Well, it isn't all that late. There is still time to change. Perhaps you and Victoria could join me."

He had work to do, the final papers to review on the real estate transaction. Still, he had promised Victoria he would take her and it didn't set well that he had broken his word.

"All right. We'll go over to the house, see if she still wants to go."

It was ten minutes later that he and Rafe walked into the foyer of his town house.

"I'm afraid her ladyship isn't at home," Timmons informed him. "She accompanied her friend, Miss Chastain, and Miss Chastain's parents to the duke of Tarrington's ball."

Cord felt a trickle of irritation. He didn't really mind that Victoria had gone. It was the way of the *ton* to lead separate lives, and that was exactly what he wanted.

"Since your wife is already there," the duke said, "you might as well get dressed and come along."

He started to say no, that he had a million things to do, but Rafe caught his arm.

"There have been rumors," the duke said softly, "whispers about your wife and Julian Fox. I don't believe for an instant they are true, but still…it would serve both of you well if you escorted your wife on occasion."

Rumors, he thought. Whispers about his wife and another man. Anger burned through him. He had warned her not to see Fox again. Had Victoria disobeyed him?

"I won't be a moment," he said. "Why don't you pour yourself a drink and I'll be right down."

Sixteen

He would not be a cuckold, by God!

Riding in the duke's impressive black-and-gilt carriage pulled by four black horses, Cord and Rafe traveled the busy streets of London toward the outskirts of town and reached Tarrington Park half an hour later. Cord said little along the way, but his temper simmered the entire length of the journey.

He wasn't sure exactly what he would discover at the ball, or what he might do if he found Victoria with Fox, but Rafe's words had jolted him out of his apathy where his wife was concerned.

The ball was in full swing when he arrived, the orchestra music soothing some of the heat that pumped through his veins.

But if he found her with Fox…

He spotted Percy and Claire, staring adoringly into each other's eyes in a corner of the main salon, a huge room with gilded columns, gold brocade sofas and urns overflowing with blooming pink roses. In the gaming salon, Dr. Chastain sat at a green baize table, a sizable stack of chips resting in front of him.

Cord found Mrs. Chastain in the entry, coming back from the ladies' retiring room.

"My lord, it is so good to see you." She smiled. "Lady Brant said you wouldn't be able to attend the ball tonight."

"Fortunately, I was able to make a last-minute change of plans." He glanced down the hallway, but saw no sign of his wife. Instead he saw Julian Fox in conversation with the duke of Tarrington's son, Richard Worthing, marquess of Wexford. He was only mildly relieved to see Victoria nowhere near.

"Do you know where I might find Lady Brant?" he asked the doctor's wife.

"She was with Grace when last I saw her. They were going into the ballroom to dance."

Cord smiled politely. "Thank you." So she was dancing. Better that than spending time with Fox. But when he walked through the door, Victoria wasn't on the dance floor. She was standing next to Grace, surrounded by a circle of admiring men.

As he crossed the room, he watched the group conversing and realized each of the men were smiling, vying for his wife's attention. He had never thought of Victoria as any sort of temptress—though she had tempted him mightily from the start.

Now, as his gaze ran over the low-cut bodice of her gold satin gown and he watched the rise and fall of her luscious breasts, he realized she had blossomed into exactly that. Along with her beauty, she radiated poise and self-assurance, making her one of the loveliest, most intriguing women in the room.

Even if she didn't seem to know it.

She smiled at something someone said, and Cord noticed the upsweep of her thick chestnut hair, saw the way it glinted in the light of the candles burning in the crystal chandeliers. He wanted to pull out the pins and watch it tumble around her shoulders, wanted to feel the soft strands curling around his fingers.

Her feminine laughter drifted across the ballroom and a wave of desire washed over him. His blood heated and his groin grew thick and heavy. He didn't like the way the men were looking at her. She was his wife, dammit! She belonged to him and no one else!

Jealousy mixed with the lust he was feeling and his temper inched up. It was mollified only a little by the warm, welcoming smile that lit her face the moment she saw him walking toward her across the room. It was a smile that cut right through him, made him want her more than he ever had before.

Or perhaps it was knowing every man there wanted her as much as he did.

"My lord," she said, still smiling. "I am pleased that you came."

His eyes remained on her face as he made an elegant bow over her hand. "You're looking quite fetching this evening, Lady Brant."

"You, as well, my lord. I am glad you changed your mind."

He thought of Fox and wondered… "Are you, indeed?" He turned to the other men before she could answer and the smile he gave them held a note of warning. "Gentlemen, if you will excuse us, I need a moment with my wife."

The circle nervously parted. "Of course, my lord," one of them said, a Viscount Nobby or Nibby or some such thing.

Cord rested Victoria's gloved hand on the sleeve of his coat and led her toward the door of the ballroom.

"Where are we going?" she asked as he guided her down one of a maze of various hallways.

"Someplace we may be private." There were no bedchambers on this floor. He opened a door, saw that it led to Tarrington's impressive study and that several guests were chatting away inside. He closed it and kept on walking.

"Cord, what is it? Is something wrong?"

There might be. If there were, he couldn't be sure. "Not that I'm aware of."

Another door proved useless, but the third provided exactly the space he needed. A linen closet with rows of freshly folded sheets and towels would absorb any sounds they might make.

"Cord, what are you—"

She stopped midsentence as he hauled her inside and firmly closed the door.

"I missed you when I got home. I didn't realize exactly how much until I saw you in that ballroom."

"But this is a linen—"

He cut off her words with a kiss. A long, hot, very thorough kiss that ended her questions and had her leaning against him, softly whispering his name.

It was dark in the closet, smelling pleasantly of starch, soap and lavender. Victoria's slender arms wrapped around his neck and she kissed him back as fiercely as he was kissing her. Her tongue was in his mouth and he was sucking on it when he shoved up the skirt of her gold satin gown to find her softness.

She was already damp, he discovered with a feeling of triumph, and growing rapidly more so as he began to stroke her.

"Cord, you…you can't possibly mean to…to…"

Another kiss warned that was exactly what he meant to do. He managed to unfasten enough buttons to lower her bodice, giving him access to her breasts. They spilled into his hands and he gently pinched the ends, turning them diamond hard, and heard her soft intake of breath.

Darkness surrounded them, forming an erotic cocoon where the senses of touch and feel enhanced their rapidly escalating desire. His hand moved over a warm, satiny breast and he inhaled the faint scent of her perfume.

Bending his head, he took the fullness into his mouth and Victoria arched toward him. She trembled as he reached for her gown once more and slid it up past her waist, his hand brushing her thighs, smoothing over her bottom. Lifting her up, he wrapped her legs around his waist, leaving her open to him, completely exposed. He found her softness, stroked until he had her trembling, begging him to take her.

Unbuttoning the front of his breeches, he freed himself and positioned his shaft at her core. A single deep thrust had him buried to the hilt.

Ah, heaven couldn't be sweeter. Victoria made a soft sound in her throat urging him to move, but he held himself back, absorbing the feel of her body fitted so snugly around him, the rightness of being inside her. Her arms tightened around his neck and her lovely breasts pressed into his chest.

She wriggled, making him throb. "Cord…please…"

He started to move then, aroused by the need he heard in her voice, a need that urged him on. Holding her hips in place to receive his thrusts, he began driving into her, taking her deep and hard, feeling the heat rush through him.

Little mewling sounds came from her throat and it spurred his desire, urging him faster, deeper, harder. She came with a cry of pleasure he hoped was silenced by the padding in the closet and the voices and music outside the door.

A rush of triumph tore through him as he felt her come again.

She was limp in his arms by the time he allowed his own release, a fierce, pulsing climax that left him completely sated. It took a moment to recover, to regain his control, seconds longer to convince himself he had to let her go.

Easing her down his body, he set her on her feet, then in the darkness, felt along the closet shelves in search of a linen towel. He found one and handed it over. While Victoria freshened herself, he turned her around and refastened the buttons at the back of her gown.

"I must look a fright," she said. "I can't believe we did that."

In the darkness Cord smiled, pleased with himself. "I can." It wasn't the first time he'd had a woman in an unusual sort of place, but it was certainly the most satisfying.

The only thing that bothered him was how badly he'd wanted her.

And that the woman was his wife.

* * *

Tarrington Park was exquisite. Claire danced beneath crystal chandeliers to the music of a twenty-piece orchestra in blue satin livery and white powdered wigs.

A score of servants, also in the duke's blue livery, bustled about the ballroom, carrying silver trays laden with every sort of exotic food from oysters to caviar, roasted swan to lobster, and the most delicious assortment of fruit tarts, egg crèmes and petits-fours.

It was a fairy-tale night, the sort she had dreamt of but never really thought to see. And she owed it all to her husband, the white knight who had saved her from a fate she dared not imagine.

Claire danced with Percy's cousin, Julian, who doted on her like a younger sister. When the orchestra finished the tune, he led her off the dance floor, returning her to her husband. Percy managed one of his rare, sweet smiles and she gave him a shy smile in return.

His gaze wandered along her shoulders, down to the swell of her breasts. He shifted uncomfortably and his smile slipped away. He was always so serious. She couldn't help wondering if, as Emma had said, he would smile more often, once they had made love.

But so far that hadn't occurred, and instead, each night after he returned her home, she slept alone in her big four-poster bed while Percy slept alone in his.

"She is yours once more," Julian said gallantly, bowing over her hand. "As for me, I believe I shall call it a night."

She was a little tired herself, but she didn't want to spoil the evening for Percy. Tonight, she would like to go home a little early, spend some time alone with him, kissing and touching. Perhaps they might even do some of the things she had read about in the book.

She wished she were brave enough to ask him to make love to her. Tory would probably have the courage, but Claire wasn't anywhere near that bold.

"Well, if it isn't my beautiful *daughter*."

Claire's gaze jerked away from the glittering jeweled buttons on the front of Percy's coat to the man who had walked up beside her. Her legs started to tremble and her mouth went dry. She thought of the night her stepfather had come into her bedchamber, and she wanted to turn and run.

Instead, she inched a little closer to Percy and his arm went protectively around her.

"Baron Harwood," he said. "I didn't know you were in the city."

"I had some business to attend. I hope you received my note of congratulations. I presume the two of you are rubbing along well together."

"Very well," Percy said.

"I am glad to hear it."

But Claire could see that he wasn't. The baron was angry at being duped and it showed in his cold, dark eyes. She searched to find something to say. She had hoped, now that she was married, she would never have to see her stepfather again.

"I—I hope all is well at Harwood."

He nodded. "Aside from the usual problems with wayward servants. You will have to come for a visit some time." He flicked a glance at Percy. "You *and* your husband, of course."

Percy's jaw looked like granite. "Do not hold your breath, my lord."

Claire's eyes widened. Her husband was such a soft-spoken man. The last thing she expected was for him to stand up to Harwood.

"I see," said the baron.

"I hope that you do," said Percy.

Harwood made a stiff, very formal bow and excused himself, and Claire fought to stop trembling.

"It's all right, love," Percy said, his gaze still following Harwood. "I would never let him hurt you."

"We must tell Tory that Harwood is returned to the city." But her sister and her husband had already left the ball.

"I'll send word to Lord Brant in the morning."

She caught a last glimpse of her stepfather's retreating figure. "I would hate to spoil your evening, my lord, but if you wouldn't mind so very much, I should like to go home."

"You are not spoiling anything." Percy bent and pressed a kiss on the top of her head. "I believe I should like to go home, as well."

Leading her out of the ballroom, he summoned his coach, and within the hour they were returned to their town house. Percy guided her upstairs to her bedchamber as he did each night, but when he turned to leave she caught his arm.

"Do you think you might stay…just for a while?"

He looked at her and his hand came up to her cheek. "I will stay as long as you like, sweetheart."

She wanted to ask if he would stay with her all night, but she knew she would be crushed if he refused. Instead, she led him over to the sofa in the cozy little sitting room and they sat down in front of the hearth.

"I know I am being a coward, but my stepfather frightens me so much. I am glad you were with me tonight."

A hardness came over Percy's features that wasn't usually there. "You're my wife. You don't have to be afraid of anyone."

She gazed into his handsome face, determined not to think of Harwood. "Would you…kiss me?" It was a bold request, she knew, but she needed her husband's comfort tonight.

Percy swallowed and leaned toward her, then very tenderly settled his mouth over hers. The kiss began to deepen and Claire kissed him back, letting the wondrous sensations wash over her. If this was only the act that the book called foreplay, what must it be like to actually make love?

Percy began to draw away, but tonight she refused to let him. Instead, she caught the lapels of his coat and kissed him again. Percy groaned and kissed her back, sliding his tongue into her mouth.

Claire made a small sound in her throat at the new sensation and Percy jerked away as if he had been burned.

He shifted on the sofa and stared off toward the fire. "You are so very innocent," he said.

"All women are innocent for a time."

But Percy seemed unnerved by the fact. He cleared his throat. "You must be tired. The hour grows late. Why don't you get some sleep?"

She might be a little tired, but she was no longer sleepy. She wanted to tell him that she liked it when he kissed her and she wished he would do it again.

Instead, she merely said, "Sleep well, my lord."

He reached over and touched her cheek. "You as well, my love."

Cord received two messages the following morning, one from Percival Chezwick, informing him that Miles Whiting was returned to London, the second from Colonel Pendleton with the news that the time to free Ethan had come.

Cord debated whether to inform Victoria of her stepfather's return, but the knowledge would better prepare her should the two of them chance to meet. In the end, he summoned her into his study and handed her Lord Percy's note.

"Harwood is here?" she said from where she stood on the opposite side of his desk.

Cord came round and took hold of her hands. They felt colder than they should have. "It's all right, love. If the bastard comes within a thousand yards of you, he'll have to deal with me."

But for the next few days, he would be gone, sailing to France with the hope he would finally be returning with Ethan.

It was a far longer journey than before, sailing round the most westerly point of France, then turning south to the rendezvous point near St. Nazaire. He didn't like leaving Victoria that long, not with Harwood in London.

"Just be careful," he said to her. "While I'm gone, I want you to stay close to the house. I don't trust Harwood and I don't want you anywhere near him. I want you to be very careful."

"I'll be careful...if you promise you will be careful

as well." She had asked to accompany him, then demanded, then begged.

"The middle of a war is no place for a woman," he had said. "I want you safe, and if you think, even for a moment, of disobeying me and somehow stealing aboard that ship, I swear I shall lock you in your room for the balance of the Season."

Ignoring the mutinous look on her face, he tipped her chin up, forcing her to look at him. "I don't want you hurt, love. Can't you understand that?"

Something flickered in the green of her eyes. Her hand came up to his cheek. "I don't want you hurt, either."

Cord glanced away, the soft words moving him more than he would have liked.

He forced himself to smile. "Then I shall have to be extremely careful to return to you in one piece."

They talked a little longer, Cord explaining the plans he and Rafe had made, the danger Ethan and Max Bradley would be facing once they left the prison and tried to reach the coast. Tomorrow night, he and Rafe would sail for France.

This time, he prayed his mission would not fail.

She didn't like staying at home while her husband sailed into danger. Still, he was right. As she and Claire had learned firsthand, a ship in time of war wasn't a place she wanted to be.

Besides, with Harwood in London and her husband out of town, it occurred to her that she had been given the perfect opportunity to return to Harwood Hall in search of her mother's diary.

"You're going to Harwood?" Seated next to her on a

sofa in the Blue Room, Claire's blue eyes widened. "You can't be serious."

"I am perfectly serious. I am telling you so that should the rare possibility occur that something might happen, you would know where to look for me."

Claire worried her lip. "I don't know, Tory. I don't think you should go. What if Harwood leaves London and goes back to the hall or finds out that you were there?"

"He has only just arrived in the city. He won't be going home that soon."

"You can't know that for certain."

"Even if he does go back, Greta or Samuel will warn me of his arrival." The two were trusted servants who had worked for her family since before Miles Whiting had inherited the title. "They hate him almost as much as we do."

"Lord Brant will be furious if he finds out."

"He isn't going to find out. Gracie has agreed to help me. She and I are going to visit her friend, Mary Benton, in the country. Grace's hobby is stargazing. She knows the names of the constellations and all sorts of other things, and Mary shares her interest. In truth, only Grace will actually be going to see her. I will be leaving the coach halfway there and heading off to Harwood Hall."

"Grace has agreed to this?"

"Of course."

"Grace is as mad as you are."

Tory laughed. "It will work."

"I hope so."

Tory hoped so, too. But no matter what happened,

this was the chance she had been waiting for—the chance to prove Harwood had murdered her father—and she wasn't about to let it slip away.

Cord's ship, the *Nightingale,* sailed the following night, and the morning after his departure, Tory told Mr. Timmons that she would be accompanying Grace Chastain to visit a friend in the country. An hour later, she boarded the Chastains' coach and the two of them bowled out of the city.

Seated across from her on the tufted velvet seat, Grace plucked a piece of lint from the skirt of her cream muslin gown.

"They were glad to get rid of me," she said, a dark look on her face. "They always are."

Tory couldn't help feeling sorry for her friend. While Tory had been blessed with a loving mother and father, Grace had been shipped off to boarding school and for the most part ignored.

"Surely your parents love you. You're their daughter."

Grace lifted her eyes to Tory's face. "I'm my mother's daughter. My father—Dr. Chastain—isn't really my father."

For a moment, Tory just stared. Infidelity was a common occurrence among the upper classes, but she never would have guessed Grace's mother would do such a thing. "Surely that can't be true."

"I'm afraid it is. A couple of days ago, I heard them talking. My father had been drinking. He had lost a lot of money at the gaming tables. He started yelling at my mother. He said that if she hadn't behaved like a…like a whore he wouldn't have been forced to raise her bastard daughter."

Tory's heart squeezed for her friend. How would she have felt to discover the man she had known as her father was another man entirely?

Grace looked up and there were tears in her eyes. "All those years, I wondered why I couldn't make him love me. Now I know."

"Oh, Gracie." Tory leaned over and hugged her. She could feel Grace trembling and her heart went out to her. "It doesn't matter,' she said firmly. "You're the same person no matter who your father is."

Grace dragged in a shaky breath and leaned back against the squabs. "I suppose I am. The truth is, in a way I'm glad he isn't my father. I just wish I knew who my real father is."

"Perhaps your mother will tell you."

"Perhaps. If I ever work up the courage to ask her. The trouble is I'm not really sure I want to know."

They said no more on the subject. Her friend's parentage didn't matter to Tory, and she believed that Grace was strong enough to handle the truth of her birth. As Tory had said, she was the same young woman, no matter who her real father was.

They rode for most of the day, Grace excited to be traveling to the country, since her stargazing was much limited by the soot-darkened, often cloudy skies of London. At a crossroads in the little town of Perigord, Tory bid farewell to her friend. She spent the night at the Black Dog Inn, a place she had stayed with her family when they had traveled to London, and caught the mail coach to Harwood Hall the following morning.

By late afternoon, she was inside the familiar walls of her family home, the servants pleased to see her, especially Greta, the housekeeper, and Samuel, the butler. She swore them to secrecy about her visit and they vowed to see that the others kept their silence as well.

Even if the baron discovered she had been there, he wouldn't know she was looking for the journal, and by then Tory would be long gone.

It was good to see old friends, but the search itself progressed with agonizing slowness, since she kept thinking of new places to look.

Unfortunately, when the following morning arrived and it was time to return to London, she had nothing to show for her efforts. Greta alone knew she was there in search of the journal, though not the reason she wanted it so badly. Her disappointment must have been obvious. On the morning of Tory's departure, Greta appeared with a suggestion.

"Perhaps your mother, God rest her soul, left the journal at Windmere."

"Yes, I've thought of that. I'll try to go there next."

"Or she could have left it in the town house."

Her head snapped up. She hadn't considered the small residence in the city that her family had used only rarely. "Do you think she might have? She and Father never spent much time there. I hadn't really considered…"

"Your mother and father didn't go there often, but your stepfather always enjoyed life in the city, especially during the Season. He and your mother were there just before your mother fell ill."

"But the baron sold the town house to Sir Winifred Manning. How would I get in?"

Greta shrugged her thin shoulders. "I just thought I'd mention it."

"I'm glad you did." Tory gave the aging woman a hug. "Thank you, Greta." Her spirits somewhat revived, she set out to catch the mail coach and returned to the inn to wait for Gracie, who would be there the following day.

They arrived in London early in the evening.

It was just her bad luck that Cord was waiting when she got home.

Seventeen

Cord paced his study. He had expected Victoria to be there when he arrived home late that afternoon. He was exhausted, more weary from his failure to rescue Ethan than the sleepless hours he had spent at sea.

On arriving at the rendezvous point off St. Nazaire, instead of finding Ethan, a battered, beaten Max Bradley had tumbled over the rail, spilling blood and water onto the holystoned deck. He carried a lead ball in his shoulder and a bad gash on his face.

"The captain escaped from the prison just as we planned," Max had wearily told them. "We made it nearly to the coast before they caught up with us. We gave them a bloody good fight. Then one of them shot me. They thought I was dead or I wouldn't be here now."

"And Ethan?" Cord asked, his stomach in knots.

Bradley released a shaky breath as the surgeon Rafe had had the foresight to bring along worked over him. "He's alive. They'll haul him back to prison. He's made an enemy somewhere. I don't know who it is." He winced at the needle and thread being pulled through the cut on his forehead. "They're determined he won't escape."

"So it's over," Cord said darkly, his hands biting into the back of the wooden chair next to Bradley's bunk.

"I didn't say that." Max managed a crooked smile. "It isn't over till Max Bradley says it is and that time has yet to come."

The words made Cord feel better, but not much.

He tried to push his worry away and instead think of Victoria, imagining her slim arms around his neck, her slender frame pressing against him as she comforted him with her womanly warmth. He imagined the way she would fuss over him, trying to make him feel better, imagined carrying her upstairs and making love to her, using her welcoming body to forget what Ethan suffered.

Instead, when he walked through the door, Timmons had informed him that his wife and Grace Chastain had gone to visit one of Grace's friends in the country. The butler wasn't exactly certain when her ladyship would return.

Cord stopped pacing and sat down at his desk. He tried to fix his mind on the stack of paperwork piled on top, but he couldn't concentrate.

Where was Victoria?

He had told her to stay close to home. He had warned her that Harwood was in London. Had something happened? Was she in some kind of trouble?

Shoving back his chair, he got up from the desk and started pacing again. The hands of the gilded clock on the mantel read seven in the evening when he heard voices in the entry and knew his wife had returned.

Cord walked out of the study, his strides lengthening in proportion to his anger. He caught sight of Victoria, smiling at Timmons as if she hadn't a care in the world, and his fury threatened to explode.

He stopped a few feet from where she stood and lounged back against the wall, folding his arms across his chest.

"So, you are returned."

In the midst of untying her bonnet strings, she spun at the sound of his voice, her hat flying off into the corner.

"You...you are home. You got back to London sooner than I expected."

"So it would seem."

The butler bent and retrieved her hat and stoically handed it over.

"Thank you, Timmons," she said.

"That will be all, Timmons," Cord said curtly, then waited impatiently for the man to depart. He turned a hard look on his wife. "Is this the way you obey my orders? Heading off to God knows where is your idea of staying close to home?"

"I—I...the opportunity came up rather unexpectedly."

"Is that right?"

"I didn't realize you would be upset."

He grabbed her small tapestry overnight bag and inclined his head toward the staircase, indicating he would carry it up for her. Victoria brushed past him, hurriedly climbed the stairs and headed down the hall into her suite.

She turned as Cord walked in behind her and firmly closed the door.

"What of Ethan?" she asked, changing the subject,

trying to sound casual—without the least success as far as Cord was concerned.

"His efforts to escape were a dismal failure. My cousin remains locked up in France."

She started toward him. "Cord, I'm so sorry."

He held up his hand, stopping her in place. "Why did you disobey my orders? Why did you leave when I told you to stay at the house?"

"I didn't…didn't really think you would mind. Harwood was in London, after all. What safer place for me to be than out of the city?"

He frowned. There was something in her expression…. "Who was it again that you visited?"

"An acquaintance from school. Mary Benton. She and Grace are chums."

He didn't like the way her gaze wouldn't quite meet his. "Benton…Benton… Would Mary be Richard Benton's daughter? Or perhaps she is Robert's child, Richard's cousin."

She swallowed. "Mary is Simon's daughter. Simon is related to both Robert and Richard, but I am not…not quite sure how."

"I see." He saw, all right. He saw that his wife was lying. "I find that extremely interesting, as there are no such persons as Robert or Richard Benton. I just made them up."

Her face went utterly white. "I—I must then be mistaken."

Cord strode across the room, gripped her shoulders and dragged her up on her toes. "You are lying, Victoria. If there is a woman named Mary Benton, you were clearly not with her. Where were you? I want the truth and I want it now."

She looked up at him, her eyes big and round, then the stiffness went out of her shoulders. "All right, I'll tell you the truth if you promise you won't get angry."

He clamped his jaw down hard, set her back down on her feet. "I am so angry now it is all I can do not to throttle you. Tell me where you have been."

Looking as though she wanted to bolt, she nervously moistened her lips. "Harwood Hall."

"Harwood Hall! That isn't possible. You can't be that insane."

"It isn't as bad as it sounds. The baron was in London. It was the perfect opportunity."

His temper was raging. He worked to pull himself under control. "You disobeyed my direct instructions and left the safety of the house to hie off to Harwood Hall—the very viper's nest itself? I cannot credit why in God's name you would do something so utterly harebrained as that."

Her chin went up. "Because Miles Whiting killed my father. Or at least I am convinced that he did. I found my father's ring hidden among my mother's possessions. He was wearing it the day he was murdered. I believe the baron took it from my father the day he was killed and my mother somehow found it. If she did, there is every chance she wrote about it in her journal. That's what I was looking for at Harwood Hall. It is the only way I can prove that he is guilty."

Rage still pumped through his blood as Cord mulled over her words. He remembered Victoria speaking of her father's murder, telling him she hoped to see the man responsible pay for the crime. She hadn't mentioned she believed the baron was that man.

As insane as traveling to Harwood was, Victoria was certainly brazen enough for such a scheme. She had stolen aboard the *Nightingale,* hadn't she? Still, Rafe's words whispered through his head.

There have been rumors about your wife and Julian Fox.

"So…you traveled to Harwood unaccompanied? How did you get there?"

For a moment she looked uneasy and his suspicions returned.

"I went by mail coach. I knew the road well. I had traveled it a number of times when I was a girl."

A muscle tightened in his jaw. "With your parents, Victoria! Not by yourself!" His temper was heating up again. "Do you have any idea how much danger you put yourself in? An attractive young woman on the road alone? There are footpads and highwaymen on those roads, just lying in wait for a morsel as tempting as you. You could have been ravished, perhaps even killed. I ought to lock you up in your room and throw away the key!"

"Nothing untoward happened, my lord. As you can see, I am home now, unharmed and in perfect health."

"And the journal? Did you find it?"

She shook her head. "As it was not at Harwood, likely it is somewhere at Windmere." Her mother's family estate. She had spoken wistfully of the place on several different occasions.

"If it is, it will have to stay there. If you even think of haring off again, I swear I shall thrash you within an inch of your life."

She dutifully bowed her head and lowered her eyes, but a small smile tugged at the corner of her lips. Damnable woman knew he wouldn't lay a hand on her, though on occasions such as these, he was sorely tempted to put her over his knee.

"Say you are not angry," she said, looking up at him from beneath a thick fringe of lashes.

He was, but less so. Then she moved closer and all he could think of was the soft look on her face and the feel of the gentle hand she rested against his cheek. Desire curled through him…and something else he refused to name.

"You must be exhausted. Why don't you lie down and take a nap before supper?" She eased his coat off his shoulders, beginning to fuss over him as he had wanted so badly for her to do. "Let me help you undress. In a little while you'll feel better."

He let her remove his white piqué waistcoat. When she started on the buttons on the front of his shirt, he caught her hand and pulled her into his arms.

"I'll lie down if you will join me."

She glanced toward the door. "I've been away. There are matters I should attend."

He wished she hadn't reminded him. Recalling the danger she had put herself in reignited his temper. The painful erection her soft body aroused did the rest. "You'll stay if I say so, and I do."

Spinning her around, he began to unfasten the buttons on the back of her dress. A few minutes later, he had her beneath him and he was inside her. She was making those sweet little mewling sounds he loved, her fingers digging into his shoulders.

If only he could keep her naked and in bed, he wouldn't have to worry. She arched toward him, urging him on, and he bent his head and kissed her, began to surge deeply inside her. At least for a while, his body would take control and his mind could rest.

For a while, at least, he wouldn't be consumed with thoughts of the troublesome creature he had wed.

Cord was ignoring her again. For the first few days after his return from France, he had been brooding and bad tempered, burdened by yet another failure and consumed with worry for his cousin. He had buried himself in his work and she had let him, hoping he would come to terms with something he was helpless to change.

That had been two weeks ago. During the entire time, she had spent every night home alone. She was sick unto death of sitting in the drawing room embroidering, or couched in the library reading a book. When her sister dropped by for a visit, Tory voiced her complaints and Claire urged her to once again join their evening activities.

"In a way it is funny," Claire said. "You are tired of sitting at home and I grow weary of going out."

"I wouldn't be tired of staying home if my husband didn't spend the whole night locked up in his study. Half the time, I think he has forgot that I exist."

Claire smiled. "He didn't forget the night of the Tarringtons' ball. I saw the way he looked at you. He was green with jealousy. He looked as if he meant to ravish you right there."

As she thought of what had happened in the linen closet, Tory's face heated up. "What do you know of ravishment? Have you and Percy…have you finally made love?"

Claire's smile slid away. "We have engaged in foreplay."

Tory nearly choked on the sip of tea she had taken. "Foreplay?"

"That is what they call it in the book."

"You're speaking of a man fondling a woman's bosom…and other things."

"Mostly the other things haven't happened yet, but last night he caressed my breasts. He says they are quite wonderful."

Tory grinned. "You won't have long to wait now."

"That is what I am hoping. We are traveling to Tunbridge Wells for a week to take the mineral waters. Perhaps it will happen then."

"Lord Percy is extremely shy. You have told me he worries about your innocence. Perhaps he is afraid that once he starts making love to you he won't be able to control his passions."

Claire set her cup down in her saucer. "You really think so?"

"From what you have said, I would say it's a strong possibility."

"If that is so, what should I do?"

Tory sipped her tea, mulling the question over. "I think you should tempt him. Drive him mad with desire, then tell him you want him to make love to you. At that point, there'll be no way he can resist."

Claire began to smile. "I am ready to become Percy's wife in every way. I shall do it! Percy says the estate he had let is quite large. A small number of guests have been invited. You and Cord could join us. I should like to have you near in case something goes wrong."

Tory sighed. "I should love to go, dearest, but Cord will never agree. He is always too busy."

"Then you must come by yourself. I would have ever so much more courage. I would only have to think, Victoria would not be missish, and my fear would go away."

Tory pondered the notion. She was tired of Cord's inattention. They were newly married, but except when they made love, he treated her as if she didn't exist.

"All right, I shall come."

Claire excitedly hugged her. "Oh, Tory, thank you ever so much."

And if Cord didn't like it, he could simply pack his bags and come with her.

Cord didn't like it. Not one little bit. The sale of the Threadneedle property had stalled after his last meeting with the owner and he needed to see the matter resolved. But it was obvious Victoria was determined to go, whether or not he went with her.

In the end, he grudgingly conceded to joining the house party for a couple of days, though he couldn't afford to spend the five full days Victoria would be gone.

Cord sighed. In truth, he would love to take a break from the grueling hours he'd been putting in since his marriage. Aside from his determination to add to the earldom's coffers, he spent extra time working to avoid what he really wanted to do—spend more time with Victoria. He was attracted to her mind as well as her luscious little body, which didn't bode well, as far as Cord was concerned.

Every time he looked at Percival Chezwick and saw

the lovesick expression on his face, Cord's resolve to keep his distance from Victoria strengthened.

Over the years, he'd been careful never to let a woman get too close, though a number had tried to sink their hooks in him. A wife was supposed to know her place—making him happy in bed and running his household. Victoria was adept at both and he intended to see that was as far as it went.

Rafe's words flickered through his head. *There have been rumors...about your wife and Julian Fox....*

Still, perhaps he should pay a bit more attention where his wife was concerned. He made a mental note to do something about it once he and Victoria returned to London.

Cord leaned back against the carriage seat, listening to the spinning of the wheels. Outside the window, cows grazed in the rolling green fields. A hawk swooped down on a ground squirrel in the meadow but flew off empty-handed.

The carriage would arrive in Tunbridge Wells late in the afternoon. It bothered him that Victoria had left only yesterday and already he missed her.

It was lucky he knew the pitfalls to avoid where a woman was concerned.

And he would be interested to see if Julian Fox happened to be on the guest list.

Eighteen

Evidence of fall had set in, the leaves turning shades of rust and orange and gold. A cool breeze swept over the lush green fields surrounding Parkside Manor, the sprawling stone house Lord Percy had rented for his weeklong sojourn in the country.

"Tory!" Claire raced toward her, arms open, and Tory went into them, giving her sister a hug. "I'm so glad you could come."

"Thank you for asking us. I must admit it does feel good to be out of the city."

Claire glanced around the entry. "I thought Cord was coming with you."

"He couldn't leave town quite yet, but he said he would be here. I am hoping he won't change his mind."

Claire linked arms with Tory. "He had better not. And in the meantime, I will show you around the house and introduce you to the guests."

Tory smiled and let her sister lead the way. She and Cord had been assigned a large, airy set of rooms at the opposite end of the hall from the master's suite. There were two rambling guest wings, each lined with doors that opened into elegantly furnished bedchambers, and the downstairs was impressive.

The house was old, built in Jacobean times, with heavy hand-carved beams and mullioned windows. Added onto over the centuries, the three-story gray stone structure spread out beside a small, tumbling stream.

The place was large and welcoming. As Claire had said, there was no lack of privacy for any of the guests, and the "small" list of visitors included an interesting mix of people, including Percy's father, the marquess of Kersey; Percy's brother and sister-in-law, the earl and countess of Louden; Cord's cousin, Sarah, her husband, Jonathan, and young son, Teddy; and Rafael Saunders, Duke of Sheffield.

Cord arrived late the following afternoon. "Good afternoon, Victoria," he said, a polite smile on his face.

"Good afternoon, my lord," she replied with equal courtesy.

"I trust your journey was not overly taxing."

"Not in the least."

"The road was a bit muddy, but we made fairly good time, considering."

Considering what? she wanted to ask, considering he didn't want to be there, which he was making perfectly clear by his bored but polite attitude. He greeted a few of the guests who wandered into the entry, then Tory led him to their assigned room upstairs. Though they chatted pleasantly, his smile remained bland, his attitude slightly indulgent. The perfect aristocratic husband,

Tory thought, and as the day progressed, she found his distant regard more and more annoying.

She was his wife. His lover, for heaven's sake! Not just some woman who shared his quarters. Tory was determined to do something to shake his cool facade, but in the end, she didn't have to. The moment he realized Julian Fox was one of the guests, his entire attitude changed.

"I see your friend, Mr. Fox, is in attendance."

"Why, yes. He is Lord Percy's cousin, after all."

Cord didn't say more, but when she looked up at him, his bland expression was gone, replaced by the subtle hardening of his jaw.

It was a heady thing to realize one's husband was wildly jealous of another man.

And far too tempting.

More than anything, Tory wanted Cord to love her. She wanted the kind of marriage her father and mother had once had, a loving relationship that encompassed their children.

At least Cord had worked diligently at his duties in that regard. The moment he stepped across the threshold of their bedchamber, his eyes darkened with desire. Sooner or later, Tory was certain, she would find herself with child.

Which would keep her busy and out of his hair, seemingly his greatest desire.

Tory wanted children, of course. She adored them, had always dreamed of having a houseful. But she had hoped to have them with a husband who loved her.

She watched the way his eyes fixed on Julian Fox whenever the man came near. He didn't like Julian, though she thought the reason had more to do with the friendship she and Julian shared than it did with the man himself.

"I think your husband is jealous," Julian said as they stood in the drawing room before supper, purposely leaning over to whisper in her ear. He didn't seem to care in the least that Cord stared at him with eyes sharp as daggers. If anything, it seemed to make him bolder.

"I have told him that we are merely friends," Tory said.

"And so we are. Still, I think a little competition is good for him."

She had never complained about her marriage, but it didn't take an Oxford scholar to guess that when one's husband rarely accompanied his wife something must be wrong.

Tory flicked Cord a glance. He was speaking to his friend the duke, but his eyes continually strayed in her direction. When she smiled at something Julian said, his eyebrows drew into a frown.

"It is well known," Julian continued, "that where women are concerned, the earl of Brant is far too cocksure of himself."

She pondered that, knowing it was true. "So you think making him jealous might teach him to appreciate me more?" *Might even make him love me?*

"Sometimes a man doesn't realize what he has until he thinks he might lose it."

Her mind spun with possibilities. The thought had occurred to her more than once. Perhaps it could actually work. "Are you saying you would be willing to risk the earl's displeasure in order to help me?"

He smiled, displaying a row of teeth that gleamed like

pearls against his dark skin. He was entirely too handsome. She wondered again what had happened in his past that made him avoid most women. Of course, the way they fawned over him, she didn't really blame him.

"As you say, we are friends. I would be pleased to help in any way I can." He looked up. "In the meantime, I think we have goaded the tiger enough for the present. I believe I shall take my leave." Bowing over her hand, he made his exit just as Cord approached.

He walked up beside her, his eyes still fixed on Julian. "You and Mr. Fox seemed to be enjoying yourselves. What did Fox have to say that was so intriguing?"

She shrugged. "Nothing unusual. We spoke of the change in the weather. He mentioned a new play opening at the Haymarket Theatre next week."

Cord's gaze followed Julian across the room. "I would prefer you conversed with someone else."

Her gaze followed his and her defenses went up. "You aren't saying I should ignore him? I refuse to be rude, Cord. I told you before—Julian and I are merely friends."

"Yes…that is what you have said."

They went in to dinner, and though he was charming to the rest of the guests, he said little to Tory. She knew she was playing with fire and yet… She had to take the chance, had to do something to breach the wall he had build around himself where she was concerned.

Like her sister, if she wanted to succeed, she would have to be bold.

Tory looked down the table to where Claire sat to the right of her husband. The gown she had chosen was cut exceedingly low and Percy could barely keep his eyes off her breasts.

Good luck to you, darling, she thought, then turned to see Cord scowling at Julian, who sat next to Claire, obviously believing it was Julian that she had been watching.

Good luck to both of us.

The hour grew late. Determined to carry through with the plan she and Tory had made, Claire pled a headache and asked Percy to escort her upstairs. He didn't hesitate.

She was counting on that as they walked into the sitting room of the master's suite and her husband closed the door.

"I hate to wake Frances," she said sweetly. "Would you mind unfastening my gown?"

Percy's expression turned guarded. "Of course." He did so with a hand that shook only slightly, dispatching the buttons, then taking a step backward when the task was complete.

Claire turned to face him, holding up the front of her gown. "Remember the night you caressed my breasts?"

He swallowed, color rising in his cheeks. "I have not forgot. Nor could I, even should I try."

She let go of the front of the gown, a pale blue silk with a bodice Frances had altered daringly low, letting it fall open. Percy's eyes widened as she lowered the straps on her chemise, leaving her bosom exposed to his gaze.

Percy seemed rooted to the floor. "Touching you that way…it is only the first step in making love. That night, I came very close to losing control. If I were to…to touch you that way again, I am afraid of what might happen."

"I am not afraid, Percy."

"You're delicate, Claire. Fragile. I promised I would wait, give you time to get adjusted to the idea of being married. Waiting, where one's wife is concerned, is not an easy thing for a man to do—particularly when the woman he has wed is as lovely as you. Should we start, I might not be able to stop. If I should hurt you in some way—"

"I would get over it. All wives submit to their husbands. I wish to submit to you, my lord."

Percy swallowed, his eyes full of turbulence. "Are you…are you certain, Claire?"

"Yes, my lord."

Percy took a long, steadying breath. He swallowed so hard, his Adam's apple went up and down. "We will take this very slowly. If you wish to stop, I shall do my best to—"

"My only wish is for you to make me truly your wife."

Percy's light eyes darkened. In the faint glow of the lamp, he looked older, more of a man than the boy he had been when she had first met him. He took her into his arms and kissed her and she began to forget her fears. She wanted this. Wanted it so much.

Percy carefully undressed her, then carried her to his bed. He kissed her and touched her all over, spent hours making certain that she was ready to accept him, hours that filled her with joy and the most marvelous sensations. When his body joined with hers, there was only a moment of pain and then it was gone. Her body burned with heat and a wild sort of need that during the long and wondrous night, Percy filled.

As her sister had said, making love was wonderful.

But then, Tory was nearly always right about everything.

She hoped she was doing the right thing. Subtly flirting with Julian, never openly, of course. She didn't want to fire any untoward gossip.

Just occasionally, when she saw Cord looking her way and Julian happened to be near, which he made a point of doing, she would laugh or smile or ply her fan. She'd had little practice at flirting. She hoped she was doing it right but she wasn't really sure.

As Julian had promised, he cast her smoldering glances and graced her with sensuous smiles.

That night, Cord made very thorough love to her, as if he wished to claim her in some way. She was limp and sated, barely able to move when he finished. Before dawn, he took her again.

Lounging next to her on the bed, he wrapped a lock of her hair around one of his fingers. "I've decided to postpone my return until the end of the week. We can ride back to the city together."

She wanted to shout with glee, jump up and yell in triumph. Instead she kept her reply purposely casual. "Really? I thought you had work to do."

Cord's features darkened. "I had hoped you would be pleased."

Tory smiled, unable to hide her pleasure any longer. "I am very pleased, my lord."

But she didn't think Cord was convinced, and she thought that might be good.

Their last few days in the country passed far too

quickly. She spent most of her time with her husband, who seemed to enjoy himself almost as much as she did. They laughed together and took long strolls along the little stream that ran beside the manor. One day the entire party went into Tunbridge Wells to enjoy the mineral baths that were said to have healing properties.

"In the last century the place was a favorite of the *ton,*" Cord explained. "It was founded back in 1609 when Lord North discovered the chalybeate springs."

It was less popular now, but Tory and the others enjoyed themselves. Even Cord.

Then finally it was time to leave.

As she descended the stairs for the return trip to London, she chanced upon Julian in the entry. He looked unbelievably handsome in buckskin breeches and a dark green tailcoat. He winked as she approached, then leaned close.

"I believe our plan has succeeded. I have never seen a man behave more possessively toward his wife."

"You were wonderful, Julian." She wanted to give him a grateful kiss on the cheek but did not dare.

Julian inclined his head, turned and smiled as Cord walked up. "I hope you have a pleasant journey home, my lord."

"Thank you. The ride can be tiring, but I'm sure I can think of a way to entertain my wife along the road." The hot look he gave her said exactly the plans he had for her—right there in the carriage.

He was sending a message to Julian, a warning of sorts that she belonged to him. She couldn't help feeling a shot of exhilaration.

"Shall we go?" Cord took her arm and guided her

down the front porch stairs. He helped her into his traveling coach and she settled herself on the seat. She couldn't resist a last glance at Julian, who stood on the porch stairs watching them, a smile on his sensuous lips.

Tory bit back an answering smile that was nearly the exact opposite of the scowl on Cord's face.

"Enjoying the play, my love?" Cord leaned close and a tremor of awareness shot through Tory. They had been home from the country less than a week. Last night he had taken her to the opera and tonight they were attending *The Mistral's Journey*, the play at the Haymarket Theatre that Julian had told her about.

"Yes, very much. And you?"

"I am, indeed." He traced a finger along her cheek. "But I am enjoying your company far more."

A little thrill bubbled up inside. Her plan was working! Since their return, Cord had been wonderfully solicitous. They were having a marvelous time, Cord smiling more often, relaxed with her in a way he had never been before. She thought that his affection for her was growing, as she had so hoped it would.

Then a messenger arrived at their door.

"What is it?" Tory asked, walking up beside him in the entry.

He tossed the linkboy a vowel for his service and tore open the wax-sealed message he had received. "News of a mill I'm interested in buying in Lemming Grove. It looks like a marvelous opportunity. I've been hoping to purchase the business, improve working conditions and make a few other changes that will help increase profits. If I'm lucky, I'll be able to sell it for a considerably larger sum."

"Perhaps I could go with you," Tory offered, determined not to let their relationship slide back to where it had been before.

"Lemming Grove is a mill town. There isn't much to see. I'll be leaving late in the day, staying only one night. While I'm there, I'll be busy, and I'll be home again the next morning. Perhaps next time..."

Tory reluctantly gave in. It was only one night, after all. Besides, she had been thinking about what Greta had said about the property her family had once owned in Greenbower Street, just six or seven blocks away.

She had quietly made inquiries of Sir Winifred Manning, the man who had purchased the residence from her stepfather, and discovered he and his family were at present in the country. The house was closed up for the few weeks Sir Winifred would be gone. If she could find a way inside...

A memory arose of her husband's furious face when he had discovered her trip to Harwood Hall. Cord would be even angrier this time. Still, the house was nearby. She would only be gone a couple of hours.

She wasn't sure what she would find, but the baron had sold the house just as it was, so all of the furniture remained. She would recognize the pieces that had been in her mother's bedchamber and those in her sewing room, two of her favorite places. This time Cord wouldn't find out and even though he might, she had to take the risk.

As he had planned, Cord left for Lemming Grove late in the afternoon of the following day. Immediately after supper, Tory retired upstairs to her bedchamber. She changed into a simple rust-colored gown, removed her kidskin slippers and put on a pair of sturdy shoes.

She paced the floor for a while, waiting for the house to quiet, listening to the maddening tick of the clock and wishing the minutes would hurry past. Just before midnight, she opened the door, checked to be certain no one was about and headed down the servants' stairs at the back of the house.

Instead of hiring a hackney, she had decided to walk the seven blocks to the town house. Mayfair was the most elegant section of London, and as far as she was concerned, perfectly safe.

She was only a block from Greenbower Street when she heard the whir of carriage wheels behind her. She adjusted the shawl around her shoulders, lowered her head and kept on walking as the carriage drew near. Then she heard the crisp tones of authority, instructing the driver to pull over to the edge of the paving stones.

"For heaven's sake, Victoria, is that really you?" She recognized Julian's familiar voice floating toward her through the window of his very fashionable carriage, glossy black with yellow stripes round the fenders, pulled by matching gray horses. "What on earth are you doing out here all by yourself?"

With a sigh of resignation, she turned to face him. She had so hoped no one would see her.

"Good evening, Julian." She knew he lived in Mayfair, though not exactly where. It was just her luck to run into him. "I haven't time to explain. I'm on a rather important errand. I hope you won't mention you saw me."

One of his black eyebrows lifted in interest. "Of course I won't...as long as you tell me where you are going. I'm not about to leave you out here at this hour on your own."

Sweet Lord, just what she needed, another complication. "It's a long story, Julian."

The door of the carriage swung open, beckoning her in. "I have plenty of time. Your sister and Percy would have my head if I were to leave you unprotected at this hour of the evening and something untoward happened. You may as well tell me what sort of an errand takes a young woman into the streets in the middle of the night and accept the fact you are stuck with me until said errand is completed and you are safely returned to your home."

She could tell by the look on his face he wasn't going to change his mind. And she trusted Julian. He would keep his silence, no matter what she told him.

Lifting her skirt, she climbed into the carriage and settled herself on the seat across from him. Very concisely, she explained how her father had been murdered and conveyed her suspicions that the man to blame was his heir, Miles Whiting, Baron Harwood.

"I believe my mother may have uncovered the truth before she fell ill, but she died before she could do anything about it. If that is what happened, she would have written about it in her journal. All I have to do is find it."

"I see. And you think this journal might be somewhere in Sir Winifred's town house?"

"Yes."

Julian rapped on the roof with his silver-headed cane and instructed his driver to point the carriage toward Greenbower Street, then the coach turned down the alley at the rear.

Once they reached their destination, they departed the carriage together, made their way past the mews and began to search the back of the narrow two-story brick house for a way to get inside.

"Here," Julian said softly. "There's a window left unlatched. I'll go in, then come round and open the door for you."

She nodded, grateful he was willing to risk his reputation to help her, equally glad he was the one climbing over the sill and feeling only a trifle guilty when she heard the rip of fabric and Julian's soft-muttered curse.

A few minutes later she was standing inside the house, a small brass lamp burning to help light their way. The place looked much the same as she remembered, a cozy residence less concerned with fashion than comfort, with overstuffed chairs and glass-fronted cabinets filled with books. Julian held up the lamp and she followed him up the stairs.

"My mother's room was down at the end of the hall," she said softly. Though mostly Lady Harwood slept in the same room with Tory's father. She wished she and Cord shared that kind of closeness. "Her sewing room was right next door."

Memories flooded her: the warmth of her parents' laughter, she and Claire playing in front of the hearth, her father reading and her mother dabbling at writing poetry or making entries in her journal.

"Things might have changed since then," Julian said.

Yes, things were very different now, she thought, her mind running over the vast changes that had taken place in her life since her parents had died and she and Claire had been left at the mercy of her stepfather.

But as luck would have it, with the exception of new striped damask bed hangings, a new counterpane and thick Persian carpets, the room looked mostly as it had when last she was there.

Hurriedly, Tory searched each familiar piece of furniture, looking for a place that might hide something the size of the journal and not be discovered.

"Perhaps one of them found it," Julian said.

"I'm sure if they did, they would have returned it."

"Perhaps."

Whatever had happened to the diary, a very thorough search that expanded to possible places downstairs turned up nothing.

"It's time to go," Julian said gently. "Every moment we remain increases the risk of being discovered. I would prefer not to be arrested as a common thief."

She hated to leave without finding the journal, but they had covered the house fairly well and there was still the very real possibility the diary was somewhere at Windmere.

Shoving aside her disappointment, Tory followed Julian out of the house and back to the carriage. The conveyance returned her to Berkeley Square and she made her way back home, sneaking in the rear door and being careful not to be seen.

She was tired as she undressed without Emma's help and climbed up in bed, disappointed but not discouraged.

Windmere. The word whispered softly through her head. The beautiful Cotswold manor house on a hundred glorious acres of rolling hills and tumbling streams might still hold the key. The place she and her mother had loved—an estate that should have belonged to her and Claire.

Now that she had told Cord about the murder, perhaps he would help her find some way to search the house.

She sighed at the notion. Stealing into Windmere was scarcely something her husband would be willing to do.

Tory shuddered to think how furious he would be if he discovered she had broken into Sir Winifred's town house—accompanied by none other than Julian Fox—and prayed he would never find out.

Nineteen

Cord returned to London later than he meant to. The cotton mill needed more work than he had guessed, and the conditions the employees worked under bothered him.

Making money was important, but so were people's lives. He didn't want to increase his wealth at the expense of those less fortunate than he. In the end he decided against buying the business, and though he would have to work harder to make up for lost profits, he felt good about his decision.

And he was eager to get back home. Fortunately, this time when he arrived at the house, Victoria was waiting. She greeted him with a warm smile that turned into a look of surprise as he caught her round the waist and very thoroughly kissed her.

She responded with her usual abandon, pressing herself against him, leaving him hard when the long kiss ended and impatient to get her upstairs.

He had missed her, dammit. He should have taken her with him.

"I'm so glad you're home," she said, smiling up at him.

His gaze moved over her breasts and he noticed that her nipples had tightened. "Why don't you come upstairs and you can show me how much?"

She blushed and glanced toward the stairs. For a moment, she looked tempted, then she shook her head. "Grace is coming over. She'll be here any minute."

Cord nodded, but he wasn't happy about it. He noticed an errant dark curl at the nape of her neck and desire licked through him. He bent his head and kissed the spot. Perhaps once Grace had left…

His arousal still throbbed as he started up the stairs. If he couldn't have Victoria, he would change out of his wrinkled traveling clothes, then take a long, hot bath and relax. He tried not to think of his wife's luscious breasts and nicely curved bottom, but the image nagged him all the way to his bedchamber.

He was soaking in the copper bathing tub in his dressing room, trying to focus his thoughts on something other than his wife's delectable body, when he heard the sound of voices in the room next to his. Mrs. Rathbone conversing with one of the chambermaids. He settled himself more deeply in the tub he'd had made especially to fit his long frame, rested his head against the rim and closed his eyes.

He didn't mean to eavesdrop, but when he heard his wife's name, his eyes popped open and he sat up in the tub.

"I was gettin' ready for bed when I saw her slippin' down the back stairs," Mrs. Rathbone said, her rusty voice loud enough to carry through the walls. "Went out the back door, she did, must have been just afore midnight. 'Twas some past two in the mornin' when I heard her come back in."

The pressure was building in his chest. Cord couldn't seem to breathe for the lead weight that had settled there.

The chambermaid's voice was softer, harder to hear. "Ye don't think 'er ladyship were meetin' another man?"

"His lordship found her on the street, didn't he? Who knows what kinda woman she is."

The women said more, but he couldn't hear. They finished their cleaning and left the room, closing the door behind them. Cord sat in the tub unable to move, his mind numbed by the things he had heard. Eventually, the water turned cold enough to pierce his stunned senses and he abandoned the tub, dripping water on the floor as he toweled himself dry, all the while thinking of Victoria.

His wife had gone out of the house late last night, using the back stairs to avoid being seen. She had been absent several hours before returning home. The last time he had left town, she had also gone out—had traveled to Harwood Hall, she had said.

But had she actually gone in search of her mother's diary? Or had she gone off with Julian Fox for a lovers' tryst?

His stomach knotted. The pressure on his chest turned almost painful. He had tried to keep his feelings in control where Victoria was concerned.

It was obvious how miserably he had failed.

Cord dressed to go out and summoned his carriage. He left word for Victoria that he had an errand to run and made his way down the front porch stairs, passing the seated lions on his way to the carriage. He instructed his driver to head for Bow Street, then leaned back in the seat, hoping Jonas McPhee would be working in his office.

Cord had to know the truth, and confronting Victoria wouldn't help him find it. She had lied to him before, lied to him since the moment she had met him. If she hadn't lied about who she was, he never would have made love to her. He never would have taken her innocence and never been forced to marry her. She had deceived him again and again. How could he believe her now?

Anger swelled inside him. If Victoria had betrayed him with Fox... He forced himself to stay calm. McPhee would sort through the facts and ferret out the truth. He would discover if Victoria had actually gone to Harwood Hall, perhaps even find out where she had been last night.

In the meantime, as difficult as it might prove to be, he would pretend that nothing was wrong. He would treat her with the courtesy she deserved as his wife and pray that his fears proved false.

Should his physical need of her arise, he would not deny himself. But he would be careful to distance himself from his feelings, protect himself and insulate his heart.

As he now painfully realized he had utterly failed to do.

Tory sighed as she moved through the house on her way to a meeting with Mrs. Gray to go over the menus for the week. Except for the night she had sneaked out of the house, lately her life had been so boring she almost envied Mrs. Gray her housekeeping job.

Last night was the third evening in a row that Cord had left the house on some sort of business matter.

Afterward, he had stopped by his club for a hand or two of cards, or so he said this morning. Days like today, he rarely came out of his study unless he had somewhere to go, and he had come to her bed only once. Their coupling had been brief and unsatisfying and he hadn't joined her there again.

Tory paused outside the door to the kitchen, enjoying the smell of fresh-baked bread seeping into the hallway. After their return from the country, for a time her relationship with Cord had improved. But since his return from Lemming Grove, he had become more remote than ever, and even their occasional lovemaking felt distant and empty, as if he kept himself carefully apart from her.

It was growing more and more difficult to believe his affections might ever deepen into love.

"I've a list of suggestions for the week, my lady," Mrs. Gray said, bustling toward her. "Perhaps we could use the breakfast room to go over them." It was a gentle reminder. Mrs. Gray ran the world downstairs. She didn't think a countess should lower herself by becoming involved in such menial affairs.

Tory didn't tell her she often felt more comfortable below stairs than she did in the lonely world she lived in with the earl.

Still, she made her way to the main floor of the house, Mrs. Gray close behind her. Beginning to believe her marriage would forever be a loveless one, she had started to think of children to fill the emptiness inside her.

If she couldn't have Cord's love, perhaps she could have his child. She prayed a son or daughter would soon be growing in her womb.

Then she thought again how remote he had become, how he had even begun to stay away from her bed, and sighed to think that even the gift of a child might be denied her.

Cord stared out the window of his carriage as it rolled through the crowded streets. An hour ago, he had received a message from Jonas McPhee, requesting a meeting at his earliest convenience. Cord had replied that he would be there at eleven o'clock.

More than a week had passed since his journey to Lemming Grove and his wife's midnight rendezvous, if that was what it had been. Time enough, apparently, for McPhee to have done his job.

Anxious to reach the runner's office, Cord swore at some sort of delay. Turning his gaze to the window, he saw a regiment of soldiers marching past, decked out in scarlet-and-white uniforms. A dozen cavalry officers, mounted on high-stepping blacks, accompanied them, temporarily blocking the street. Watching them pass, Cord couldn't help thinking of Ethan, wondering if he had been returned to the prison he had escaped from or been moved somewhere else, wondering if his cousin even still lived.

And if he did, would they ever find a way to free him before this long, bloody war was over?

But Ethan slipped to the back of his mind as the carriage again rolled toward Bow Street. Cord had prepared himself for his meeting with Jonas McPhee. Still, he was filled with dread as McPhee opened the door to his small, cluttered office and invited Cord to take a seat in front of his desk.

"I am afraid the news isn't good, my lord." With his balding head and wire-rimmed spectacles, Jonas McPhee looked little like a man who spent his days hunting criminals, delving into the darker side of London. But his shoulders were muscled and his hands knotted and scarred, reflecting the dangerous work he often did.

"Whatever you have to say, say it."

Seated behind his battered desk, McPhee glanced down at the sheet of papers in his hand. "In regard to the first incident you asked me to look into, your wife's supposed visit to Harwood Hall. According to the servants, her ladyship was never there."

His chest constricted. He had told himself he was prepared for whatever news McPhee had to convey. Now he realized he wasn't prepared at all. "I take it you spoke to more than just one of them."

"That is correct." He looked down at the paper. "Specifically, a housekeeper named Greta Simon and the butler, Samuel Sims. I spoke to one of the chambermaids as well."

"And the baron? Where was he when you called?"

"Lord Harwood is still in London."

"Any chance my wife could have been in the house and no one knew she was there?"

"The servants seemed very certain, my lord."

He told himself to stay calm. He knew how clever Victoria could be. "What else did you find out?"

"You mentioned a man named Julian Fox in connection with your wife. I did some checking. Fox owns a town house in Mayfair. I located his residence and spoke to one of his footmen, greased his palm a bit, you understand. I'm sorry to tell you that the footman said that sometime round midnight of the night in question, Mr. Fox picked up a lady a few blocks from Berkeley Square, the location of your residence. The woman's description matched that of Lady Brant."

Cord's stomach balled into a painful fist. "Go on."

"The coachman was instructed to carry the two of them down the alley behind a house in Greenbower Street. Mr. Fox and the lady departed the coach and went in through the rear of the house. They were inside for more than an hour. Afterward, Fox ordered the driver to return them to Berkeley Square. The lady left the carriage and disappeared into one of the houses down the block, presumably yours."

His chest squeezed. There were other questions he wanted to ask, but he couldn't bear to hear the answers. "I presume you have all of this down in your report."

"Yes, my lord."

"And a bill for your fee is included as well?"

McPhee nodded and handed over the file.

"I'll have a bank draft sent over first thing in the morning."

"Thank you, my lord. I wish the news had been better."

Cord's fingers tightened around the file. "So do I."

Turning away from the runner, he forced himself to walk calmly out of the office. As soon as he gained the privacy of his carriage, he dropped down heavily on the seat, his head in his hands. His wife was involved with another man.

She was having an affair with Julian Fox.

Despair and loss washed over him. They had only been married such a very short while and already he had lost her. His eyes burned. He hadn't understood until that moment how much she meant to him. How could he have let down his guard? How could he have been such a fool?

Then the anguish and grief he was feeling began to change direction, turn into a simmering rage and a feeling of bitter betrayal.

How dare she! He had been faithful to Victoria since the day they were wed. Bloody hell, since the night he had stormed into her below-stairs bedchamber, he had never had the least desire for another woman.

And she had wanted him, too. Victoria was a vibrant, passionate young woman. He had introduced her to pleasure and she had enjoyed every damned minute.

Then Fox had come along. Cord itched to call him out, to shoot the man for stealing his wife. Victoria was his! She belonged to him, dammit! But Fox had been handsome and charming, flattering her and—

Cord paused mid-thought. *Flattering her and paying her attention.* Squiring her all over London, to the opera, the theater, escorting her to lavish balls. Fox had danced with her and dined with her and laughed with her, while Cord had been holed up in his study, thinking of ways to avoid her. He couldn't even manage time enough for a single game of chess.

The knot in his stomach twisted. Knowing Victoria as he did, he knew with certainty this wasn't a casual affair. Her affections had to be involved—Victoria had to be in love with Julian Fox.

He thought of the months since their marriage. Never once had she told him she loved him or said anything that remotely implied she felt that kind of affection for him. Perhaps if he'd had the slightest suspicion how deeply his feelings ran for her….

But he hadn't known then. At least he hadn't admitted it to himself. Not until now. Not until it was too late.

For the first time it occurred to him that, in truth, he was the one who had insisted they marry. He had *forced* Victoria to wed him. First he had bullied her, then he had tricked her. He had always had a way with women and he knew Victoria desired him. Aside from that, she needed him to protect her. It never occurred to him that he was pushing her to do something she really didn't want to do.

All the way back to the town house, he considered his options. Victoria was in love with another man. Fox was Percy's cousin, nephew to the marquess of Kersey. The family had plenty of money. Fox could take care of her.

Acid swirled in his stomach. Victoria was everything to him. He couldn't imagine life without her. Still, it wasn't fair to keep her locked in a marriage she had never really wanted.

Cord leaned back in the carriage seat, his chest aching, his stomach tied in knots. It was blazingly clear he had committed the unpardonable. He had allowed himself to fall in love.

It was a stupid, idiotic thing to do.

The only thing worse would be to stay married to a woman who didn't love him in return.

Twenty

Victoria hadn't seen Cord all day. Supper was over and he still had not come home. She was beginning to worry. A storm was coming in and she didn't like the idea of him being out in the rain. Then she heard masculine footfalls in the entry and felt a wave of relief.

She walked in to greet him, noticed the hard look on his face, and her relief turned into a sharp stab of fear.

"What is it, Cord? What's wrong?"

"I need a word with you. Perhaps upstairs would be best."

Her heart was beating oddly. She had never seen quite that look on his face. She climbed the stairs ahead of him, went into her room, and he followed her in and closed the door. She searched his eyes for any sign of what he might be thinking, but they remained shuttered and hard.

"You might want to sit down."

He didn't have to ask twice. Her legs were shaking. Something was dreadfully wrong and she couldn't imagine what it was. She walked over to the small settee in the sitting room and sank down onto the seat.

"I've been to see a man named Jonas McPhee, an investigator of sorts. I've worked with him a number of times before."

"I believe you mentioned him...the man who discovered that Claire and I were Miles Whiting's stepdaughters."

"That is correct."

"Why...why did you go see him?"

"There were things I needed to know...things I hoped Mr. McPhee would be able to find out for me."

Dear God, had he discovered that she had broken into Sir Winifred's town house? Had McPhee found out she had been with Julian Fox? She told herself to stay calm, perhaps that wasn't it at all.

"What sort of things did you wish to know?"

Cord walked over and poured himself a brandy. "Would you like one? You're looking a little pale."

She moistened her lips. "I am fine." But she wasn't fine at all.

Cord took a drink of his brandy, swirled the amber liquid in his glass. He was so calm. Unnervingly so. Her fear inched up another notch.

"I had some questions about my wife."

"Your wife," she repeated, barely able to force out the words.

"Yes, and in that regard, McPhee was very helpful. To begin with he informed me you were never at Harwood Hall."

Her stomach turned completely over. "That isn't true!"

"Isn't it? Jonas spoke to the butler as well as the

housekeeper and one of the chambermaids. You were never there, Victoria."

"The servants…th-they are my friends. They were sworn to keep their silence."

He swirled his brandy. "And then there was the matter of the night I was away in Lemming Grove. You were gone that night, as well."

She fought to draw in air. How had McPhee found out? How could he possibly have known? "I can explain."

"Really? Why don't you, then?"

Why wasn't he shouting? Why wasn't he raging at her, telling her how he meant to throttle her or at least lock her up in her room? This deadly calm was worse than anything she had ever faced before.

She took a deep breath, released it slowly. "This is all very easily explained. When I was at Harwood Hall, Greta—that is the housekeeper you mentioned—she said something about the town house my family once owned in London. She said that perhaps Mother's journal might still be somewhere inside."

"Ah—the elusive journal. I should have guessed."

"The town house is in Greenbower Street, which isn't all that far. I knew you wouldn't approve, so I decided to go by myself. I left here just before midnight." She looked at Cord.

Should she mention Julian Fox? If she did and he didn't already know, he would be even more upset than he was already. Her mind spun, trying to think if McPhee could have somehow found out, thinking she owed it to Julian to keep her silence.

"I—I walked the few blocks to the town house and I was lucky enough to find a window open behind the house." She tried to smile. "My stepfather sold the place to a man named Sir Winifred Manning, but Sir Winifred was out of town. I made a search of the residence, but—"

"But again, unfortunately, you came up empty-handed."

"Yes."

"That's a shame, Victoria. Perhaps if you'd had someone along to help you, you would have been successful. Someone, perhaps, like Julian Fox."

She nearly swooned. For an instant, dark circles swirled in front of her eyes. Maybe for a moment she did swoon, for when she opened her eyes, Cord was pressing his glass of brandy against her lips.

"Take a drink, Victoria. In a second or two, you'll feel better."

She swallowed, felt the quick burn of the liquor as it raced down her throat. "This…this isn't what you think. Julian and I—we met simply by chance. He lives in Mayfair, you see, and he was in his carriage, on his way home. He saw me on the street and he wouldn't leave until I told him what I was planning to do and then he wouldn't let me go alone."

"I'm sure Mr. Fox is extremely protective."

"Yes, he is. We are friends, after all. He didn't want anything untoward to happen to me."

He was standing over her, dark and imposing, looking down at her as if she were someone he barely knew. She had to reach him. She couldn't stand the remote, completely unreachable expression on his face.

She closed the distance between them, took the glass from his hand, reached up and slid her arms around his neck. The fragrance of his cologne drifted over her. His dark hair teased her fingers. She pressed her face into the hollow between his neck and shoulder and felt the rapid pulse beating there.

Not nearly as calm as he seemed.

"I'm sorry I lied to you," she said. "I shouldn't have done it. I should have told you the truth but I was afraid of what you would say. I knew you would be angry." She leaned toward him, pressed her lips to the side of his neck, raised on tiptoe and kissed him. Cord made no response, just stood there unmoving, his hands hanging limp at his sides.

It was frightening.

Terrifying.

She kissed him again, coaxed his lips apart and slid her tongue over his. She pressed herself more fully against him and felt the reassuring hardness of his arousal. He wanted her. Just as he always did.

"Victoria…" he said, and there was anguish in his voice. Dear God, what had she done? She hadn't meant to hurt him. She loved him. Somehow she had to make amends.

"I'm so sorry, Cord." She pressed small butterfly kisses to the corners of his mouth, kissed him deeply again. Using the little erotic tricks he had taught her, she slid her tongue over his, teasing him, urging him to respond. "I should have told you the truth. I wish so badly that I had. I won't ever lie to you again. I swear it."

He seemed not to hear her. His body remained rigid and unyielding. She thought he meant to push her away.

Her hands were shaking. Frantically, she slid his coat off his shoulders, worked the buttons on his silver waistcoat, pushed it off and tossed it away. Capturing his face between her palms, she dragged his mouth down to hers for another scorching kiss.

Still, he seemed reluctant. She tugged his shirt from the waistband of his breeches and hastily unfastened the buttons, desperate to touch him, to break through his terrifying calm. He wasn't helping, but he didn't resist when she pulled off his shirt and pressed her mouth against the bare skin just above his heart.

She could taste the salty tang of him, feel the ripple of muscle and sinew when he moved. He was breathing hard, his wide chest heaving in and out. She ran her tongue around a flat copper nipple, used her teeth to nip the end.

Still, he didn't reach for her.

Four tiny buttons closed up the front of her high-waisted gown. She swiftly unbuttoned them, lifted one of his big hands and slid it inside her chemise to cup a breast. Her nipple hardened and she heard Cord groan.

"Victoria, this isn't going to change—"

She silenced him with a kiss, even more frightened than before. She took his hand and led him toward the bed, urged him to sit down on the edge. He seemed so weary, too exhausted to protest when she knelt and removed his shoes, then began to work the buttons at the front of his breeches. His shaft sprang free, thick and swollen, more eager for her than he seemed to be. In minutes, she had stripped him of his clothes and removed her own.

Still, he didn't reach for her.

Dear God, he had always been so passionate, so fierce in his lovemaking. Something was terribly, terribly wrong. She kissed him and kissed him, hoping he could feel her love for him, praying she could somehow heal the pain she had caused him.

She nearly wept when she felt his hands on her breasts, giving in to his desire for her at last. His mouth followed his hands and he began to suckle her there, filling her with heat and need and an overwhelming love for him.

Tory arched her back, giving him better access. When he made no further move to take her, she blinked against the tears that burned her eyes, urged him back on the bed and followed him down, kissing him and kissing him, determined to show him how much she loved him.

Tory gasped as his big hands wrapped around her waist and he lifted her and settled her astride him. His eyes found hers and the pain in them nearly tore her apart.

"I'm so sorry," she said. "So sorry."

He whispered her name and the sound, filled with such sadness, was more alarming than anything that had gone before. Reaching up, she pulled the pins from her hair, let it tumble down around her bare shoulders. Cord lifted a hand and ran his fingers through it, spreading it around her.

"I always loved your hair," he said, and she thought she heard a catch in his voice.

Lifting her again, he eased himself inside her, lowering her slowly, until he filled her completely. He was joined with her, part of her, and no matter what happened, she knew he always would be. Her hair swung forward, enveloping them in a silky cocoon as she bent her head and kissed him. She loved him. She wanted to give him the kind of pleasure he had always given to her.

She drew herself up, then slowly sank back down, trying to find the rhythm, determined to please him. She could feel the muscles in his body tighten, feel the strength of him each time she moved.

Her own pleasure built. Heat and need rushed through her, mixed with her desire and her fear of losing him. Cord gripped her hips, began to thrust deeply inside her, and pleasure washed through her, quaked through her limbs. Love for him swelled in her heart. Combined with his powerful thrusts, it sent her over the edge.

Seconds later, Cord followed her to release. Limp and sated, she sank down on his chest, praying that at last he would forgive her.

For a moment, she must have fallen asleep. When she awakened, Cord stood next to the bed, almost fully dressed. He fastened the buttons on his cuffs and dragged his jacket on over his waistcoat.

"That wasn't necessary, Victoria," he said coolly, his maddening calm back in place. "But I'll admit it made for a pleasant parting interlude."

The fear returned, so strong it threatened to choke her. "What are you talking about?"

"I'm talking about ending this sham of a marriage. The paperwork to begin annulment proceedings is already under way. If all goes well, in a few short months, both of us will be free."

"You're…you're going to set aside our marriage?"

"You should be pleased, sweeting. Once you gain your freedom, you can have your Mr. Fox."

She swallowed, tried to make her mind work, struggled against the hot burn of tears. "I don't want Julian. I never have. I told you, we are only just friends."

Cord straightened his jacket and shot his cuffs. "I wish you the best, my dear, I truly do." Turning away from her, he started for the door.

"Cord, wait!" Tory dragged the sheet around her and raced after him, frantically gripped his arm to stop him before he escaped. "Please don't do this. I know I shouldn't have lied to you. I should have trusted you with the truth. I...I love you, Cord."

His golden eyes turned to flint. "Odd that you never thought to say so before. Perhaps being a countess holds more appeal than I thought."

"I don't care about your title! I never did!"

A corner of his mouth edged up. "Lucky for Mr. Fox." And then he closed the door.

Tory collapsed on the floor in front of the door in a tangle of bedsheets and chestnut hair. Great sobs tore from her throat and shook her body. She cried for hours, cried until she had no more tears. In the room next door, she could hear her husband moving around, speaking to his valet, then the closing of the door. He was leaving her, setting aside their marriage.

He could do it. He was an earl and a powerful man.

And why shouldn't he? She had lied to him from the moment she had met him. Lied to him time and time again. The years she had spent with her stepfather had made her wary of other people and particularly of men.

But she had come to trust her husband. And she loved him more than life itself. She had wanted to make him jealous, wanted to make him love her in return. Now he believed she had betrayed him with Julian Fox.

She had to prove her innocence, had to find a way to convince him.

She would ask Julian to help her, to explain to Cord that nothing had happened. Surely Cord would believe him. But Julian had left London to visit an ailing relative in York. She had no idea when he might return, and even if he did, she wasn't sure what would happen should the two men come face-to-face.

Thoughts swirled like flotsam round and round inside her head. She had to think clearly, had to figure out which path to take. She was madly in love with her husband and she couldn't bear to lose him.

Cord planned to leave town, to spend some time at Riverwoods, to forget Victoria and his failure as a husband. At the moment, he simply wanted out of the house, away from his wife, away from the memory of her kisses, of her softness, of how sweet she had felt in his arms.

Grabbing his high beaver hat on the way out the door, he climbed aboard his carriage and headed straight for his club. For the next several hours, he sat by himself and quietly got drunk.

It was sometime after midnight that he stumbled upstairs into one of the guest rooms, a place he could stay without speculation as to why he hadn't gone home.

In the world of the aristocracy where marriages were mostly arranged, couples often felt little real affection for each other. They lived separately so each could carry on his or her private affairs.

Surprisingly, Cord had no desire to begin such an affair. His heart was badly battered, and after losing Victoria he didn't feel the least desire for a woman.

Except his wife, of course, and she was the one

woman he could not have. He tried not to think of their last frantic coupling, the desperation, the sadness that seemed to surround them both as their bodies joined one final time. He hadn't meant for it to happen, never considered that it would.

But he was attracted to Victoria as he had never been to another woman, and her innocent seduction had been impossible to resist.

He envied Fox.

Thinking of Victoria's lover, his hand balled into a fist. The image arose of Julian caressing her beautiful breasts, spending himself in her luscious body, and Cord's stomach churned. He closed his eyes to block the image and crossed his small, rented, upstairs guest room to the dresser. Lifting the stopper off a decanter of brandy, he poured himself a glass.

He was drinking too much, but he didn't care. He drained the glass and filled it again and took another long mind-numbing swallow. The liquor dulled the pain, but only a little, not enough to make him forget.

The week crept past. It was time he went home and got his things together, made plans for his stay at Riverwoods. He tried not to think whether Victoria would be there at the house or if she had gone off with her lover.

Lucky for Fox, the man had been away during those first wild moments when Cord had discovered his wife's affair. According to McPhee's report, Fox was on his way to his family estate in York. If the man had been in London, he would have been facing a duel, or a horsewhipping at the very least.

Fortunately, Cord's common sense had finally returned. He had accepted the unpleasant fact that he was the one who had betrayed Victoria, not the other way around. He had left his bride alone and lonely, keeping her at a safe distance, except when they were in bed.

If only he could do things over. He would tell her the way he felt, admit that he loved her. Better still, he would show her. He would spend every second he could with her, do whatever it took to make her happy and erase the lonely expression he had so often seen on her face.

Why had he done it? Why had he been so afraid to let himself love her?

But in his heart he knew. He'd been thirteen years old when his mother had died, a slow, agonizing death that took weeks and had nearly destroyed him. He'd been tortured by her suffering and his inability to help her. He'd hated himself for not being stronger, not being tougher. He should have been able to handle the loss instead of letting it tear him apart.

But he had learned his lesson. In the years that followed, he had learned to insulate himself from his feelings, to protect himself so he wouldn't be hurt that way again. He had taken the easy way out. He had indulged the wild side of his nature, immersed himself in his hedonistic pleasures. He had become so wrapped up in himself that he had failed his father when he needed Cord the most.

Now he had failed his wife.

Cord made his way downstairs to the card room. It was time to go home, to leave the sanctuary of the club and prepare for his trip to the country.

Soon, he told himself.

But instead of leaving, he headed for one of the big

overstuffed leather chairs in front of the hearth. He was about to sit down when he spotted the duke of Sheffield walking toward him. He wasn't certain if he should be glad to see his friend, or dread the coming conversation.

"I went by your house," Rafe said. "When no one seemed to know where you were, I figured I might find you here. Mind if I join you?"

Cord nodded his head. "Though I should probably warn you, I'm not the best company."

Rafe signaled to a waiter, and a few seconds later had a glass of brandy in his hand. They sat down in the big leather chairs, for the moment by themselves.

"You look like hell," Rafe said, swirling the liquor in his glass.

"Thanks."

"There's talk on the street. Rumor has it you are filing annulment papers."

Cord sat up straighter in his chair. "How the hell could anyone know that?"

"A talkative clerk, perhaps. Or one of your servants overheard something that was said. I presume you've told Victoria."

"I've told her." Cord looked down at the brandy he held in his hand but didn't take a drink. "You were right about Fox and Victoria. I had Jonas McPhee look into the matter."

Rafe's blue eyes narrowed. "Are you certain? I rather thought your wife was in love with you."

Cord glanced away, wishing it were true. "It's my fault. I virtually ignored her. I practically drove her into the arms of another man."

Rafe took a drink of his brandy. "Damned women.

They get at you one way or another." Cord knew he was thinking of Danielle, the girl he'd been engaged to marry. Rafe had found her in one of his closest friend's bed. He had never gotten over the betrayal.

"As I said, the fault was mine. From the start of the marriage, I handled things poorly. Hell, even before we were wed."

"Perhaps. Still, I can't credit a woman giving up on a man so soon. Particularly one with whom she seemed so thoroughly in love."

"Victoria never loved me. Perhaps, for a time, she thought she did."

"What about you? Did you love her?"

He sipped his drink, thinking of the night he had confronted her in his study over moving the pieces on his chessboard and she had soundly trounced him in the match.

"I loved her almost from the start. I was a fool, Sheffield. I deserve exactly what I got."

Rafe made no reply.

"If you don't mind, I think I'll go on up and get some sleep." It was only nine o'clock, but he felt bone-tired.

"This will pass, my friend," Rafe said gently. "There are other women to love."

But Rafe had yet to find one.

And Cord didn't think he would, either.

Tory tried to pretend her life was normal. She had been lonely before, even with Cord in the house.

She was completely miserable without him.

Little more than a week had passed since he had moved out, but it seemed more like years. She hadn't told anyone about the annulment. Not Gracie, not even Claire. Eventually, she would have to say something. Once the filing was posted in the newspaper, everyone in London would know.

When Claire burst through the front door unexpectedly that afternoon, Tory was certain her sister had found out. Dear God, the filing must be public. He stomach squeezed as Timmons announced her sister's arrival. Tory pasted on a smile and went to greet her.

"Tory!" Claire was grinning so broadly, a dimple appeared in her cheek. "The most wonderful thing has happened!"

It was hardly the greeting she had expected. It was stupid to feel relief that the end had not yet truly come.

"Calm down, darling." She took Claire's hand, led her into the drawing room and closed the door. With Cord away, there was enough gossip in the house already. "All right, now. Tell me what has got you so excited."

"It's Percy. He loves me! I was so afraid he had only married me out of pity." She released a tinkling laugh. "Last night he said he loves me so much sometimes he simply can't breathe. He said he looks at me and love fills him to overflowing. I told him I loved him, too, and he kissed me, and it was so wonderful, Tory."

Tory opened her mouth to tell Claire how happy she was for her, but a choking sound came out instead. Her eyes filled with tears and a great sob tore loose from somewhere deep inside her. Her legs went weak and she feared they would buckle beneath her.

"Tory!" Claire caught her round the waist and helped her over to the sofa. Tory sank down, holding on to her sister for support.

"What is it, Tory? Dear God, what has happened?"

The tears just kept coming. Claire hastily dug into her reticule and pulled out one of her pretty lace handkerchiefs.

Tory accepted the cloth and wiped at her tears, trying to find the right words. "Cord has left me."

"What are you talking about? Cord is your husband. He can't just leave."

She closed her eyes, but moisture leaked from beneath her lashes. "I wanted to make him love me. I thought if I made him jealous...if he believed other men found me attractive, perhaps his affections would grow." She sniffed back a fresh round of tears. "Julian agreed to help me. We both...both thought it was a good idea at the time."

She told Claire all that had happened, how Cord believed she had never gone to Harwood, how the servants had lied to protect her and wound up convincing him that she had never been there at all. She told Claire about going to their old family town house in Greenbower Street and how she had run into Julian and he had gone with her and how Cord had found out they were together and thought it was a lovers' tryst.

Claire squeezed her hand. "It's going to be all right, Tory. You can straighten all of this out. You just have to find a way to make Cord see you are telling the truth. Go to Harwood and bring Greta back. She can tell Cord that you really were there."

"He won't believe her. He'll think I paid her or something."

"Perhaps Percy and I could speak to him. We could tell him you and Julian are only just friends."

"He would simply think you were too naive to see the truth."

"Then you must write to Julian. Ask him to come back and explain."

Tory only shook her head. "At first, I considered doing all of those things. I believed I could find a way to prove my innocence and everything would be all right. Then I realized that maybe this happened for a reason."

"Reason? What kind of reason?"

She dragged in a shaky breath. "Don't you see? Perhaps this is the perfect opportunity for Cord to escape the marriage. He wanted to marry an heiress, not a woman who came to him without a farthing. This is his chance, Claire."

She had known the truth from the start. If he hadn't been forced to marry her, Cord would have wed Constance Fairchild or any of a number of eligible women. Half the young ladies of the *ton* had been devastated to learn the earl of Brant had married a nobody from the country.

"Once he has his freedom," she finished, "Cord can have the woman he wanted before I trapped him the way I did."

Claire put her arms around her. "You didn't mean to trap him. Sometimes things just happen."

Tory rested her head on her younger sister's shoulder. Claire was growing up. She was a woman now. A wife. If felt good to have someone to talk to.

"I have to let him go, Claire. Cord deserves to be happy. He was never happy with me. He did everything he could to stay away from me." Tears welled again.

Tory cried against her sister's shoulder and felt Claire's slender body shaking.

Tory knew that her sister was crying, too.

Twenty-One

It was late in the afternoon, a gray, cloudy day that hinted at the coming of a storm. The dismal weather exactly fit Tory's mood.

She sighed as she walked out of the drawing room, trying not to notice how empty the house felt without her husband's presence. She was headed for the entry when the sound of men's voices drifted toward her. For an instant, she thought it might be Cord and her heart took a leap.

Instead, Timmons spoke to Colonel Pendleton, who stood stiffly in front of him. The colonel turned at her approach and his face looked grim.

"Lady Brant." He made a polite bow, the light of the chandelier reflecting off his silver hair and the gold epaulettes on his shoulders. "I apologize for the intrusion, my lady. I come in search of your husband."

Her insides painfully twisted. In the weeks ahead, how many more times would she face such a moment?

"I'm sorry, Colonel. At present, my husband is not at home."

"Do you know where I might find him? I bring urgent information regarding Captain Sharpe."

She shook her head, not having the slightest idea where her husband might be. Or with whom.

"I'm sorry, Colonel. You might look for him at the home of his friend the duke or perhaps he is at White's, his gentlemen's club. You may certainly leave word for him here." Not that he was likely to get it, since she had no idea when or if he might return.

"Thank you. I would appreciate if you would tell him the news is urgent. Ask him to get in touch with me as soon as he possibly can."

"Of course. Is there anything else I can do?"

"I'm afraid not, my lady. Except, perhaps, to remember the captain in your prayers." Turning, the colonel strode out of the house, leaving Tory to worry what terrible things might be happening to Cord's cousin.

It was evening, a light drizzle dampening the ground outside the house, when she heard Timmons speaking to another man. She recognized her husband's deep baritone and her heart leaped, his familiar masculine drawl filling her with longing.

She stood frozen in the hall, drinking in the sight of his tall, athletic frame and beloved features, aching to feel his arms around her.

Then she remembered the colonel's urgent news and forced her feet to move along the passage. Cord started up the stairs, his foot pausing on a step near the bottom when he saw her.

"Good evening, my lord."

"I won't be here long. I only stopped by to pack a few

things. I'm leaving for the country in the morning." He started climbing again.

"Colonel Pendleton was here," she said hastily. "He is looking for you. He has urgent news of your cousin."

Cord turned and came back down the stairs. "Did he tell you what the news might be?"

She shook her head. "I'm afraid not. I think he wanted to impart the information himself."

The muscles across his shoulders subtly tightened.

"I don't think Captain Sharpe is dead," she told him, reading his thoughts. "I think it was something else."

"I pray you are right." He turned toward the door, and she had never wanted anything so much as to go with him.

Cord lifted the latch and started out, but stopped abruptly as he spotted Rafe and the colonel striding up the walk. Stepping back, Cord waited as they moved past him into the entry.

"Thank God you're here," Rafe said.

"I've been trying to find you," the colonel explained. "I stopped by to see His Grace in the hope he might know where you were. He had only just left you at the club. He said that he thought that you were on your way here."

"Ethan's in trouble," Rafe said, cutting to the point. "We haven't got much time."

"What's happened?"

Colonel Pendleton answered. "I'm afraid the captain is scheduled to be executed the day after the morrow."

"Bloody hell."

"Word from Bradley should have arrived two days ago, but a storm blew up and the ship was delayed. The note just got here this afternoon."

"We'll have to sail tonight," Rafe said. "Fortunately,

the *Nightingale* is in port. We swung by the docks on our way over here. The good news is Ethan's been returned to the prison in Calais. If we can get him out, he won't have far to go to reach the ship."

"That is good news. He may not be in shape to make too long a journey."

"We'll take the surgeon along, just in case," Rafe said. "He came in handy the last time."

The men continued speaking, their conversation so urgent they seemed to have forgot that Tory was there.

"I'm afraid there's another problem," the colonel said. "In his former efforts, Max Bradley always had a plan. The decision to execute the captain came up so quickly we have no choice but to make the attempt without the usual preparations. He says he is going to need help. A couple of men and someone who can provide a diversion."

"A diversion," Cord repeated. "What the devil kind of diversion?"

"Someone to distract the guards so that Bradley and the men can get inside the prison."

"Perhaps we can find a woman," Rafe suggested. "Nothing diverts a man's interest like a pretty bit of muslin."

"She would have to speak French and be someone we could trust," Pendleton added.

"There isn't time to find someone like that," Cord said. "We'll have to think of something once we're aboard the ship."

"I could do it." Heart pounding, Tory stepped out of the shadows, drawing startled looks from the men.

Cord scowled in her direction, obviously unhappy to find her still there. "Don't be ridiculous."

"It isn't the least ridiculous. I speak flawless French. I could dress as a young woman in from the country, a lady who wishes to inquire of…of her brother, perhaps. She is desperate. She pleads with the guards to let her inside the prison or at least provide some information as to his welfare."

"What if they agree to let you in?" Rafe asked, eyeing her with speculation.

"Then I shall have to stall them until one of you can come to my rescue."

"No," Cord said flatly. "I'm not about to put you in that sort of danger. Not even for Ethan."

"Please, Cord, I can do this. I want to help."

"I said no and that is the end of it."

Tory gently touched his arm. "You don't have time to find someone else, Cord." She wanted to do this, to give him the one thing he truly wanted. "So much has happened these past few weeks. Give me this chance to make things right."

He started to shake his head, but Rafe clamped a hand on his shoulder. "We need her, Cord. One of us will keep an eye on her. If anything goes wrong, we'll get her out of there in a hurry and back aboard the ship."

A muscle ticked in Cord's cheek.

"It's Ethan's life," she reminded him softly. "It's worth the risk."

It was clear he didn't want her along, but finally he nodded. "All right, she can come, but I stay close enough to make sure she doesn't get hurt and that she gets back safely."

"Done," Rafe said.

The colonel offered the use of a couple more men, but

Cord declined. This was Ethan's last chance. Too many men might be worse than too few, and Cord and Rafe believed they could handle the job better themselves.

"At least you'll have Bradley along. He knows every nook and cranny of that prison. He spent nearly a year there before he was able to escape."

And he had risked himself again in his efforts to save Ethan. It said a good deal about Max Bradley's character.

"Well, that's it, then," Pendleton said once everything was settled. While Cord went to change and collect the gear he needed, Tory ran up to her room and began to dig through her trunks, looking for the worn, dove-gray gown she had been wearing the day she had come to the earl of Brant's town house.

Emma hurried in to help her. "Be sure to take your cloak," the maid reminded her, stuffing the clothes into a tapestry satchel along with a pair of brown leather shoes. Tory took the satchel and her cloak and started for the stairs.

In minutes, they were ready to leave. In the carriage on the way to the docks, the men reviewed the information Max Bradley had sent in his message and began to formulate plans. When they arrived at the ship's berth, they found the *Nightingale* fully crewed, ready and waiting to sail.

Cord led Tory across the deck, down the ladder to the cabin they had shared the time she had stolen aboard the ship, and memories washed over her.

He had made love to her here in this cabin. He had claimed her innocence—and her heart. She would never forget the tenderness he had shown her, or the pleasure.

She had never thought to marry him, never thought to fall so completely in love with him.

Never known how badly it would hurt to lose him.

"I can stay in the cabin next door," Cord said. "Or if you are worried what the crew might think, I can stay in here and sleep on the floor."

She swallowed. Once they returned, he would leave her. She should distance herself, protect her heart from more pain. But she wanted this time with him, wanted these last few precious hours.

"I would rather you stayed in here."

For an instant, Cord's tawny gaze searched her face. Then he simply nodded. "Very well."

Brushing past her, he tossed his satchel onto the berth, turned and strode out the door. He was dressed as he had been before, in snug brown breeches, knee-high boots and a full-sleeved white lawn shirt.

He paused for a moment in the doorway. "I'll give you some time to get settled, then come back and take you down to the galley. We'll need to go over what will happen when we get to the prison."

Tory nodded. But she was more concerned with what would happen when Cord returned to the tiny cabin they would share for the hours that lay ahead.

Cord gripped the starboard rail, letting the cold night wind wash over him. The last thing he needed was another torturous night in company with his wife. He didn't want to hear her soft breathing as she slept, didn't want to watch the rise and fall of her breasts, or remember the silkiness of her skin as he had taken the rose-tinted crest into his mouth.

His body hardened with desire just to think of the night ahead, and he knew the throbbing ache would not leave him.

Still, part of him craved her nearness, felt almost sick with need of her. Cord tried to imagine Victoria with Fox, but the image would not form and his desire for her remained. He wanted her. Worse yet, he loved her.

His fingers tightened around the rail. He needed to think of Ethan, not Victoria. His cousin's life was at stake and Cord vowed he would not let the bloody damned French take it without a fight.

Once the ship was under way and the three of them were settled, Cord returned to his cabin to escort Victoria down to the galley. Their meeting took several hours, but the plan they developed seemed a good one. According to Bradley's information, there were only two guards at the front gate of the prison, though a number of others prowled the corridors in front of the cells.

If Victoria could succeed in drawing the guards' attention, then he, Rafe and Bradley could get inside. Once they were there, they would post a guard to give them cover. There was a good chance they could get Ethan out without raising the alarm.

Confident each understood their roles, Rafe and Victoria had retired to their cabins. Cord had stayed on deck, dreading the moment he would have to be alone with her. But the night was slipping away and he needed to get some rest. Perhaps the cold floor would numb his lust enough he could manage a couple of hours of sleep.

Cord sighed as he turned from the rail and started toward the ladder leading down to his cabin.

* * *

Tory couldn't sleep. With every creak and groan of the ship, her eyes flashed to the door in search of Cord. Where was he? Why hadn't he come down to the cabin?

Their meeting in the galley had ended sometime earlier. The ship was quiet now, except for the heavy spray of the ocean against the hull, the shrill of the wind, and the clatter and clang of the rigging.

The seas were getting rougher. The *Nightingale* plunged into one trough after another, then battled its way up the opposite side. But the captain remained optimistic that the storm would not worsen. He kept the ship under sail and driving toward their destination—the inlet off the coast of France just south of Calais that they had used before.

Tory stared up at the ceiling above her berth, thinking of Cord, her heartbeat increasing at the sound of the cabin door creaking open. In the low-burning light of a ship's lantern swinging in the passage, she caught a glimpse of her husband's beloved face as he stepped inside and closed the door.

She heard the rustle of fabric, then the sound of his knee-high boots hitting the floor. He swore at the noise, magnified in the confines of the cabin.

"It's all right," she said. "I wasn't asleep."

"You should be. We'll reach France on the morrow and begin our journey inland. You're going to need your strength." He reached up and pulled a blanket down from a shelf above the teakwood bureau, began to spread it out on the floor.

"The floor is cold," she said, surprised at the words

but somehow unable to stop herself. "The bed is wide enough for both of us to share."

He turned to her and she thought that his breathing seemed to quicken. "I don't think that is a very good idea."

She remembered the way she had practically attacked him the last time they had made love and was glad for the darkness that hid the color in her cheeks.

"You will be perfectly safe," she said, forcing a lightness into her voice. "I promise I won't ravage you, my lord."

She could almost imagine the faint curve of his lips.

"It's not you I'm worried about." But he finished undressing and climbed up beside her and she scooted closer to the wall to give him room.

Her heart was pounding. She prayed he could not tell. They lay there in silence, careful not to touch each other. Each time he shifted on the bed, Tory imagined the muscles moving beneath his skin, the sinews in his long legs flexing and tightening. She wanted him to turn to her, to reach out and touch her. She ached for him so badly she almost relented and begged him to believe the truth.

I never betrayed you with Julian! I don't want an annulment! I've never loved anyone but you!

But she didn't say the words. She might love her husband, but he didn't love her. He had been unhappy in their marriage, had spent as little time with her as he could. In the end, he had made her unhappy, too. Perhaps this way, they could both find a measure of contentment.

The wind blew outside the cabin, washing great sprays of water against the hull, splashing up onto the porthole, but the storm didn't strengthen. The *Nightingale* fought her way through the night and the turbulent seas, and Tory's eyes drooped closed as fatigue settled over her.

She must have fallen asleep. When she awakened, faint gray light seeped through the porthole. It was cold in the cabin, but her body was infused with a radiant heat and she realized she was curled up next to Cord, his long frame wrapped around her. He was naked, the way he usually slept at home, his chest pressing into her back and his hips cradling her bottom.

Her eyes widened as she felt the swollen length of his sex pressing hard against her, hot through the folds of her cotton night rail, rucked up to the tops of her thighs. In the night, she had shifted toward him. She relaxed as she heard his even breathing and realized that he was asleep.

Tory tried to ease away, but a muscled arm draped over her shoulders and a long leg pinned her to the bed. It occurred to her that perhaps she could simply enjoy this moment of closeness, the sort that would disappear from her life once they got back home.

Her eyes drifted closed and she imagined the night that they had made love in this very cabin. He had wanted her so desperately then. And she had wanted him.

She still did.

Desire slipped through her at the memory of his hands on her breasts, the feel of his mouth moving hotly over hers. Heat drifted out through her limbs and dampness slid into her core. She shifted restlessly and his shaft stirred, grew thicker and harder.

"If you move…even a fraction of an inch…I won't be responsible for my actions."

Tory's breathing quickened. There was nothing she

wanted more than for Cord to make love to her. It couldn't happen. It wouldn't be fair to either one of them.

Still, her hips moved of their own accord. Her body seemed unable to resist.

Cord swore softly, shoved her nightgown up to her waist, gripped her hips and impaled her. She was wet and ready, he discovered, and she heard him groan. Tory gave herself over to him as she always did, reveling in his need of her, the sweetness of having him inside her.

Cord moved deeply and his voice whispered softly against her ear. "Can he make you feel this way?" He eased out and drove into her again. "Can he, Victoria?"

Her eyes stung. "No," she answered truthfully. "No one but you, Cord."

He filled her and filled her, increasing the rhythm, driving into her until they both reached a shattering release.

Tory drifted contentedly, but Cord didn't linger. He rose from the bed, leaving an empty space where his warm presence had been. A weak light filtered in through the porthole, outlining his magnificent body. His chest expanded and lean muscle tightened as he reached down to pick up his clothes.

"I knew this was a bad idea." His face looked drawn and filled with regret, and she felt a stab of pain.

"Was it?"

His lion eyes pinned her to the bed. "You don't think so?"

"I think in this we have always been a perfect match."

Cord said nothing for several long moments, but his eyes looked dark and troubled. Turning away, he busied himself with the task of pulling on his shirt, breeches and boots.

"You had better get dressed. Cook will have breakfast prepared and you need to have something to eat."

The storm had delayed the ship and it was late in the afternoon by the time they reached their destination—the quiet waters of the well-hidden cove near Cap Gris-Nez that had provided the ship protection before. At dawn on the morrow, Captain Ethan Sharpe was scheduled to stand before a firing squad, guilty of having spied for England, which in fact, he had.

They had only tonight to make their way inland, manage the captain's rescue and return to the ship. Since both previous missions had failed—each of them better prepared than this one—it seemed a Herculean task.

Still, they were determined. Just before dark, Tory donned her frayed dove-gray gown and joined Cord at the rail. She watched as he checked the load in his pistol and Sheffield did the same.

"Are we ready?" Rafe asked.

Cord cast her a glance. "It's not too late to change your mind. We can still find another way."

"I am not changing my mind."

Cord set his jaw and Rafe nodded, then cocked his head toward the rail. They descended a shaky rope ladder into the small dinghy bobbing next to the hull of the ship. A young blond sailor manned the oars, his muscled arms pulling rhythmically, making the task look easy. He rowed them ashore, beached the craft on the sand, and Cord helped her out of the boat.

They found Max Bradley waiting in the shadows not far away, his harsh features recognizable from the time she had seen him before.

"Thank God you got my message," Bradley said in French. "I was afraid something had happened and you wouldn't get here in time." Now that they were ashore, it was too dangerous to speak English. Both Cord and Rafe spoke French passably well. Max, who had lived in the country for years, and Tory, who had always had a knack for languages, could pass for French citizens.

"How long will it take to reach the prison?" Cord asked.

"I've got a wagon waiting. The cove is an hour southeast. We need to get under way." Max flicked Victoria a glance.

"My wife," Cord said, by way of introduction, a firm hand at her waist. "She's volunteered to distract the guards long enough for us to get in." But he planned to remain just inside the front door to keep watch if anything went wrong while she spoke to the guards.

Cord helped her up on the seat of the wagon next to Max, then he and Rafe climbed under a heavy canvas tarp that covered the flat bed of the wagon. Max flicked the reins and two big-boned gray horses lurched into motion. As the vehicle pulled out onto the rutted dirt road, Tory's fingers curled over the edge of the hard wooden seat.

When she had offered to help, she hadn't been afraid. But with every mile the wagon rolled closer to the prison, her fear edged up and her heart beat a little faster.

The hour-long journey seemed to take forever, but going any faster might draw unwanted attention. They couldn't afford to make the smallest mistake. This was Captain Sharpe's last chance and all of them knew it.

And the captain was no longer the only one in danger.

A sliver of moon rode high in the black night sky by

the time they reached the hill outside the prison, and Bradley pulled the wagon to a halt beneath the concealing branches of an ancient tree.

The tarp folded back and Rafe and Cord climbed out of the wagon bed, their attention fixed on Max.

"The prison lies just over that rise." Bradley pointed east. "If your wife can manage the team, she can drive up to the gate and pretend she has just arrived from the country."

Her heart jolted sideways. Since they weren't sure what arrangements Max might have made, their plans hadn't included her means of arriving at the prison. She had driven a single-horse gig when she was younger, but never anything remotely similar to a two-horse team and wagon.

She kept her eyes on Bradley. "I think it would be better if I walked to the gate. I can say that I hitched a ride from my home to an inn down the road and walked from there. That way the wagon can stay hidden, ready to haul us all to safety."

Cord cast her a look that said she wasn't fooling him for a moment. "That sounds good to me. All right with you, Bradley?"

"I think it's a good idea. We'll leave the wagon where it is. That way no one will see it." He turned to Tory. "The closest inn is the Lion d'Or, if the guards should happen to ask."

And so they set off. A biting wind swept over the rough terrain, buffeting her cloak and seeping through her gown and chemise. She had left the hood down and her hair loose around her shoulders as an enticement to the guards at the prison gate. Dark curls whipped around her face and stuck to the corners of her mouth. She shook her head and the wind tore the strands away.

They paused at the edge of the trees. Cord caught her shoulders and turned her to face him.

"Get them talking. While you keep them busy, we'll slip round to the other side of the courtyard."

Max had bribed the guard who stood watch outside a small wooden door some distance from the main gate leading into the prison. But once inside, the men would have to cross the open courtyard to reach the main access to the corridors lined with cells.

That was where Tory came in. Her job was to keep the guards busy while the men crossed the dangerous open space.

"Once we get in," Cord said, "I'll keep watch from just inside the front door. If anything goes wrong, you know what to do." She was supposed to faint dead away. That always threw a man off track, Cord said.

She remembered exactly the plan, knew that while Cord stood watch, Rafe and Max would make their way down to Ethan's cell in the bowels of the prison. She knew Cord would rather go in after his cousin, but he was worried about her safety. He had always been protective of those he cared about.

Apparently, in some way, he still cared for her.

She reached out and touched his cheek. "Be careful." Then she turned and hurried away, her cloak billowing out behind her.

Twenty-Two

The prison sat at the bottom of a gently sloping hill, a three-story building fashioned of rough gray stone. A row of tarnished brass lanterns hung from the heavy iron fence surrounding the courtyard, but much of the open area was dark.

Two guards stood at the entrance, one tall and thin, the other older and heavier. They straightened, their casual posture disappearing the moment they spotted her heading for the gate.

Tory pasted on a smile and kept walking, praying they couldn't tell how fast her heart was beating, how slick her palms had grown. As she drew near, she could see their faces, see their suspicion building.

"You there! Stop where you are."

Her heart was racing, trying to pound its way through her ribs. The pudgy, older guard left his post and walked over to where she stood. He was carrying a pistol and he pointed it in her direction.

"What are you doing out here in the middle of the night?"

"Please, *m'sieur,* I am only here to discover what has happened to my brother."

He motioned with the pistol and she walked over to the entrance where the second guard, younger, thinner, with a missing front tooth stood stiffly at his post.

"My brother's name is Gaspard Latour. He has been in prison for nearly six months." Tory told them how she had come all the way from Saint Omer hoping to see him, explained how worried she and her family were about him.

Finally they seemed to relax, and a few moments later, she actually had them smiling. She didn't see Cord, Rafe or Max, but she knew that unless something had gone wrong, by now they were inside the prison. She focused her attention on the guards, kept smiling, and kept them talking, determined they wouldn't notice any movement in the courtyard behind them.

The pudgy guard cast her a faintly suggestive glance. "Are you sure it is your brother you have come to see and not your lover?"

Tory looked away, pretending to be embarrassed. She shifted a little and slowly shook her head. "It is my brother, truly, *m'sieurs.*"

The thinner man shrugged. "If he is your brother, or if he is not, you will have to come back tomorrow. There is no way to know which cell he is in until the clerk arrives in the morning."

Thank God. She wasn't sure what she would have done if they had offered to let her inside.

Over the skinny guard's shoulder, she caught a flicker of movement. While the guards laughed and she pretended shyness, she saw the men emerge from the prison and start running across the shadowy courtyard. One man had his arm draped over another. The injured man had to be Captain Sharpe, who limped along, barely managing to walk as they made their way toward the side door leading out of the prison. She only caught a glimpse of the third man, but a fourth man followed, his pistol pulled as protection for the other three.

She forced herself to stay calm. They had retrieved Captain Sharpe. Now if they could just get out of the prison and safely back to the wagon.

One of the guards started to turn toward the courtyard, but Tory caught his arm, capturing his attention once more.

"Thank you, *m'sieur.* I shall return to the inn and wait until morning, as you suggest. I am so grateful for your help."

The plump guard moved closer, his blunt fingers circling her wrist. "I think the lady should stay here with us. What do you think?"

The skinny guard gave her a missing-tooth grin. "I think she should stay…at least for a while." They started pulling her farther inside the gate and Tory's fear kicked up. She tried not to let it show.

"I must go," she said. "I have family waiting at the inn. They will come here looking for me if I do not return."

The fat guard spat in the dirt. "What kind of fool would let a beauty like you go off on her own? No, I think there is no one."

"Please let me go." She could pretend to faint, but Cord would undoubtedly rush to her aid and all of them might be captured. "I am telling you the truth. One of them is my husband. He forbade me to come, but the prison was very near and I wanted to see my brother. I must get back before he comes looking for me."

"I'm afraid he is already here." At the sound of Max Bradley's voice, relief washed over her. The guard let go of her wrist and stepped warily away. There was something about Max Bradley, a hardness that warned of danger.

Tory caught Max's arm and gave him a beseeching look. "These men have been very kind. They say if we come back in the morning, someone will check on Gaspard. Perhaps we might even be able to see him."

Max's features grew even harder. "Your brother is not worth the trouble." He shoved her a little ahead of him. "And you had better not disobey me again."

Looking properly contrite, Tory kept walking. She could hear Max's boots crunching on the ground behind her. They topped the hill, dropped down out of sight, then she spotted the wagon. The seat was empty, the tarp over the back tightly drawn.

"Come. The men are already in the wagon." Max helped her up on the seat, climbed up and released the brake, then set the horses into motion.

For the first time she wondered why Max had come to her rescue instead of Cord, who had been so determined to protect her. Probably because he spoke better French. Still… "Everything…everything went as planned?"

"For the most part."

"Then Captain Sharpe is all right?"

"The captain is in very bad condition. He is lucky to be alive." He turned the horses onto the road, jolting the seat of the wagon. "And there was one mishap."

A trickle of fear went through her. "What sort of mishap?"

"There was a guard posted at the end of the row of cells where the captain was being held. He must have been standing in the shadows and we slipped right past him. He took off to sound the alarm. Your husband stopped him before he could reach the front door."

She forced herself to breathe. Cord was all right. Four men had left the prison. "What happened?"

"There was a struggle. Lord Brant knew he would bring a dozen men running should he fire his pistol. The guard pulled a knife, and in the fighting, your husband was wounded. He took the blade in his chest."

She made a strangled sound in her throat and whirled toward the back of the wagon. Max caught her arm and jerked her back around in the seat.

"Stay calm. We can't afford to draw attention. We've got to get back to the ship."

"But we have to help him! He must be bleeding. We have to get it stopped!"

"We've done that. He'll be all right till we reach the *Nightingale.* The surgeon will take care of him once we get there."

She glanced toward the back of the wagon. "The road is bumpy. What if he starts bleeding again? Let me look at him. Maybe there is something I can do."

"The best thing you can do is keep your eyes on the road and pretend there is nothing whatsoever wrong. We aren't out of this yet. If we get stopped before we reach the ship, it might be better if his lordship took that blade in the heart."

Tory gripped the wagon seat and sat there shaking. Cord was injured, perhaps very gravely. And there was nothing she could do!

"What about the guard who attacked him? Won't he sound the alarm?"

Max's lips went thin. "You needn't worry on that score. He won't be making any sound at all."

Tory said nothing more, but a shiver went through her. All she could think of was Cord and how badly he might be hurt.

The ride back to the ship stretched on interminably, accompanied by the frantic, sluggish beating of her heart. No one stirred in the back of the wagon and no one appeared on the little-traveled road in search of them.

Finally, she heard the crash of waves against sand, and relief, mingled with her terrible fear, threatened to swamp her.

"Easy now," Max said, eyeing the pale hue of her face. "We're almost there."

But they couldn't get there fast enough for Tory.

Her throat closed up to think that beneath the tarp, her husband might be dying.

Cord was unconscious when they carried him aboard. His eyes were closed, his face deathly pale. Each breath seemed an effort, and as Tory looked at him, her heart squeezed so hard it hurt. The doctor stripped away his bloody shirt, exposing a deep wound in his chest that continued oozing blood.

Don't let him die, Tory silently prayed. *Please don't*

let him die. She had told him she loved him, but she knew he didn't believe her. Now he might never know.

"The blade went in deep, but straight," the surgeon said as she hovered next to where Cord lay in the cabin they had shared. "That is good news, but he has lost a lot of blood—which is not."

The surgeon, a man named Neil McCauley, was short and slightly built, not more than five-and-thirty, with dark hair and a mustache. He shifted a little with the roll of the ship, whose sails had been unfurled, the anchor weighed. The *Nightingale* was heading into deep water, away from French shores, back home to England.

Tory prayed that Cord would survive the journey.

He stirred on the bunk and groaned as the doctor poured sulphur powder into the wound, along with a mixture of herbs and a thick substance McCauley said was made with axle grease.

Cord groaned and her hand shook as she reached out to touch him. Starkly pale, his skin icy cold, he still exuded the magnetic, vibrantly powerful presence that drew her as no other man ever had.

And yet he could die, just like any other man.

"We'll have to keep a close eye out for putrefaction," the surgeon said as he threaded his needle with catgut and began the lengthy process of stitching his patient back together.

Tory frowned at the haphazard way the man drew the needle through Cord's torn flesh. She had always loved his smooth, hard-muscled chest. She didn't like to think of the scars the surgeon's coarse work would leave.

"Perhaps I could do that, Dr. McCauley. I've never

sewn a man's skin back together, but I have done a good bit of needlework over the years."

"Be my guest." The inside stitching was already done. McCauley handed over the threaded needle and she took a steadying breath.

She could do this, do it for Cord. She would do whatever she could to help him, as he had once helped her.

Her hand trembled for an instant, then steadied as she determinedly set to work, taking small, delicate stitches that would mostly disappear once the wound had healed. Cord's body stiffened a little with the pain of the needle sliding into his flesh and his eyes slowly opened. She could read the pain in his face and a lump rose in her throat.

"I know this hurts," she said. "I'll try to do it as quickly as I can."

"I'll get him some laudanum," the doctor said. "It will help ease his discomfort."

As Tory continued to work, the surgeon poured the bitter liquid into a cup, added a bit of water, then lifted Cord's head and trickled the mixture between his lips. Cord swallowed the substance and lay back down, and his eyes came to rest on her face. For an instant, his golden gaze softened. Seeing her there beside him, he seemed to relax and breathe a little easier.

"The doctor is taking good care of you," Tory said, smoothing back his hair. "You're going to be all right."

He must have seen the fear and worry in her face for he tried to smile. Instead, his eyes slid closed and he slipped back into unconsciousness.

Tears welled in her eyes. She clamped down on an urge to weep and continued her stitching, pulling the thread taut, taking another small stitch and pulling it taut again. When the wound was completely closed, she tied off the thread they had used and clipped it neatly. The moment she was finished, she burst into tears.

"It's all right, my lady," the surgeon said gently. "The knife didn't hit any vital organs. It is losing so much blood that makes him so weak."

She nodded, but the tears kept rolling down her cheeks.

"He'll need plenty of rest and care, but with luck, there is a good chance he'll recover."

He would, she told herself. Cord was young and strong. He would survive this and soon be back on his feet.

Tory stayed with him that night, sitting in the chair next to his bed. Both Rafe and Max Bradley came to check on him, but he didn't wake up while they were there.

It wasn't until just before dawn that he stirred.

When his dull, pain-glazed eyes slowly opened and fixed on her face, Tory almost started crying again. Instead, she swallowed against the thick lump in her throat and busied herself tucking the covers around him.

"You need to lie still," she said briskly. "You will open my very handy stitches."

The edge of his mouth barely curved. "I never thought your…needlework…would come in so…handy."

She brushed the hair back from his face, just so she could touch him. "Yes, well, I suppose it did."

The doctor knocked just then and came in to check on his patient. "So you are awake."

"Only just a moment ago," Tory told him.

McCauley drew back the covers and looked down at

the bandage. "The bleeding wasn't excessive during the night. I believe we have got it mostly stopped."

As the doctor stripped off the bandage and replaced it with a clean one, Cord's gaze fixed on the surgeon's face.

"What of Ethan?" he asked. "Is he…all right?"

McCauley frowned, debating how much to say to a man so gravely injured. "He is doing as well as can be expected."

Cord didn't look satisfied with the answer, but his eyelids drifted down and, seconds later, he was once again asleep.

The sun was up and Cord was awake when the doctor returned to check on him a second time. His color was better, Tory thought, and his gaze more alert.

"I insist on knowing Captain Sharpe's condition," he said with authority.

The doctor straightened, mildly irritated by his tone. "You want the truth? The captain is near starved to death. He's so weak he can barely stand. He was infested with lice and beaten within an inch of his life. What can be done for him has been. He is bathed and shorn of his beard and filthy mane of hair. Right now he needs to eat and sleep and try to recover his strength. Is that what you wished to know?"

Cord relaxed against the pillow. "Thank you," he said softly, letting his eyelids drift closed. The sheet draped over his hips, leaving him bare to the waist. The white of the bandage stood out against the dark hair on his chest.

"See that he takes the medicine I've left and a bit more of that laudanum. It will keep the pain at bay. I'll be back to check on him one more time before we dock."

The doctor left the cabin and Tory moved a damp cloth gently over Cord's face, down his neck and over his powerful chest and shoulders. His skin quickly warmed the cloth and she worried that he might be starting to run a fever.

"The doctor says you should have a bit more laudanum. It will ease the pain and you will be able to sleep."

Cord stared past her out the porthole. Several times, he seemed to have drifted back in time, his thoughts returning to the man he had found in the prison.

"I didn't even know him," Cord said. "He looked nothing at all like Ethan. He looked like a man who was already dead."

Tory's hand shook as she dipped the cloth into the porcelain basin of water and wrung it out. "Captain Sharpe will recover and so will you. You saved his life, Cord. If you hadn't persisted as you did, he never would have left that filthy prison."

Cord turned his attention to her, reached out and caught her hand. "Thank you for what you did for him tonight. We couldn't have gotten him out of there without you."

Tory brought his fingers to her lips. "I'm just glad I could help."

Cord's gaze held hers for a moment. Then weariness forced his eyes slowly closed. Tory continued to bath his heated skin and press cups of water to his lips, and Cord seemed comforted by her presence.

They reached the London docks a little after noon and carriages were summoned to return them to their homes. With Cord injured, it was decided that Captain Sharpe should recover at Sheffield House, the duke's palatial residence. Dr. McCauley promised to continue his care of both men.

Tory got her first look at Captain Sharpe as he was helped into one of the carriages, limping slightly, leaning heavily against the duke. A tall man with high, carved cheekbones, he had the hard, dangerous look of a man like Max Bradley.

His gaunt frame and the loose fit of his clothes emphasized the width of his shoulders and hinted at what he must have suffered in the prison. His lips were well shaped, but carried a cynical twist.

It was his eyes that were most disconcerting. She had never seen eyes the pale hue of a frozen sea, and yet she thought that once he recovered, Ethan Sharpe would be a very handsome man.

As it was scarcely the time for introductions, she returned her attention to her husband, helping him aboard a second carriage for the ride back to his town house. All the way there, she thanked God that he had survived and prayed that his wound would heal.

The week passed in a blur of activity. Tending to Cord consumed most of her time, seeing to his meals, bathing him, making certain he took his medication, changing the dressings on his wound.

By the end of the week, there was no sign of putrefaction and, to Tory's great relief, it was clear that Cord would completely recover.

"I've a houseful of servants to do my bidding," he had grumbled, clearing recovering his strength. "Considering our present circumstances, you are under no obligation to take care of me."

But she wanted to take care of him. She loved him. "It isn't a burden."

He didn't say more and she thought that he was as pleased to have her there as she was pleased to be there.

On Monday, after eight days of confinement, when she entered his suite, she found him dressed and standing in the middle of the room. He looked a little pale and somewhat shaky—and so handsome it made her heart hurt.

"You're up," she said, selfishly wishing she could have spent a few more days taking care of him.

"I am out of that blasted bed, as I should have been several days past. As I would have been if it weren't for Dr. McCauley's high-handedness and your constant bullying." A corner of his mouth edged up. "Thank you, Victoria. I appreciate your care of me."

She didn't reply. She wasn't certain what would happen now. If he would move out or expect her to leave. A lump formed in her throat at the thought of how much she would miss him.

She worked to keep her voice even. "Are you going to the duke's to see your cousin?"

"I'm headed there, yes…eventually. I hope Ethan has had half as good a nurse as I have."

She flushed and looked down at the toes of her slippers, peeking out from beneath the hem of her cream muslin skirt. "Are you…are you certain you're feeling well enough? Perhaps I should go with you."

"I don't think Ethan is ready for visitors yet. And I'm feeling perfectly fine."

She studied him a moment, trying to memorize his features, hoping he would come home, though she had no idea if he would. She expected to receive the annulment papers any day. She pasted on a smile and ignored the way her heart was squeezing inside her chest.

"Well, then, if there is nothing else you need..."

"There is one more thing. Before you go, I'd like a word with you. There is something of importance I'd like to say." His gaze flicked over her, making her heart hurt even more, then he moved off toward the sofa in front of the hearth.

"If you don't mind, perhaps we might sit down."

She rushed forward. "Yes, of course! Here, let me help you."

He brushed away her assistance and sat down with only a grimace or two, then waited as she took a seat across from him.

"Being abed this week, I've had a good deal of time to think. Or perhaps it was having a brush with mortality." He seemed so serious her nerves grew even more frazzled.

"Yes, I can understand that."

"I spent a good deal of that time thinking about our marriage."

She swallowed. Dear God, she had thought of nothing else. That and her worry for him had kept her up night after night.

"We have only been wed a little over three months, not long enough to really know each other. And the circumstances of our marriage were not what either of us would have preferred."

She clasped her hands together in her lap, trying to keep them from shaking. "I'm sorry I forced you into such a position. It was never my intent."

"I'm the one who forced the marriage, not you. I can be somewhat high-handed. At the time, I thought it the best solution all round."

"You saved my sister. That is all that mattered."

"Your happiness also mattered, Victoria."

Tory made no reply. Her heart was beating too hard, her nerves stretched too thin.

"The truth is, I wanted to marry you. In fact, I was determined to have you. At the time I refused to admit it to myself, but taking your innocence onboard the ship merely gave me the excuse I needed to wed the woman I wanted for my wife."

Something was happening inside her. She couldn't seem to get enough air into her lungs. "But you…you wanted to marry an heiress."

"There was a time I believed that sort of marriage was important. I thought I owed it to my father to increase our family's wealth. It didn't take long to discover it really didn't matter."

"But—"

"Hear me out, Victoria…please. I have the courage to say this only once." His eyes found hers and there was so much turmoil in them, she wanted to reach out and touch him.

"In life, sometimes people make mistakes. I made a very big mistake in the way I treated you after we were wed. I should have spent time with you. I should have showered you with flowers, bought you expensive gifts. Bloody hell—I should have given you anything you wanted."

Her throat was aching. She was going to weep any moment. "I didn't want gifts. I only wanted you, Cord."

Cord looked away, then seemed to collect himself. "Last week onboard the ship, you asked me to stay with you in your cabin. You gave yourself to me as you did before we were wed. Since my injury, you have shown great care of me, and obvious concern. And so there is a question I must ask. I need to know if what happened between you and Fox was also a mistake, or if he is truly the man who will make you happy."

The ache built until she couldn't swallow. "I don't love Julian. I never did."

"And what feelings do you carry for me?"

What feelings? She was in love with him. Desperately, heartbreakingly in love with him, and she always would be.

She took a shaky breath. Cord said he had made a mistake. Dear God, she had made mistakes, too. Conspiring with Julian had been a terrible mistake.

And now she knew that her husband had wanted to marry her. Her—not an heiress or anyone else.

"I love you, Cord," she said softly. "I only wanted you to make time for me. Julian and I, we never—"

"Listen to me, Victoria. What happened between you and Fox is past. The future is all that matters. What I need to know is if you wish to make a future with me—or with Julian Fox?"

Blessed God! How could he think she would ever choose Julian over him? How could he not look at her and see the love for him that was there in her eyes?

"I love you," she repeated, praying she could make him see. "The thought of losing you is tearing me apart."

Cord maintained his carefully controlled expression.

"Then you are willing to give up Fox? You will never see the man again?"

She couldn't find her voice. He was willing to continue their marriage even though he believed she had betrayed him.

"Please, Cord, you have to believe me—Julian and I were never—"

"Don't say it! Don't say another word about that man. I don't want to hear Fox's name in this house again. I want your answer, Victoria. If we're going to continue this marriage, I want your vow of fidelity. I want you to cleave to me and only to me."

Her eyes welled with tears. "We were pretending," she whispered. "It never really happened."

His handsome face hardened. It was clear he didn't believe her. Rising from the sofa, he started to walk away and her aching heart painfully twisted. He didn't feel trapped into the marriage. He wanted her to remain his wife.

And if he felt that way, there was a chance he might come to love her.

He was almost to the door when she finally grabbed hold of her courage, the tears in her voice freezing him where he stood.

"I swear to you that I will forever be faithful. I will cleave to you and no other. I will bear your children and love you for all the days of my life. This I pledge on my life—on my sister's life—on everything that I hold dear." Tears spilled down her cheeks. "You are the only man I want, Cord. The only man I have ever wanted."

He turned toward her. She yearned to know his thoughts, but his expression remained carefully guarded. She wanted to go to him, wanted to throw herself into his arms, but it could not be. Not yet.

"We'll start over," he said softly, "begin as we should have done before."

"Yes..." she said, aching for him, loving him more than she ever had before.

And silently she vowed she would find a way to prove that she had never betrayed him with Julian Fox.

Feeling an unsettling mix of emotions, Cord left the house. Giving his coachman instructions to take him to Sheffield House, he settled himself in the carriage and leaned his head back against the seat.

He was still a little shaky, but his wound was healing and he was beginning to recover his strength. He hoped Ethan was recovering, as well.

Leaving Berkeley Square, the carriage rumbled through Mayfair, making its way beneath leafless trees, the wind kicking up dust and leaves on the street beneath the spinning wheels. Cord watched the blur of activity outside the window, but his mind was fixed on Victoria.

He had meant to tell her he loved her. In the end, he found that he could not.

It had taken all his courage to expose his feelings for her, to humble himself enough to admit his mistakes and ask her to remain his wife. In return, she had told him that she loved him and vowed life long fidelity.

He wanted to believe her. He prayed she was speaking the truth. But trust wasn't something a man could summon at will, and her betrayal was too recent, too raw.

Time would prove the truth of her words. She loved him or she did not. She would be faithful or she would not.

In that regard, he had meant what he had said. What had happened with Fox was in the past. Cord had slept with more women than he could count. He could scarcely condemn the innocent young wife he had unthinkingly thrown to the wolves.

He had made any number of mistakes and he meant to repair the damage.

And he prayed Julian Fox would stay in York until his mission was complete.

Twenty-Three

Cord climbed the front porch stairs of the duke of Sheffield's palatial mansion and lifted the heavy brass knocker, anxious to see Ethan, worried about him, still uncertain how he had fared after his lengthy ordeal.

Following the butler into the Club Room, an intimate salon done in dark green and heavy oak, Cord turned as Ethan walked in, pausing just inside the doorway, neither man knowing exactly what to say. So much had happened. The war had changed so much between them. His cousin seemed a completely different person, and Cord could see he wasn't ready to accept the cousinly hug Cord desperately wanted to give him.

Cord managed a smile. "You're beginning to look yourself again. I am glad to see your health is improving." Cord was grateful to see the dark hollows gone from beneath his friend's light blue eyes. Still, he looked thin and pale, especially with his hair shorn, his skin lacking the tanned, robust quality it usually carried.

"And you are back on your feet."

"Yes. Thanks to God—and to my wife." Both men were physically healing, but Cord thought that emotionally his cousin had a long way to go before he was back to the man he had been before he'd been thrown into prison.

Ethan crossed the room to the sideboard, a noticeable limp in his left leg. "Brandy?" He lifted the stopper off a crystal decanter filled with burnished liquid.

"None for me," Cord said, already beginning to tire as he sank down into an overstuffed chair. "I've a good bit yet to do this afternoon."

"Still working as hard as ever, I imagine."

"Actually, I've decided to slow down a bit. It's time I began to enjoy life again."

One of Ethan's black eyebrows went up. "I'll believe that when I see it."

"It's a long story. Suffice it to say sometimes there are more important things than making money."

"You're speaking of your wife…the lovely lady who proved so useful in getting me out of prison. There aren't many women who would risk themselves for a man they didn't even know."

"Victoria has always been a woman of exceptional courage."

"I look forward to meeting her. I'd like to thank her in person."

"What happened out there, Ethan? No one really seems to know."

Ethan took a long drink of his brandy. "To put it bluntly—we were betrayed. There is a traitor among us, Cord, and I mean to discover who it is." His long, tapered fingers tightened around the glass. "And when I do, I am going to make him pay."

"Do you have any idea who he is?"

"Not yet. But now that I am a marquess, my resources are nearly unlimited. I'll find him. When I do, I'm going to kill him."

A finger of ice slipped down Cord's spine. Ethan wasn't a man to make idle threats. He wanted vengeance, and Cord didn't blame him. If he had been locked up, tortured, and beaten for nearly a year, he would feel exactly the same.

"If there is anything I can do to help, let me know." Cord rose from the chair, his strength waning, not nearly as recovered as he had hoped.

"You've already done enough," Ethan said as he approached. For the first time he seemed to let his guard down, resting a hand on Cord's shoulder. "If it hadn't been for you," he said softly, "I would have died in that prison. You're the best friend a man could ever have."

For an instant, the men embraced, both knowing how close each had come to dying.

"I'm glad you're home," Cord said gruffly as they broke away. "I know Sarah is, too."

He nodded. "She and her family are due at the town house this afternoon. Which I suppose is mine now, along with everything else."

"She refused to stay there until you were safely returned."

"I can't say I'm looking forward to all of that crying and female carrying on, but I will be sorely glad to see her, and Jonathan and Teddy, of course. Sheffield has been an excellent host, but I shall be very glad to be sleeping once more in a bed of my own."

"I imagine you will."

"Why don't you and Victoria join us for supper? I know Sarah would like it."

Cord smiled. "So would I. And you can finally meet my wife."

He found himself wondering what Victoria would think of Ethan. His cousin had changed so much in the year he'd been imprisoned. He had always been intrigued by danger, facing it with a kind of reckless abandon. But he had also been a man who laughed often and found great joy in life.

He was more cautious now, more withdrawn. He hadn't smiled once since Cord's arrival. Ethan was just twenty-eight. Cord hoped, in time, he would return to the high-spirited man he had been before.

Limping a little, leaning on his silver-headed cane, Ethan headed upstairs to pack and leave for his town house. The leg injury was permanent, the doctor had said, a result of a beating he had received from one of the guards, though in time, the limp would lessen.

As Ethan disappeared up the stairs, Cord went in search of Rafe, uncertain what his friend would say to his reconciliation with Victoria.

"I have always admired your wife in a number of ways," Rafe said, surprising him. "She is smart and courageous and protective of those she cares about. As you say, sometimes people make mistakes. I don't think I could be as forgiving as you, should the lady belong to me, but I am happy for the two of you. I hope this time things work out."

So did he, Cord thought. But it would take time to know for certain. Perhaps even years.

It wasn't a comforting thought.

Cord was living in the house, and though he hadn't come to Tory's bed, he had kept his word and spent a good deal of time with her. It was obvious he wanted to be the sort of husband he believed he should have been before.

He wanted to make things right between them this time round, and it broke Tory's heart to think that he still believed she had betrayed him with Julian Fox.

She considered writing her friend a letter, asking him to send a message to Cord explaining that nothing untoward had ever occurred between them. But she didn't think Cord would believe anything Julian had to say, and any sort of correspondence might only make things worse.

For the present, she was forced to let the matter lie, though it was one of the hardest things she'd ever had to do.

"All you have to do is wait," Claire said during one of her morning visits. "Give him time to see how much you love him. It is obvious that he loves you. No man would forgive so terrible a thing if he did not."

"But I didn't do anything!"

"No, but he thinks you did and he loves you still. In a way it is very romantic."

Tory had no idea what Cord's feelings for her might be, but she knew that she loved him and she was enjoying the time he spent with her, something he had rarely done before. Escorting her round London, he accompanied her to the opera, the theater, and took her shopping in Bond Street.

Cord lavished her with gowns and gloves and bonnets, purchased skimpy silk lingerie she was embarrassed to carry out of the shop yet yearned to wear for him. He bought her exotic perfume and hand-painted fans and a dozen pairs of kidskin slippers, even her own personal carriage. And there was the jewelry: a lovely sapphire brooch, a pair of garnet earrings, a diamond-and-emerald ring so big it dwarfed her hand.

"It belonged to my mother," he said a little gruffly. "She was larger than you. We'll have to have it sized."

Still, her favorite gift remained the exquisite Bride's Necklace he had given her on the day they were wed. Whenever she put it on, she felt an odd sort of comfort, a serenity that helped to ease her troubled thoughts.

She wore the necklace the evening they joined Cord's family for dinner at the marquess of Belford's town house, though secretly she still thought of the man as Captain Ethan Sharpe.

Tory wasn't sure what to make of him. As the flesh returned to his lanky frame, he grew more and more handsome. But he was cool and remote, a little too quiet and often forbidding, his pale eyes somehow disturbing. She knew he had suffered and that he was bent on revenge for what had happened to him and his men.

She hoped, for Cord and Sarah's sake, that in time, the marquess would give up the notion.

In the meantime, she focused her attention on her husband. She worried about the injury he had suffered, knowing that it often still pained him, but he seemed determined to ignore it.

Tonight they were attending a soiree at the duke of Tarrington's mansion. They waltzed together as they had never done before, and every time his tawny gaze touched her, warm color rushed into her cheeks.

She knew that look. He wanted her. And yet he denied himself, denied both of them. He was giving her time, letting her set the pace. He wrongly believed she had made love with another man and undoubtedly that was the reason.

Tory couldn't help thinking of the last time she and Cord had been to Tarrington Park, the night he had hauled her into the closet and made passionate love to her. What would happen, she wondered, if she tried that tactic in reverse?

She might have had the nerve to try if Cord were close at hand, but at the moment he stood next to the punch bowl speaking to his friend, the duke. She started to join them when she spotted her stepfather walking toward her. She didn't miss the smug smile pulling at the corners of his lips.

"Well, Victoria... How long has it been?"

A little shiver went through her. *Not long enough,* she thought. *Not nearly long enough.* She stiffened her spine. "Good evening, my lord. I hadn't heard you were in London."

"Actually, I am here on business." He toyed with the glass of champagne in his long-boned hand. "You see, I've had an offer for the purchase of Windmere."

Her stomach instantly tightened. "Someone wishes to buy Windmere?"

"That is correct. I intend to finalize the transfer some time next week."

Her head spun. "You...you can't possibly do that. Windmere has been in my mother's family for three hundred years. You can't just sell it!"

Now she understood why he had looked so smug. He knew how much the place meant to her, the memories it held, knew that selling it would be like a dagger in the heart. "Who has offered to buy it?"

"I'm afraid I'm not at liberty to say. I hear the new owner intends to do extensive remodeling, though, perhaps turn it into some sort of an inn."

The knot in her stomach grew almost painful. It was probably a lie. He knew how much it would disturb her, therefore it was just the sort of thing the baron would say. Still, it might well be the truth.

"If you want the place so badly, perhaps you can convince your husband to buy it for you. The price would have to be a great deal higher, of course, perhaps double—no, let's say triple the existing price—but I'm sure we could come to some sort of agreement."

The baron hated Cord nearly as much as he hated her. He would extract every farthing he could get. Cord might agree to the purchase, but Tory refused to ask him.

She had come to him penniless when he had wanted a marriage that would increase his family's wealth. He had paid the extravagant price Lord Harwood had demanded for the necklace she and Claire had stolen, then bought it and given it to her as a gift. Lately he had lavished her with expensive presents.

She refused to ask him for more.

If the cost was losing Windmere, so be it.

"I believe I see your husband coming. Perhaps I should mention the offer to him."

"No," she said firmly. "We are not interested in buying the house." But she was extremely interested in getting inside. Windmere posed the last chance of finding her mother's journal. If the new owners began to tear the place apart, she might never find it.

She studied the baron's razor-thin face, the smug smile still on his lips. The man had murdered her father. Tory was sure of it. She wanted nothing so much as to make Miles Whiting pay.

The baron made a timely departure as her husband drew near. Cord was frowning by the time he reached her.

"What did that devil, Harwood, want?"

"He was just being obnoxious, a knack that comes to him quite readily."

She gazed up at her husband, who looked impossibly handsome in his dark evening clothes. His shoulders were so very broad, and she knew exactly the hardness of the muscles across his chest. She wanted him to kiss her right there in the ballroom, wanted him to drag her off to the closet and shove up her skirts, as he had done before.

He must have read her thoughts for his eyes darkened to burnished gold. She thought that if she touched him, she would find him heavily aroused.

Then his careful control slipped back into place and the moment was lost.

Tory flicked a glance across the dance floor to where the baron stood speaking to a group of his friends, and ignored a faint shiver.

"If you don't mind, now that Harwood is arrived, I would like to go home."

Cord followed her gaze and nodded. "Come. We'll collect your wrap and summon the carriage."

Protective as always, he didn't stray from her side again, but when they got home, he retired to his room, leaving her alone. Instead of a restful night's sleep, she had erotic dreams of Cord and disturbing dreams of Windmere.

The afternoon of the following day, Grace showed up at the town house. Teary-eyed and shaken, she let Tory lead her into the Blue Room and waited while Timmons closed the sliding doors.

"For heaven's sake, Grace, what is it? You're pale as a ghost."

Grace wet her trembling lips. "My father—I've found out who he is."

"Come, you had better sit down. Shall I ring for tea? You look as if you could use a bit of a bracer."

Grace shook head. "I can't stay long. I wanted to show you these."

For the first time, Tory noticed the small wooden box tucked under Grace's arm. "What is it?"

"Letters. Written to me by my father."

"Good heavens, how on earth did you get them?"

"I finally found the courage to speak to my mother. At first she was upset that I had discovered her secret, but I told her what had happened was in the past. I simply wanted to know who my real father was."

"And?" Tory prompted.

"She cried and begged me to forgive her and then she went and got the letters. She said she had received one each year since the day I was born. She said that she should have given me the letters as soon as I was old enough to know the truth, but she didn't want to cause any more trouble with her husband."

"You mean Dr. Chastain."

"Yes. Mother said he has never been able to accept me as his daughter. She was the one who had been unfaithful, but he took it out on me."

Tory looked down at the small, carved wooden box in Grace's lap. "Have you read them?"

"Yes."

"What did your father say?"

Her hand stroked lovingly over the box. "Mostly he said that if he could, he would raise me as his own. He said that if I ever got into trouble, I should go to his aunt, a woman named Matilda Crenshaw. She's the widow of Baron Humphrey. He said that she knew all about me."

Tears welled in Grace's eyes and she fumbled for a handkerchief, dragged it out of her reticule. "As I grew older, my father said he wanted to meet me. I wrote to him, Tory. I asked if he still wanted to see me and he wrote and said he did. I am meeting him tomorrow night."

Tory reached over and took hold of Grace's hand. "Are you certain, Grace? Are you sure that is what you want?"

"More than anything. My father is a man of some prominence in the government. He is married, with children of his own, but I have vowed to keep his secret. They will never know anything about me."

She sniffed into the hankie. "He never forgot me, Tory. Not in all of these years."

"I'm happy for you, Grace. I know how much you've always wanted a father who loved you."

Grace smiled through her tears. "I have to go. I ordered a new gown for our meeting and I am due for the final fitting." Grace leaned down and hugged her. "I'll tell you all about it after I see him."

Tory nodded and rose to her feet. “Good luck, darling.”

Grace swept out of the room with her usual vibrancy, and Tory could almost feel the energy left in her wake. Perhaps it was Grace’s departure that made the room seem suddenly cold. Whatever it was, her head began to spin and her stomach started to roll.

The nausea worsened. Hurrying upstairs, Tory reached her bedchamber just in time to empty the contents of her stomach into the chamber pot. God’s breath, the same sickness had plagued her yesterday and the day before.

“Milady?” Emma stood in the doorway. “Are ye ill again today?”

She fought down another wave of nausea. “I can’t imagine what is wrong with me.”

Emma poured water into the porcelain basin, dampened a cloth and handed it to her. “When was yer last menses, milady?”

“I’m not sure.” She used the cloth to wash her face. “It must have been some weeks back—” She broke off as she realized the direction of Emma’s thoughts. “Dear Lord, you don’t think that I…that I might be with child?”

“You have been married some months, milady. And your husband is a most virile man.”

Sweet God, she was going to have Cord’s baby! A surge of exhilaration collided with a sharp stab of fear. Cord still believed she had made love with Julian Fox. Which meant there was a very good chance he would think that the child was not his.

The notion made her stomach roll again and perspiration broke out on her forehead.

"Perhaps ye ought ta sit down, milady."

She sank down on the padded bench in front of her dresser, frantically trying to think. She would have to take the chance and write to Julian, beg him to speak to Cord. She would talk to her sister, beseech Lord Percy. Maybe together they could convince her husband that she had never been unfaithful.

"What is it, milady? Are ye not happy about the babe?"

Tory looked up at Emma and managed to muster a smile. "I am very happy, Emma."

But she couldn't tell Cord the news. Not yet. Not until she found a way to persuade him the child belonged to him. She had to convince him of her love and fidelity—and that wasn't going to happen as long as they lived separate lives.

Tory turned to Emma. "I need your help. I need to pack my things."

"Are ye goin' on a trip, milady?"

Tory stood up from the bench. "Yes, Emma, a very short trip. We are moving into the master's suite."

Cord was tired when he got home. He'd had supper at the club, stayed a bit longer than he meant to, and now the wound in his chest was aching. Added to that, his earlier meeting with his banker hadn't gone as well as he had planned.

Tomorrow, he needed to make a two-day trip to Watford to check on what appeared to be a promising business opportunity. This time, he intended to take Victoria along.

Just thinking about her made his body clench with desire. He hadn't made love to her since they had shared the cabin aboard the *Nightingale*. In the past few days, he grew hard every time she walked into a room. It took sheer force of will to maintain his careful control, but he wanted to give her time, wanted her to be certain that he was the man she truly wanted.

As he stepped into the house, his gaze went in search of her. "Do you know where I might find Lady Brant?" he asked Timmons, trying to sound nonchalant.

Timmons collected his hat and gloves. "Aye, my lord. Her ladyship retired to her room just after supper."

The butler helped him out of his greatcoat and he started up the stairs, more eager to see her than he would have liked.

He was in love with Victoria. It was a feeling he couldn't seem to shake. Still, he didn't have to behave like a callow schoolboy.

She wasn't in her bedchamber. He asked one of the chambermaids, but the girl had no idea where his wife might have gone.

"She were here a bit earlier, milord. Must 'ave gone out for a breath of fresh air."

An instant of unease slipped through him as he thought of Julian Fox, but he shook it away. She was there. He simply had to find her.

Beginning to feel the chill of his damp clothes, he went into his bedchamber to change. He untied and pulled off his cravat, tossed off his coat and waistcoat, then pulled his shirt off over his head. He was about to summon his valet to help him remove his boots when he heard voices in his bathing room.

The door was closed. Wondering if one of the maids was working in there, he turned the knob and walked in, then froze at the sight of Victoria sitting in his copper bathing tub.

"That will be all for tonight, Emma," she said. "Thank you."

The blond woman blushed and hurried out of the room, and Victoria smiled up at him. It seemed a bit tentative, a little uncertain, and Cord wondered at the cause.

She leaned back in the tub, her lithe body naked beneath a thin layer of frothy white bubbles. They parted whenever she moved, exposing the rounded tops of her breasts and the small rose nipples at each crest. She had piled her chestnut hair up in soft curls, though a few glossy strands escaped at the side of her neck.

Her lips curved prettily in welcome, but a trace of uncertainty remained. "Good evening, my lord."

He was already beginning to throb uncomfortably inside his breeches. He had never seen a more fetching sight. Victoria rarely came into his rooms and she had never used his bathing tub before. Seeing her like this, he wondered why he hadn't invited her to share it long ago.

She moved a bit, her breasts peeking through the bubbles again, and desire hit him so hard his stomach muscles contracted.

"I was looking for you," he said, having to force out the words. "It didn't occur to me to look for you in here."

"Perhaps it will from now on."

One of his eyebrows went up. "Oh? And why is that?" He tried to concentrate, but she was lifting a slim, shapely leg, trailing a small square of linen over her wet, glistening skin.

His member swelled. He could feel each heartbeat throbbing in his groin. He wanted to touch her, to press his mouth against her moist flesh. He wanted to be inside her so bad his hands clenched into fists.

"From now on," she said, "I plan to use this tub whenever I wish. I intend that from this day forward we will share this room. I plan to sleep in your bed each night, to wake up with you in the morning."

It sounded like heaven. Still, it would only increase the power she held over him. "What if I refuse to allow it? This is my room, after all."

She stood up from the tub and soapy water sluiced down her body. "Think how handy it would be, my lord. Should you want me, I would be close at hand. I could satisfy your desires whenever you wished. I would be available for whatever wicked things you might—"

His control simply snapped. He dragged her wet body against him, and claimed her mouth in a ravaging kiss.

It had been so long. Too bloody long.

His arousal strengthened as she yielded, then kissed him back and slid her arms around his neck.

"Cord..." she whispered, and he could feel her trembling. She was trying to work the buttons at the front of his breeches, but he caught her hand and brought it to his lips.

"Not yet. Not until I've tasted every wet, delicious inch of you." Lifting her out of the tub, he set her on her feet and kissed the side of her neck.

It was warm in the bathing room. Her skin tasted like hot, wet silk. Her head fell back as he kissed her shoulders, took the fullness of her breast into his mouth. Her nipple puckered and tightened and he heard her soft moan. Her fingers dug into the muscles across his shoulders, and his erection continued to throb.

He pressed his lips against the skin above her rib cage, moved to the slight protrusion of her belly, then nudged her legs apart. She cried out as he knelt to kiss the inside of her thigh, then invaded her moistness with his tongue. He laved and tasted, refused to stop until he had brought her to a trembling climax.

She was sobbing his name when he lifted her into his arms and carried her out of the bathing room, over to his big four-poster bed. Still, he didn't take her, not until he had her squirming on the bed, once more on the edge of release. Victoria arched upward, and he positioned himself at her core. Surging deeply, he filled her, slid out and filled her again. Her nails scored his back as he took what he so badly wanted.

What he could no longer do without.

They reached release together and afterward lay entwined, Victoria curled against him. She looked up at him with eyes still clouded with doubt.

"May I stay?" she whispered softly.

Cord ran a finger along her cheek. "I forbid you to leave. In fact I think I shall chain you to the bed—just in case I decide to do one of those wicked things you mentioned."

He could feel the pull of her smile as she snuggled closer against him and his body stirred, wanting her yet again.

A long chestnut curl wrapped around his finger and he smiled. Then he thought how well and truly she had him snared and prayed he had done the right thing.

Twenty-Four

Cord awakened more rested than he had been in days. He turned on the mattress to reach for his wife, but found the place next to him vacant. Pulling on a burgundy silk dressing gown, he padded over to the door adjoining their two chambers.

At first he didn't see her. Then he heard a sound and found her behind the painted screen in the corner, emptying the contents of her stomach into the chamber pot.

"Victoria!" Cord started in her direction, then turned and went over to the bureau instead. Pouring water into the basin, he wet a cloth, poured her a glass of water and carried it to where she bent over the pot.

Victoria accepted the cloth with a shaking hand. "I was hoping I wouldn't wake you." She used it to wash her face and neck, then managed to muster a smile. "I must have eaten something that didn't agree with me."

Cord frowned. "I was planning to go to Watford this afternoon. I was hoping you would come with me. I think now I had better stay home."

She shook her head. "Don't be silly. There is nothing you can do to help and I am already feeling better. How long did you plan to be gone?"

"Two days, three at most."

She washed her face again, then accepted the glass of water he held out to her. "I want you to go. There is nothing you can do for me here."

"If I left, I would only worry the entire time I was away."

"Please go, Cord. If you're here, I won't rest as I should." She looked down at the chamber pot and her cheeks reddened. "And I would rather you not see me this way."

Cord studied her face and thought there was something different about it, a soft sort of glow he hadn't noticed before. He remembered the plumpness of her breasts as he had caressed them last night, the slight protrusion of her belly.

She was ill in the morning.

Cord had been with any number of women. They felt comfortable with him, confided in him. Sarah confided in him. Victoria might not yet know it, but Cord had a very strong suspicion he knew exactly what was wrong with his wife. Victoria was with child.

The possibility staggered him.

As earl, it was time he set up his nursery. It was his duty to provide an heir to the Brant title and fortune. He wanted children very badly. As a boy, he had yearned for a brother or sister and felt blessed at the arrival of his three Sharpe cousins. He adored young Teddy and looked forward to the day he would have a son of his own.

He only wished he knew if the child his wife carried were his own.

He looked down at Victoria. She still looked pale, but the tremors had eased. "If you're certain you'll be all right, I think I'll go ahead with my plans."

He needed to get away, needed time to adjust to this new complication. He had to come to grips with the fact the child growing in his wife's womb might belong to another man.

It wasn't a possibility he had imagined when he had married Victoria. It wasn't something that was easy for a man like him to accept. Time was what he needed. With a few days to think things through, perhaps he could resign himself to the knowledge that Julian Fox might be the father of Victoria's child.

Tory saw Cord only briefly before he left for Watford. Perhaps she shouldn't have moved into his bedchamber until her morning sickness had passed, but she couldn't stand to sit by another day doing nothing to mend the terrible rift between them.

And she had hoped she would be able to hide her illness and that it would quickly pass. She would have to be more careful in the future—at least until she received a reply to the letter she had written to Julian.

She only prayed he could help her find a way to straighten out the coil she had managed to get herself in.

It was two hours after Cord's departure that Tory received an urgent message from Claire.

Tory had told her sister about their stepfather's intention to sell Windmere and her own determination to get in and search for the diary. But Claire had never been as taken with the lovely Cotswold estate, and she believed Tory should leave the past behind and look to the future.

"Every time you have tried to find Mama's diary, it has caused you nothing but trouble. Whatever Miles Whiting might have done is in the past. It isn't worth putting yourself any more at risk than you have already."

They were sitting in the Blue Salon. At least Claire was sitting. Tory paced in front of the hearth.

"The man murdered our father, Claire. He ruined our mother's life and stole the home she loved and always meant for us to have. Proving he is guilty is worth any sort of risk."

Claire fiddled with the skirt of her plum velvet day dress. She seemed older now that she was married, but she looked no less lovely. Perhaps she was even more so.

"I suppose you are right," she said. "I came by to tell you the sale is supposed to close day after the morrow."

"What!"

"That is what Percy told me." Tory had asked her sister to keep her ears open. Lord Percy was quite the man about town and he always seemed to know the London gossip. "Percy says the buyer's name is Baldwin Slaughter. He is to begin work on the house the day the deed is transferred into his name."

"Oh, dear Lord! Once they start tearing things apart, there is almost no chance we will ever find the diary. I have to get inside before the new owners take over."

"Perhaps Cord will take you."

"Perhaps he would. Unfortunately, Cord is out of town." And she didn't really think he would help her break into what yet remained her stepfather's house.

"He isn't due back until after the sale has already been concluded."

But she wouldn't make the mistake she had made before. She would write him a letter, explain to him just how important this was and how little time was left and beg him not to be angry with her for going.

"At least Windmere isn't that far away," she told Claire. "And I shall be traveling in my own carriage."

And she would take Evan along. She had known the young footman since she had been employed as Cord's housekeeper and she trusted him. Along with Griggs, her big, burly coachman, she should certainly be safe enough.

"As I said, time is slipping away. I shall leave for Windmere first thing in the morning. It shouldn't take more than four hours each way. I'll have time to search the house and still be back by tomorrow night."

"Maybe I should go with you."

Tory shook her head. "The last thing we need is for you to get involved in this. If anything happened, Lord Percy would never forgive me."

"I don't think you should go, Tory."

"I have to, Claire. It's our last chance to bring Miles Whiting to justice and I am going to take it."

Claire didn't say more, but Tory knew she was worried. Her sister would be even more concerned if she knew Tory was carrying a child. But the babe wouldn't arrive for a good long time and she would be careful.

Tory was more concerned with how furious Cord would be when he read her letter. Still, she couldn't just sit by and let her last chance to catch Miles Whiting slip away.

She penned the note that evening, having to rewrite it twice in the hope she could make him understand. Once she finished, she carefully sanded it, sealed it and placed it on top of his desk where he would be sure to see it.

If everything went as planned, he would never have to read it. She would be back before he returned and she could explain the situation herself.

Hopefully, she could also show him the journal. If she did, Cord would finally realize she had been telling him the truth all along. He would know she had never betrayed him with Julian Fox.

Finding the journal was more important than ever and Tory was determined to succeed.

By nightfall, a bitter wind howled outside the windows. Branches scraped against the mullioned panes and a weak moon filtered in between the crack in the damask curtains. Tory spent restless hours tossing and turning, thinking of the day her father had died and remembering her mother's terrible grief.

She awakened later than she meant to, feeling achy and tired but determined. She suffered a brief bout of nausea, but it didn't last long, and an hour later, she was ready to leave, the fancy black calèche Cord had bought her waiting out in front, the horses dancing nervously in their traces.

The carriage wasn't fashioned for this sort of journey, more for bowling about the city in warmer weather with the top down. But Cord had taken the traveling coach so the calèche would have to do.

Dressing in a warm blue woolen day dress with a matching fur-trimmed bonnet, she waited impatiently for Emma to settle her fur-lined cloak around her shoulders and headed downstairs.

Evan helped her climb into the carriage, then tucked a heavy horsehide lap robe over her legs and feet to help keep her warm. The young blond footman mounted the coach and sat down next to the driver, facing the chilly November winds far more readily than she.

The four-hour journey stretched into more than five. Tory entertained herself with an edition of *Castle Rackrent* she had taken from the library, but it was hard to concentrate with her hands and cheeks gone numb. They stopped several times to warm themselves at inns along the way, which helped, but slowed the journey.

It was late in the afternoon by the time they reached the tiny Cotswold village of Windingham and turned toward the yellow stone manor house sitting on top of a gently sloping hill.

Windmere.

The name whispered through her, filling her with memories and longings, stirring a soft ache in her heart. The house had been closed up for the last two years. Only a gardener and his wife lived on the estate to care for the house and grounds.

She hoped that the woman, Mrs. Riddle, she recalled, would remember who she was and allow her inside the house.

There was no way the woman could know the last person Lord Harwood would welcome was his stepdaughter—trying to prove him guilty of murder.

Cord had hoped to find respite in Watford, a small town in the country away from the noise and soot of the city—away from Victoria. Instead, he spent an uncomfortable night thinking about her, wishing she were there with him.

By late in the morning the day after his arrival, he had collected all the necessary information on the property he hoped to purchase and decided to head on home.

It was a short ride back to the city. He arrived a little after noon. He still wasn't certain how he felt about the very likely prospect that his wife might be with child—one that perhaps belonged to another man—but staying away from her hadn't made things any clearer.

Perhaps being with her would.

"Welcome home, my lord." Timmons greeted him in the entry. "We hadn't expected your return for at least another day, perhaps two."

"Yes, well, business progressed rather better than I expected." Of course, he might have stayed an extra day in the charming inn on the river he had discovered—if Victoria had been with him.

As it was, he had fought an urge to be home nearly from the moment of his departure. "Where might I find Lady Brant?"

"I'm sorry, sir. Her ladyship left for the country just this morning. I believe she left a note for you in your study."

Victoria was gone? His stomach instantly knotted. Twice before—as soon as he had left town—she had gone off to meet her lover.

Cord strode down the hall, anxious to read the note. Surely there was some explanation. Victoria had said that she loved him. She had promised to be faithful. He wanted so much to believe her.

But a search of his study turned up nothing and the knot twisted tighter in his stomach. He returned to where Timmons worked brushing the dust from his greatcoat.

"Are you sure Lady Brant left a note?"

"Not for certain, my lord, but I saw her carrying a letter into the study. I presumed it was for you."

He went back and searched again but still found nothing. He went up and made a thorough search of his rooms, then shouted for Emma, who came on the run.

"Yes, milord?"

"Apparently Lady Brant has left for the country. Do you know where she might have gone?"

Emma shook her head, moving a swatch of kinky blond hair. "Not exactly, milord. But she said the trip wouldn't take too long and she would be home sometime tonight."

"Thank you, Emma."

"I believe she left you a note, milord. It were there in the study."

Cord shook his head. "I looked. There is no note."

Emma's pale brows knit together. "That's a bit odd. I was sure I seen her writing it."

"Perhaps she left it in her room." But most of her things had been moved into the master's suite and he found nothing there.

His chest squeezed. He'd had such hopes for them. He wanted a future with Victoria. He thought they might well have one.

Returning to the master's suite, he sank down in the chair next to his bed, feeling sick inside. Sick and empty.

He had trusted her. Again.

He had actually believed she cared for him.

He sat there for several long moments, feeling the sluggish beat of his heart, the deep ache in his chest. She must have gone to Julian. Perhaps to tell him about the babe.

Cord swore foully as he came up out of the chair.

Victoria had lied to him from the first day she had met him, lied to him and duped him. It was time he faced the fact that he meant nothing to her at all and never had. It was time he did what he should have done weeks ago when he had first discovered her betrayal.

Striding down the hall, he shouted for his carriage to be returned to the front of the house, then rapidly descended the stairs. He had made a fool of himself for Victoria for the very last time.

A grim smile curved his lips. The way to forget one woman was to find another.

His stomach twisted viciously, arguing that wasn't the answer, but his legs kept moving toward the street. He couldn't go another day feeling like this—never certain, never really trusting. His marriage was over. He had to get out, get away from Victoria before it was too late. An annulment wouldn't be easy to accomplish, but he believed he could see it done.

His coach was rounding the end of the block. He wasn't quite sure of his destination, someplace he could find feminine companionship of the paid-for sort, the kind who expected nothing of him in return.

Someone who might help ease the pain that gnawed at his heart.

The carriage pulled up in front of the house and a footman raced to open the door. He started to climb the narrow iron stairs when he caught sight of Emma streaking toward him, kinky blond hair sticking out from beneath the mobcap sitting askew on her head.

"Wait, milord! Ye must wait—please!" She was waving a scorched piece of paper and there was soot all over her hands.

Cord steeled himself. He could almost feel the hardening of the wall he was erecting around his heart.

"What is it, Emma?" he asked coolly.

"'Tis the note, milord." She was out of breath, trying to gasp in air. "The one from her ladyship. Mrs. Rathbone—she stole it off your desk. She were tryin' to burn it when I walked into her room."

Cord reached over and took the piece of foolscap out of Emma's trembling hand. He prepared himself to read Victoria's words, thinking that no matter what she said it wouldn't change the way he felt.

He told himself to remain objective, and foolishly believed he actually could. But the lines, written in her familiar, feminine script, made his eyes burn.

Beloved husband,

I know that you will be angry when first you read this note, but this is something I must do. I only hope, once you have read my letter, that you will understand.

This day, I travel to Windmere in search of my mother's journal. My stepfather has sold the estate and today is my last hope of finding it. I know you have never been truly convinced of its existence, but I believe my mother discovered Miles Whiting to be the man responsible for my father's murder and that her writings may hold some proof.

If you return before I get home, please forgive me. I say again how much I love you. When I am returned, I shall find a way to prove it.

Your loving wife,

Victoria

Cord reread the words, more dispassionately this time. She said she had gone in search of the journal. It was the same excuse she had used two times before. He hadn't believed her then. Why should he believe her now?

He refolded the letter. He could climb aboard his carriage and drive away, forget Victoria, forget his marriage, forget that his wife might be carrying another man's child.

Or he could believe her.

He could take a chance on love one more time.

He thought of Victoria the last time they had been together, looking up at him so sweetly.

May I stay?

In his bed? In his heart? She seemed to have always had a place there.

He thought of the days when he had first met her, remembered her courage the night she had helped them free Ethan from prison. She had always been reckless and determined. If there were a diary, she would not give up her efforts to find it as long as there was the slightest chance.

He looked toward the house, thought of the years stretching out ahead of him, years without Victoria, and his decision was made.

His jaw hardened as he turned his attention to Emma. "Where is Mrs. Rathbone?"

"Upstairs, milord."

Cord started back toward the house. He took the stairs two at a time, then climbed the narrower set leading up to the servants' quarters.

Mrs. Rathbone's door stood slightly ajar. She was pacing the floor in front of her tiny, still-smoldering hearth when he walked into the room.

Her face went chalk-white at the sight of him. "M-my lord?"

"Why did you take the letter?"

She moistened her dry, thin lips. "It…it were just a mistake, my lord. I was cleaning up in your study. The letter got mixed into a stack of trash. I tossed it into the fire by mistake. I—I didn't know it was for you."

He glanced at the hearth. There was no reason she would have brought the paper up to her room.

"You're lying. You've hated Victoria since the day she arrived. You didn't want me to see the letter. You were trying to cause trouble for her."

"No, my lord. That's not true."

A memory trickled in and something clicked in his brain. "You knew I was in the bathing room the day you spoke to the maid about Lady Brant—didn't you? You wanted to make trouble for her then."

"She did go out that night—just like I said."

"What my wife does is none of your concern. You are dismissed, Mrs. Rathbone—without references. While you are scurrying around the city, looking for a way to feed yourself, you might remember that my wife could have terminated your employment months ago. It was only through the goodness of her heart that you continued to work in this house."

Her scarecrow face turned hard. "She always thought she were so smart. Better'n the rest of us. Well, I won't be starvin', I can tell ye. I been paid well and good by his lordship, her stepfather. I don't need your piss-pot job no more."

Cord's mind reeled. The older woman started marching past him, but Cord stepped in her way. "You've been spying on us? You've been feeding information to Harwood?"

"I didn't do nothin' against the law. He were just concerned for his daughter's welfare."

Like bloody hell he was. "You read what was in the letter. Did you tell Harwood that Lady Brant was going to Windmere?"

A smug smile twisted her narrow features. "It's his house, ain't it? Man's got a right to know who comes and goes in his own home."

Cord clamped hard on his temper. "Pack your things and get out. You have fifteen minutes." Turning, he strode out the door and down the hall, down the three flights of stairs to the entry.

"How long ago did Lady Brant leave?" he asked Timmons.

"Late this morning, my lord. She took the footman, Mr. Kidd, with her."

Thank God for that. Her coachman was a big, burly fellow and the footman was young and loyal. Still, if Harwood actually *had* murdered her father, or even hired it done, he would do anything in his power to keep her from finding the proof.

Cord remembered the welts he had seen on her back on their wedding night and his stomach tightened with fear. Harwood was utterly ruthless. If he believed Victoria posed any sort of threat…

"Saddle my horse. I won't be needing the carriage."

"Aye, my lord."

Fifteen minutes later, he was on the road to Windmere, pressing his big black gelding as fast as he dared. He would rent a fresh horse at one of the inns and make even better time.

He just hoped Miles Whiting didn't get there first.

Twenty-Five

"There it is!" Tory pointed toward the knoll. "Just up the hill." But instead of urging the horses ahead, Griggs pulled the carriage over to the side of the road.

Tory heard him mutter a curse. "We got us a problem, milady."

"What sort of problem?" But just then she heard it, a grinding crack as two of the carriage spokes snapped and the conveyance tipped sideways.

"Broken wheel, milady." He jumped down to examine the damage. "The iron band's come off. Looks like we'll 'ave to find a smithy to fix it."

Tory gazed back up the hill toward the house. That wasn't the very best news, but neither was it much of a problem.

"There is a blacksmith in the village. And I can walk the rest of the way quite easily. Once you get it fixed, you can come up to the house and get me. I'll probably be busy for quite a while, so there is no reason to hurry."

"I'd better come with you." Evan jumped down from

his perch next to the coachman and started walking toward her.

She thought of the hours she might need to spend. "As I said, I may be there quite a while. The gardener and his wife live on the property, so I shall be perfectly safe. I'm sure Mr. Griggs could use some help, and there is a tavern in the village. While the blacksmith is working, the two of you can get yourselves something to eat."

Evan helped her down, then turned toward the yellow stone house on the knoll. The danger lay on the road, not in her childhood home.

"As you wish, milady."

As the men began working on the wheel, Tory started up the hill. It didn't take long to reach the house, and once she did, getting inside proved not to be a problem.

Mrs. Riddle, who lived with her husband, Jacob, in the gatehouse, remembered her from the last time she had been there with her mother and sister, after her father had died.

"Why, praise the saints! 'Tis Lady Victoria come home to Windmere." A big-boned Irish woman with graying auburn hair, Mrs. Riddle had a smile that still contained all of her teeth. She and her husband had been at Windmere since Tory's grandfather had owned the house.

"Good afternoon, Mrs. Riddle. It's good to see you."

The woman glanced toward the empty drive leading up to the carved front doors. "How did ye get here? 'Ave ye come by yerself, then?"

"There was a problem with one of the carriage wheels. The coachman took it in to the village to have it fixed."

"What brings ye here, child? After so many years?"

"I just learned that my stepfather is selling the house. I wanted to see it one more time before it belonged to someone else."

"Aye, Windmere's a special place, and no doubt. Queen o' the valley, she is, and always will be." Mrs. Riddle shook her head. "Ah, but 'tisn't joyous, the way it once was. Not with your da and ma gone."

"That is one of the reasons I came. I think my mother may have left a few of her things in the house."

"Well, then, 'tis past time ye came to collect them."

Mrs. Riddle led her up the gravel drive to the front of the big stone manor house and opened the door. "I'll be goin' into the village for the rest of the afternoon. Jacob's workin' the fields. Take all the time ye like."

Tory watched the woman leave and turned to survey the inside of the house. Memories enveloped her. She could almost hear the sound of laughter coming from upstairs, hear her father's deep baritone and her mother's saucy reply. Tory closed away the painful thoughts. She didn't have time for the past. She had to find the journal.

Pulling the ribbon on her fur-trimmed bonnet, she tossed it onto the table in the entry along with her cloak. For more than two years, the place had been locked up. White sheets draped over the sofas and chairs, and most of the curtains were closed, but the heavy oak tables had recently been dusted, and the carved wooden beams and leaded glass cabinets gave the house a familiar air.

Considering the size of the house and knowing her search might take some time, Tory set to work. But two hours later, she was still searching. She found some of her mother's clothes still hanging in an upstairs armoire, found a stack of stitchery with the threads beginning to fade, a few of Claire's baby toys, and some of her own infant clothing.

But no sign of the journal.

She went through the sideboards in the dining room, but really held no hope of finding the journal there.

If it's here, it has to be somewhere Mama would feel it would be safe.

But where would that be? She made her way back up to her mother's bedchamber. When her father was alive, her parents had slept in the master's suite. After her mother's disastrous second marriage, she had moved into the adjoining room.

If she had kept the journal in there, the baron might have seen her putting it away. He might have discovered her hiding place.

Tory made another thorough search, but wasn't surprised to find it not there.

She had twice checked her mother's sewing room, which seemed the most likely hiding place. Still, she went back down the hall, into the small room her mother had favored. A rosewood settee sat in front of a small stone hearth. Next to it perched the rocking chair her mother had sat in while she stitched samplers, crocheted or read.

A portable oak writing desk sat on a table in the corner. When Tory's father was alive, the journal had been kept inside. But she had already looked there and found it empty.

Where did you put it, Mama?

It struck her then—if her mother had gone to the

trouble of hiding it, perhaps she had hoped that one day her daughters would find it.

Tory left the sewing room and hurried down the hall. During the last week of her life, her mother had begged the baron to take her and Claire home to Windmere. Tory had been away at school, unaware how desperately ill her mother was. She had died here in the house before Tory had time to get there.

If her mother had wanted her to find the journal...

She raced into the bedchamber that had once been her own. She had chosen the soft rose counterpane herself, to complement the heavy rose damask curtains at the windows. Memories of the fun that mother and daughters had shared the day they went shopping crept into her head, but she ruthlessly forced them away.

Hurrying toward the bed, she lifted the feather mattress and made a thorough search beneath, then checked the drawers in the armoire in the corner.

Nothing.

There were still a few items of her clothing in the rosewood dresser against the wall.

And in the bottom drawer, beneath a shawl her mother had knit for her one Christmas, rested the journal.

Tory's hand shook as she lifted the shawl away and ran her fingers lovingly over the smooth red leather cover, worn over the years from so much use. Dear God, she had actually found it! She swallowed against the lump that formed in her throat as she lifted it out of the drawer, and the book fell open, revealing her mother's feminine script.

She didn't read the beginning, those first years after

Charlotte Temple had wed the handsome young man she had fallen so deeply in love with. Her mother's thoughts were her own.

Instead, she skipped to the final days of her mother's life, those last weeks when she had been so desperately ill. And there it was—the proof Tory had been searching for—exactly as she had imagined.

Today I found William's ring. It was in Miles's jewelry case, wrapped in white satin and hidden away, a trophy—an irresistible prize that proved how clever he was.

Tory stopped reading and took a deep breath, fighting to control her racing heart. *Oh, Mama.* She turned the pages, revealing her mother's growing suspicions—and her fear.

I think he knows I have discovered his part in William's murder. Beloved William—how could I not have seen the man Miles truly was? How I loathe him. And I am frightened of him, frightened for the children.

Every page filled Tory with anger and pain.

He goads me at every turn, warns me with a look what will happen should I give him away.

How could her mother have married him? How could she not have recognized the sort of man he really was? But her mother had been so desperately lonely, so deeply buried in grief. And in the end, she *had* seen.

> *I grow more and more ill with each passing day. I am certain that Miles is poisoning me, but I have no idea how he is going about it. I grow weaker and weaker, too ill to stop him.*

Tory stared at the lines that were beginning to blur in front of her. She blinked to clear her vision and tears rolled down her cheeks.

He had killed her mother, too!

She brushed away the wetness, despising Miles Whiting, vowing she would see him hang.

She forced herself to continue, though little more was written over the next several days. Then,

> *The end is near. I am so afraid for my daughters. Somehow I must find a way to protect them. Dear God, what shall I do?*

It was her final entry. She had died that same day. But somehow she had found the strength to hide the journal in a place she believed Tory would find it. Perhaps she had meant to warn her.

Or to see justice done.

"Well…I see you have finally found it." Miles Whiting's voice sent an icy chill down her spine. She whirled to see him standing in the doorway. "It would have been far better had you not…but then you never were a sensible sort of young woman."

"You killed her! You killed them both!"

"Ah, so that is what your mother had to say. She was delusional, you know…there toward the end. No one will believe a word of what she has written."

"Oh, I think they will—once I show them my father's ring! It was supposedly stolen by the men who killed him. My mother found it in your jewelry case and now I am the one who has it."

His lean face hardened. "Is that so?" She saw his hand move inside his coat, and an instant later, his long fingers wrapped around the handle of a pistol. Sweet God, confronting him here was the worst possible thing she could have done.

"A ring is hardly proof enough to see me hanged, though your accusations would certainly be enough to cause me unnecessary trouble."

"How did you find me?" she asked, trying to control the tremor in her voice, trying to give herself time to think. "How did you know I was here?"

He gave her a tight little smile. "Your Mrs. Rathbone has been quite helpful in that regard. She doesn't care for you much, you know."

She glanced toward the door, but Harwood blocked her way and the second-story window was too high off the ground. She had the babe to think of. She couldn't possibly jump.

He motioned with the pistol. "Come. You began this game. Now it is time we finished it." He backed away from the door so that she had room to get past him, then fell into step behind her, close enough a pistol shot wouldn't miss.

"Where are we going?"

"You were searching for your mother's journal. Surely you would want to look in the basement."

A shiver of fear went through her. Unconsciously her hand came up to the slight rounding of her belly where the babe nestled. She shouldn't have come. Nothing was worth putting her unborn child at risk.

"I'm not going down there." She stopped in the hallway and started to turn, but he shoved the pistol into her ribs.

"If you prefer, I can shoot you right here."

He would do it, she knew. He would murder her and the child.

"I didn't come here alone. If you pull the trigger, one of my men will hear the gunshot. They'll come looking for me." That wasn't true, of course, since the men were still in the village.

"Perhaps, but by then you'll be dead. Since no one knows I am here and I shall be gone within seconds after I fire, it really won't matter."

"My husband will know. I left him a letter explaining where I have gone and why. Cord will know you are the one who murdered me and he'll kill you."

He laughed. "There is no letter. I instructed Mrs. Rathbone to burn it. Your husband will believe you have gone off with your lover, as you did before. Perhaps he'll think the man is responsible for your death. Yes…I believe he might think that exactly."

She clamped down on another round of fear. God in heaven, he knew everything about her! And he had destroyed the letter! If she weren't at the house when Cord returned and she had left no word of where she had gone, he would believe she had gone to Julian.

He pressed the gun into her ribs, nudging her forward, and she started walking, her legs trembling beneath her skirt. Evan and Griggs had not yet returned. Jacob worked somewhere in the fields, but even if he heard the shot, it would be too late.

"A little faster, if you please. I have plans for the evening."

Plans that would prove he had been in London the night she disappeared. There had to be something she could do!

Outside the windows, dusk had begun to fall, a soft purple haze that floated over the landscape. She thought the dim light might work in her favor, but Harwood paused on the landing and instructed her to light the small glass lamp on the Sheraton table.

She held it out in front of her, the flame wobbling, the unsteady light betraying her fear. Continuing forward, she went over her options, of which there seemed none, and fought to control her growing terror.

Perhaps Mrs. Riddle or her husband would come up to the house. Perhaps Evan and Griggs would get the wheel fixed and come to get her. She thought of calling out, but there was no one to hear, and Harwood might simply shoot her.

Still, she couldn't give up hope. She refused to let him win again.

She held up the lamp and kept walking. Down the broad staircase, along the hall to the short flight leading down to the big, low-ceilinged kitchen. It smelled of long-dead fires, dust and old yeast. As they entered, she glanced toward the wall near the back, where a stairwell led into a storage area below the house.

"Set the lamp on the table."

She considered throwing it in his face, but he was

pointing the gun directly at her and she knew if she made the slightest move, he would pull the trigger. She set the lamp down on the table.

"Very good. Now open the storage-room door."

She saw the anticipation in his face. He had wanted to be rid of her for years. "Why?"

"Because you are going to have an accident. You are going to take a terrible fall, poor dear. You're going to crack your head wide open—fitting, don't you think, since you once did that to me. Only when I do it, I won't leave you alive."

Fresh fear trickled through her. He was going to kill her and the child she carried and she still had no idea how to stop him. She glanced frantically around the kitchen in search of a weapon. There was a row of butchering knives in a wooden rack on the wall. If she could somehow get to them…

She bolted in that direction, but the baron's long fingers caught the coil of her hair, ripping it free of its pins and sending a shot of pain up her neck as he yanked her backward, slamming her hard against the door leading down to the basement.

"I would really prefer not to shoot you, my dear. So messy, you know. But I swear to you that I will."

A deep voice resonated from the doorway. "I wouldn't advise it. Should you do anything other than let my wife go, I shall take great pleasure in killing you—as slowly and as painfully as I possibly can."

"Cord…" Tory whispered, her eyes filling with tears. Dear God, she had thought never to see him again.

Cord didn't so much as glance in her direction. Every ounce of his concentration was focused on the man with the gun. In the pale light of the lamp, the blue metal barrel of his own pistol glittered.

"Step away from her, Harwood. Move very, very slowly."

"So you saw the letter. A pity Mrs. Rathbone proved such a disappointment." Still, he didn't back away from her. Instead, he jerked her in front of him, up against his chest, and pressed the gun to the side of her head.

"See how quickly the game can shift?" he said. "Now, I believe it is my move. I would advise you to do exactly as I say."

Keeping the pistol in place, he slid an arm beneath her chin and locked it around her throat. "Set the gun on the floor, then shove it over here with your boot."

"Don't do it, Cord! He'll kill us both!"

"Shut up!" the baron warned, tightening his hold until it was hard to breathe.

Cord's jaw hardened as he bent down and placed the gun on the floor, sent it spiraling across the room with the side of his foot.

"There is a man working in the fields," Cord said. "He'll be in here the instant you fire that weapon."

Harwood laughed as he turned the pistol away from her and aimed it at Cord. "Then I suppose I shall have to leave through the storage room. The door opens into an area on the other side of the carriage house. There isn't the slightest chance anyone will see me."

He looked from one of them to the other and shook his head. "Terrible what happened here tonight…the unfaithful wife shoved down the stairs, killed by her jealous husband, who then took his own life. Men can be such fools."

Tory heard the hammer being cocked, knew Cord had only a moment to live. Clamping her teeth, she shoved Harwood's arm up as hard as she could and at the same instant, hurled herself against him with every ounce of her strength.

The gun went off, the sound deafening in the closed-up kitchen. Tory screamed as Harwood bolted past her, racing for the door, but Cord caught his coattail and brought him crashing down, both men hitting the floor in a tangle of thrashing limbs.

She heard Cord's softly muttered curse and knew he had reinjured the wound in his chest. He delivered a couple of vicious blows to Harwood's face, but the baron managed to tear himself free and run for the door. Cord raced after him, both men pounding up the stairs to the main floor of the house.

Tory grabbed the brass lamp off the table and ran after them, hoping Jacob had heard the gunshot, but knowing he was probably too far away.

She glanced around, caught sight of the baron running into the drawing room, Cord close on his heels. Above the hearth, in a crisscross pattern, her grandfather's dueling sabers glinted in the light of the lamp she carried into the room.

Harwood grinned as he dragged one of the weapons down and tossed it to Cord, then reached up and yanked down the other.

"See what a sportsman I am? I am giving you a chance. Perhaps you yet will live."

But Miles Whiting was an expert swordsman, and the way Cord was favoring his left side, the match would hardly be fair.

Ignoring the pain, Cord tested the blade. "You've just made your second mistake, Harwood. It's going to be your last."

The baron just laughed, the sound echoing through the deserted house, sending chills down Tory's spine. The men stepped toward each other, raised their arms and crossed blades. Sabers clashed. Steel clanged against steel, ringing across the drawing room. Harwood thrust and Cord parried, the baron slashing one way and then another, driving his wicked blade toward Cord's heart.

Tory saw that Cord was more skilled than she had imagined. Far more. But he was not in the same league as the baron.

Some might have called it a duel.

Tory thought that it was the baron's excuse for murder. Harwood had killed her mother and father. She wasn't about to let him kill her husband, too.

Heart pounding, she took off for the short flight of stairs leading down to the kitchen. She considered trying to find Jacob, but even if she did, Cord might be dead by the time they got back to the house.

As soon as she reached the kitchen, she went down on her knees in search of Cord's pistol. Her hands shook as she ran her fingers over the planked wooden floor where the weapon had disappeared.

Please, God... Frantic now in the semidarkness, she groped the surface beneath the table and her fingers closed over the grip of the gun. Tory dragged it toward her and leaped to her feet.

By the time she reached the drawing room, the men had stripped off their jackets and waistcoats. As they circled each other in the center of the room, a scarlet blossom of blood spread over the sleeve of Cord's white shirt, and her heart squeezed with fear for him.

"You surprise me, Brant," the baron said, showing only the least bit of exertion. "Perhaps in time, you might make a descent swordsman. Unfortunately, time isn't something you have."

"It would seem to me that you are the one whose time has run out." Cord found an opening and his blade sliced into Harwood's shoulder. The baron hissed in pain. Furious that Cord had drawn blood, he started slashing in earnest. As Cord fell back, Harwood circled his blade, caught Cord's saber near the hilt and sent it flying into the air.

Tory bit back a scream as the tip of Harwood's blade found the spot above Cord's heart.

"You did very well…considering. Unfortunately, as I said, I have plans for the evening. And there is still the problem of disposing of your troublesome wife."

The muscles in the baron's forearms tensed as he prepared to thrust home—and Tory fired.

The blade trembled in Harwood's hand. An expression of disbelief appeared on his thin, dark face. The saber wobbled and fell from his nerveless fingers and he crumpled onto the floor.

Tory stood there shaking. A sob escaped as the pistol dropped from her hand, hitting the Persian carpet with a quiet thud.

The sound jolted Cord into action. Turning away from the baron's lifeless eyes, he crossed the room to where Tory stood, tears streaming down her cheeks. She started to weep as he hauled her into his arms.

"It's all right, love." He held her hard against him, trying to ease the tremors coursing through her body. "I've got you now. Everything's going to be all right."

Her fingers curled over the lapels of his coat. "I never imagined you would come."

"I had to. I was afraid for you. Afraid something like this might happen."

"He would…would have killed you."

"Yes. But you were there with the gun and I knew you wouldn't let him."

Her voice shook. "Harwood said Mrs. Rathbone burned my letter. I thought you might not believe what it said, even if you read it."

His hold tightened around her. He thought of the letter and how close he had come to casting it aside. How close he had come to giving in to his jealousy and fear, to running away from his overwhelming feelings for her.

"I'm going to have a baby," she said, looking up at him through her tears.

"I know."

"The child is yours—I swear it on my life."

"It doesn't matter." And it didn't. He knew that now, knew it with every ounce of his soul. From the moment he had stepped into the kitchen and realized the danger she was in, he had understood the depth of his love for her. The depth of his feelings for both her and the child. "I just thank God that you are safe."

Fresh tears rolled down her cheeks. "I love you. I love you so very much."

Cord looked down at his brave, beautiful wife and captured her tear-streaked face between his hands. "I love you, too, Victoria. As God is my witness, I do."

Twenty-Six

It was full dark outside by the time the wheel was repaired and the carriage rolled up in front of the house. Jacob had left to fetch the constable, who arrived at great speed a few minutes later. Cord answered questions for more than an hour, but finally he and Victoria were allowed to leave.

"There is something I need to tell you," Cord said.

Victoria looked up at him, worry creeping back into her face. "What is it?"

"You didn't have to make this mad journey. Harwood didn't know it, but he was selling Windmere to me. The house needed a good deal of repair, which I hoped to begin right away. Then I planned to give it to you as a birthday gift."

"But Claire said a man named Baldwin Slaughter had bought it."

"I knew the baron would never agree to sell it to me for any sort of reasonable price." Cord grinned. "Bald means white...as in Whiting? Slaughter...well, Mr. Slaughter drove a very hard bargain."

Tory grinned and threw her arms around his neck. "You are the most wonderful man!"

Cord winced and Victoria hurriedly released him. "Darling, I'm so sorry. Is it hurting very much?"

"It's just a little sore, is all. Nothing to worry about, though I don't relish the long ride home." Victoria climbed into the carriage and Cord climbed up beside her.

The wound in his chest was aching, the muscles and tendons still sore. With Mrs. Riddle's assistance, Victoria had bandaged the gash in his arm, but there remained an uncomfortable four-hour ride back to London.

In the end, fussing over him as always, she insisted they stop for the night at a place called the Black Dog Inn.

"I told you it is only a scratch," he grumbled. "Nothing to get worked up about."

Victoria simply ignored him. She helped him undress and checked the bandage on his arm. She insisted he take a dose of laudanum before he went to bed, to which he agreed—only if she would join him. Unfortunately, the damnable laudanum put him almost immediately to sleep.

It was just before noon of the following day that they arrived back in London. As the coach pulled up to the house, Cord was surprised to see the duke of Sheffield's extravagant four-horse rig parked out in front.

It wasn't like Rafe to arrive unannounced. Cord worried what new crisis might have arisen while he was away.

"It appears we have company," he said to Victoria. "Are you certain you're up to it?"

"I would love to play the invalid a bit longer, love, since you take such good care of me, but aside from a bit of soreness, I am feeling just fine."

They made their way toward the town house just as Sheffield walked out on the porch.

"Timmons said you had left for the country," he said. "I suppose I should have sent a note ahead, but I didn't want to waste that much time."

Cord climbed the front porch stairs, Victoria on his arm. "I don't know if I should be glad to see you or terrified of what news you may have brought."

The duke chuckled softly, then frowned as he noticed the coat draped over Cord's shoulder. "Problems with your wound? I thought you were pretty well healed."

"I was," Cord said.

"My stepfather tried to kill him," Victoria said. "He tried to kill both of us. Cord was injured during a saber duel."

"The cut is minor. It's a long story," he said with a sigh. "Why don't we go inside?"

Rafe flicked a glance at Victoria. "Good idea. If your wife can spare you for a bit, I'd like a word with you in private. There is a matter of some importance we need to discuss."

Cord's eyebrows drew together. "I was afraid of that."

"Buck up, old friend. This is news you'll want to hear."

"I'll arrange something for luncheon," Victoria said diplomatically. "Will you join us, Your Grace?"

He smiled. "Thank you, I believe I will."

Mollified a little by his friend's congeniality and more than a little intrigued, Cord led Rafe down the hall into his study.

"Something to drink?" he asked.

"Not at present."

"Will I need one?"

Rafe chuckled. "Perhaps later, to celebrate what I'm about to tell you."

"Now I *am* intrigued."

The men sat down in front of the fire. "I had a visitor earlier this morning."

"Is that so?"

"His name was Julian Fox."

Cord felt a rush of blood to the back of his neck. "What did he want?"

"He came to discuss your wife. It seems he recently received a letter from her."

A pulse began to pound in his temple. "Victoria wrote Fox a letter?"

"Take it easy, my friend. It is not what you think. Apparently your wife wrote to the man in desperation. In the letter, she explained the series of events that led you to the erroneous conclusion that their relationship went far beyond friendship. She begged him to help her set things right. She told Fox that she was with child—"

"Did she tell him the child might be his?" Cord shot to his feet. "Perhaps that is the real reason she wrote the letter."

"Dammit, man, sit down and listen. This is the very reason Fox came to me instead of approaching you directly. When you hear what the man had to say, you will know your wife has been telling you the truth."

Cord took a deep breath, Rafe's last words beginning to sink in. He sat back down in his chair, his chest starting to ache again. "What did Fox say?"

"He said that he and Victoria were never more than friends. He said that he didn't like the way you ignored her and he believed making you jealous would force you to realize how lucky you were to have married such a woman."

"And why, exactly, should I believe him?"

Rafe cast him a glance. "You're acquainted with my younger brother, Simon?"

"Of course. What does Simon have to do with any of this?"

"Fox came to me because of my brother. The two of them are friends, you see. Julian knew that I was aware of Simon's er…sexual preferences, and yet I've never condemned him. Fox trusted me with his own, similar secret and asked that the information go no further than you."

Cord worked to get his mind around exactly what Rafe was saying. "Are you telling me that…that Julian Fox is a—"

"I'm saying Fox prefers intimacy with members of his same sex."

"Good God."

"As I said, he and Simon share a similar preference. Fox and your wife are nothing more than friends."

For several long moments, Cord simply sat there, mulling over Rafe's words.

Then a slow smile broke over his lips. "Victoria never betrayed me with Fox."

"According to Fox, your wife is desperately in love with you."

He wanted to cheer, to shout into the streets. "She tried to tell me. She said that she and Fox were only pretending. But she had lied to me before and I refused to believe her. And there was McPhee's report."

"I believe your wife convinced the servants at Harwood Hall to keep their silence in regard to her visit. The night Julian happened to run into her, she was headed for her father's old town house in search of her mother's journal, just as she said."

Both men came to their feet. "You're a lucky man, Cord," Rafe said a bit wistfully.

Cord thought of Victoria and how close he had come to losing her. "Yes, I am." He smiled. "And in the not-so-distant future, I'm also going to be a father."

Rafe laughed and Cord chimed in. The future had never looked brighter.

"If you will excuse me," Cord said. "I believe I need to speak to my wife."

Rafe nodded. "I wish you great happiness, my friend."

Cord just smiled. "I appreciate that—but I already have it."

Epilogue

An icy December frost settled over London. Thick tendrils of fog drifted through the streets, the heavy mist making the cobbles slick and difficult to navigate. But in the master's suite of the earl of Brant's town house, a warm fire snapped and crackled pleasantly in the hearth and the chill remained outside the windows.

Several lamps had been lit, giving the room a soft, golden glow. Tory sat on the blue velvet stool in front of the dresser. In the mirror, she could see her husband behind her, so handsome in his dark evening clothes and gold brocade waistcoat, leaning forward a little as he draped the beautiful diamond-and-pearl necklace around her throat.

"Have I told you lately how beautiful you are?"

She turned to look up at him, the netting on her copper silk gown rustling with the movement. Though she was several months gone with child, her pregnancy had only barely begun to show. "Have I told you lately how happy you make me?"

The diamond clasp made a soft click as it went together. Tory felt the cool, comforting weight of the strands, then the press of her husband's lips against the side of her neck.

"Have I told you how much I love you?" he whispered softly.

She rose from the stool and went into his arms, slid her own arms up around his neck. Her throat felt too tight to speak so she simply held on to him.

His mouth traveled up to her ear. "Are you certain you don't want to just stay home and forget the ball? I imagine I could find a way to keep you entertained." He nuzzled her ear and little shivers ran over her skin.

Tory leaned back to look up at him. "I am certain, my lord, you could persuade me with very little trouble to do most anything you wished. But we have promised your friend the duke that we would attend his ball and I think we should do as we have said."

He sighed, though his eyes held a smile. "I suppose you are right."

She turned away from him and went to retrieve her reticule. When she turned toward him, Cord must have noticed the slight crease that had settled between her eyes.

"What is it? You're worried about something. Tell me what it is."

Tory hung the cord of her copper silk reticule over her shoulder. "I saw Gracie today." Cord knew the truth about Grace and her real father. There were no more secrets between them—not anymore. "She was extremely upset. It seems her father—her real father—has been tossed into prison."

"Prison? What in God's name for?"

"The charge is high treason with the French. Grace is afraid they are going to hang him."

"There's been nothing in the papers. When did this happen?"

"Only just this morning. She told me some time back that her father was a man highly placed in the government."

"Perhaps he was privy to information that would be valuable to the French. Did she tell you his name?"

"Yes, just this morning. His name is Harmon Jeffries, Viscount Forsythe. Do you know him?"

"I've met him once or twice. A man in his forties. I don't remember much else about him."

"Perhaps he is innocent."

"For Grace's sake, we can only hope."

She walked to where he stood, reached for his hand and brought it to her lips. "There is something I would ask of you."

Cord smiled. "Anything, my love. By now, you must know that."

She let go of his hand, reached up and touched the pearls at her throat. Each precious diamond glittered in the lamplight.

"I've never believed in legends or curses. I don't know if what they say about the necklace is true. But my stepfather once owned it and now he is dead and no one ever had a blacker heart than he."

"And no one has a purer heart than you, my love."

"Though the road was not always smooth, in the end, I've been blessed with everything I've ever wanted. I have a husband who loves me that I love more than my own life, and soon we will have a child. Claire is safe and never been happier." She felt the burn of tears and blinked to hold them away. "We all have so much and Grace has so little."

She looked up at him and prayed he would understand. "I want to give her the necklace, Cord. I want Grace to find the kind of happiness I have found with you."

Cord's gaze held hers. "The necklace was a gift. It belongs to you, Victoria. It's yours to do with as you wish."

Tears filled her eyes. "Thank you."

Cord bent his head and very softly kissed her. "You won't be disappointed if the necklace doesn't work, will you?"

She shook her head. "At least Grace will have the joy of wearing it."

"Then I wish her just that." Cord straightened away from her. "Now that I have behaved like such a prince, can we stay home?"

Tory laughed. "You are shameless! We are going to His Grace's ball." She cast him a look. "But as I recall, the house is quite large. Perhaps we might find some small room not in use, a place where we might be private?"

Cord's golden eyes darkened. A corner of his mouth edged up. "I imagine that can be arranged." Far more eager than he was before, he settled a hand at her waist and guided her out the door.

Tory bit back a smile, certain he was already thinking what place he might find—and exactly what he would do with her once they got there.

Author's Note

I hope you enjoyed Cord and Victoria and the tale of *The Bride's Necklace.* Grace Chastain and Captain Ethan Sharpe, marquess of Belford, meet for the first time in Grace's story, *The Devil's Necklace.* It's a clash of wills and a tale of high adventure.

Find out if the necklace will bring Grace the same happiness it brought Tory. Look for *The Devil's Necklace,* coming August of this year.

Till then, all best wishes and happy reading,

Kat

* * * * *

Grace stood rooted to the deck of the *Sea Devil,* fear a living thing inside her. She could hear the thunder of her heart, feel the tightness in her chest that made it hard to breathe. The captain stood in front of her, long legs braced against the roll of the sea, a cold, triumphant smile on his face. It took sheer force of will to keep her shoulders squared and her head held high, monumental strength not to let him know how terrified she truly was.

Dear God, she should have fought him! She should have refused to go with him, should have shouted for help, begged the passengers and crew of the *Lady Anne* to come to her aid. But there was Captain Chambers to consider and she didn't want the man harmed, perhaps even killed because of her.

She was guilty of a terrible crime, and in that brief, terrifying instant when the black-haired Captain Sharpe had walked into the salon it was obvious he knew what she had done.

What kind of a man was he?

The devil, he had said, and Grace believed him. She had never seen eyes such an icy shade of blue, never seen a jaw so hard it appeared carved in stone.

He was tall, his legs long and sinewy, the shoulder pressing into her stomach as he had carried her down the rope ladder wide and solid. There was no extra fat over the lean muscles in his back, she knew, her face growing warm at the memory of the intimate contact.

His skin was dark, his face tanned, with little crinkles at the corners of his eyes. Sun lines, not laugh lines, she was sure. She couldn't imagine the devil captain ever laughing at anything, except, perhaps, someone else's pain. Instead, his features were hard and unforgiving, brutal, even cruel.

And yet he was handsome. With his wavy black hair, winged black brows, and well-formed lips, Ethan Sharpe was one of the handsomest men she had even seen.

"Follow me." Captain Sharpe's words sliced right through her thoughts. Sweet God, why had she ever let him force her off the *Lady Anne?*

She mustered another shot of courage. "Where are you taking me?"

"You'll need a place to sleep. You'll be staying in my cabin."

She stopped dead still, the deck rolling just then, causing her to stumble. "And where, exactly, do you intend to sleep?"

His mouth barely curved. "This ship isn't all that big. I'm afraid you'll have to share the cabin with me."

Grace shook her head, unconsciously taking a step backward. "Oh, no. There is no way you are sleeping in the same room with me."

One of his black eyebrows went up. "Then perhaps you would rather sleep on deck. I can arrange it, if that is your wish. Or perhaps you would rather bunk with the crew? I'm sure there isn't a one of them who would mind sharing his bed with you. What will it be, Miss Chastain?"

She stared at those hard, cruel features and a wave of nausea hit her. She was completely at this man's mercy. What in God's name should she do?

She glanced frantically around the deck. There was nowhere to go, no place to run. Half a dozen crewmen stood in a semicircle around them. One man smiled and she could see the black stumps of his teeth. One of them had a wooden leg, another man was big and dark and covered with tattoos.

"Miss Chastain?"

Surely the captain was the lesser evil, though she wasn't completely sure. At the nod she managed to give him, he turned and started walking. Grace forced her feet to move, her legs shaking as she followed him down the ladder that led to his quarters in the stern of the ship. At the bottom of the stairs, he turned and reached for her hand, helping her down with a chivalry that was more mocking than gallant.

She swallowed, collected herself, forced up her chin. "I demand to know why you brought me here. What do you want with me?"

He slowly turned to face her, his expression cold and completely unforgiving. "That is the question, is it not?"

Instead of fear, anger rose inside her, bringing a wash of color into her cheeks. "Who are you?"

The captain looked into her face, making no attempt to hide the hunger in his eyes. "You want to know who I am? Well, I am the devil incarnate and you, my love, are about to pay the devil's due."